ECLIPSE

SHADOWS SERIES
BOOK FIVE

SAM BLOOD

Edited by S.K. O'Connor and Alicia Lee
Cover Illustration by Lindsey Wakefield
Cover Design by Jenna Brockett

First Published by Blood Enterprises, 2021

ISBN: 978-0-473-49941-9

www.samblood.com

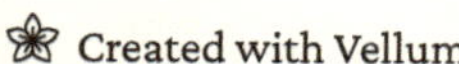 Created with Vellum

CONTENTS

To Beren. Off-stage: my best friend. On-stage: the Hector to my Patroclus, the Tybalt to my Mercutio. Kings to you.

LAST TIME, IN 'BOOK FOUR: MAJESTIC'...

Griffin Cameron unites with a fellow teen hacker named Phoebe. Phoebe has been frozen in stone for ten years and used to work with Griffin's Mum Melissa Cameron. Together the pair discover that Melissa secretly built a back-up portal station on an isolated island in the Bermuda Triangle. This facility could remotely activate all the others which Cameron Technologies have built around the world, opening portals and finally allowing all Shadows and humans to find their counterpart and create a happier, more harmonious universe. All of the other stations have already been seized by the human governments, who suspect Griffin and his brother Calvin of having conspired with the Shadows to commit an act of terrorism against the human world.

Griffin and Phoebe's mission to activate the portals is complicated upon arriving in the islands when the world suddenly shifts around them, transporting them to a parallel pair of islands over in the Shadow world. In an effort to let Phoebe survive to complete the mission, Griffin is captured by an incredibly powerful being who is half human and half Shadow: a being known as a Majestic. Griffin is imprisoned along with some other human teenagers in an ancient gothic palace named Aeyu, only to discover that their captor is none other than Raven.

Raven was once known as Taylor, Phoebe's genius best friend who she worked with alongside Melissa Cameron. However once Taylor showed his true colours Phoebe banished him to the Shadow world. There he rose as the formidable Raven, a human who hid his true identity while using his Empress puppet, the young faerie called Hanna, to rule the human-hating Empire.

With Griffin as his prisoner, Raven confesses that the last time they met it reminded him of who he used to be, back before he lost himself to darkness and anger. However it's clear that Raven hasn't changed when he reveals the terrifying reptilian Majestic that has been pursuing Griffin is under Raven's control, and is actually Griffin's brother Calvin. Calvin has been fused with his Shadow Zephyr into a single form. Raven has been perfecting the process of fusing Shadow and human counterparts together, and the young prisoners he has been holding in his palace are used for these experiments.

Meanwhile, Griffin's Shadow Eclipse, the powerful golden dragon-parrot who was once Cirrus, arrives in the Islands of Sun and Moon along with his companion Hanna, the ex-Empress. Eclipse and Hanna have formed an alliance to find their human counterparts. They arrive in the islands searching for an entrance into the subterranean Underworld which will allow them to cross over to the human world. On arriving in the Islands the pair are greeted by refugees fleeing the civil war that is consuming the Shadow world, fought between the human-loving Resistance and the human-hating Empire. The refugees' leader tells Eclipse that most of their world's inhabitants are still deciding who will control the Shadow world. She claims that most Shadows don't care about humans either way and that they want only to live in peace. The refugee's leader tries to convince Eclipse to stay in the Shadow world with them and use his power to protect those affected by the civil war. However, she refuses to take in Hanna because of the ex-Empress' past crimes, so Eclipse rejects the offer for him to stay.

The small island community that the refugees have formed is blown apart when human soldiers inexplicably appear in the camp, shooting and killing the innocent Shadows. Eclipse blacks out with rage when he sees the humans poised to hurt Hanna. When he comes to he discovers that he has killed the human soldiers, violating his vow not to take life, a vow that he had made in honour of his human, Griffin.

Hanna and Eclipse continue toward Aeyu Palace in search of the Underworld's entrance. On arrival they witness a fusion machine creating a Majestic. Hanna betrays Eclipse, stabbing him with a poisonous stinger, incapacitating him. Eclipse passes out. He wakes in princely chambers and Raven comes to him, revealing that Hanna was bringing Eclipse to him all this time. Raven tries to persuade Eclipse to join him, so that they can rule the Shadow world together. An old part of Eclipse is tempted, as he once dreamed of attaining power and conquering this world, winning the awe and loyalty of its people through sheer force. However, Eclipse refuses Raven, saying he is no longer that Shadow. Later Hanna comes to visit Eclipse, wracked by immense guilt and remorse. In seeing how much disregard Raven, the man who raised her, has for her, she frees Eclipse. The pair break out the Shadows being kept prisoner in the palace, making for the Underworld together.

Meanwhile, thanks to Phoebe distracting Raven by revealing to him that she's still alive, Griffin frees the human prisoners. Their team manages to escape from Raven down into the Under-

world beneath the palace, but they are closely pursued by Raven's army. Griffin finally reunites with Eclipse down in the Underworld, and Griffin is ecstatic to finally be with his Shadow again.

Calvin and Zephyr's Majestic is turning increasingly volatile and bloodthirsty, and Raven is now struggling to control it. Griffin and Eclipse battle the all-powerful being but lose and fall deep into the Underworld. Stumbling upon an ancient temple, the pair encounter a new Majestic; the Majestic of Griffin's Mum and her Shadow Silvaluna. However this Majestic is not corrupt and mutant like the Majestic Raven has created; it is more angelic than demonic, and Griffin shares an emotional reunion with his mother before the Majestic vanishes. Eclipse and Griffin then find one of Raven's fusion machines. Griffin suggests they combine together into a Majestic of their own in an effort to gain the power they need to fend off the one pursuing them. Eclipse refuses Griffin's offer and Griffin is deeply hurt, taking this as a personal rejection.

Unexpectedly Griffin and Eclipse are reunited with Phoebe and the other human prisoners who explode into the temple, followed by the Shadow prisoners led by Hanna. In the chaos, one of the traumatised human girls, believing all Shadows to be threats, shoots at Eclipse... but Hanna takes the bullet for her friend instead. She lies bleeding out on the floor of the temple. The other humans and Shadows finally recognise that they are each other's counterparts, and they embrace, overwhelmed. At that moment Calvin and Zephyr's Majestic smashes its way into the temple to kill them all. However, as Phoebe, Griffin and Eclipse appeal to the terrifying Majestic they are able to break through to Calvin and Zephyr. The Majestic splits back into two, but only after Calvin and Zephyr use their joint power to create a Rip between the Shadow and human worlds.

As Eclipse has the power to mimic the ability of any Shadow, Zephyr gifts Eclipse his ability to heal others. Eclipse uses this to heal Hanna's wound and save her from death, as the rest of the team escapes through the Rip into the portal facility over in the human world. Phoebe and her team of humans and Shadows hold back Raven's frenzied soldiers as Griffin runs to the control room of the facility to activate the portal. He's soon joined by Eclipse. As Griffin powers up the facility, Eclipse stuns him by revealing that he, Eclipse, is still Cirrus. Griffin thought that Cirrus had been lost when he died and mutated into Eclipse. Eclipse also tells Griffin that through his experiences in the Shadow world he's come to believe that Shadows and humans don't belong together; that when counterparts get too close to each other, bad things happen in the long run. He believes the Shadow world needs to look to heal itself, rather than looking to humans as a miracle cure for their troubles. Griffin is powerless to stop Eclipse, who activates the facility's self-destruct sequence using the knowledge he gleaned from Griffin through their tele-pathic connection. Heavy-hearted, Eclipse destroys the controls, ensuring Griffin cannot complete his mission. Eclipse emotion-ally farewells Griffin, but a furious and grieving Griffin refuses to be touched by his Shadow. Eclipse then returns to his true home, the Shadow world, for good.

Phoebe arrives as the facility begins to flood. She finally manages to get through to the grief-stricken Griffin, and with her encouragement Griffin figures out how to activate the facility despite Eclipse's meddling. Recalling how he once released Phoebe from the stone statue that Cirrus sealed her in by chan-nelling his Shadow's power, Griffin coaches Phoebe to reach deep within herself. Phoebe is shocked and overjoyed when she manages to once again call on the fire powers of her Shadow Ember, the Shadow she's been separated from for a decade. She takes this as a sign that their connection is still as strong as ever and that Ember hasn't forgotten her. Phoebe manages to use Ember's flames to weld the broken fuel line and help her refuel the rocket, which Griffin then hotwires. The rocket launches up to the surface far above to open a giant portal, just as nine other facilities release similar rockets in synchronisation around the world. Phoebe uses her body to shield Griffin from the rocket's exhaust, Ember's flames protecting them both. In their moment of euphoric victory, Phoebe and Griffin share a kiss. Griffin, Phoebe, Calvin, Zephyr and their small team of human and Shadow prisoners ascend in an elevator toward the surface of the island. Griffin is heartbroken by the loss of his Shadow and best friend. He is told by the unnerved prisoners that Eclipse took out the soldiers of Raven who refused to surrender, demonstrating terrifying power. Griffin is further saddened when his brother Calvin tells Phoebe that since he lost her ten years ago he never stopped loving her. Griffin realises that things aren't over between Phoebe and his brother, and it looks like there may be a chance of them rekindling their relationship.

High above the island, the portal is opening, the reflective sphere growing larger and larger in the sky. Griffin comforts himself with the thought that his Mum's dream and her Shadow's dream have finally been made real and that all of the losses have been worth it. But with shock he sees human fighter jets approaching the island, just as winged Shadows and flying ships explode out of the portal to meet the humans in battle. Griffin and his team make it to their own jet just in time to escape the island as the conflict erupts, the powers of the Shadows clashing with the firepower of the humans. Griffin's team wonders where they can possibly run to now, given that Calvin and Griffin are still wanted fugitives. Griffin also realises that this conflict means that the two worlds have both chosen hate and fear of the other over cooperation and compassion... and that instead of healing the two worlds by opening the portals, both him and his team have unknowingly unleashed a war of unimaginable proportions. A war with Griffin and Eclipse stranded on opposite sides.

And now the story continues, in the fifth book of the Shadows Series... Eclipse.

1

THE GSA

"My name is Griffin Cameron. These initiation challenges are extremely dangerous, and should not be attempted by anyone, anywhere, anytime. If a contestant is too afraid to complete a challenge, they're eliminated. But if they and their counterpart succeed, then they will be one step closer to the grand prize: being initiated into the GSA."

Epic, intrepid theme music blasts from the speakers over my head. Five new teenage recruits, my only audience in the near-empty lecture hall, stare back at me dumbly.

A girl raises her hand. There are three humans including her, and only two Shadows.

"Yes,' I say solemnly, "confused-looking Selena Gomez."

"It's Blanca," the girl corrects me. "Is this meant to be a parody of the *Fear Factor* TV Show?"

"Yes," I say promptly. "Maybe. I don't know, I've never watched an entire episode, so I took a real big risk with this one."

"What's Fear Factor?" one of the Shadows murmurs, a

wild bear with fur the colour of honey. She looks like a more ferocious take on Winnie-the-Pooh.

"It's like, a really old reality TV show," a young German girl explains, rubbing the Shadow's neck. "I think."

We're in a small lecture hall aboard the ship we now call home. If everything had gone as planned when we opened the portals, this room would have been used for the education of Shadows and humans who were being transported to meet their counterparts for the very first time. Instead it's dusty with disuse.

"Introducing our contestants!" I declare. "We have Sam from Nairobi. He was fighting in the war until he met his Shadow, Solace, on the battlefield. They asked for sanctuary with the GSA."

Solace, a giant hulking panda with boulder-sized fists made of rock, looks stunned. His gawky human with thick specs grins uncertainly.

"Then we have Grindelbark," I continue, "who was sucked through a Rip into our world and met her human: Molly Kahnwald from Germany. The two of them enjoy listening to K-Pop and taking long walks on the beach." The golden bear and her human are both staring at me. Their mouths are hanging open slightly, as if they're awestruck. I choose to ignore it. "And last but not least, Blanca Rodriguez. An expert in political campaigning for a range of causes." The sassy Spanish girl with her legs crossed seems to be the only one who's quietly amused. She's been assessing me over the rim of her glasses.

"No Shadow," Blanca explains, seeing the others' curious, probing looks. She smiles, a glimpse of vulnerability showing through her confident exterior. "Yet. I just volunteered my services."

"For your first challenge," I continue, "you must choose between either eating the Madagascan Hissing Cockroaches in jar number one..." I gesture to the sealed jar on the desk, "or spending twenty minutes in a bath filled with African Cave Spiders. You decide." Blanca raises her hand, looking at the others for support.

"Yes?"

"I'm pretty sure that we've already qualified for the GSA?" she says, arching an eyebrow. "That's why we're here, in the base. We had to leave behind our old lives and all that. Aren't you meant to just be giving us an inspirational speech about what the organisation stands for and... I don't know. Housekeeping stuff?"

"I could. But it doesn't take a genius to know that Madagascan Hissing Cockroaches sounds like the more fun option." Sighing, I scratch my head. "Okay, I'm going to fess up," I tell them. "I've never done one of these initiations. I'm mainly here because I lost a bet with Calvin. Usually these sorts of things fall to Phoebe."

Phoebe can't get enough of them, but she's away right now. She's been bringing in a whole lot of tools and strategies into our little underground organisation for what she calls 'culture-building', 'group-consensus decision making' and 'horizontal-hierarchies', or something like that. Now you can walk past any room in the base to see the members sitting in circles, wiggling their fingers silently in the air to show they're resonating with what's being said. Phoebe also brought in laughter yoga and something called '*cuddle-puddles*' as team-building exercises to encourage positive mental health while we're all stuck down here. She eats this team-building stuff for breakfast. *'Grassroots social justice movements for the win,'* as Phoebe would say brightly. Whatever that means.

At least *her* inner child clearly isn't dead.

"It's just...." Molly flushes when I look at her, embarrassed. But then she meets my gaze shyly. She and Grindelbark are only thirteen. Jeez. It's really come to throwing thirteen year olds into warzones just to get scraps of intelligence.

"We've all watched your video you made a year back, the one about what happened to you the first time you went to the Shadow world," Molly says quickly. "It's why most of us are here, Griffin. Er, sir. Are we allowed to call you *'Grif'*?"

Of course they've seen it. I sigh inwardly. I'd recorded that video aboard the jet, back when my whole world had fallen apart and Phoebe and I were on the run together. A home video that went viral around the world, no matter how hard the UN tried to quash it. It helped us to get out the truth to those who would listen: the truth that Shadows aren't the enemy of humans, but the other half of us. The truth that for every Shadow, there's a human who they've been missing their entire life. Their counterpart.

"You guys are heroes," Sam gushes, gulping as I look at him. "Even the UN seem to know they can't get away anymore with telling everyone that you and Calvin are terrorist double agents for the Shadow world."

"No, that's good," I agree. "Now we're just traitors for trying to *stop* the war."

"The GSA are legend. We just can't believe that we get to be a part of this."

My smile flickers, but holds.

Oh, kid. I don't look forward to the moment where they

realise the brutal reality. They've been told that the GSA isn't some fun summer camp; they know that joining as members means forsaking most of your personal connections, means being on the run from the authorities of both worlds. The UN and the Empire would both love to see us pay for sabotaging their war operations whenever we can. We warned these kids before they came how tough it can be mentally to be in here, about the struggle to keep your spirits up. They're brave, these recruits. Of course they are, or they wouldn't be here. But they still won't really know what this is like until they experience it.

How did I ever end up in this situation? I swear just yesterday my only worry was whether Sophie at Burger Max would notice me or not.

Sophie. Yet another person I don't know what's happened to in this war. We'd dated in the end, even if briefly, even if it had lost us our friendship. I deeply hope she's still alive.

So many of my old classmates aren't.

I jerk my head out of the past, force myself into the present. That's becoming harder and harder lately.

"We want to make a difference, like you do," Grindelbark is saying, her snout twitching in excitement. They're freaking irrepressible. Look at them now, all beaming in their new khaki GSA uniforms, each with the medal pinned to their right breast: two identical world globes in gold, a blue ribbon looping around them in the symbol for infinity.

I can feel my heart rate escalating, and realise my hand has curled into a fist, the nails biting into my palm. I force myself to breathe. They're watching me, and I have to be their example: eternally optimistic and upbeat, while still keeping them grounded in reality.

"That's great," I say to them, smiling. "I like your attitude. But it's important to be cautious, too. You have to be aware of the stakes we're up against, you have to be prepared for the dangers. All right, as for the security briefing: some of the doors in this ship are locked for safety or because they're off-limits, but in the event of an emergency they'll automatically unlock. However, the access hatch on the top of this ship stays locked at all times, except when cleared to open so the jets can leave from the on-board hangar out on field missions. Both the UN and the Empire would like to see us dead, and that hatch is the one line between us and the threats out there, understand? We're only safe in here as long as the bad guys stay on the outside."

"I thought we believed there were no *bad guys*?" Solace rumbles carefully. "That everyone in the two worlds is just misguided because they don't know the truth of how we're connected?"

"True that," I agree, "but that doesn't mean that they won't misguidedly destroy us by any means necessary if they get a chance. The work we're doing here, it's as deadly as being right on the frontlines, people. Working for peace puts a target on our back. So you can never let your guard down, not for a single moment. You'll be drilled about what to do in the case of the base being discovered or breached. Also no sharing classified information with your peers; we're very careful about controlling who knows what so that if anyone is captured and interrogated for information our operations aren't totally compromised." I see their grim expressions at how run-of-the-mill I'm making this sound. I think about telling them not to worry about it, that that's the worst-case scenario, but I stop myself. That would be a lie. We're not kids anymore, and they signed up to this because they understand the stakes, and the consequences. "Whenever members leave this base on a field mission, which is the only reason you should ever have for leaving this base, they go out in teams. We have gas masks and safety gear for any trips to battlegrounds and environments on the surface that are no longer hospitable. Those are the main points; you'll be taken on a guided tour of the base. Someone will drop by your bunks later to tell you about showers, laundry etc.," I add. "Not my area."

Grindelbark has her paw up.

"Yes, Winnie?" I doubt the Shadow gets the Winnie-the-Pooh reference, but it doesn't seem to matter. She's toying with her claws uncomfortably.

"We're so sorry about what happened to Cirrus," Grindelbark says in a small voice.

My pulse spikes. I'm blindsided.

"Ah, what?" I say.

"Molly showed me the video you made, of everything that happened to you the first time you went to the Shadow world. And the second one you made, when you talked about activating the portals from the island near Bermuda, and how Raven manipulated the worlds to start the war once the portals opened. About how Raven had been friends with Phoebe and your brother once."

"Ah-huh." I clear my throat. It's stupid, of course they've seen the videos. That's why they're here. But still. Making that first video had felt so personal; it's weird sometimes to realise that millions if not billions of real people who I've never ever met have actually watched them and now know intimate details about my life and the lives of my family.

"We were so sorry when we heard about Cirrus," Molly says. "I cried."

"Thanks." I frown at myself. That doesn't seem like the right response. *Thanks for crying.*

I feel a pain in my chest. Voices from the past press in at me. I try to ignore them.

"I saw some quote online once," Cirrus had said to me beneath Winghold. *"Some friends move through your life like waves, but others are like an octopus that sticks onto your face."*

"You're saying I'm your octopus?"

"What?" the green dragon-parrot had blinked at me, his crest-feathers straightening in puzzlement. *"No, dude, you're a human."*

"And you're my Shadow," I'd whispered proudly.

"It was hearing about your friendship that made me want to meet my own Shadow," Molly says breathlessly, jerking me out of the memory. "So we were all just wondering..." She looks at the others for support, who all look equally eager. "Where's your Shadow, the one that Cirrus transformed into? Where's Eclipse?"

Their hopeful faces blur in my vision. I feel my own face getting hot, the room getting fuzzy. I'm overwhelmed by being placed on the spot.

"Eclipse?" I manage.

"Yeah. Are you two still best friends? Is he different than when he was Cirrus, or is he still the same?"

"Well... sure," I say, my voice sounding strange to myself. "Yeah. Um, we found each other again. I met him in the Shadow world. And I found out that he was still Cirrus. He had been, all along. It had just taken him a while to come to terms with having a new identity and personality. New look, new name... but still my friend."

They're all staring at me, literally gaping at this revelation in joyful excitement. Like me and my Shadow are some kind of serialised TV show they've been vicariously pinning their own hopes and dreams on.

"So... me and Eclipse had just reached the station," I continue carefully, with them hanging onto every word. "We were ready to open the portals to connect the worlds, ready to bring all humans and Shadows together. Then at the last moment, out of nowhere, Eclipse, my own Shadow, the other half of me... he told me that he'd decided that humans and Shadows were bad influences on each other. That he had... he'd changed his mind, basically. He'd seen all the bad things humans had done to Shadows, what Raven had done by creating the Empire over there, and now Eclipse believed that both of our worlds were never meant to meet. That the human and Shadow worlds being in contact will always end badly for his people and mine. So..." I close my eyes. "Eclipse turned on me, and he used our connection to see in my head how to set the portals to self-destruct, and I nearly drowned when the base flooded itself."

The silence that follows is total and deep. Nobody speaks for a while.

"That... doesn't make sense," Blanca whispers.

"Tell me about it."

"Where is he now?" Sam finally asks.

I shrug, casting my gaze down at the floor, lost. "I don't know," I mutter. "I haven't heard from him since the war broke out."

"Is he fighting for the Empire now?" Molly says, her voice hushed. "Against the humans?"

"I don't know," I repeat, swallowing. I look back up to see the five new recruits staring at me, ashen.

I smile crookedly. So much for a rousing, inspiring initiation ceremony.

"Any questions?"

I'm interrupted by a deafening, artificial howl.

All the others jerk, afraid, and in the same moment I'm already on my feet.

No. Not now.

"What is it?" Sam shouts, his and Solace's soldier training kicking into gear as they fall in behind me.

"There's someone trying to dock without authorisation," I yell over the din of the screaming alarm, rushing to the exit. "Everyone to the hatch. Follow me."

But only one thought is playing over and over in my head in a building sense of horror.

They've found us.

I think the ship that we call our base can be best compared to a haunted, abandoned hotel, or the sunken Titanic. It was built by Cameron Technologies and modelled on the flying metal ship of New Redemption, with the exception that this vessel was meant to be a symbol of utopia, a place of luxury built on hope, dreams and ambition. There are gold and midnight blue carpets and gleaming big pots of lush decorative plants, many of which are now dead. The corridors are lit by trails of soft glowing lights. But somehow all the empty corridors and landings with their fancy décor just make it feel more sinister to me. Our new home is a constant mocking reminder of our failed attempt to bring the worlds together.

The alarm is still howling. As we run, more humans and Shadows rush to fall into line with us from connecting corridors: Sien and Pixie, Nam and Ashwind, April and Celeste. We collectively charge to the defence of our home, heading up to the top floor and then toward the back of the ship. Soon we're running down a dark, almost industrial corridor.

We arrive at a giant metal door the colour of rust. A few other GSA members are already standing there, weapons trained on it. Beyond the sealed door is the on-board hangar where jets can take off through the hatch.

I quickly type on a keypad mounted on the wall, unlocking a weapons cache. I pull it open and start passing out swords and guns to the new recruits, who are about to get a harsh *'throw them in the deep end'* lesson, Griffin-styles.

"What's the situation?" I say, turning my gaze to that thin layer of metal, our only source of protection.

"An unknown aircraft landed a minute ago," Pixie says beside me. The cat-unicorn scrapes the floor with her hoof restlessly, and shivers. "It ignored all of our transmissions and refused to identify itself."

"Landed?" I repeat. "*Inside* the hangar bay?" That means this door of reinforced steel is our only barrier between us and whatever lies on the other side. "How did they open the hatch?"

"I don't know."

The metal panels above us slide away, revealing self-targeting tranquiliser rifles and cannons capable of firing electrified capture nets. Luckily our ship isn't without its own defence mechanisms.

We stand in rows, weapons trained at the door. Ashwind's feathers burn with cold blue light and Woo-min's dragon-dog Pouncer snarls bravely despite his small stature. I can hear our panicked breaths in the tight space, tense with anticipation. We're all wondering what horror could possibly lie on the other side.

Then from beyond the door, barely audible, someone speaks.

"Sorry for the red alert, our comms died. But are you eggheads going to open up or what?"

It's Phoebe's voice. Collective relief ripples through our ranks. I feel a wave of giddy euphoria. Phoebe's alive. She's here. She and her team made it back okay.

But as quickly as my excitement at hearing Phoebe's voice came on, I'm suddenly reminded that I should actually be kind of almost anywhere else.

"Griffin?" Sien says in surprise as I start hastily moving away.

"Excuse me, excuse me, thanks," I say, awkwardly stepping and weaving through the others as I make my way back down the corridor.

"Griffin?" Sien tries, chasing after me. "Don't you want to be here to welcome them back?"

"Nah, you've got this. Also, do you mind giving the newbies a tour of the place? 'Kay, thanks, bye. Oh! And welcome to the GSA!" I say. I give a taken aback Grindlebark a high-five. Then I slip away as fast as possible.

Later that night, once the lights are out, I pass the dormitories with their rows of bunk beds, coming to a stop outside one of the rec rooms. The room is exuding the sound of gentle snoring. It's dark in there, lit only by the artificial glare of the screen. An action movie is still playing, one of the Men in Black movies, I think. I slide inside, taking in the teenage Shadows and humans who've all fallen asleep before the end of the film, passed out on the beanbags and couches scattered through the movie room. Each counterpart is a unique expression of the other.

This is all I have. The work here is the only thing that keeps me from flipping out or going off the deep end. At the risk of sounding dramatic, it's the only thing I really have to live for. Since splitting ways with my own Shadow I haven't had the energy for any friendships. The work itself, our purpose here, is the one shred of light and hope that keeps me fighting with everything I have... and still it's not enough. We're fighting a losing battle, just like the two sides in this war are. If nothing changes, all of us are going to lose.

I don't even know how to put into words the scale of my longing for a way out of all of this, what I would give to figure out a solution. I mean, I'm to blame for this war breaking out in the first place. It's not just about me feeling it's my duty to fix my mistake either. It's also about wanting to honour Mum. I still want to give her some kind of legacy, to make her most important work mean something in the grand scheme of the universe.

I look around at the familiar faces. Apart from our new recruits, the GSA is mainly made up of the prisoners we helped free from a terrifying fate in Raven's island palace, Aeyu.

There's Little Marty and his Shadow, a lithe primate with the legs of a tarantula (nicknamed 'Spider-Monkey-Spider' by his human. Nice one, Marty). Rihäm and her pegasus Stalia, with wings like stained glass.

I see Molly shiver, trying to snuggle closer into the big,

fuzzy golden bear beside her. Softly, treading on the carpet so as not to wake anyone, I take a fallen blanket from the floor and gently lay it across Grindelbark and Molly. They both sleep on undisturbed, and Molly's shivering stops.

I stare down at the human and her Shadow for a moment, both caught in a blissful hug.

I'm sorry, Griffin.

No, Eclipse... NOOO!

Suddenly there's water all around me, churning, and I'm locked in with no way out. I'm gasping, fighting to stay at the surface and to keep breathing as the water level rises... the last thing I hear is an awful roar, from a being almost more beast than bird. Then I jerk back to my senses.

I gasp a mouthful of air. Disorientated, confused, I look rapidly around me, scared, taking in my surroundings: the lounge, the sleeping teens. Nothing has changed. It's all just in my head.

But it's getting worse.

I steady myself against the wall. I'm not trapped in the self-destructing portal facility, fighting the rising tide. That's in the past now. I'm safe. As safe as any of us are, at least.

Something lunges out of the darkness and grabs me.

When I see who it is, I stop myself swearing just in time.

"Could you make it any *less* easy?" Phoebe chuckles. She wears a mischievous grin, a radioactive grin which holds me in its power while slowly killing me. What's worse is it feels like it's worth it. "You're really starting to take all the fun out of it." She follows my gaze to where I was watching over the sleeping recruits. The grin spreads even further across her face, almost from ear to ear. "Oh my God, were you just having a proud Daddy moment?"

"I feel nothing," I say in denial.

"How'd the initiation go?" she asks knowingly. "Did you emotionally scar our new recruits with all your sass?"

"I resent that implication."

Phoebe just waits.

"I may have scarred them a *teensy* bit," I confess. "Accidentally."

"Griffin," I hear her sigh.

"I didn't mean to! I tried *so* hard," I brood.

"Of course you did."

Finally I turn to her, carefully arranging my face to hide the fact that I'm still shaking from the sudden terrifying vision. Phoebe can't know. No one can. I try to focus on my racing heart, to make it slow. But it's a lost cause, because when I see Phoebe it always goes into overdrive. It doesn't help that her face lights up like a Christmas tree whenever she sees me.

I've never wanted to kiss anyone so damn badly. To hug her, to hold her close to me and be able to call her mine. To have one bright, gorgeous, dangerous thing in the middle of all this misery. Phoebe is a single flame that the darkness and the horror of the war seems unable to touch.

"So, why have you been avoiding me?" Phoebe asks determinedly, her joking tone dropping without warning.

I stare at her, flummoxed. I'm caught off-guard.

"I'm not..."

"I don't appreciate being lied to. I heard you practically ran away when my team landed. You're my best friend. I don't know if I'm yours, but... you're mine. We live in a ship, Grif. It's pretty damn obvious when you're avoiding someone."

Man, I've forgotten the terror of being fixed in one of Phoebe's blazing, righteous glares.

You know why, I want to say, staring at her helplessly. It must be written all over my face. I wear my emotions on my sleeve.

"You've had your own... new things going on," I say carefully, "and I've been trying to focus on finding a way through this war."

"We all have. You know that. You're pulling away from everyone, Grif, ever since *he* left. You're giving every spare minute you have to this place. You barely sleep. You can't stand to be around the others, to talk to them, as if you feel you don't deserve it. Like you're spoiled, stained. But you're not. And you don't get to pull away from me, even if you pull away from everyone else. Deal?"

"Deal," I smile, masking the bittersweet sadness of the word.

How I wish Eclipse was here to talk to about Phoebe... no. I can't keep thinking like that. He chose to leave.

Phoebe and I stare at the slumbering recruits together protectively, proudly.

"They have your eyes," I tell her.

She punches me in the arm, rolling the eyes in question. The punch actually hurt quite a lot.

This is who she is to me, the real Phoebe. It's in how she looks at the sleeping members of the GSA before us. She's a lioness, and this is her pride. I heard that when Phoebe was homeless she would look out for the other young people living on the streets. Defend them and fight for them when they were picked on. Phoebe needs a tribe to care for, to defend. She needs something outside of herself. Now she has that again. She has a home. Even at the end of everything, she finally feels like she's where she's meant to be.

"I think I should join you on your next field mission," I say lightly.

Phoebe snorts.

"Yeah, because being shot at is fun."

It's amazing what passes for a normal conversation these days.

"I mean, I suppose our glorious leader gets the final say," Phoebe adds, "but I think the general consensus will be that you should stay put here. Your brain is way too valuable."

"That's a nice way of saying that I'm really unfit, isn't it?" I stretch. "It just messes with me, being cooped up in here. It might be nice to get out before it turns into something from *The Shining*."

"Um... I've never seen it," Phoebe confesses. "Or read it."

"Pheebs!" I gasp, as if personally offended. "You'd love it."

"I guess I just haven't been in the mood for psychological horror lately," she says wryly.

"You're confused. It's a heart-warming comedy about a family who goes to take care of a charming hotel over the winter so the loving father can work on his novel."

She nods.

"I'm sure that was a totally accurate synopsis."

Our members all look so peaceful asleep, as if their two kinds aren't warring up on the surface right now.

"Just look at them," Phoebe says softly. I follow her gaze to Blanca. I realise the new arrival is still awake, her eyes open. She must have heard our conversation so far. She's staring at the humans and Shadows slumbering alongside each other, full, happy and whole.

I know what that ache is really like, how that longing for your own counterpart feels.

"Doesn't it break you a little bit?" Phoebe says quietly. "I wish more than anything that I could hear Ember right now, that I could speak to her in my head. I keep thinking about the station, how her flames flowed from my skin. I haven't been able to pull it off again since. But, it's kind of comforting. No matter how far she and I are from each other, I know that our link still exists as strong as anything."

"So you made flames appear from your bare skin, so what?" I say casually. "I managed to bring you back to life after you were a stone popsicle for a decade."

Phoebe rolls her eyes.

"I know. Last time I was here you emotionally blackmailed me with it just so you could win a game of Go Fish." She hesitates. "Look, I know I've said it before, but if you ever want to talk about Eclipse..."

"You know that I don't," I say, shutting down instantly.

"What, so all your feelings toward him are dead, and your memories together mean nothing?" Phoebe says, flaring with anger for a second. Then she sighs. "Sorry, it's just... I know you. I don't like hearing you giving up on hope. Every single night before I go to sleep I imagine wrapping Ember in my arms, feeling the heat of her fire. I imagine having stupid slumber parties or just talking to her about nothing. I wonder if she'd be as happy to see me as I would be to see her again."

It's the most tender and honest that I've heard Phoebe be about her feelings toward Ember. Usually I think it hurts too much for her to talk about. But her reason for neglecting to mention her Shadow is very different from mine.

"Of course she would be," I say, shocked. "You're doing things here that are just as good and important, Pheebs. You're doing exactly what Ember believes in, looking after a place where Shadows and humans can be together safely and fighting for everyone else to have that same right."

Phoebe smiles but then presses her lips together, troubled.

I wish I could bring Ember back to her. I'd do anything to stop her feeling pain like this.

The last time I'd met Ember was when I'd been in the Shadow world with Cirrus. Ember's the charismatic and tough-as-nails phoenix who created Winghold, a safe hideaway for the humans and Shadow counterparts who wanted to escape the persecution of the Empire. When Winghold was destroyed by the Empire, Ember's movement had grown into a global Resistance, taking on the Empire... until attacks by humans on the Shadow world secretly orchestrated by Raven had broken the support for the Resistance, causing the Empire to consolidate all of its power again and take full control of the Shadow world. We've been trying to get in contact with Ember, wherever she is. Because if the Resistance still exists over there in some form, they could be important allies for the work we're trying to do here to stop the war. But so far we've heard nothing.

"I just want to speak to her again," Phoebe says softly, vulnerable. "I'd do anything to hear Ember right now, wherever she is. To hear her voice, even if she is all the way over in the Shadow world."

It hits me, in a dramatic shower of mental sparks. Wheels start vigorously turning in the back of my head. An idea, seemingly impossible and simultaneously thrilling, grips my imagination.

"Phoebe?" I whisper. I realise I've grabbed hold of her without thinking, elated. "You are brilliant."

A confused smile illuminates her face in the hushed dark, visible only by the flickering light from the movie. Suddenly I'm remembering our kiss down in the station together, surrounded by flames. The kiss we've never spoken about. I feel myself yearning to gently stroke the curve of her cheek.

But that would be the deepest and cruellest of betrayals, so I do what I always do and bury it down, swallowing it, even as it hurts.

The widescreen television playing the movie cuts. The sudden motion startles me. I let go of Phoebe as if I've been burned. She steps away from me too, tucking a lock of hair behind her ear with a flicker of something. Awkwardness? Did she see too much of me in that moment of intensity?

But then the black of the TV screen is suddenly replaced with something far worse, something far more terrifying than any horror movie. Instantly all of our attention is transfixed on the screen.

The TV is showing a live feed. We're staring at a dark, jagged throne. Sitting upon it is a Shadow.

Her gelatinous purple eyes are like swollen domes, fractured into countless reflective mirrors. She's covered in an emerald exoskeleton, a violet cloak flowing from her shoulders, padding the throne beneath her. A pair of antennae quiver in anticipation, and her mandibles work the air hungrily.

Empress Galvanize. Leader of the Empire and ruler of the Shadow world. The one who replaced Hanna on the throne as Raven's puppet. Deranged, sadistic, dangerous.

Also, somehow she's on our home cinema screen.

I grab the remote from beside where Little Marty is snoozing and crank the volume.

"You are all sick, you who so futilely oppose us," Galvanize leers. *"Perverted. Abominations. You who call yourselves the GSA."*

The hairs on the back of my neck are fully on end. The high, twisted voice that exudes from the screen is waking the others from their slumber.

"Everyone," I command, feeling cold sweat down my back. "At attention. Now."

Suddenly everyone is up, throwing off their blankets, on their feet with adrenaline storming through their systems. Ready for a fight.

"You have interfered in this war for the very last time. No one believes your wicked teachings. You presume that humans and Shadows are part of each other, that we are somehow entwined?" She sounds amused. *"Shadows are your superiors, your rulers. Fools. You humans rely on your tools, your bodies too weak to match us in single combat. Storm and flame runs through our veins. The human world will be dominated, enslaved, and those who aren't slain for their crimes will be grateful to serve us. Not even you, the GSA, will survive. The Shadows who work with you will be executed as the traitors that they are, their bodies buried far from the humans they share their sickness with."* Galvanize rises from her throne, a demented queen, berserk with desire. Her mandibles writhe at the air, thirsting for blood and flesh. *"You will be the first to be eradicated,"* she hisses in anticipation, *"and I*

look forward to sating myself on the divine chorus of your screams."

The screen cuts back to the movie. We all stare into it as if the secret of our fates is held there. I can hear Phoebe breathing beside me.

"Well," I say evenly. "That's not great."

2

EMERGENCY TEAM MEETING

"Galvanize transmitted the same message across most screens in the human world," Calvin tells the rest of us. "The Empire hacked human satellites and used emergency alert systems to cut through normal transmissions. It's all over the web too. Why go to all that trouble just to taunt us?"

"Galvanize takes shows of power seriously," I muse. "She likes building fear."

"We've never seen anything to suggest Shadows were capable of doing that," Phoebe says, perturbed.

"It must be some kind of technology they got from Raven. It was a warning to any humans who might be helping us. But at least it means the Empire hasn't found us... yet."

We're in the bridge of our ship. Our ship doesn't get to fly like it was intended to, so this space is now the office of our oh so glorious leader, where our core leadership team gathers to deliver their progress reports and debate any sticky issues to do with the war or how the

GSA is run. A long tunnel connects the other offices and meeting rooms to the bridge. The bridge itself is a wide, round room with lit-up display screens at empty control stations for piloting the ship. Comfy faux-leather seats face a control desk at the front of the room. Looming behind the desk is a backdrop of giant windows. They stare out into darkness, because the ship is hidden underground, invisible to the surface and to the rest of the world.

Our team is standing before the empty desk, all too amped to take our seats.

"I wish eradicating us was just the Empire's priority," I say, thinking of the United Nations who've declared the GSA a public enemy. Since the war breaking out, the human UN has been transformed into something unrecognisable. Now they're responsible for coordinating the war efforts of every human country against the Shadow threat. "We seem to have been a royal pain in the arse for both sides. It's like not wanting both worlds to be destroyed makes us super uncool or something."

I study the other members of our core leadership team. Other than me it's made up of Phoebe, my brother Calvin, and Calvin's Shadow, Zephyr. The white-feathered dinosaur is eating an apple with a knife, which would look more bad-arse if it wasn't so hard for him to transfer the pieces of apple from his short stumpy arms into his jaws. He subtly mirrors Calvin's movements as if he's orbiting him or vice versa. The tip of his tail sweeps back and forth. Despite past troubles, Calvin and Zephyr's trials in the Underworld have brought them closer together than ever. They're not as cuddly as say, Cirrus and I were. But the love and respect between them can't be missed. The two of them move in perfect synchronisation, more like one entity than two.

"So now that we're all clear we're not under imminent attack," Calvin says smartly, "How are you all?"

"Um, excuse me?"

Calvin's glasses slide down his nose, and he presses them back into place with a finger. He's traded out his contact lenses for the geeky, black-framed specs he used to wear as a teen. I guess it humanises him. But it's also a physical reminder of his promise to Phoebe, to try and be more like the boy that she'd fallen in love with, and that makes me squirm.

"I mean, er, how are my three favourite people in the world?" Calvin smiles sheepishly.

Yeah, I know. It makes me uncomfortable too. My brother has turned from an alpha-predator of the corporate world into this smiling caricature who wants us to all sit in circles and discuss our feelings all the time.

"I have a question," I say, putting up a hand. "How long is this new freakish Calvin persona going to last for?"

"Indefinitely, Grif," Calvin answers seriously, without missing a beat. "I've switched from coffee to tea. It changes a man."

Personally, I'm going to need more than six months to believe this change is permanent. I'm still convinced it's a temporary outcome of his near-death experience in the Underworld, and him wanting to believe that it really meant something.

Calvin and I became really close in the Underworld. I said some things to him which I hadn't thought I'd ever confess, all to bring him back from being under Raven's control. I love my brother. It's just that since Eclipse left me,

I don't know if I'll ever be able to trust anyone again. Trust just isn't something I do anymore. Also, trusting Calvin in the past has never stopped him from ending up hurting me, every time.

I recall Calvin's horrific transfigured face, black eyes radiating rage, his skin covered in white scales. The face of the twisted form that he and Zephyr had been a part of. A 'Majestic,' one corrupted by Raven and twisted into a demonic form. Raven had used the two of them as his puppet, their god-like powers under his command. But even Raven had lost control of the warped being. Calvin and Zephyr's Majestic had nearly killed me along with the others but we'd managed to get through to them, causing the darkness possessing them to leave. As it did, for a moment they'd been the Majestic they were meant to be; a being of purest light.

When I look at Calvin I see the shining angel and I also see the demon.

Blind to my musings, Calvin sweeps around the desk. He seems charged with energy.

"We have to keep focused," he informs us, sliding himself into the chair to survey us, toying with the files in his hands. "Galvanize is trying to rattle morale, and she's succeeding. But what we need..."

I clear my throat.

"Sorry, I'm going to stop you for just one moment." Stepping up to the desk, I lean into the microphone and switch it on. "Message for Calvin? This is Frigga," I say with my best impression, twirling a lock of hair. "We were on the cleaning roster today, and we weren't going to say anything but... we beg you, please stop blocking the toilet."

"Very mature," Calvin says, rolling his eyes.

"There is… it's just, we've never seen anything like it," I broadcast into every room and corridor of the ship. "You really destroyed the place."

Phoebe's just shaking her head beside me, trying to look disapproving, but losing it to a silent fit of laughter.

"I mean, how sick would a person have to be to even contemplate *doing* something like that? Three of us are in therapy."

Calvin massages his temples, exasperated. I switch off the mic, smiling brightly.

"You are a terrible human being," Phoebe tells me.

Still, Calvin doesn't blow up like he would have back in the day. Hmm. Interesting. I wonder what it will take. Further testing is required.

"I'm not *entirely* sure that was necessary," Calvin says.

"I think it was," I say pointedly. "You're in my seat."

Calvin blinks, as if slowly becoming aware of his feet up on the desk, reclining like he used to in his office at Cameron Technologies.

"Sorry," he says sheepishly. "Old habits." He gets out of the seat, gesturing for me to take his place. I take it. It's been months now, but taking the seat of command over my brother still feels mighty strange.

We've been improvising as we go along, and it's been chaotic trying to turn what started as a bunch of young human and Shadow prisoners we rescued from Raven into the cohesive anti-war organisation now stationed in this ship, with proper job titles, chains of command and everything.

Phoebe, Zephyr, Calvin and I had been the original team making decisions, but it quickly became evident if we were to move as fast as we had to we needed someone overlooking everything, someone to make the hard calls when people were locked over a decision. Phoebe didn't want the job, she loves being in the field with her team on crazy dangerous missions. Zephyr didn't want it. I think he's sworn off positions of authority since it corrupted him last time. So the whole organisation voted, democracy-styles. We agreed there'd be no hard feelings whatever happened.

I was elated and also felt weirdly guilty when they chose me over Calvin. I mean, okay, I did invent this organisation. While Calvin was paralysed, watching one of the first battles of the war above our heads, I got him out of there alive. I made a plan of how we could take some kind of action against this.

But still. Calvin's smart, charismatic. He *did* sorta invent and design revolutionary new technologies all while managing a global billion-dollar corporation. Plus he's twenty-seven, ten years older than I am.

Now the roles are switched. I put my legs up on the desk, crossing them. I look across the desk at my big brother as he stands there in my office, hugging a pile of files to his chest, smiling respectfully.

It gives me a serious case of the heebie-jeebies. I remember the number of times in my childhood, when little Griffin, all wide-eyed in awe of his genius big brother, would happily waddle up to Calvin's work desk, waiting patiently for whatever absent minded task or order he'd be given next. He was so proud to be working for his brother at Cameron Technologies.

Phoebe is grinning, presumably at Calvin getting booted out of the seat by his little brother.

"Oh, you find this funny?" Calvin teases her, arching an

eyebrow in challenge. But there's a rueful, goofy grin on his face.

"Hilarious," Phoebe tells him plainly, but smiles as he steps shyly in toward her.

I feel strangely short behind the desk and try to slide up higher in my chair. I clear my throat.

Phoebe reaches up to Calvin and wraps her arms around his neck. Tentatively they bring their lips together in a kiss. I feel a grinding deep inside my stomach. Like something shredding.

Now Calvin and Phoebe start full-on making out. Her bum actually seats itself on my desk. I jerk my feet off the desk at the speed of light.

Seriously, do they not realise I'm right here? Can they not see me?

I stare at the files on my desk as if they're suddenly fascinating, sliding them away from Calvin and Phoebe before they get dirty.

"You know you don't have to do that *every* time," Zephyr says dryly. I'm glad someone says it, but I think Zephyr is amused to see his human so happy. Thankfully Calvin pulls away, smiling at Phoebe like a goofy school boy. So weird.

"So," Zephyr says with a fanged smile, "what's this meeting about? Are we voting on a new name for ourselves?"

It's a running joke. Zephyr pushes for this at every meeting.

"Yeah, Calvin is still peeved with you about that too," Phoebe smirks at me. "On the down-low."

Calvin looks exasperated.

"If you'd just told us in the first place that GSA stood for

'*Griffin's Shadow Academy*', I never would have gone for it. We had no idea it was a joke suggestion."

"I wasn't joking," I say, feigning hurt.

"So we had to invent new words to fit the letters," Calvin says. "Do you know how awkward '*Generation Shadow Alliance*' sounds? Or how un-catchy it is?"

I ignore him, still haunted by the heavy-petting that almost transpired on my desk. I notice that Phoebe as always looks strangely amped for a leadership meeting despite the super dystopian times it's taking place in.

She catches my look.

"What?"

I shake my head, smiling.

"You love this."

"What?" she says, hugging her files self-consciously.

"You love everything about this place," I say, amused. "Leading a team, facing an impossible crisis head-on. It's what you were born for."

"Well, clearly I'd prefer it if we weren't in the middle of a devastating war," Phoebe points out casually. "I'd rather we were hanging out with our Shadows at Burger Max."

It's an appeal to me, and a very pointed one at that. I can feel myself lose control of my features as my face goes numb.

"I don't want to talk about him," I mutter.

"Griffin, can't you find it in yourself to..."

"He's not my concern," I snap, more heated than I meant to. I try to soften the emotion from my voice. "You all are. Everyone else in these two worlds is. Ending this is our priority. If he doesn't want to be a part of that..."

Zephyr misses the apple with his knife. Damn, I forgot he was here. It's his little brother I'm talking about. After the Underworld I'd told Zephyr about Eclipse, how he was really still Cirrus after all. Zephyr was as rocked by that as I was. Now he feels guilty for not following his little brother back to the Shadow world. He thinks he should have tried to get through to Eclipse.

Zephyr resumes his slicing, more carefully.

"You know what *he* did in the station," I say, "what he tried to do."

"I wish Eclipse had succeeded," Calvin says quietly. "Need I remind us all why this war started?"

There's a tense silence.

"It started because of Raven," Phoebe says darkly, crossing her arms. "And he's going to pay."

"He's your best friend," I say, troubled.

"He was... until he betrayed everything that I care about. Besides, I've got a better bestie now. An upgrade." Phoebe winks at me.

"We all carry the weight of breaking the worlds," Zephyr interrupts gruffly, "for not guessing Raven's plan in advance. That's on all of us. It was our naiveté in thinking Shadows and humans would vote for peace, for friendship, when they were faced with their true selves. Now we know how hard it is for people to unlearn their pasts."

Calvin nods. His expression is easy and relaxed, but looking into his eyes I wonder how much he wishes he could get his hands around Raven's neck: the friend who'd betrayed him, and taken away everything good in Calvin's life.

I remember the last time I encountered Raven. He'd made me pancakes in the palace kitchen, and talked about my Mum with so much love in his voice... before he'd killed Calvin's friend, Mr Falco, in cold blood right in front of me.

I push those memories down. My feelings around them are too troubling.

"Well, that gets me back to my report," Phoebe says, handing out folders to each of us, "and what my team found back in Auckland."

"Nice trip home, was it?" I say, flicking through the pages, scanning their contents.

"Not really," Phoebe says, troubled. "Everywhere's unrecognisable now, especially home. But what's important is what we found."

All of us go still, watching her expectantly.

"I visited the house that Taylor and I used to squat in," Phoebe says, clearing her throat, "before he took the name Raven."

"You're telling me they haven't rebuilt that wreck?" Calvin says, raising an eyebrow. You'd have to have known him as long as I have to see the sudden tension in him. I know how much he dislikes the idea that once upon a time Phoebe and Raven were inseparable.

"Someone has tried to do it up, but to be honest it's still a bit of a hole. I think some new people had been squatting there recently. There were broken beer bottles and signs it had been lived in. But just when I was about to leave... I touched a space on the wall that he and I used to cover with photos of us. Happy things. Somehow touching it activated a switch, and part of the floor started to sink into the ground, forming steps down underneath the house. I'm not kidding. It was some top-notch spy stuff."

"And?" Zephyr prompts her quietly.

"What did you find?" I whisper. Phoebe has all of our attention.

She hesitates.

"We found tech. Contraptions. I don't have the slightest idea what they do. We're talking a lot of storage down there, a state of the art subterranean warehouse beneath a falling-apart house in Grafton. But there's no doubt about it. It's Raven's, or at least someone working for him. This was technology that no other human could have created. It had his signature all over it."

We digest this, gaping. Just for a moment, I see a flash of something on Calvin's face.

Something that looks like hunger.

"Why is Raven storing equipment in Auckland?" I say, bamboozled. "When he could store it anywhere in the Shadow world?"

"Who knows? Maybe it's nice to have a secret stash where nobody will think of looking for it, for a rainy day? But we know from experience he's able to cross between the worlds fairly easily. He has a way to manipulate the Rips. That's how he sent the Shadows to destroy Cameron Technologies and how he hired those human soldiers to attack Sanctuary City when he was trying to spark this war. Maybe some part of him is still sentimental about Auckland? Because of everything that happened there. I guess..." she shifts uncomfortably. "Living on the streets was hard, but we also had some good times there together. I mean, enough for me to go back and visit it, right? So I suppose it still has meaning for him too."

"Forget all that for a moment," Calvin says, fired up. "Did you manage to bring any of the tech back?"

Phoebe bites her lip. She looks unnerved by Calvin's sudden intensity.

"We had to commandeer a bigger ride, but we managed to get the equipment loaded up. It's all in the hangar bay."

Calvin marches away from us toward the door, with a signature purposeful stride that I haven't seen since his days in Cameron Technologies.

"We need to be careful," I shoot at him, and he halts. "Anything Raven spent his time building and hiding can't be good news."

"We should just destroy it," Zephyr mutters, haunted. I know he's recalling what the Majestic machine did to the two of them, placing them at the mercy of Raven's mind control.

"Whatever it is, it might be crucial to Raven's plans," Calvin argues, turning back to confront his Shadow. He looks luminous, as if victory is suddenly near. "We have enough on our hands without him plotting some new hellish horror in the wings."

"Calvin's right," I muse. "Figure out what it is and what it does, big bro. Whether or not Raven was in Auckland himself, the tech Pheebs recovered might be a clue to where he's headed next."

Calvin nods, satisfied. He, Zephyr and Phoebe get ready to head out.

"Anything else, oh glorious leader?" Phoebe smirks.

I survey the three of them, thinking deeply. Phoebe's find was very interesting, but most of these meetings usually go the same. I hear about field missions at various stages of completion, our attempts to scramble human and Shadow communications to stall the fighting for as long as possible. We run guerrilla campaigns for peace online, trying to get the truth out there about the connection between humans and Shadows. Yet every day, more people die across the worlds. Every day, the darkness seems to move in, inexhaustible, gleeful, eating away at the last spots of light.

My fingernails scratch at the arms of my chair, restless. The hopeful, fierce idea that struck me when I was talking with Phoebe in the lounge has been growing. It's been gnawing inside me ever since Phoebe mentioned her deep desire to hear Ember's thoughts, even from a world away.

For a moment I wonder whether or not I should share my idea with the others. Part of me is scared that it might fall apart in exposure to the light of reality.

"I've had an idea," I burst out, surprising myself. I stand up. There's too much energy fizzing through me to sit. "What if we've been going about all of this wrong? What if rather than trying to get both worlds to come to the table for peace negotiations, we could create something that could bring all human and Shadow counterparts together instantly?"

"I'd know that wishes really do come true," Phoebe mutters.

"I say we get some of our members to start researching the telepathic connection between Shadows and humans," I say in a rush. I move over to my whiteboard and the others follow me. I start scribbling on it. "We find a way to amplify the signal," I say, illustrating my point, "so that all humans here can hear their Shadow's thoughts a world away, and vice versa. Like... turning every single person into a long range radio. Who's going to raise a weapon against the other world when they can hear their counterpart on the other side? The UN and Empire don't even realise that if a Shadow dies, the human dies too. They're in denial of the connection between them. This would fix that." I spin to face the others, breathless. "It would fix everything."

I'm expecting slowly dawning expressions of hope, if not for them to look outright thrilled, like I am. I'm unsettled to see that instead they all look openly horrified.

"What?" I say, confused, my enthusiasm slipping slightly. "This is literally what you just talked about downstairs, Pheebs. Being able to hear Ember, even all the way from another world. I'm talking about making it a reality."

"That was wishful thinking," Phoebe says softly. "What you're suggesting doing to make it real..." She shakes her head, troubled. "This might sound different to you from what New Redemption was doing: breaking the connection between a Shadow and a human, fostering an artificial one instead... but what you're talking about is still mind control."

"What?"

"Listen to me. This would still mean messing with the most private inner being of a person. Some people just aren't *ready* to meet their Shadows. Being confronted with your true self suddenly can be... violent," she says honestly. "Traumatic. I've seen it. Being forced to hear them by some kind of... device? There's no way of telling how someone will react. That's the whole reason why Melissa's original plan of bringing humans and Shadows together was a process. People would be briefed in advance, they'd spend time alongside their Shadow to get to know them and come to realise their connection over time."

"I didn't hear Zephyr straight away when I first met him," Calvin agrees. "Same with Ember and Phoebe. Sometimes coming to accept your Shadow, to allow their consciousness into yours, takes time. It's a big adjustment. Forcing billions of people to hear their counterparts thoughts, amplified... messing with their minds like that..."

He looks overwhelmed. "It could have unimaginable conse-quences. Plus the telepathic connection doesn't work over long distances, let alone between dimensions." Calvin folds his arms, troubled. "I don't even think I could figure out a way to make it work if I tried. It's science fiction. Impossible."

"You're just saying we don't know anything about how it would work, which is my point," I vent, "that we should commit more resources to finding those answers. And are we really in a position to say what solutions are *tasteful?*" I roll my eyes. "Especially considering the war that's about to end all of existence."

"Griffin," Phoebe says softly. I force myself to avoid looking at her, because I know she can always get through to me, damn her, and I need this. I need this to hold onto. "You're talking about messing with people's minds, breaching their innermost privacy. This isn't the way."

"What, and putting up posters and gathering online petitions is?" I shouldn't say it, but it slips out.

"You know that's not all we're doing," Zephyr says sharply. "We're retrieving actionable intelligence so that we can create a meaningful dialogue between the two worlds. The worse the war gets for both sides, the more likely they are to sit down and make a deal."

"Can you really see that bat-crazy Empress Galvanize making a deal?" I say sarcastically. "Or the United Nations? The two sides could have shut down the portals themselves years ago using the stations, if they wanted this to end. They're both too hungry for the land and resources in each other's world. This isn't about survival, it's about greed."

"We agreed that this was the way we would try and make a difference," Zephyr says quietly, "and we're sticking to it." There's a quiet danger in a voice that makes me stop dead. Still, I can feel myself shaking.

"We're making progress," Calvin tells me gently. "I know it's hard to keep faith, but we have to stay our course."

'What progress?' I want to scream in frustration, but I don't. I know the hope and morale of everyone in this base hangs on a knife edge. Hope and morale are all we have. I don't want to risk breaking that. But I also don't want us blindly walking off a cliff, if what we're doing is taking us nowhere fast.

Clearly, my words are falling on deaf ears. Phoebe, Calvin and Zephyr are all looking at me as if my idea's ludicrous and dangerous, as if this is a sign of me cracking from spending too long in here.

"An extreme situation requires an extreme response," I tell them evenly, silently begging Calvin to understand most of all. He's Mum's other son. He knows how important this is. He must get that this is the piece we've been missing. "I don't think it's fair that the four of us in this room get to turn down something that could save fifteen billion lives. We need to dedicate resources to this. I'm happy to head the project and take full responsibility for it."

"Griffin, it's a no," Calvin says calmly.

"Do I really need to remind you who's in charge now?"

"You know you can't move forward without our support. This is the war getting to you; it's getting to all of us. But once you calm down, you'll see that we're right. Even if what you're talking about wasn't insanely complex and beyond the scope of your abilities, or the scope of anyone here... it's morally reprehensible."

I stare at him. The old Calvin Cameron would not have

hesitated. He would have done whatever it took to end this. I wanted him to believe in me. I thought he did.

"What gives you the right to make the decision for *them*," I say angrily, "the people out there who might die never having met their Shadows? Mum would have understood."

There's a heavy, uneasy silence.

"We can't know what Mum would have wanted," Calvin says quietly, "or Silvaluna. They never imagined that a day like this would come. And with respect, Grif... you were just a child. I know she meant everything to you, but you never met the Melissa we knew."

"Yes," I say thickly, recalling the moment I'd encountered her Majestic in the Underworld, a sacred moment that I still haven't shared with any of them. "Yes, I have."

My blood feels hot in my veins as I leave the desk and stride toward the exit. I'm so angry I'm storming out of my own office. I reach the start of the tunnel that leads from the bridge, then jerk backward in shock.

A girl about my age is standing there right in front of me, pale. I stare.

I know who it is. But that's impossible.

It's a girl who I know for sure has never stepped into the base before this moment. But I recognise her. She's a girl that I know from another time, and another place. Seeing her here, in the midst of all this... for a moment, I'm sure that I'm hallucinating again.

"Griffin!" the girl gasps, flushing. Then she runs at me, throwing her arms around me and nearly bowling me over.

"I knew you weren't a terrorist," she whispers in my ear.

"Sophie?" I say in disbelief.

3

BEFORE NOW

It's her. It's really Sophie. A face that I so associate with home, who has somehow just popped up in our top-secret underground base.

She's still clinging to me.

"How are you...?" I splutter, overwhelmed. "*What* are you...?"

Sophie pulls away, embarrassed.

"Hey, Griffin," she says, strangely shy all of a sudden.

I think my brain is going to implode. But at the same time, I feel an overwhelming wave of relief. She's here, she's safe. She's alive!

"Do I know this human?" Zephyr asks uncertainly. He and the others have come up the ramp to the back of the bridge to investigate.

"This is Sophie," I say, everything feeling unreal. I look to Calvin. He seems utterly clueless.

"Sophie," I repeat impatiently. "My friend. My co-worker at Burger Max." Calvin stares blankly. It's like I can see the tumbleweed blowing idly through his brain. *You know,* I think inwardly, *the one I had that massive awkward crush on through most of my school life.* "We were in a relationship."

"Are you sure?" Calvin says uncertainly.

"Am I *sure?*"

Sophie has gone red.

"Well, we only dated for two months."

"I was very crushed over it," I mutter.

"Um, you're the one who broke up with me," she says.

"I thought we broke up with each other?"

There's an awkward silence.

"It sounds like you two had something quite special," Zephyr offers diplomatically, to fill the silence.

Sophie's eyes are looking determinedly skyward, like she wishes she could be sucked into the floor, not put on the spot by me about our love life in front of the leaders of the last resistance on the planet. She seems a little in awe of them.

"My first proper girlfriend, ever," I repeat for Calvin's benefit. Incredulous that he still doesn't recall.

"Yes. *Yes,* Sophie!" Calvin reaches out and grasps Sophie's hand earnestly, with clumsy enthusiasm. "It's a pleasure to meet you."

"We have met. Just a few times," Sophie says. A giggle escapes her, seeming to surprise even herself.

I sigh. I wish girls I liked were physically repulsed by my brother.

"Excuse us all asking," I say, still reeling, "but how are you here? We don't usually allow walk-ins. We're meant to be top-secret, impossible to find and all that. For obvious reasons."

But then I follow Sophie's gaze to Phoebe. Phoebe's

smiling at me. My heart rises in gratitude.

"You found her in Auckland?" I whisper to Phoebe. "You brought her here so she'd be safe."

"I know you don't have any other friends or family back there," Phoebe says softly. "But I knew you were worried about her."

"It's a good thing Phoebe found me when she did," Sophie says, looking at Phoebe as if she's some kind of action hero-slash-patron saint. "Things were getting ugly and my family..." Sophie cuts off, choked. "Sorry." She shakes her head. "I'm just really tired, and this is all... this is a lot."

"You're safe here," I say, still trying to accept that Sophie is actually here. "Come on. This meeting's over, I'll show you to your room."

When Calvin and Zephyr aren't looking I turn to Phoebe.

"*Thank you,*" I mouth at her, touched.

Phoebe nods.

For a moment I wonder if Phoebe had an agenda literally importing my ex-girlfriend into the base. Like she's trying to set me up. But I dismiss that instantly. Phoebe did it because she's a kind friend, because she looks out for people. Phoebe knew that I'd been trying to find word of Sophie, to find out if my friend was still alive, if she was okay. And it hurts that after all of my own searching, I've been unable to find Phoebe's Mum or her sister, the only family she has left.

I show Sophie to her room so she can stow her stuff. She greets her new dorm mates we run into shyly but warmly.

As much as I'm itching to get down some of the thoughts circulating through my head from the meeting, I give Sophie a tour of the base. It's bizarre having her here. I mean, I had a crush on her back when I didn't even know that Shadows were real.

I do see the wild longing in Sophie's eyes as she sees each person's Shadow. I thought she'd be afraid of them, grossed out, or angry. It can be hard to shake the feelings from only seeing Shadows in war news clips on TV, even if you know so much of it is just propaganda. But I don't see any of that in her. As Sophie looks at the Shadows we pass I notice her hand softly reaching out to the empty air beside her, like if she concentrates very, very hard, she might be able to feel her own Shadow's hand.

"Griffin, can I ask you a question?" she asks. "Where's your Shadow? Can I meet Eclipse?"

"Ah..." I feel a lump in my throat. So she watched the video I'd posted online too. "He's not here."

"Well, I hope I can see him when he gets back. I wonder what my Shadow looks like," she sighs. "Or if I'll ever get a chance to find out."

I look across at Sophie. That ache in her voice for her other half stokes the fire burning inside me at my new idea.

"I'm sure you will." I open my mouth again, then hesitate. "Hey Sophie, there's something I've got to say. You and me dating..."

"Yes?" she says, suddenly alert.

"We... we weren't great at it, were we?" I say sheepishly. "I think we did friendship much better. I'm sorry I didn't see that."

"Um. I guess... I guess maybe dating wasn't the best idea..." She looks weirdly flushed.

"I was going to say it was an unmitigated disaster," I say with a grin.

"Oh…" She smiles strangely. "Oh, yeah."

"Friends?"

"Friends," she says, her head bobbing up and down until she remembers to stop it. "We never stopped being friends, just so you know," she adds, softly.

"I'm sorry how I acted the last time I saw you," I mutter, ashamed, "the day of our break-up. I should have told you about everything, about Shadows…"

"I would have called you crazy. I didn't believe that hours later pterodactyls would be attacking Cameron Technologies. I was sick with worry about you, Grif. It looked like nobody made it out alive. They turned it into a burning wreck. Seeing all those people…" She's pale. "I cried for weeks. And when I found out you were alive, I didn't believe anything the news was saying. Auckland's pretty dire right now, I was lucky to get out. They started building obstacle courses with barbed wire and shooting ranges on our rugby field. Military manoeuvres became part of the school day as much as homeroom. It was all like some nightmare we couldn't wake up from."

I feel sick thinking of our old school. I was miserable there, but somehow that makes me miss it all the more. I miss hating it. I miss when school was the worst thing I had to worry about.

"Hey, if you don't have anything to do right now… do you maybe want to watch some Gilmore Girls?" Sophie says, upbeat. "We could see if some of the others want to watch with us too?" She smiles. "It's a timeless classic."

"I've got stuff I should be doing…"

"Oh, yeah. Of course." Sophie reddens. "Don't worry, I brought some magazines, I'll just read those."

"You might want to try and make those last," I say, smiling weakly. Something occurs to me. "Sophie, where's your family?" I ask.

"My family got out of Auckland, away from the portal," she says. Her lips tremble, but otherwise her face is brave. "But Tim… he was drafted. I stayed to try and sneak him out of the city. My family had told me not to, that they didn't want to lose me, but I went after Tim. I failed him anyway. I couldn't get to Tim in time before he went through." She turns, and I see her trying to wipe away tears without me noticing. Tim is Sophie's older brother. He should still be shooting hoops behind their house, instead of being sent by our government to fight in an alien dimension.

"I'm so sorry." I can't imagine Sophie leaving her family during the evacuation, knowing she might get separated and never see them again, to try and sneak her brother out of the military. Risking her life. I realise that she's changed as much I have.

Sophie shrugs, trying to be upbeat again. It's unconvincing at best.

"Everyone has people in this war that they've lost, right? Everyone has someone they miss. School seems a really long time ago now, doesn't it?"

"Yeah. Yeah, it does."

She looks at me closely as if she's glimpsed something in me.

"Griffin… are you okay? I know that's a stupid question, but… it feels like something is different with you. Something deeper." She looks closer at me, carefully. "Who have *you* lost?"

• • •

My quarters are utterly quiet. Apart from the night shift, everyone else is in bed trying to get some rest before another busy day tomorrow. No matter how many hours we put in, it never seems to be enough. All the while the loneliness and silence of this place are closing in.

Since being the appointed grand 'Leader' of this place, I suppose my rooms are nicer than the others, but it's still pretty simple. I have a small ensuite bathroom and a writing desk in the bedroom between two single beds. The other bed is meant to be for my Shadow. I've buried that bed under papers and reports to try and erase it from sight. I would've removed it entirely but it's fixed to the floor, a constant reminder.

I connect my phone to the room's speakers and hit play. I have a playlist set up where all of the emails I've saved from people around the world who've seen my video are dictated aloud. Instead of hearing the cool, artificial voice of the AI though I feel like I can hear each individual voice, reaching out to me. I hear the excitement in their words on finding out another half of them exists. I hear their burning hope that one day they'll get to meet their Shadow.

Phoebe, Calvin, Zephyr... they're all wrong. Somehow, in my gut, I can feel it. I haven't felt this strongly about something for as long as I can remember, not since my journey with Phoebe to activate the portals, before it all went to crap. My idea to amplify the Shadow-human telepathic connection isn't impossible; it's not as wrong as the others seem to think.

It's just daring.

Making up my mind, I grab my pen and start sketching on the back of one of my files. Suddenly I'm lost in the excited, feverish designs spilling out on the page, glad to play in a playground that's all my own.

What matters is that *I* believe I can do this. I'm not putting this idea of amplifying the connection between humans and Shadows into action for myself, or out of some far-flung hope that Eclipse and I will reunite and be friends again. There's no saving me or my Shadow. I know that. The two halves of my soul are divided, at war with each other. Whatever there was between me and Eclipse is gone.

No. I'm doing this for everyone else. Everyone who deserves to be as happy as me and Eclipse once were.

I think of the moment Eclipse and I saw our Mums' Majestic down in the Underworld. His Mum and mine, Silvaluna and Melissa Cameron, as one. I don't know how real it was, if it was an illusion, or if it was really them.

But I felt their love. I know it was Silvaluna. I know it was Mum.

I'm going to finish this for both of them.

"I'm going to make you proud, Mum," I whisper, staring down at my sketches as a tear blurs a fresh line of blue ink.

At the centre of my sketches is a device. A small device with a touchscreen, like a smartphone. It's shaped like an oval, with appendages shaped like hooks curving out from both ends in opposite directions. It looks like the black, innocent-looking Oracle that we lost in the collapse of Cameron Technologies.

Looking at my design is seeing the old reborn as something new. A device truly with the power to bring Shadows and humans together. But in my mind this device isn't black. Instead it's encased in glimmering gold.

4

THE BATTLE OF TROY

THREE MONTHS LATER

The City of Troy, the Shadow World

An arrow whistles past my head. A split-second later it's accompanied by countless others. My life doesn't end, thanks to a matter of inches. Cries and screams come from all around me. My soldier's uniform is heavy with water. The rifle clasped in my hands shakes uncontrollably as Phoebe and I run from the beach toward the enemy-infested hills, hundreds of other soldiers screaming and firing in chaos all around us.

Somewhere along the line, this field mission went very, very wrong.

The regiment of humans Phoebe and I have disguised ourselves amongst can't be any older than we are. Teenagers, their faces lit by sickly sunlight. They're made up of soldiers from the Australian and New Zealand Army Corps, in an operation led by the Turkish Armed Forces. Some of the soldiers are wetting themselves, others are anticipating the stories they'll tell of their first victory in battle. Not knowing there's a chance they'll kill or be killed by their own Shadow.

If my path hadn't led me where it did, if I hadn't already been at the centre of everything to do with Shadows, then this is where I'd be right now anyhow. Storming a bloody shore along with other students I'd known from high school, shipped off to kill strange creatures in an alien dimension before I'd even earned my University entrance.

But the whole reason Phoebe and I are trapped in this madness right now is because of me. I uncovered whispers within Shadow communications of an important source of intelligence that we desperately need, hidden in the ancient Shadow world city of Troy. Intelligence that will be a big win for us if we get our hands on it. Yes, I said *Troy*. Like the ancient city in our world wrapped in myth.

I'd insisted on coming, despite Phoebe being pretty super against it. We couldn't take any Shadows from the base with us either, due to our plan of passing ourselves off as human soldiers. Thanks to the GSA's allies in some high-up places, we'd used fake identities to pass through the Istanbul portal with other soldiers. It started out real smooth. Phoebe and I had made it across to the Shadow world city of Azure Nazar. The human army had moved out, down the Black Strait toward the city of Troy which was supposed to have been abandoned. The humans were after the fuel stockpile left behind in the abandoned city.

So anyway, a great big hovercraft had taken us up onto the beach. The Shadow world's Troy has ancient walls standing tall and imposing on the hilltops. Below them there's a long stretch of beach, the rocky shoreline scattered with deep pools of water.

Our Armoured Personnel Carriers (or APCs) rolled off the hovercraft and headed up across the beach, toward the hills leading up to the city. Everything was going exactly to plan.

Then it was revealed that reports of the Empire abandoning the city were clearly greatly exaggerated. Shadow soldiers hiding in hillside trenches started firing. The APC that had been transporting Phoebe and me was hit by something explosive. We managed to clamber out with the other troops just before it was struck a second time. We watched it flip through the air, a burning wreck. All of the human soldiers around us were screaming, returning fire as they tried to make for cover behind the other APC's storming the beach.

Which brings us to now. You're pretty much up to date.

Phoebe and I run toward the hills in a suicidal sprint, in the direction of the enemy-infested trenches. The Empire may have managed to cloak itself from the human drones that surveyed the city somehow, but Phoebe and I have a mission in that old city we need to complete, whether it's occupied or not.

I really, really hope we don't die. If I'd known it was going to be this dangerous, I never would have told Phoebe about it.

I slip and fall into one of the rock pools with a splash. My feet touch on something at the bottom that feels far too much like a body. Phoebe grabs my arm.

"Griffin!" I see her shouting at me, her voice stolen away by the cacophony around us. "*Griffin!*"

Then she's hauling me up and I clamber out after her. Reeling from shock we blindly press on toward the hills. Arrows penetrate the sand and pools across the beach, killing everyone they touch. An explosion scatters sand and rocks with stunning force. The sound is deafening. We dive aside to avoid the falling shrapnel.

The walls of Troy loom high above us. A proud and ancient city of the Shadow world, it's everything you'd imagine. Giant flaming torches are fixed to its high stone walls. Chiselled statues of titanic horse heads survey the sloping hills and the ocean below. I can make out tall towers and the domes of what look like grand mosques peaking above the walls. Their midday prayer call drifts down from the city, mingling with the sounds of war and death.

Another volley of arrows needles down at us, hungrily finding their victims. The Shadows learnt long ago that improvements had to be made to the arrows to keep up with human weaponry. These arrows are flung with such force they can puncture through armour, and some explode after piercing their victims. It's pretty horror-show.

We're still racing across the rocky shore, almost to the base of the hills, when Phoebe falls without warning, crashing into one of the rock pools and vanishing from sight. It feels like the world ends.

"Phoebe!" I scream.

I scramble after her, hunting for her in the water. I imagine her choking on water as blood spills from an arrow through her heart... but then my hands find her, and I heave her back up so that her face can breach the surface. I feel like I'm holding my own heart in my hands.

"I'm okay, I'm okay!" Phoebe gasps, and I'm nearly sick

with relief. She grips my shoulder as I help her to her feet, and I'm relieved to see there's no arrow shafts stuck in her. "I just tripped into it..." Phoebe's voice cuts off abruptly as she looks back at the rock pool. We can both make out a face in the water. Skin waxy white, the soldier's hair billowing around her like seaweed, looking like she's smiling up at the heavens.

Soldiers flounder around us as they're wiped out under enemy fire. Others float lifelessly in the rock pools, the water pink and frothy with the fallen. Others vanish from sight into the pools but struggle to surface again with their heavy outfits streaming water. I see others struggling before their lives are extinguished.

There's nothing Phoebe or I can do. We're in hell.

How we're still alive I have no idea, but it's not over yet. Overturned APCs litter the beach, flaming. The air is alive with gunfire, humans taking shots up at the high walls of the city and the hills below it where the Shadows are flinging arrows down at us like we're sitting ducks. Catapults launch giant chunks of red gemstone that detonate violently into flame when they strike the beach. Not to mention the barrage of Shadow powers being cast down at us; bursts of ice that can freeze off limbs, flashes of lightning that sear down at us, melting metal helmets and mowing down everything in their path.

It looks impossible for any human to remain alive. Hundreds, if not thousands of them will have already been killed or wounded before reaching the land, their bones turned to dust, washed out with the tide, forgotten far from home.

Seeing Turkish, Australian and New Zealand soldiers fighting side by side is overwhelming. I feel a strangely acute bout of homesickness. Over a hundred years ago the Australians and New Zealanders had been fighting the Turkish on the beaches of Gallipoli. That's what exists where we are now, but over in the human world. Now Turkish, Australian and New Zealand forces are finally united together... all so they can fight another pointless battle in a meaningless war. That's been the one silver lining of all this, that it's brought all the nations of the human world together in peace. Unfortunately, that's just so that they can more effectively kill their mutual enemy.

Phoebe and I make it to the base of the hills. A tall wall of stones and barbed wire runs along it. Keeping low, using the wall as a shield, we move away from the centre of the fighting. Phoebe stoops to extract the C4 from the bag.

Jeez, I almost forgot we had that. Thankfully we haven't been shot yet and blown sky-high.

I try and cover Phoebe as she sets the explosives, then at her shout we both scramble away. The blast reverberates through the wall. It looks like the explosive survived any water damage. There's so much chaos and misery all around us that I doubt anyone even heard the explosion.

Phoebe checks that I'm behind her then surges forward, scrabbling through the hole in the wall and up the slippery mud into the trenches.

I follow after her as we make our way up through the sliced wounds in the side of the hills, trying to skirt around the main fighting as we make for the city. It sounds straight forward. In reality it's insanity. It feels like it takes several lifetimes, all while a battle of biblical proportions crashes on, dangerously close.

I'm still carrying my army issue rifle, clasping it in my cold hands. As we push up through the bunker, I pray I won't have to use it. I'm not sure if I'm more afraid for myself if we run into Shadow soldiers or for them if I have to kill.

High in the air above us, human choppers and jets are engaged in aerial combat with the Shadows defending the city. I watch as two choppers are sent spinning through the air, crashing into each other in a fiery inferno as a great, winged goblin traps them in a mini-tornado with its wings. I see an electric eel with the wings of an eagle shot down by machine-gun fire. A flying wooden ship, its sails the violet of the Empire, is defended by an invisible force field until it falters, missiles striking its hull. The burning wreck nearly crashes down into me and Phoebe, too close for comfort, but we push on.

I pause as I hear shouts coming from around the corner to our right. I just catch a glimpse of violet-armoured soldiers, running to aid their fellow soldiers in combat.

Seizing our chance, I rush forward and drop into the recently emptied bunker... but I trip suddenly, my leg caught, and I'm sent sprawling to the ground. My rifle flies from my grasp and I spin around, ready to fend off whoever's grabbed onto my legs...

But there's no one. I'm entangled with a corpse. A giant Shadow in violet plates of armour, slain by human bullets. The golden-feathered, scaled Shadow lies lifeless, his serpentine tail stretched like an anaconda along the wooden boards lining the trench.

I put a hand to my mouth, moaning. I'm immobilised with fear.

"Griffin. Griffin." Phoebe's hand is on my shoulder. "It's not him," she says quietly.

She's right. This dead Shadow is big, but not nearly as

big as Eclipse. Its body is more round too, like a hen crossed with a snake. I breathe again, angrily trying to get control of myself.

Apart from the dead Shadow, this trench is unoccupied by Imperial soldiers, as it's too far from the main battle. I can't believe we survived that. I know Phoebe's thinking the same thing.

It's my fault. This is my Intel that we're acting on. My mistake that nearly cost her her life. She came because she trusted me.

I find I'm staring down at the dead Shadow again.

"One minute," Phoebe says to me, barely out of breath. "Drink some water, then we'll slip into the city before we get any more unwelcome company." She doesn't say a word as to what we just endured. We both know there's nothing to talk about. It can only to be felt.

As I catch my breath I look down at my trembling hands. They're covered in blood. The Shadow's blood.

Phoebe comes up to me. Removing the lid of her water bottle, she tips some of the contents over my hands.

"Pheebs, what are you doing?" I say, incredulous. "We're going to need every drop..." I stop as she gently rubs my hands, using the water to clean off the blood from the dead Shadow. The Shadow that looks like mine. I swallow. I look up and meet Phoebe's eyes. Her hands are still holding mine.

Then, as if catching herself, she slowly slides her hands away. Wordlessly, she turns and stalks back over to survey the battle for Troy unfolding down on the beach.

I take a moment, staring down at the dead golden Shadow. Then I rejoin Phoebe.

"So... do you think this Troy is somehow based on the Troy in our world?" I wonder, staring up at the high walls.

"Maybe," Phoebe answers thoughtfully chewing on an escaped lock of fiery hair. "Or, like, is this the exact same Troy that existed in our world, except it never got destroyed over here, because history happened differently? I still don't get how the Shadow world works." Phoebe gazes down at the bay, at the horror below. It's one of the worst sights that will follow us for the rest of our lives. However long those might be. "This is officially the worst birthday ever," she says.

"Wait, it's your *birthday?*" I say, turning to her. "You didn't tell me that."

"I've told you before, Grif. You're missing the key part of friend's birthdays, where you're the one supposed to *remember them.*"

The hours go by, and the siege of Troy is vicious but short. The winged Shadows defending the city are shot down by human jets and surface-to-air missiles from the ships out on the water. The fighting carries on in the hills but it won't be long before the humans are landing their aircraft within Troy's walls to deploy troops... and the city will surely be theirs not long after that.

Phoebe and I use the trenches as cover as we make our way up to the walls of the city. The air is choked with black smoke from the human missile strikes against the hillside, and for a moment everything is as dark as night as it drifts across us. The maze-like trenches ahead of us are obscured. We feel the ever present danger of running into armed Shadows, or of another human missile striking the hills and blowing us up without warning. We scramble through the dark, almost blindly, like mice in a maze.

I carefully study the images displayed in my Cameron Glasses™ as we navigate our way through the trenches. I'm looking at some drone photos taken of Troy a few months back. The trenches were already dug in then as a defence. I'm zoomed in, trying to read which routes we need to take to get us closer and closer to the city walls. I try to keep us away from the paths with the best vantage points of the beach that are more likely to be occupied by Imperial soldiers.

"This way," I say. Then: "Next left."

As I reel off the directions Phoebe reacts instantly, trusting me implicitly, responding as if we're psychically linked. I've missed this: the two of us being in the field together, completely in sync.

The acrid-smelling smoke from the flames and explosions drifts in a dark, ominous cloud around us, reducing our visibility. We squint, smoke stinging our eyes, trying to make out the way forward.

"Did you see that?" I whisper abruptly.

"See what?

I stare high into the black haze. For a moment, I thought something pale had flashed there. Something alive.

Was it even real? Am I starting to imagine things again? I'm learning slowly that the demons within are even more dangerous than the ones without. Phoebe's life is my responsibility. If I start seeing things, if I lose my grip on reality... I need to be able to trust my own mind. It's all I've got left.

Then we hear something. A sound like nails on a blackboard.

Phoebe presses herself up against the side of the trench. Turning, I look up... and see a fearsome claw reaching toward Phoebe from the rooftops, long talons blindly feeling their way down toward us.

Somehow we keep ourselves from screaming. We step slowly away from the claw, keeping low. Then we're racing away, as quiet as possible, zigging and zagging madly to escape it.

When I look over my shoulder, I suddenly realise I'm staring at a Shadow. It slowly stands up, towering high above the trenches. A gargoyle, its skin as white as bone. Long leathery wings stretch slowly outward as it turns its head, searching for us; a silent titan of death. Then black smoke drifts across, obscuring the terror once more.

We make our way into the city, leaving the dark haze of smoke behind us for the light of the sun. The imposing walls show the skeleton of what the city once was, but they've crumbled in places and no longer fully encircle the city. Instead modern streets and malls have been built around the fragments of the old city, like if Middle-Earth had suddenly found itself having to haphazardly modernise.

We slip into the city undetected, evading the patrolling guards as best we can, knowing that at any moment, the city could fall to the humans.

"I can't believe you actually forgot it was my birthday," Phoebe exhales.

"You're focusing on this right now?" I say, incredulous.

"I'm not having a go, I'm just asking. Where's my present, Grif? Clearly, this merry mission your Intel has led us on doesn't count."

We stop to hide in the shade, watching as sobbing families of Shadows stumble past us in fine-coloured silks, fleeing for their lives to God knows where. It wasn't just Imperial soldiers who had reoccupied this city then.

"There are children here," Phoebe whispers, watching the smallest of the terrorised innocents.

"I know," I say quietly.

My attention is caught by graffiti on a wall opposite us as the Shadows run past it. The bright splashes of paint read: '*I LOVE MY HUMAN.*'

Something inside me strengthens. We're not alone. There are still those who resist, in this city, here and everywhere. There are those who can still imagine a universe of diversity, one where we're not at war with our very selves.

"Grif," Phoebe says tensely. "Let's move."

I look up, and my spirits plummet. Human aircraft are landing on the rooftops of the city's towers. The battle in the air is finished. Soon human troops will be running freely through the city, and Troy will fall to my world. For whatever reason, the Shadows here are under-equipped and weakened, ill-prepared to fend off a human invasion.

Taking Phoebe's arm, I guide her the final few turns to reach our prize: the golden-fleece that's hopefully going to make this bonkers mission worth it.

"Three moves until you reach your destination," I say, imitating the smooth voice of a satnav.

"Which is what, by the way?" Phoebe says, sounding irate for the first time. "What's worth risking our lives for this time? You've been awfully tight-lipped about it."

I don't answer. We enter through the open face of a huge stone building. All that is left of the façade is rubble and shredded timber. I'm glad the rest of the building seems to be intact.

We rush down the stone corridor. It sounds like the sounds of battle are getting closer.

"These are the coordinates," Phoebe says edgily. "What is this, some kind of prison?"

She's right about that. But I'd thought there would still be guards here for the high value prisoners, since the city hasn't been as abandoned as last thought. I feel a squirm inside me.

Please, please let her be here. Let her be okay.

I weave back and forth between the doors on either side, sliding open the small grills in each one. Every cell is empty. I feel a gnawing fear in my gut.

But then I slide open another grill and see what lies beyond it. I feel an intense rush of relief.

"Phoebe, has the rest of that C4 blown up yet?"

"I think you'd know, Grif," Phoebe says, extracting it from her backpack. I can *hear* her rolling her eyes. "Or you wouldn't, because we'd be very dead." She makes to look through the grill in the door but I nudge her away from it.

"We have to be fast," I remind her, as she fixes the C4 to the lock.

Phoebe hesitates.

"The noise might attract attention."

"All the soldiers are off defending the city, and the noise should be masked by the other big explosions," I say. "We'll be okay."

"So what, we get the asset, then we commandeer one of

the human choppers and tail it back to the portal without being found out?"

"Yup. Easy peasy. I'm sure everything will go swimmingly."

Phoebe clears the blast radius, pulling me with her.

"Three, two, one..."

We clamp our ears as the lock detonates. Then we run forward, just in case we did draw attention after all. Phoebe scans the room with her rifle, waiting for the smoke to clear.

I hear her breath as it's sucked from her body.

We're both staring into a grim, dark prison cell. A feathered Shadow is strapped to an X-shaped metal frame, her wings stretched wide. Her head is bowed, her body unmoving. I stare, an awful, terrifying feeling seizing me. That after all this, after coming all this way for her... we may be too late.

"What...?" Phoebe breathes, her voice barely a whisper. "How..." She sounds like a little girl again.

But then the Shadow slowly stirs, lifting her head in a struggle to gaze at us. She's alive. She's still fighting.

"Phoebe?" the phoenix croaks.

"Ember?" Phoebe whispers.

Phoebe rushes forward to hug her Shadow, then stops herself. Her hands hover delicately, urgently around Ember's head, afraid that her touch might hurt Ember in her current state. Phoebe is trembling like a leaf.

"It's you," Ember whispers in wonder. "When I felt you in Sanctuary... it was real. You're real."

"I am," Phoebe half-sobs, half-laughs. She pulls a knife from her belt and starts slashing urgently at Ember's bindings.

"You've been alive all this time, and I never knew," Ember says, wretched. "I failed you."

"You've failed me?" Phoebe chokes, stunned. She slices the final binding, and Ember slumps forward. Phoebe catches her, a tough thing when Ember is almost as tall as she is. Phoebe falls to her knee to hold the phoenix's weight, enveloped by Ember's wings. Phoebe nuzzles her head into Ember's neck. Ember nuzzles her back, tears running from her beak. As I watch the love in that moment between a human and a Shadow who haven't seen each other in eleven years, I feel an intense pang of jealousy and a longing so sharp that I have to look away.

"How can you even say that?" Phoebe is saying, shocked. "Look at you. Look at who you've become. All the time I was gone, you never stopped fighting. You're my Ember, you're everything..." Phoebe seems torn between being awe-struck, and aghast at seeing her Shadow's state. "Oh, Ember, I'm so sorry. But we're going to fix it."

"Oh good. How?" Ember smiles wryly, looking her human in the face. She seems overwhelmed.

"We get you the hell out of here," Phoebe says. "We're getting you back to base, back to our home. Where you belong."

"In your world?" Ember whispers.

"It's your home as much as it is ours. You know that." Phoebe smoothens Ember's fiery feathers. "We're going to have to carry her," Phoebe says to me anxiously.

"I'm fine, stop fretting." Ember nips playfully at Phoebe's hair with her beak, like a mother with her baby chick. "Jeez, just a little joint in prison and some long-term torture and you blow a fuse." She sees Phoebe's traumatised expression. "I'm sorry," Ember says hastily. "My humour did get pretty dark when I was in here. But I can walk." She struggles, but manages to take her own weight with her claws. "I'm strong enough for this," Ember says, looking up determinedly. "Let's get the hell out of this hole."

The sounds of gunfire and the screams of Shadows are all too audible through the stone walls of the prison.

"We need to get out before this place starts rolling out the UN flag and building Burger Max franchises," I agree.

"No way," Ember says, hearing my voice. She blinks at me with bleary eyes. "Griffin, is that you?"

"Hey, Ember," I say nervously. I respect her more than anything, but there is the small matter that last time I saw her I secretly manipulated the Resistance into attacking Sanctuary City in the hope of making a morally questionable trade with Raven.

"We have to stop only catching up during sieges," Ember comments with a hint of her old, signature glibness.

"I am one hundred percent with you on that," I nod with a quick smile.

"I heard you were alive, that you survived the Battle of Sanctuary," Ember tells me, "but I'm really glad to see it and know it's true."

"You too."

"Griffin," Phoebe says through her tears, dazed. She looks between Ember and me. "How did you..."

I smile softly.

"Happy Birthday, Phoebe."

Phoebe stares at me.

There's another explosion, far too close to the prison.

"Do you have anyone else here?" Phoebe asks Ember

urgently. "Your people, was anyone else captured from the Resistance?"

"The Resistance is dead," Ember says heavily.

In the time that I've known her, the leader of the Resistance has been playful, tongue-in-cheek, infuriatingly righteous, honourable, calculating, and infinitely resilient and courageous. But I've never heard her like this.

Broken.

The Resistance is dead.

The words hit me like a wave. A cold sensation washes right through me.

Ember had founded a safe haven for humans and Shadows on this side who wanted to live together, much like the GSA base on our side. Except Ember's had grown into a movement locked in civil war with the human-loathing Empire. Lately we'd heard barely anything from the Resistance in this world, and all this time we'd thought if we could just make contact, perhaps the GSA and Ember's Resistance could pool our resources and somehow bring an end to this war. Finding and rescuing Phoebe's Shadow still makes this mission worth it, of course it does... but it also extinguishes one of the last hopes we had of bringing an end to this war.

I'm still numb from her words, barely able to process the news after coming so far. The Resistance, completely wiped out. *How is that even possible?*

But I can't give that another thought right now. We have to fight through it; we can't let that sense of defeat weaken us. We need all our focus right now for the three of us to make it out of this warzone alive.

I move through the other cell doors in the corridor, checking through each of the slats in search of other prisoners. There might be other enemies of the Empire here who could help our cause. Empty, empty... It seems that most of these cells are unoccupied. I reach the last grate and slide it open to check it, expecting it to be barren like the others.

There's someone inside. A human man. He seems to be restrained in what looks like a white straitjacket. His long dark hair falls across his face and his black beard is unkempt and shaggy.

"Hello? I call to him through the grate. There's no response. The guy doesn't even stir.

If it is a human, then he'll be released anyhow when his people take this place. We don't have to worry about him. I should leave.

"Hello?" I repeat, tersely.

The figure stirs at the sound, and he turns his head ever so slightly toward the stimulus of my voice. His hair falls away from his features, revealing a terrifyingly familiar face.

I see who it is. But it makes no sense. The walls start to close in.

"Griffin?" the dishevelled prisoner croaks.

Well, I think, stunned, staring at Raven. This complicates things.

5

AND I FEEL FINE

Raven. A cold hatred blooms in my belly, seizing me with a sudden desire to grab him by the throat and suffocate him with my bare hands.

I gasp for oxygen. The prison spins around me.

It was because of Raven that Cirrus and I grew up apart from each other. He killed my parents, he killed Mr Falco. But my last meeting with Raven had also shaken me to my core. What was so simple before is no longer anywhere near as simple. Staring at him, cowering, dirtied, with a haunted look in his eyes, I'm at a loss to name the emotions I'm feeling.

I shake my head fiercely. This is the man who betrayed my family. This is the creator of the Empire, the individual who planned the war between the two worlds.

What the hell is the genius mastermind, the dark puppeteer of the Empire, doing rotting in an Imperial cell?

It's a trap. It has to be. Everything Raven does is intentional. He's always thinking seven steps ahead of us.

So what *is* this trap exactly? What should we do with him? What does he expect us to do with him?

Why is he *here?*

That's when I glimpse something else through the slats in the door. What I thought was just a pile of old blankets on the hard stone floor suddenly moves. There's someone else in the cell too.

A Shadow.

Slowly it clambers onto its two legs, head bowed as if asking for mercy. I stare at it in recognition. It's like a human crossed with a crow, its eyes small, black and beady. I know that it's large, feathered black wings are capable of unleashing streams of ice are strapped to its sides, are bound by another white straitjacket.

Winter. Raven's creepy, servile Shadow. The one who attacked me and Cirrus when we were just children, the night that my Mum died. He's haunted my nightmares ever since, long before I discovered that the nightmares were actually memories. But right now Winter looks more pitiful, more beaten than ever. They both do.

But I'm not one to take anything on appearances when it comes to Raven. This can't be a coincidence, me finding them here.

Surely it isn't.

"Is there someone in there?" I hear Phoebe call to me, and I start violently. "Who is it?"

I don't even know how to begin to answer that, knowing that the truth will inflame Phoebe and Ember beyond all reason. Ember might even kill Raven. And she'd have every right to.

I take in the straitjackets again. Jeez. The Empire really wasn't taking any chances with either of them. Smart.

What the hell do I do?

For the millionth time, I wish that Eclipse was…

Shaking my head, I sigh.

The prison trembles, and I can hear what sounds like the roar of a chopper landing, as if it's right on top of us.

Human soldiers. It sounds like they're landing on top of the prison. Dang. It won't be long until they're storming down those steps, trigger-happy and high on adrenaline.

"Ember!" I shout. "There are two prisoners in here, I need you to blast it open! Do you have any juice?"

"I can try." Ember limps up behind me. Her feathers spark, flame licking across them, but it's much less dramatic than her usual fiery plumage. "Fire in the hold."

I duck out of the way as a volley of flames blasts from her body, smashing the door off of its hinges in a miniature eruption. Guess she's still got it. I charge into the cell. It stinks. There's a handful of dirty sacks on the floor, like some kind of makeshift bedding. I grab a sack and pull it over Raven's head to hide his face from the others, then do the same to Winter. There's time to deal with that distraction later. Raven flinches in surprise, but otherwise he barely resists, his shoulders sagging. Winter complies limply with no argument, as if he's barely living at all.

I grab hold of the two of them at the back of their necks, feeling a shudder as I touch them.

"Don't you dare move," I whisper into their ears. "Either of you, or I'll tell Ember who you are, and risk her obliterating you on the spot. Understood?"

Already I can hear the sound of boots coming down the stone steps toward our level. Shoot. The troops from the chopper.

"Hide!" Phoebe hisses, and we all take cover, flattening

ourselves against the wall on either side of the cell door. I peek around the corner, and I'm shocked to see violet-armoured Shadows instead of humans. They don't notice us though; they're in a rush to join the fight to protect their falling city. I'm guessing those humans who just landed on the roof must have lost whatever battle just transpired up there.

"They're gone," I say finally, exhaling in relief.

"Who are *these* guys?" Phoebe says, casting an eye at my masked captives. I push Raven's head down instinctively, even though he has the sack over his face. He complies meekly.

I catch Ember's gaze lingering on Winter's talons and his black moulting legs emerging from the strait jacket. But if she suspects anything, she holds her tongue. Out of tact or utter exhaustion, I'm not sure which.

"Let's just say they might be useful," is all I say, my tongue feeling thick and clumsy in my mouth. "Now we just need a way out of..."

Phoebe and I catch each other's look. We can still hear the sound of the slowing rotor blades up above.

"I think those soldiers brought me a birthday present," she says flippantly. Then with a flash of her signature devil-may-care grin, she makes for the stairs, Ember shuffling stoically along beside her. I march after them, taking my hostages with me... one of them the most dangerous and intelligent man in the entire universe.

Our luck holds when we get to the roof. The chopper blades are spinning to a slow stop, the aircraft undamaged. The troops and pilot have been hauled from the chopper, their lifeless bodies strewn around us. I don't even look at them. I'm not sure if it's the shock or if I'm just desensitised to death after what we've been through.

The chopper is a Chinook. It's a long, powerfully built aircraft meant for carrying heavy loads and capable of containing large numbers of troops. Phoebe helps Ember struggle up into the back of the chopper, the phoenix weakly flapping her wings to help propel herself in. I force a stumbling Raven and Winter toward the chopper. We reach an awkward hurdle though when it's time for them to clamber into it.

"Raise your left foot," I mutter into Raven's ear, shivering at our proximity. I can barely believe what's happening. "No... the rail is... yeah." I give him a shove, and he collapses onto the floor of the chopper, hands still bound within the straitjacket. Ember moves automatically to help him.

"No!" I say, holding a hand up at her. "Don't touch him, and if either of them tries anything... burn them."

Ember gives me a suspicious look, almost like she knows... but then I'm busy helping Winter clamber blindly up into the back.

I pull open the passenger door and grab a headset, fitting it onto my head. I swing myself up into the cockpit beside Phoebe. She's firing up the chopper, familiarising herself with the controls. She grips the control stick convincingly.

"You do know how to pilot this thing right?" I say, shutting the door behind me.

"Of course. We study all the vehicles used by human and Imperial military." Phoebe hesitates. "I'm just re-familiarising myself, that's all."

"Very reassuring for the passengers. Let's haul arse back to the portal before our luck runs out."

The scream of the rotor blades increases, and then we're defying gravity as we start to rise from the roof of the prison tower. The city of Troy comes more into view as we ascend: the chaos down in the streets, the fires starting to eat at the buildings.

While Phoebe does the heroic bad-arse piloting I do the heroic... um, DJ responsibilities.

"Any '*Mission Impossible Theme?*'" I ask, fiddling with the music system. Then I laugh. I've hit a song by REM that couldn't be more fitting or more exquisitely ironic.

"*It's The End Of The World As We Know It...*"

"*...and I feel fine,*" Phoebe and I sing along as we launch into the air. We try to ignore the fiery apocalyptic scenes below as Troy falls. The Chinook carries us, Ember, the most dangerous man in the universe and his Shadow back out to sea. Somewhere across it is the portal back to our own world.

Suddenly I hear a roar. An unnervingly familiar sound that rises above every other noise from the battle. Something in it makes me seize up. It's a deep roar, more avian than mammalian. A silhouette passes over the buildings of Troy. Something great and winged, a tail swooping behind it.

"What was that?" Phoebe yells. But we don't have long before a more pressing emergency arrives.

"Look to sea, we've got trouble!" I hear Ember shout in warning through the ears of my headset. Ember's only just started speaking when Phoebe banks right, trying to change the chopper's course as she sees through her Shadow's eyes whatever Ember has seen.

Craning my neck, I see what the problem is. A giant freaking problem.

We're approaching the Trojan shore, headed straight to the ocean. But the human military ships drifting just offshore seem to have spotted us. Worse, I can see even from up here that their missile launchers are swivelling definitively in our direction.

"No," I whisper. Beside me, Phoebe swears. Escaping without the humans finding out we're imposters was our only hope. The amount of firepower training itself on us right now is inescapable.

"Why are they aiming at their own chopper?" I yell.

"One of the humans on the roof must have still been alive. I bet he called it in."

"That or your slightly erratic flying!" I growl, holding on for dear life.

No. We didn't go through all of this to get Ember for nothing. If we all die here, our deaths are on me.

"If I could make a suggestion..." I hear someone croak into my headset. Not Ember, someone else. A muffled voice, distorted through Raven's face-sack.

"No!" I snap back at him in frustration. "Shut up! Damn it, Ember, don't give him headset privileges."

But Phoebe is frozen, and I see how white she suddenly is. Her entire body has seized up. She's recognised the voice from under that sack.

"Was that...?" Phoebe begins, her voice hoarse.

And then all of it, the battle, the missile launchers, our hostage in the back, suddenly fades into the background as a boom reverberates through the air. It's a kind of prehistoric roar. We heard it before, but now there's no mistaking who it belongs to.

No. It can't be.

Something is coming after us, across the towers and rooftops of Troy. Something great in size, its wings beating slowly. It's nothing but a silhouette in the smoke from the siege.

I'm shaking. Scared to believe it's really him. I tell myself I don't care but tears are streaking down my cheeks.

I turned my back on him for so long, I've buried the thought of ever seeing him again. It can't be. I won't let myself feel all of that hurt again. But every part of me, every atom of my being is drawn toward him. I know. I know it's him.

He's flying from the direction of Troy's walls, directly toward our chopper. As if the human missile launchers swivelling to train on us aren't enough of a sign that this is the end for us.

The smoke clears, and I see him in all of his glory, damn him. Even from here, it feels like we're staring directly into each other's eyes, facing off high above the siege.

The upper half of his body is that of a proud cockatoo, one of those crested parrots from Australia. His feathers are as golden as the sun, exuding warmth. His wings flap steadily, and the reptilian body that trails behind him has scales like gleaming coins from a dragon's hoard. His tail is enormously long and slender like a whip, ending in a splay of tail-feathers.

My heart feels like it just got pulled apart.

There's no way this isn't a hallucination. Having Ember, Raven and Winter all in the back of our chopper? Ridiculous. There's no way Eclipse just happens to be here too, right at this time.

But of course he is. I was drawn here, and somehow, he was too.

My Cirrus. My Eclipse. My other half.

I snap to my senses. Eclipse is on the other side now, I tell myself. He's our enemy, and he's flying right at us like he's going to attack us and tear us from the very air. We're stuck between him and the missile launchers preparing to fire...

"Griffin," Phoebe gasps. "Look."

I rip my eyes away my Shadow as if I've been drinking in the sight.

Now I see what Phoebe has seen.

The ocean seems to shiver with a blue luminosity that's rippling outward from the shore. The water begins to churn and the human ships sway dangerously. Waves rise up to smash down on the boats, threatening to capsize some as the water pushes them away from us and out to sea.

I gape. I think every single human and Shadow stops their fighting, awestruck, to turn and watch, like they're witnessing a once-in-a-lifetime miracle.

It's Eclipse. I can sense it. He's doing it. Eclipse is single-handedly turning back the human forces in the water, single-handedly altering the course of battle with his sheer power.

This is like nothing I've ever seen. Not even from him. I remember when he had felt dizzy just from turning Nugwai's arm into stone, so long ago. Back when he was Cirrus.

He'd done it to save me.

Some of the floundering ships manage to fire off a couple of missiles at Eclipse before they're swept away... which means the missiles fly straight at us as well.

Eclipse surges past us, and the Chinook wobbles in the air flow created by his powerful wings. We watch as the dragon-parrot summons sheets of water up out of the ocean purely with a single thought. The water spins together, flying through the air to collect in a giant liquid orb. It crashes into some of the missiles, knocking them off course to sail into the distance. Eclipse barrel-rolls through the air to dodge the remaining missiles...

Then one detonates right on top of him.

"NOOOOO!" I scream.

An agony tears through every one of my nerve endings, as physical as it is emotional. I feel like I'm dying. Darkness encroaches on my vision as I watch him fall. Eclipse hurtles downward, descending in slow motion toward the hills at the foot of Troy. He flips through the air, falling, his wings faltering like a bird that has died mid-flight.

"Eclipse!" I gasp, jerking upward.

I blink.

Covered in cold sweat, I look around me. I'm in my own bed back at base. How did I get here?

My walls are barren. I haven't put any posters up like some of the others do. I find that having a blank canvas feels safer for some reason.

I roll out of bed and my bare feet touch the cold metal floor. I moan as a sharp pain lances through my head.

Troy. Was it all just a nightmare? I wonder. The heat, the violence ... it feels surreal. But how on earth did we get back here, and how did I sleep through the entire journey?

Phoebe. Ember. Are they okay? Did they make it back too?

I groan, trying to collect my thoughts, to make sense of everything. My skull is pounding, and I clutch it. I've never had a hangover, but I imagine this is what it feels like. My skin feels raw and painful. It feels like I've been hit by a missile.

The room swims around me.

Eclipse.

The last thing I remember is... him. I see him in my mind's eye again, the missile flying up at him, the explosion...

His body falling lifelessly to earth.

I'm barely aware of pulling on a shirt and hitting the button on the mic beside my bed.

"Core team meeting in the bridge," I say. "Right now."

Then I'm barrelling out into the corridor, racing as fast as I can.

The others I pass in the corridors all look alarmed as I shoot past.

Eclipse. It had really been him. I remember seeing him struck out of the sky... but if I'm breathing, that means he's still breathing too. He has to be. The Shadow can't survive without the human, and vice versa.

I must have passed out when Eclipse was hit, but that seems crazy. It's as if the link between us is stronger than ever. I'd felt Eclipse's pain as if it was mine. That's never happened before, not at that level.

I try to shake off the troubling implications of that. Still. If I survived... he must still be alive somewhere too.

I have to find out from the others what happened. I have to know that Phoebe and Ember are okay too.

That's when I feel it. A tingling. An electricity down through me into the extremities of my body. It's a sensation in every part of me, more instinct than anything. That sixth sense that tells me, even if I can't hear him in my head... He's alive. Eclipse is still alive.

I breathe out heavily, steadying myself against the wall. But as I feel that wave of relief, it suddenly crashes into simultaneous paralysing fear.

"No," I say in shock.

Eclipse is close. Somewhere very close. I can feel him.

No. They can't have possibly have brought him *here*.

With a rush I remember Raven and Winter. Does this mean they're here too?

Suddenly a voice speaks, resonating from every corner of the ship.

"Griffin will be able to fill you in now that he's conscious," Calvin is saying over the intercom system, *"but as I was saying, it's thanks to Intel acquired by him, and a mission led by Phoebe, that we've recovered two very special new recruits: their Shadows."*

Feeling sick, I triple my running speed.

Excited chatter reverberates around me as I hurtle toward the bridge. Never before has anyone here outside of the leadership team ever met the Shadow of Phoebe, the hero of our base, or the Shadow of Griffin, the reclusive Leader/YouTube sensation.

"Ember founded the Resistance in the Shadow world," Calvin's voice continues from above. *"She's been fighting for peace longer than any of us. Eclipse has the ability to mimic one Shadow's power at a time; using some form of telekinesis, he was witnessed singlehandedly parting opposing forces during the siege of Troy. I don't have to tell you how valuable Ember and Eclipse will be to our operations."*

Excited whispering fills the corridors. I can tell that all

our members are mentally trying to picture how one Shadow could possibly be capable of that.

"*This is a major triumph for every single one of you.*" Calvin's in his element again making a speech. He always loved the performance, the chance to play the charismatic leader. He was known as the man of conviction who could raise his employee's morale and their corporate bloodlust with a single rousing speech. It's a role I think he really, really misses playing. Maybe a little too much.

I'm almost at the bridge.

"*I hope you're all proud of what we're accomplishing here,*" Calvin continues. "*It's thanks to your hard work that two of our heroes are home safe.*"

I pass campaign offices as the people inside applaud and cheer. I hear Rihäm call out to me cheerfully in congratulations, but I just put on a tight smile like a mask as I stampede toward the tunnel at the end of the hallway.

There's no need for any of them to know what a fudgestorm my brother has brought into our base until I have some idea what we can even do about it. It won't help anyone to tell them that Eclipse could be working for the Empire, not after Calvin just told them how Eclipse can control oceans with his mind and send armies scattering. The last thing we need is a panic in close quarters.

"*Eclipse has been through a lot,*" Zephyr adds over the intercom, with his customary gruff, military stiffness. He's still surprisingly awkward interacting with so many young people. "*Please don't overwhelm him, use him for games or do anything alarming.*" Zephyr's voice becomes emotional. "*He's a very special boy.*"

"*Yes, well,*" Calvin says, and I can hear the quirk of a

smile in my brother's tone. *"Give the very special seventeen-foot boy lots of space if he needs it."*

I race down the tunnel and burst into the bridge. Calvin and Zephyr are there waiting for me in front of my desk. Phoebe is there too.

Thank God. My knees nearly buckle with relief. If she'd been hurt...

"You're okay," I gasp. "Ember?"

"She's fine," Phoebe assures me in a rush. "We were worried about *you*. After Eclipse was hit..."

"Killer headache, but I'm fine."

I stride toward Phoebe and hug her, without thinking.

"Eclipse," I croak. "Is he... is he hurt? Is he all right?" I can feel him here, in the base, but his mind is dark, subdued.

"He's okay, Grif," Phoebe says, quietly. "Any other Shadow would have been killed. But he's..."

"... not normal," I finish for her. Relief pours through me, and I flush, dropping my arms.

"Grif," Calvin says, his face lit up. "You're awake. We were worried, we weren't sure exactly what was wrong with you."

"Get off," I scowl, pulling the microphone away from him. "This is mine. The intercom is not for you, okay? It's special. Now can someone please tell me what the heck is going on? I know I was unconscious, but are you telling me you brought Eclipse back *here*?"

"Yes," Phoebe says.

"Why?" I explode at her.

"You're lucky either of you got back to base at all," she shoots back, a sharp edge in her voice.

"Phoebe landed your chopper," Zephyr says quietly.

"After you and Eclipse passed out at Troy. Phoebe and Ember used the cargo haul net they found on board as a sling to carry Eclipse beneath the aircraft."

"I wasn't sure the Chinook would take Eclipse's weight," Phoebe says, shrugging, as if landing in an active warzone to airlift a giant dragon-parrot hadn't been suicide. "Good thing it turns out he has hollow bones so he was lighter than I expected."

I look at Phoebe, suddenly forgetting everything else.

"You did that for me?" I whisper.

"Of course," she says, narrowing her eyes. "And I would again, in a heartbeat. I was just lucky that a contact forged the paperwork for us in time. I managed to pass Eclipse and Ember off as hostages and fly them back through the portal. As if that wasn't stressful enough, we only just made it back here before a battle broke out above the base."

"Wait. This base?"

"The humans tried to take back territory around the Brisbane portal, and some of the fighting drifted out to our location. The Empire unleashed a cloud of that new gas against the humans. If we hadn't made it into the hatch in time we would have been toast."

Shoot. The Empire's invented a new compound. We don't know what they call it, but it's deadly. A highly corrosive, super-fine agent developed to target human technology, for the purpose of disabling jets, human transport and weapons. But it's also pretty lethal for any living person that happens to breathe it in.

"It's too thick for anyone to land or take off," Phoebe concludes. "We're all grounded until it rains and clears away the vapour."

"Which according to the forecast, could be at least a few days," Calvin says.

I feel a shudder of foreboding at the thought that we're all trapped down here, in an even more literal way than normal. No way in. No way out. There's nothing to do but pray that the vapour clears sooner rather than later.

But the slight panic of claustrophobia is overridden by my thoughts of Eclipse, and of the other prisoners.

"What about the others?" I say, looking to Phoebe.

Zephyr frowns.

"Others?" he asks.

Phoebe shakes her head slightly, almost imperceptibly. So she hasn't told them yet about Raven and Winter. I don't know exactly why, but it does explain why everyone isn't going crazy right now.

"I meant Ember and Eclipse," I say, trying to play off my pause as a result of my brain-fog. "Eclipse, is he...?" I swallow. "Where is he?"

I'm half-scared, half-hoping that Eclipse's head is about to emerge through the entrance into the bridge.

"He's recovering down in the bottom level."

"What, in the Lab?"

"No, there's that chamber down there that was always meant for bigger Shadows," Phoebe says. "It's the only room big enough for him to sleep in. Zephyr healed him up as best he could."

"You should go see him," Zephyr says. "He'd want you to."

"He doesn't want to see me ever again," I mutter, my face burning.

"Griffin," Calvin says carefully, "I know that you and Eclipse had a falling out..."

I snort.

"…but he just proved that he has the kind of power that could prevent massacres. Do you know what we could do with that kind of power? What a dent we could put in each world's war efforts? Eclipse could help us protect the worlds from each other as we convince them to sign a peace treaty."

"That's wishful thinking, trust me. It's a mistake bringing him here," I say coldly.

"A mistake?" Zephyr scowls. A scowl from a velociraptor is about ten times more terrifying than one from a human. "So what do you want us to do with him: reject him and put him back out onto the street? Shouldn't we ask him what *he* wants? He belongs here with us. He always has. A lot has changed since the portals opened."

"I just…" For a moment, I wonder if I should speak my real fears aloud. But I can hear it in the protectiveness in Zephyr's voice for his little brother, and I hear Calvin's firm conviction. They see this as a coup for our organisation, for our family. To them, I'm the stubborn, emotionally immature one, still not letting go of a simple fight which happened months ago.

"You think I'm paranoid?" I say, raising an eyebrow, even as my chest is palpitating at the thought of being able to see Eclipse again, to speak to him.

"This is my little brother's Shadow you're talking about," Calvin reminds me with a smile, kind but firm. "He's part of the family, and a hero, and we're welcoming him home."

"I believe that's my decision," I remind him curtly.

"Eclipse is awake too, since you asked," Zephyr cuts in.

"Do you know what the first thing he said was? *I want to see Griffin.*"

My insides squirm. I try to keep my face carefully neutral, not betraying my monsoon of emotions.

It looks like none of them are going to be receptive to my theory that Eclipse could be working for the Empire. The longer I push it, the more unhinged I look to them and the less reliable as their leader. I'll just have to handle this myself.

"Did I miss anything?" a voice says lightly. I turn to see Ember limping into the bridge. "Sorry. After prison, using a real toilet again is a luxury. I had to savour it." She looks around, amused. "What did I miss?"

Then Ember lays eyes on Zephyr. I see the shock on her face. She cries out in anguish and hatred.

Ember bursts into flame and spreads her wings, preparing to attack.

6

BAD BLOOD

Ember and Zephyr circle each other dangerously. Ember's wings are splayed wide, her feathers metamorphosed into flowing flames. She looks like a burning spectre of vengeance. Meanwhile Zephyr's small claws are held palms-outward, asking for mercy.

Before Ember can unleash a blistering blast of flame at Zephyr I rush forward to stand between the two of them, holding out my hands. Ember holds in an attack just in time, but her flames crackle and spit feverishly, hungry to be unleashed.

"I'm sorry! I'm sorry!" Aghast, Phoebe joins me, waving her arms frantically at her counterpart. "I haven't caught Ember up on everything yet," she gasps in apology to the rest of us. "Em, please don't burn Zephyr."

"Out of my way!" Ember demands, walking to the side to try and get a clear shot. I manoeuvre as well, keeping myself as a shield between the livid flaming bird and the distraught velociraptor. "Don't you know what that wretched scum has done? Who he *is*?"

I wish I could contradict her, but no matter how much good Zephyr has done since then, you can't change the past.

"He's Zephyr!" Phoebe pleads. "He's Calvin's Shadow. He used to be your friend."

"He was there at Winghold." Desperation and grief enter Ember's voice. "He could have tried to stop the Empress' destruction of our home, but he didn't. My people that were lost, that was because of him. You saw Winghold fall Grif, you know I'm right! He has to pay!"

"Ember," Zephyr says, choked with guilt, "I regret everything I did. I left you when you needed me and I walked down the wrong path, I know it. There's no way of redeeming myself. But I'm fighting now for the same cause as you. The same mission we once worked on with Melissa and Silvaluna."

"Don't speak their names," Ember hisses, her flames spilling up toward the roof like a mini-volcanic eruption. Zephyr is quelled into silence.

"Like he says," I agree, determined. "We're all on the same side now. Ember, it's so good to see you again, but if you barbeque my brother's Shadow it's going to be hella awkward in here. Understand?"

"I needed you when we got back to the Shadow world," Ember shoots at Zephyr, enraged. "You were all I had but you'd have nothing to do with me! You wouldn't even let me explain what had happened, how Taylor was to blame for everything. Then when I was trying to build a safe place for counterparts, you were helping the Empire spread fear and hate. You were the Empress' executioner, her loyal pet hound."

"He knows," Phoebe murmurs, stroking Ember with

feeling. The flames don't hurt her, I notice. "I know how hard this is, but you have to let it go for now. Zephyr's on our side, and he's done a lot for us. Yeah, he's made some colossally horrible choices, but he's different now. We need him. Also, he's the one who healed your injuries when you were napping. You were in bad shape and you know it."

I see the effort it takes as Ember, shaking with fury, shuts her eyes and calms her flames. They slowly shorten, until they're gone. All that's left is a faint angry glow to her normal feathers.

"I won't forget," Ember says, her voice like metal.

"I'm so sorry," Zephyr tells her, his voice super quiet. "I hope someday I can prove to you I've changed, and how ashamed I am about who I was. In the meantime, I'll try to stay out of your way."

He leaves the bridge. We watch him go.

"Well, that wasn't awkward," I mutter, "or at all terrifying."

I realise that Calvin and Phoebe seem to be avoiding looking at each other. I know it's wrong, that it's awful, but maybe I do get a teeny squirm of satisfaction that their Shadows are so clearly at odds. Like, maybe it's some small sign that they're not meant to work out romantically.

Calvin walks up to Ember, smiling.

"Hello, old friend," he says. He offers his hand.

"Ah, just as weirdly formal as you were as a teenager," Ember snorts. She's clearly still hot-blooded, still ready for a fight. But she shakes it off and steps into Calvin, wrapping him tightly in her glowing wings. Then she steps away to examine him properly, suddenly shrewd.

"Did I see in Phoebe's head that you two are *dating* now?"

Calvin flushes. I don't know if I've ever seen the great Calvin Cameron flush.

"Um..." he stammers.

Stammering! It gets even better.

"Dude," Ember recoils from him, revolted. "She's ten years younger than you."

"We haven't done anything," Calvin says quickly. "Just... kissing. I mean..." He gets redder.

It's horribly awkward. No one wants to be here.

"...I wouldn't want you to think I was doing anything... untoward," Calvin says. "It's just that there's still, *I* feel, a link between Phoebe and myself, just as there was before she was petrified into stone for ten years. A connection which I, for one, would like to explore. Not sexually! Well, yes, perhaps eventually..."

"Oh God," says Phoebe, her face in her hands. "Please stop. For all our sakes, just *stop*."

"You were always too easy to mess with, Gecko," Ember smirks. "I knew you two had a thing back in the day. You were always perfectly awkward for each other."

I shuffle slightly.

"Just to get the topic back on track..." I say, clearing my throat. "Ember, how did the Resistance fall? How can it be completely gone?" I shake my head, overwhelmed. We'd been counting on the fact that there was a Resistance in the Shadow world who could help support us in stopping the war.

"When most of the Shadow world voted to become part of the Empire once again, we knew we were doomed," Ember says. She shrugs her wings, but there's a weight to them, a darkness in her that shows itself just for a flicker of a moment. "When you found me I was being held prisoner at Troy for transportation to the Empress, for a nice big televised public execution: the death of the final member of the Resistance. I discovered it's hard to preach to Shadows that humans are the missing part of their souls when the humans are already killing them en masse."

"Yes. We've had some issues with that ourselves," Calvin says dryly.

Phoebe looks at Ember helplessly, caressing her neck comfortingly.

"So are we all in agreement now that Ember's back, what with all her experience running a Resistance, that she's officially inducted as a member of the core leadership team?" Phoebe asks, putting on a brave, cheerful face for her Shadow. "All those in favour, say aye!"

Calvin and I look at each other, amused, before we both raise our hands.

"Aye!"

Phoebe claps excitedly, and we both join in. It's a slightly underwhelming but poignant welcome home for Ember, for a hero returning at long last to her family.

"Thanks folks," Ember says, her expression slightly strange for a moment. "I'm going to go rest up a bit first though before I start giving out any orders."

"As long as you're okay with me being in charge this time around, you'll do great," I wink at her. Honestly, the presumption that I could tell her what to do makes me want to laugh.

"Come on everyone, that's meeting over," Phoebe says hastily, sensing something off with her Shadow. "Griffin, you go talk to Eclipse. We'll cover any other duties you have that you were planning to use as an excuse. Everything else can wait." With that, she gently accompanies Ember towards the door. "Let's get you rested up, you stubborn orange seagull."

Phoebe's so happy to be with Ember again, like she thinks she's walking in a dream. It's sweet to see.

"Can I talk to you for a minute, Pheebs?" I ask, following them both up the ramp. "Just you?"

Phoebe's mention of Eclipse has reminded me of the threat at hand. The thought of going to meet with Eclipse and talk to him again reminds me of that moment where you stand on the highest dive board at the pools, too terrified to know if you will ever be able to actually make the jump.

"Sure," Phoebe says. "As long as *just you* means Ember as well." Phoebe curls a hand around the back of Ember's neck, gently scratching her there. She stares at her counterpart in open adoration. "There's no way we're going to be apart. Not now. Give us a few weeks maybe."

I consider for a moment, then nod. I can feel Calvin's eyes following me as we leave the bridge.

"It's really good to see you two back together again," I tell them, the swarm of hungry nerves still buzzing inside me. Seeing Phoebe and Ember side by side, it's impossible to miss the likeness between them, as much likeness as a human and an oversized bird can share. "Look at you both. The dream team."

Ember nips Phoebe's hand playfully.

"At least finding out you were frozen finally explains why I haven't aged physically in ten years. Can't say I didn't wonder about that. I thought it was just my good genes."

"Luckily your maturity level froze too, so we're fine," Phoebe says, poking her.

"The other two prisoners we picked up from the prison," I murmur, stepping closer to Phoebe. "Are they…"

"Locked in a cell in the De-escalation Area," Phoebe says, her expression admirably neutral.

"Who *are* these prisoners?" Ember asks me, irate. "Phoebe keeps blocking it from me. I was pretty out of it on our way back."

"I just think it's best for us to worry about one problem at a time," Phoebe says calmly. I'm surprised by her self-control, she must be freaking out inside. But considering Ember's reaction to Zephyr being here, it's probably wise for the immediate present to hide the man who destroyed our family and birthed the Empire.

Phoebe's expression darkens as she looks at me.

"Did you know? That *he* would be there in the prison too?"

"No," I say honestly, alarmed that she could think that. "Ember was meant to be the only surprise."

"So what is it that what you want to talk about?" Phoebe says, studying me. "What are you thinking?"

"I'm glad you got out okay," I murmur, checking warily that nobody's nearby in the corridor to listen in. "I'm glad we all did. But how do we know Troy wasn't a set up?"

Phoebe is quiet for a moment. She seems thrown off-guard.

"What do you mean?"

"I'm saying," I whisper, "that I believe Eclipse could be here as a double agent for the Empire."

There's silence.

"Come again?"

"Troy may have been a set-up."

"How is saving all of those humans and Shadows from that massacre a set-up?"

"So that we'd trust him. So that we'd bring him back here." I see Phoebe's disbelieving expression, like she thinks I might have a head injury. "Look, Eclipse tried to sabotage our efforts to connect the worlds last time. He betrayed us and deserted us. He told me he doesn't believe anymore that Shadows and humans should be together. So isn't it logical to believe that he might have started fighting for the Empire?"

"I don't know about logical," Phoebe says slowly. "Eclipse knows that when a human dies, their Shadow dies too. He's not delusional like the Empire what with this war they're fighting, and he wouldn't support the Empire in all their killing and cruelty, or how they treat their own people. That's why Eclipse didn't use force to *kill* any of the humans attacking Troy."

"Maybe," I say, not certain of anything anymore, "but one thing's for sure. Eclipse doesn't support humans and Shadows uniting. What he said to me last time... he's completely against what the GSA is doing here."

Phoebe's next words are careful.

"It seems like a long shot, Griffin. You know how much Eclipse has hated the Empire, ever since he was Cirrus. Maybe he's changed his mind about Shadows and humans since the portals opened. The only way to find out is to talk to him."

"And I'm saying that he's a titan who could destroy this base with the power just in his left toe," I answer, incredulous that she's not getting it. "That's not a comforting thought, no matter where his head's at. Don't forget, he's essentially a walking, talking weapon of mass-destruction. If he hasn't already torn this place apart, it means he's here for something. That we have something he wants. And we need to figure out what that is before this damn vapour clears away and there's nothing to stop him from leaving."

"What, so you believe that Empress Galvanize leaked that intelligence on Ember's location, so that Eclipse could play the hero, make contact with us and be brought back here into our inner sanctum?" Phoebe says, disbelieving. "You really think Eclipse would work for someone as twisted and evil as Galvanize?"

"I know it sounds far-fetched."

"No kidding."

"Eclipse knew that we'd come for Ember no matter what, Pheebs. He knew that you'd come for her, and he knew that if you did that I would..." I stop, catching myself. My face goes red. "Eclipse has no idea where our base is," I say hastily, "so his only option was to draw us to him. This way nobody suspects him of being a double agent. The GSA welcomes him in with open arms."

"How could he have known we'd survive that suicidal landing on the beach?" Phoebe challenges me. At least she's playing along. "Why was that necessary?"

"I think he didn't expect the human attack on Troy. The Imperials weren't prepared for that. Eclipse was just waiting for us to bust Ember out of prison."

"You think he was keeping Ember in prison?" Phoebe says, troubled. "Using her as bait? Do you really think your Shadow would do that to mine?"

My mouth opens and closes. I can't take how Phoebe is looking at me.

"Eclipse isn't me," I finally say.

"Yes, he is," Phoebe says quietly. "And I'd trust him with my life."

"To be fair," Ember says, "I did keep Eclipse in a cage. So it would at least make us even." Her voice startles me. She's been oddly silent listening to me and Phoebe so far. She sounds strange as she talks about Eclipse, but I can't pinpoint why exactly. "But you've got this wrong, Grif. I've been out of the loop for a while, but I've made the mistake of believing Eclipse was my enemy before.... and it cost me. There's no way it was his plan to keep me in that prison. It's not who he is."

"Griffin, don't you think... that maybe you could be being a little paranoid?" Phoebe asks tentatively. "You've been stuck underground for a year, stewing over what Eclipse did last time. How can you suspect your own Shadow?"

"We're connected, but I'm not responsible for every last choice he makes."

"You have no reason to think that he's here to hurt us."

"What happened to *'we're at war*?'" I demand. "To *'trust no one?'* Just because this is my Shadow, you want to throw caution to the wind?"

"Eclipse is your friend, he'd never really try to hurt you let alone kill you, or any of us."

"He left us to drown at the station," I point out.

"He had no idea that we would be locked in there, that we'd be trapped," Phoebe says, shocked. "That was a tragic mistake."

"Have you forgotten the stakes of this war?" I whisper. "It's changed everyone. It's turned good people into monsters and pitched counterpart against counterpart. The old rules don't apply. The unthinkable is now thinkable.

People will do anything not to have their world destroyed. We have no idea what he's been up to in the last nine months, or what he's experienced. How much he might have changed."

Phoebe's mouth is screwed into an expression which looks unconvinced at best.

"Eclipse has been ill once or twice, you know," Phoebe says.

"Ill?" I frown. "What, he's sick?"

"He threw up. I think he's nervous. Scared."

"Of what?" I laugh nervously. "What in the world do you have to be scared of when you're him?"

"My guess?" Phoebe says softly. "He's nervous about seeing you again. He's excited to see you, happy to find out that you're okay and scared that things might have changed too much between you. Just like you are."

My nails are biting into my palms again.

Phoebe contemplates me for a moment, then picks up her tablet.

"What are you doing?" I ask uncertainly as she brings up a screen. She tilts it toward me, and my breath catches in my throat. I'm staring at grainy black and white footage of the room downstairs.

"We hooked up a camera to monitor him," Phoebe says. "Zephyr had to do some extensive healing work on him, and we wanted to check his recovery went okay."

"And... and is he?"

"Yes, Grif. He healed up fine. He could probably use a visitor though to cheer him up. Zephyr and him talked a little bit. But he needs his human."

"Did he say that?" I mutter.

I can make out a slinking serpentine tail in the video

feed. The ruffling of wings. He's curled up in the corner, as if trying to vanish into it. Then I see his face. I swallow. He looks worn, haggard. His eyes stare out into nothingness, haunted.

Also... he's whispering to himself. Muttering. He looks... lost. His feathers are dishevelled, even though he's already washed. Patchy, as if he's been tearing some of them out.

Just like Cirrus used to.

I stare at the screen, trying to guess what the other half of me is thinking.

"Wherever he's been, he looks pretty broken. Like he's had a hard time," Phoebe says quietly.

"We've all had a hard time," I say, glued to the screen. "And he knows we're watching him. This could all be a performance. There's no time. If we're going to act we have to act now. Get the GSA to start figuring out how to contain a Shadow like that."

"*Contain* Eclipse? You saw what he did at Troy." Phoebe shakes her head, impressed as much as intimidated. "It was insane. Eclipse can mimic any Shadow power he chooses. He could melt walls, or just fly through them."

"I don't know how, but we need to be able to trap him in a cell that can hold him, until we know for sure which side he's on."

"Calvin and Zephyr will never support that."

I wet my lips.

"I know."

"I'm dating Calvin. I'm not going behind his back."

"Even if I say pretty please?"

A heavy silence hangs between us.

"I need someone to believe me," I finally say, quiet. "Someone who doesn't think I'm crazy. Because if I'm right on this and Eclipse is here to sabotage us then every second he's here we're placing everyone in mortal danger. We're endangering the people who've pledged their lives to our organisation, who rely on us to keep them safe."

"I believe in you, Grif. I always do. I just think that when it comes to your own Shadow, you might be a little bit insane."

"So what am I meant to...?"

"Get proof. Solid proof that Eclipse put that intelligence out there for us to find, that he came here to bring down the GSA from the inside. Find out what he's been up to on the other side for nine months. Find out what it is that he's really after."

"How? We have so little intelligence on the Shadow world right now. It's radio silence over there."

"You're Griffin-freaking-Cameron. Figure it out." Phoebe sees my reproachful look, and smiles painfully. "Please, don't." She pulls Ember into a side-hug. "I have your back no matter what," she tells me. "But we're the GSA. If we start turning on our own counterparts... what hope is there for everyone else?"

7

EX-FRIEND

I take a deep breath as I descend the metal staircase toward where Eclipse is recuperating. The space is huge, more like a giant hold. It feels like I'm submerging underwater, sinking downward into the dark uncharted depths. Deep, sonorous calls like whale song play from the speakers below, adding to the effect.

I reach the bottom of the steps where the darkness glimmers with eerie blue light. Big water tanks like something from SeaWorld soon surround me. They were built for aquatic Shadows who can't leave the water and the amphibious ones that prefer to sleep in water by night. Hence the soothing whale song for them. But since we have a lack of aquatic Shadows in the GSA, we mainly use the tanks for the occasional swim. Some of them are slimy with disuse, like old fish tanks. I've had the glass painted black on some of them, fashioning them into sensory deprivation tanks for our research into the human-Shadow psychic connection.

Soft blue light from the tanks dances on the dark alloy

floor. Sometimes I swear I can see something dark moving within the tanks, as if a fin is about to breach the surface. But that's just my imagination.

I can see myself reflected in the glass. I look petrified. I consider how much I've changed since I encountered Cirrus in the clock tower in Sanctuary City. What will Eclipse see when he looks at me now?

"Come on, you got this," I say to myself. "You've faced way worse."

But my nerves are spiking like crazy. My anxiety is twisting me all out of shape. Worse: this weird, anguished kind of love is rising in me, no matter how badly I wish I could push it away.

I look at my reflection, thinking of it as my Shadow. Could that part of me betray me? The thought feels too painful to believe. I also can't forget the emotion and pain in Eclipse's face when I last saw him.

We're meant to bring in a new utopia, for everyone, I'd said to him. *And you're saying it's all for nothing?*

No. I'm saying humans and Shadows have a gift of screwing everything up, no matter what. We're not evolved enough to meet each other yet. Look at what longing for a counterpart has done to Hanna. To your Dad. Griffin, to hold you too tightly is for both of us to burn. Our longing to be united as brothers, as two halves of one self, is what living is. But the worlds weren't meant to mix.

I'd held Eclipse too tightly. We burned. So did our two worlds.

Now I have him back, and I have no idea what to do.

I mean, just by walking in there, I'm risking everything! Eclipse and I are linked at a psychic level. As leader of the GSA, I hold the most critical intelligence of our organisation in my head. Information which in the hands of the Empire or the human leadership would gladly be used to stop the GSA. I'm bringing that right to Eclipse, without knowing which side he's on.

I wonder how well I can hide the contents of my own mind. I spent so little time with my Shadow that we were still getting used to being able to share our thoughts, emotions and sensations. I can sense him now, but it's like a dim light: just the outline of his slumbering consciousness. But I could still walk toward that dim light, even in the blackest night. As long as he was close, I would always be able to find him.

I want to tell him that I love him; I want to tell him that I've missed him and that I was scared for him trapped over in the Shadow world on his own during this war, but I'm too proud to say anything like that. The hurt still burns in my veins. It owns me. I can't stand to walk in there, to look into his eyes and not know if they're the eyes of a friend or an enemy staring back at me.

Shakily, pressing on the side of the tank for support, I see something out of the corner of my vision, and turn to look.

I nearly scream.

A Shadow is standing down the far end of the row between the tanks, grinning cheekily at me. He's about my height, and covered in bright green feathers, his crest standing high. There's a happy kind of mischief about him.

"Cirrus?" I ask, one simple question, my lips trembling.

The dragon-parrot winks mischievously, then hops away out of sight, behind one of the tanks. I bolt after him.

"Cirrus!"

I round the corner of the tank and slide to a stop. All

that's in front of me is the side of the tank and the glow of the water across the metal floor.

There's no way he could have escaped. He was *right there*.

"Hello?" I say brokenly, wigging out. Maybe it was another Shadow here that I confused for Cirrus. Maybe I projected onto them. Saw what I wanted to see.

But there's, like, no one here Griffin, I tell myself. *Just you.*

Could I really have imagined it? The thought is terrifying. My chest is still pounding with longing.

I saw him just as I was fighting the idea of seeing Eclipse again. Cirrus appeared when I was trying to refuse that part of myself.

I have to stop idealising Cirrus and remember that Cirrus *is* Eclipse. Cirrus chose to leave me behind and go back to his home in the Shadow world. Now he's waiting for me in the hold of this ship.

Dragging up all the courage I have I go to meet the version of my Shadow that's actually real.

Emerging from the tanks, I can see the great glass doors of the ship's laboratory. That's where Calvin has been spending so much time since we recovered Raven's equipment from Auckland three months ago. We told him to destroy it, but he's determined that the tech will yield its secrets to him. The piece he seems most preoccupied with is a massive silver cube Phoebe retrieved. It's been x-rayed and inspected to eliminate the possibility that it's some kind of weapon that's going to kill us all. If Calvin has deciphered its purpose, he's yet to share it with us.

Instead of heading left to the lab, I turn right, in the direction of the quarters that were built for the largest Shadows we thought we might have to house on this ark of ours. I continue into the darkness until I can finally make out a wall of reinforced glass. It looks opaque black.

I breathe. Drag my feet closer to the glass. One step. Two steps.

Suddenly I feel a wild fear that makes me want to pull back. A ringing in the back of my head that doesn't want me to go anywhere near that wall of blackness.

But something in my chest forces me on. A longing.

I take a third and final step.

There's movement behind the glass. I swear I can make out a tail slithering through the air, like a giant cobra is contained in there, out of sight. I'm at the zoo again, and the glass of the enclosure is the only thing separating me from the predator on the other side that wants to eat me.

"Hello?" I whisper, with my mind and voice. With all of me.

I feel his consciousness reaching out to mine. It's a shock. I can feel him, curious and disbelieving, then overcome with emotion. I feel an urge to fall into that connection, to flow into someone else. I miss that feeling of not being alone, of being joined to something *greater*.

But I pull my mind away from his. I imagine cloaking and protecting myself with walls of black, smooth anonymity. I feel too exposed, too raw. I'm not ready to open myself like that again. His mind... he feels so tired. So exhausted. Pained.

But then the glimpse is gone. Eclipse's own mind retreats respectfully, the whispering and the rich hues fading. His mind feels different then when he was Cirrus but there are still familiar parts of it that stayed the same.

Something moves beyond the glass. Something big. As it grows closer, the faint light from behind me highlights golden feathers. I can make out a beak, a feathered head stretching out toward me...

A large claw slams into the glass palm-first, and I jump like ten feet in the air.

The area behind the glass is illuminated in very low light. It reminds me of the special inside area at the zoo back home where you could look at the nocturnal kiwis; the shy, awkward birds who were sometimes impossible to spot in the dull red light.

Eclipse is right in front of me.

I try not to jerk back. I don't know if I succeed. I'd forgotten how *massive* he is. Five, no, six metres tall maybe.

I make my way slowly along my side of the glass, tracing it with my finger as if to remind me of the boundary between us. Eclipse follows me slowly, tracking my movement. He barely has to move to cover the same ground that I take in ten steps.

He looks prehistoric, the missing link between the ancient dinosaurs and the birds they evolved into. He's like Cirrus on steroids. To me, Cirrus had always resembled one of those cute little pet cockatiels you can get. Eclipse's top half is more like a full-grown cockatoo, his crest tall and proud, his feathers morphing lower down into hardened gleaming scales. He's both parrot and dragon, a crested apex predator. Every part of him looks like it was designed to kill you, all while mesmerising you with his beauty.

I swallow, feeling faint. It's very hard not to be intimidated, even without the knowledge that his ability to mimic and amplify a Shadow's ability makes him practically all-powerful.

When I reunited with him last time in the Underworld I'd worried I wasn't worthy of him. He was so grand and powerful that I couldn't help wondering if maybe he was meant to be the other half of someone else. What if when he stopped being Cirrus, I'd lost any sort of claim to him, because I'd been found wanting?

I reach the end of the glass and my hand slides off into empty air. Above me is a tall archway, an open entryway into the oversized quarters large enough for Eclipse himself to stride through with his wings barely brushing the edges.

There's nothing standing between us now.

I wish myself courage, and force myself to look into those dark brown eyes. They're not the eyes of an adult, all-powerful double agent from another world. They're the eyes of a teenager.

They're *my* eyes.

I'm reminded that Eclipse is just a reflection of me as I am of him. He's young, scared, making stuff up as he goes. I try to tell myself that as I step into the room, but I feel like a mouse boldly stepping into the nest of an eagle.

We face each other in the entryway. Unspeaking, unthinking, unflinching. The rest of the universe rendered inconsequential.

"Hey, dude," Eclipse says, his voice cracking, and suddenly a wall of emotion hits me, and there are tears in his eyes and mine, an entire life and a war seeming to stand between us and to collapse into meaninglessness all at once.

Dude. One of Cirrus' favourite words, coming from Eclipse's beak. It throws me.

"What happened to me?" he comments, wincing and cocking his head. I can feel the lethal pulse of his headache through our connection. It's unpleasant.

"Come on, now. Self-pity doesn't suit you," I tell him. "Just one little missile and suddenly it's all about you."

"I was struck by a *missile?*"

"Almost," I say airily. "It exploded on you. A little bit." I fight an involuntary smile. "You look like hell."

Eclipse laughs.

"Hell *wishes* it looked this good."

I survey the quarters. It's hard not to admire the craftsmanship. The walls are covered in dark wooden panelling, carved with nature patterns of vines and ferns. Up above us the roof is arched, leaving plenty of room for Eclipse to stand fully upright even with his crest extended. To my right is a dividing wall and I can just make out the end of a big dining table on the other side. Over on my left, I can make out the giant nest Eclipse is in the process of constructing from sheets and odd bits and ends. Suspended above the nest is a loft with a ladder leading up to it. That's where the human counterpart is meant to sleep.

I can feel Eclipse's mind trying to coil around mine and I know I'm meant to be hiding things but my thoughts are all confused. Seeing him again... I didn't expect it to be so overwhelming. My brain is lighting up after so long alone in the darkness of the ship. He's here, and alive, and we're together again... furiously, I force myself not to start crying.

"Is it really you?" Eclipse breathes.

"I'm glad you're alright," I say, swallowing. "You're alive, which is positive." I wish I could stroke his feathers, feel the touch of my Shadow. *My* Shadow.

But it could be a trap.

"You're here," I exhale. I rub my cheeks roughly, smearing tears back. "Oh God, how are you here?"

Suddenly Eclipse lunges, a monstrous sized wing sweeping around me. I jerk backward...

Eclipse steps back clumsily, staring down at me. I realise too late what it actually was meant to be. A hug.

I open my mouth but nothing comes out. Eclipse looks hurt.

"Oh, I was... I didn't mean to..."

"That's okay."

Man, this is awkward.

"We're in the human world, aren't we?" he asks, as if nothing happened.

"Yeah." I realise if Eclipse isn't here as a spy and he didn't secretly want to be brought here, then we've pulled him away from the home he cares about. "We didn't mean to kidnap you," I say quickly. "You could say there was a slightly improvisational quality to it. Phoebe made the call because you really needed medical attention. You wouldn't have made it if Phoebe had left you there."

"Don't think for a minute that I'm not grateful," he says wryly. His voice is different since we last met. *He's* different. In the Underworld he'd sounded so... righteous, but now he sounds more relatable. He always had a charisma to him, but there's a cocky cheekiness to his words now. It's hard because it reminds me of shooting the breeze with him when he was Cirrus. The only difference being Cirrus felt like this energetic perpetual child, while Eclipse's deep voice and imposing size make him seem an adult even if he is the same age as me. I can't help but look at him as a big brother.

That's what makes it so tempting to trust him.

Eclipse swallows, uncharacteristically perplexed. He

opens his beak, closes it. He tries again. "I saw Zephyr when he came to heal me. But I was a little out of it."

"Oh. How was that?"

"Awkward." Eclipse ponders, troubled. "How... how is Zephyr? Really?"

"You mean how is he since being fused with Calvin into a super-entity with god-like powers who was pushed to the dark side when Raven brainwashed them into trying to kill us?"

"Yes."

"They bounced back."

"The two of them always do." Eclipse smiles down at me.

Zephyr is to Eclipse what Calvin is to me. The older brother that had to stand in for the absent parents while raising his younger sibling. Zephyr is the brother Eclipse will always love more than anyone, no matter how many traumatic incidents and how much conflict defines their relationship.

I haven't had many conversations with my brother about what it was like to be joined as a Majestic. For most of the time Calvin and Zephyr had been under Raven's dark control. For that one shining, beautiful moment at the end though they had been free, a real Majestic with unlimited power, directly linked to the heart of time and space. Surely being joined like that must fundamentally change who you are, even if the changes are invisible to those around you.

"Zephyr's been doing okay," I say. "He and Calvin are finally back to where they used to be with their friendship. Zephyr's really been applying himself here, giving it a hundred percent like he always does."

"He's always been a soldier at heart," Eclipse mutters,

"a warrior who needs a cause, or he self-destructs. He's happiest when he has a mission. At least he's working toward peace this time."

Just not the kind of peace you want, I think. Zephyr and the GSA want a peace without borders. A peace without counterparts being separated from each other forever.

"You guys should take time to talk while you're here," I say, looking down at the floor. "Properly. Zephyr misses you more than anything. He feels terrible for not realising sooner that you're still his little brother. He's just so happy to know you're alive."

There's a tentative pause.

"Is this your new home and HQ, then?" Eclipse says. "The new Cameron Technologies, so to speak?"

"Pretty much." I extend my arms in mock theatricality. "Welcome to the GSA."

"Interesting." Eclipse looks around doubtfully at the dark, bleak parts of the ship he can make out.

"I'm sorry that we didn't have five star accommodation available in XXL right now, okay? We'll give it a dusting, add some decorations. String some festive lights up."

"No! I like it. It's... nice."

I sit down on the floor, crossing my legs. Eclipse hunches down, arching his neck so that he can study me closer.

"So," Eclipse says with a playful smile, "what exactly is it you do here?"

"Come on," I say, feigning hurt. "You must have heard of us."

"Only rumours and stories in my world. I heard that you're trying to end the war. Bring humans and Shadows together. But I'm still unclear on how, or what the letters GSA stand for."

"Yeah, well, so are we on that last part," I admit. "At the moment it's Generation Shadow Alliance."

"And who's part of it?"

I hesitate. I'm entering a minefield, not wanting to risk giving too much information away but not wanting to seem suspiciously tight-lipped either. Also I feel the urge to impress him. To show him what we've been doing since I last saw him.

To convince him that he should have stayed.

I shake that thought off. It can't hurt to tell him the basics, at least.

"The GSA is made up of Shadows and humans," I say, "until recently it was just the prisoners we freed from Raven at Aeyu Palace. Together we've been campaigning for an end to the war. The governments in our world have been getting more and more dictator-y, cracking down pretty hard on anyone protesting the war, so we've had to go underground."

"So, how does the GSA try and end the war exactly?"

I shrug.

"Sometimes it's getting the truth out about Shadows and humans through the web, sometimes it's secretly working to build influence with certain politicians to try and get support for a peace deal between the worlds. We've managed to lessen some of the casualties from the fighting, by monitoring the two sides and warning one when a military attack is incoming so they have enough time to get to safety... but it's like a Band-Aid on a bullet wound. The death tolls are insane, and they keep rising. The humans are just as unlikely as Empress Galvanize to accept that the death toll is identical on both sides, that no one side seems to be winning. Other times we've run field missions, sending our members across battle lines to try and gather intelligence. That's why we were at Troy, to find Ember."

"Did you?" he says suddenly.

"Yeah. She's here. She's safe."

Eclipse smiles. He looks relieved.

"We didn't know that the Resistance had completely disappeared on your side," I say. "Getting Intel from the Shadow world has been sketchy, and for the last few days there's been this weird, total radio silence. We're worried Empress Galvanize might be about to make a big move. You haven't heard anything, have you?"

Eclipse shakes his head slowly.

"I've been trying to stay as far from the Empire as possible," he confesses. "So where is this base? Are we on a boat?"

"Well, you remember New Redemption..." I flush. *Idiot.* Of course he remembers that flying hellhole. His last experience there wasn't great. I didn't mean to bring back all the trauma of the place where Hanna had tried to split my connection to Cirrus, back when Hanna was still the evil Empress. The place where Cirrus had seemingly died in my arms and been reborn as Eclipse. "This place is based on... on that place," I say lamely. "We're on a kind of futuristic flying ship like that one. It was Zephyr's idea actually. When we were planning to bring humans and Shadows together by opening the portals, airborne vessels like this were going to fly between the worlds, bringing humans and Shadow counterparts to meet each other. This one is called the *Ambassador.* We built a handful of them but none of them ever got to be used, for obvious reasons. This one's never even flown. Because it's hidden below ground level it can't be easily found, so when the war started and everything came apart we came here. This has been our home ever since."

"Where are we, exactly?" Eclipse asks. "Is it back home?" He sees my expression at that word, and I think he flushes under his feathers. "Is it in Auckland, I mean?"

I hesitate. Telling him our location feels like a bad idea, but if he really wanted to find out it wouldn't be at all difficult for him.

"No," I say. "We're in Brisbane. Australia."

"That portal's controlled by the Empire," Eclipse says, surprised.

"Yeah. We're pretty well hidden. There's some of that Shadow gas up above right now," I say. "It won't clear until it rains, and the forecast says that might not be for three days or so. So I don't recommend trying to get some fresh air unless you enjoy being asphyxiated. We can't fly in the jet either or the gas will disintegrate it mid-flight."

Eclipse surveys the place again with an air of indifference, but I sense a hungry curiosity.

"So, are you going to show me around? Introduce me to all your new comrades?"

"I prefer the term 'minions,'" I clarify with a grin.

He looks at me, raising a feathered eyebrow.

"*Minions?* Why?"

"Well, you know. I'm sort of in charge now," I say, trying to play it like it's no big thing. I hide my wave of pride from him. "Well, there's a core team that makes the decisions. Phoebe, Calvin, Zephyr... Ember now too, I guess. But I'm the one who oversees everything and keeps the organisation running."

"Well, well, well," Eclipse says, his voice strangely thick. "Look at you now. You've finally been given a chance to prove your mettle. Well done, Griffin."

"Thank you," I say, hugging my knees.

"Hold on. Does this mean Calvin has to take orders from you now?"

"Kinda," I say, unable to resist a grin. Eclipse looks super amused.

"That is amazing. So you can make Calvin run to get you food and bring it to you?'

"Technically."

"Do you think you can you make him do it for me too?"

We look at each other, and some nervous, excited laughter escapes from both of us. There's a feverish energy growing, an organic camaraderie. We haven't lost how anything we say seems three times as funny as it would be to anyone else. I've missed that.

Eclipse's long, slender tail is snaking around us, coiled over itself. His tail feathers spread outward, like a golden fan trailing the floor of the room.

"This feels like one of those awkward breakups," I say. "When someone runs into their ex after a long time and they're both trying to pretend that their lives are going super well."

"*So* well," Eclipse says, deadpan. "I am so happy right now. My life's going so very well for me."

"I've just really had a lot of time to work on myself, you know?" I nod, fighting a grin.

"We should catch up some time."

"Oh, I would, but life's going so very well for me, I'm just so busy."

I've missed our banter.

Eclipse stretches his wings.

"So, do I get the grand tour?" he asks.

The elephant in the room is impossible to ignore any longer.

"Eclipse... where have you been?" I say, aching. "What have you been doing, since...?" I don't finish.

"You want the truth?" Eclipse says ironically, grimacing. "It's embarrassing. I was mainly lost in the desert."

I raise an eyebrow sceptically.

"I told you it was embarrassing."

"It's been nine months," I state.

"Deserts are big. Have you ever been lost in one?"

"You could have asked for directions." I fold my arms. Suddenly I'm not in the mood for any more crap or cute games. "Why were you at Troy, Eclipse? Did you know that we would be there? Did you know that we were coming for Ember?"

The question seems to catch him off-guard, like I was hoping it would. He's intelligent, but his wits aren't entirely with him after suffering that minor case of missile explosion.

"I heard a rumour that Ember was being held there," he says emotionally. "I came to help free her."

"Didn't I hear that she kept you in a prison for half a year?"

"Yes. I had some complicated feelings to work out around that." He hesitates, considering carefully. "But she's still the Ember that we knew as children at Cameron Technologies. Even if her conviction and do-goodery can be annoying, even if I can't see eye to eye with her anymore on bringing humans and Shadows together as she was doing with her Resistance..."

My stomach tightens.

"...when I heard where she was being held prisoner, there was nothing that could have stopped me from coming for her. She's family."

So am I, I want to say, but I hold the thought from him.

"So you came to rescue her from the Empire, and stumbled into a full-on warzone like we did," I say, trying to fill the gaps. "Does this mean you're *not* working with the Empire?"

Eclipse shoots me a look. On someone else it might look annoyed. But coming from the giant predator it's darkly terrifying.

"Work for the *Empire?* Empress Galvanize is so deranged she makes Hanna's reign look like a child's birthday party."

"Yeah, but the Empire kind of has a monopoly on the Shadow world right now," I say heatedly, "and if it's the Shadow world you're fighting for, it's not like you have a whole ton of options as to whose orders you're following."

"After everything the Empire took from me? Don't you know me?"

"Do I?"

We study each other. It feels like we're playing a game of Twister. I'm doing mental acrobatics, trying to keep check of all the things I shouldn't be thinking about. I have to calm my mind so he can't detect anything suspicious in mine. It comes strangely naturally to me. As if all the time I've spent in here suppressing and compartmentalising crap is nicely transferable.

Subtly, I try to probe into Eclipse's mind. I sneak into his consciousness like breaking through the back window of a home. I smell warm winds, and I can make out hot swirling sands beneath a night sky. Spotlights pierce the black, scanning the dunes. Hunting. If they find Eclipse... he knows he's dead.

Then the glimpse of that memory is gone. I'm just staring back at myself, through Eclipse's eyes.

I'm so tiny.

"Are you trying to read me right now?" Eclipse asks, scrutinising me.

"Yes," I say honestly.

"What am I thinking?"

"I can't tell," I say slowly. I don't tell him about the fleeting impressions I felt seconds before. "I can feel some of your emotions, the meaning behind some of the words... but a lot of it feels harder to reach than last time." *Like I'm only seeing the tip of a much bigger iceberg.*

"It's the same with you," Eclipse says. I wonder if that's a sign that blocking him is working or if he's lying, and he's still able to glean stuff from me just as I was with him. I focus harder on keeping him out. "Maybe we're out of practice," Eclipse says easily.

"Or maybe it's part of growing up," I say.

"True. Maybe we're just far too cynical and jaded now." Eclipse cocks his head. "Does it bother you?" he asks carefully.

"No," I lie. "It's good right? You're the one who didn't want us to blur into the same person." My cheeks flush as soon as I say it. The look in his eyes. "Sorry," I mutter.

I can feel how delicate this moment is. Both of us are afraid, I think. That talking about it will pop this little bubble we've found for ourselves. This bubble that's our little reprieve from the madness. Just like old times.

"I think you're hiding your mind from me," Eclipse says.

"Maybe," I whisper. "Maybe I'm just not ready for that. Being an open book like we used to be."

"Yes," Eclipse says quickly. "Yes, of course." He considers me. "I'm not working with the Empire, you know. I've tried to stay clear as much as I can even with them having total control right now. Empress Galvanize isn't my biggest fan. I don't know why, most people find me extremely charming."

"Ooh... that's a matter of opinion," I smirk.

"I'm just trying to look out for other Shadows however I can: preventing bloodshed between humans and Shadows where it's possible or stepping in whenever the Empire tries to harm its own citizens."

"What, so you're like a vigilante?" I grin. "Were you alone when you were out finding yourself in this desert, becoming a superhero?"

"I was with Hanna, for most of it." Eclipse sees my expression and smiles slightly. "Don't say anything."

"Of course not. Hanna's a lovely psychopathic ex-Empress. Glad you had a buddy with you." I pause, troubled. The very thought of Hanna makes me queasy. When I first met the beautiful faerie, I was so convinced I was in love. That's before she tried to tear my Shadow from me so that she could be my Shadow instead. Not to mention that when I rejected her, she stabbed me in the back and left me to die.

Eclipse says she's reformed. I can't trust her. The fact that he can, frankly, is a little bit insulting.

The idea that there could be feelings between them now... makes me a little sick.

"Are you two...?" I begin, unsettled.

Eclipse looks appalled by the unspoken suggestion.

Good. That's a definite no from him. I breathe out a sigh of relief.

"What?" Eclipse laughs. "No! She's my... she's my..." He seems to struggle to articulate exactly what Hanna is to him. "We helped each other survive," he says, sounding as if that can't begin to touch the depths of it. "There were plenty of refugees out there, fleeing the war. Cities burnt to ash. Hanna and I tried to help where we could. Helping them find shelter, warding off any soldiers pursuing them. I still had Zephyr's healing power at the time, so I tried to fix those who would let me." He catches my look and smiles. "When people see me and the ex-Empress turn up they tend to run a million miles in the other direction. It makes saving them hard." Eclipse's voice cracks again. "It's been hard trying to make a difference."

"I know," I say. His words make me even more aware of a dead weight in my stomach, a feeling that's been there for a while now. "It can all feel so useless."

"This war... it's horrible," he says emotionally. "Grif, the things happening back home..."

"I know."

There's a troubled silence.

"I never wanted this to happen between our worlds," he whispers.

"Me neither."

"We don't see eye to eye anymore on what's best for humans and Shadows," Eclipse says, emotional. "But I'd still like to see what you're doing here. We both want to create peace between the worlds, even if we can't agree what that looks like."

"You mean you want to shut the portals forever and separate the two worlds."

He doesn't deny it.

"Griffin," Eclipse says imploringly. "I can't stay here." His voice is tortured. "I need to get back to my world."

"Oh." I struggle to process this. "Yeah, yeah of course," I say vaguely. "I know that."

Of course that's what he wants, you moron. Why would you be surprised by that?

The news shocks me and it shouldn't. Maybe I really had wanted him to be here to infiltrate the GSA because at least then he'd hang around a little longer. Oh my... what is *wrong* with you?

"It's just that I have people back there," Eclipse says, shifting his humungous weight from one massive foot to the other. He seems desperate for me to understand. "There are Shadows who are depending on me. I need to be there for them."

"Why is it that you keep going back there," I explode, "when none of the other Shadows have ever accepted you for who you are? They never cared about you as Cirrus or as Eclipse. But we always have."

I realise I'm standing, facing off at him.

"They're my people," Eclipse says intensely.

"You'll give and give to them until there's nothing of you left. I'm just so tired of you trying to prove yourself to the Shadows when your real family is right here. We might be a bunch of misfits. But we love you." It just slipped out. I didn't mean to say it. He made me say it. *Bastard.*

"Griffin. You're the smart one, with your grand strategies and your complex programs," Eclipse says softly. "I'm most helpful on the ground, using this power that I was given to protect my people."

"You know how much more you're capable of. You

could do so much with us." He doesn't answer. "So what, you're really still against helping your people from here?" I say, bitter. "You're still against what we're trying to do?"

I can feel his remorse and helplessness pouring off of him. Well, that answers the question. I bring the walls back up between my mind and his. I can't stand it.

I turn away from him and cross my arms.

"Grif," Eclipse says, the words wrenched from deep inside him, "time is so short. Staying alive is never certain, we know that, but even with this damn war going on we've somehow been given this chance to see each other again. That vapour up above means I'll be stuck here for a few days. All I want is to make the most of this time together that we can. We can't help where each of us has ended up, but that doesn't mean that I don't miss you. Always."

I don't look at him. It's like he's saying the words he knows I want to hear most, more than anything. Like he's seen them inside me. But everything's changed from when we were just two stupid kids on the run together.

"Griffin?"

"Yeah," I say. "Sure." I can feel his anxiety that there are doors in me that I won't open to him, when once upon a time we could barely tell where one of us ended and the other began.

I burst into a run as soon as I'm out of Eclipse's sight. I don't stop until I'm up the stairs, with the glowing blue tanks far below me. I stop, panting, and press my back against the cold wall.

He's here. He's okay. Somehow he survived everything out there.

More than that, I can hide things from Eclipse. When we were talking, I could choose which thoughts to conceal. It was hard, it took focus, but I could obscure certain things. The harder part was emotions. I caught some of those little snippets of feeling from him too. Those are the dangers, the little warnings. They're the little things that could give us away.

I don't think he saw anything in me. I'm not sure if he saw the true extent of my fears about who he's become. Even if he's innocent, I don't want him to see how much him leaving me really hurt.

My best friend and I are now somehow engaged in a cloak and dagger game of mental espionage. Looking for any warning signs in each other's thoughts.

Maybe we're both bonkers. Maybe we're just two idiots turned paranoid by this stupid, outrageous excuse for a war.

Still. I'm going to find out where Eclipse has really been. I'm Griffin-freaking-Cameron. Except this time… I'm versing myself.

It's strange that as much as I wish Eclipse would leave us alone, I also wish just as much that the vapour will never clear and he and I will be trapped in this base forever.

I grab some things from my quarters then head back down toward where I left Eclipse, making my way through the glowing blue tanks.

I check my reflection in the glass of a tank, curving the corners of my mouth into a playful smile.

I have to control my mind by imagining walls around all of the things that I don't want Eclipse to see… but you know what the first thing you think of is when someone tells you to not think of an apple.

It's an apple.

I'm terrified of screwing this up in a thousand ways. It feels improvised and dangerous. But it's my only play.

"I got you a present," I say, returning to Eclipse.

His crest rises in surprise. Then he looks suddenly awkward. "It's not... it's not Fruit Loops, is it? My taste buds aren't the same as they used to b..."

I reveal the extremely oversized bottle of Fanta from behind my back.

"Something even better!"

"Oh!" he says, trying and failing to fake joy.

"A taste of the human world. Lurid orange food colouring, pure soda sugary goodness."

There are two giant bowls fixed into the floor of his place. The biggest is filled with water for him, so I unscrew the Fanta bottle and let it chug into the other Eclipse-sized bowl.

"Enjoy!"

"Oh, I will."

Something tells me Eclipse would have much preferred black coffee or something not intended for small human children. But he doesn't say anything. He's still being careful instead of risking a hurtful comment. This friendship... it's too fragile.

I can feel him wondering the same thing as me. Has too much happened between us? Have we lost too much, came too far to regain what we lost?

"I've got a board game too," I mumble, "if you want to play. Most of the rest of the team are catching some sleep right now."

Eclipse looks around his new digs.

"Well, my room is pretty bare bones at the moment. Are you sure you want to play it in here?"

"Sure. Tomorrow I can bring down the stuff from my quarters, but that seriously won't take more than one trip. We can deck this space out with some other stuff, make it homier."

"Are you saying...?"

"That I could crash in here," I say in a rush. "Just while you're here. And only if... if you want me too?"

It's to keep an eye on him in case he slips up, I tell myself, but that doesn't stop me feeling stupidly nervous at asking.

"So we would be, um..." Eclipse looks flummoxed. "We would be...?"

"Flatmates, I guess? We're nearly eighteen now. Time to move out and rent a place together, right?" I grin.

I'm worried I've overstepped... but then I watch as he relaxes. Smiling, he he dips his beak down toward the Fanta in the container before him.

My eyes follow his every movement.

If Eclipse is here to do something, if he is here to act against us, he'll do it after the vapour clears. There's no sense in doing anything when he's still going to be trapped in here for days. Eclipse may be strong, but I don't think even he could survive flying through clouds of toxic vapour that eats at your skin.

The forecast estimates I've got three days tops to find out what Eclipse is up to before it rains and the vapour clears on the surface. Three days before he can unleash whatever plan he has and bounce this place. The GSA's mission to bring humans and Shadows together may hang in the balance.

I can't relive what happened in the station when Eclipse turned on me and tried to destroy our Mum's dream. I can't go through that again, I just can't.

Three days to figure out if Eclipse is here as my friend or as my enemy.

Eclipse hovers above the drink, hesitating. Then he plunges his beak into the bowl of Fanta, drinking deeply. He throws his head back and swallows, like a seagull trying to make a fish go smoothly down into his gullet.

Eclipse's eyes bulge. Then he spews the Fanta out. I deftly step out of the way, just in time.

"Poison," Eclipse spits, aghast.

"Yeah, well, it's not everyone's cup of tea," I say mildly.

Eclipse looks at me standing there, hands casually in my pockets.

"It was hot, and... it burned. It tasted as if..."

"As if someone had mixed a few bottles of hot sauce in there?" I say innocently.

Eclipse blinks.

"You *pranked* me," he says after a long moment. There's something that wasn't there before. A sparkle in his eye.

"Sure did," I wink. "Get used to it. Flatting with me is going to be hell."

8

THE OASIS

Our *King of Tokyo* pieces are balanced precariously. The game board is resting in the big, makeshift nest Eclipse has pulled together. The game is a handmade replica which Phoebe made herself; it's meant for four players, so Eclipse and I have to have two monsters each. Phoebe told me she used to play it constantly with my Mum and the others, back in the day. Eclipse and I take turns as different monsters, some stereotypical, some ridiculous, who are all fighting for supremacy over the burning wreckage of Tokyo city, seeing which monster can kill or outsmart the other one first.

Maybe it's not the most sensitive game that Phoebe could have chosen, what with a life-sized version of it playing itself out over our very heads. I move Eclipse's pieces for him where he directs me too, as they're too tiny for his oversized talons.

Eclipse doesn't volunteer much information if any about what he's been through, no juicy details of the twists and turns his life has taken. I don't press him. I have to play this right.

Eclipse is still exhausted from his ordeal though, even if Zephyr has healed his visible injuries. We only get one game in before Eclipse falls into a deep slumber. I feel my lids growing heavy too, like sympathy pains. It must have taken it out of Eclipse, using his power like he did to push back the human ships at Troy.

"Eclipse?" I whisper. Nothing. I start packing away the game, so he doesn't accidentally crush the teensy pieces in his sleep.

I close my eyes, and I reach out toward his sleeping mind. I make my way through the sensations, the rich shades of gold and the flickering of fledgling dreams. It feels like slogging through quicksand as I search for a secret door within Eclipse's brain...

...and then I find one. Opening it, I walk through it.

I'm in a corridor of Cameron Technologies. I gasp, confronted suddenly with our old home. It's as if it was never destroyed. The walls of the corridors look taller; everything is much larger than it was in real life, like some weird Alice in Wonderland experience.

Of course. This is how Eclipse last saw this place, when Cirrus and I played in these corridors together as kids.

I'm not sure if this is a memory from Eclipse, or something that I've brought to this place. This is all very new. I'm not used to sneaking like a ninja through my own counterpart's deepest, most carefully defended thoughts. It's breaching his privacy in such a shocking way. But I can feel guilty later, once I know that we're all safe.

Now, where to start looking?

I don't have to think about it for long. I walk to the end of the hallway, feeling a pang with each small detail I see replicated from our old home. When I reach the elevator I step through the doors as they slide open. I hit the button for the place that no other employees were ever allowed to visit, the secret family lab where my mother first gathered her team to work on the project to bring humans and Shadows together.

The lift doors close, and there's a whirring as I descend, deeper and deeper into Eclipse's subconscious. When the lift doors open, I gape. I'm not staring at the lab in Cam Tech. Instead I'm staring out into a plain of swirling desert sands.

The heat is intense, like a giant, invisible hairdryer. Shielding my face from the sun, steeling myself, I leave the elevator and walk out into the desert. I survey the desolation, then turn back to the elevator I walked out of. It stands there on its own, a hole in reality. As I walk around it, it gets thinner and thinner. From behind, it doesn't seem to exist at all.

But it's what's behind the elevator that's more interesting.

An oasis. An oasis in the unforgiving heat of the desert, big enough that it's accommodating a small town. I see overgrown toadstools the size of houses, and that's exactly what they are. Houses. It's like an oversized Smurf village. Tall, leafy trees and palms cast the town in shade, and unfurling fern fronds emanate magical light.

Then I see someone I recognise. It's Hanna.

My insides lurch just seeing her. She's fallen to her knees at the edge of the oasis, staring numbly at the town laid out before her. She's cradling a small furry brown goblin in her arms, with a hat of twisted metal. Hanna's pressing something over its face, something like a ghoulish Halloween mask. No, wait. It's a gas mask.

Then a massive dragon-parrot flies out of the strange,

enchanting oasis and lands beside them, the gust from his wings ruffling my hair.

I jerk backward, scared of being caught spying here. But then I realise this isn't the real Eclipse, just the version of him in his own memory. He pays me no attention. The feathers of his right wing are matted with blood, as if he was clipped by bullets there. I can feel the throbbing pain of his wing and the tension and distress coming from him, just how I normally would through our connection. I watch as he bows down, pressing his large talons against objects strewn in the grass amongst the flowers.

That's when I realise why the town is so still. That's when I make sense of the odd cloth-coloured shapes strewn around the oasis, outside the toadstool homes, littering the wooden walkways and lying beside the crystal pools churned by miniature waterfalls.

They're the bodies of Shadows. It's as if all of the townspeople dropped dead where they stood.

I want to scream. I want to drop to my knees like Hanna with the emotion of it all. I've seen things like this, of course I have. The whole war has been like this. But this is different somehow from seeing it through a screen remotely. Troy was shocking for me, yet this strikes another chord in me entirely, though I can't say why. The silent horror, all those lives ended in an instant.

"The humans we were tracking have moved on," Eclipse says, coming up beside Hanna. "I saw them from the air, headed for the Western dunes. I've healed a few of the villagers who were still clinging to life. But there's so few." He sounds exhausted from the energy he expended healing the fallen Shadows. Still, I can feel that he's looking for a fight, looking for any way to keep moving and avoid facing the trauma. Solemnly, awkwardly, he

lowers his great head down to where Hanna is cradling the goblin.

"He's gone, Hanna," Eclipse mutters. "I... I can hear his breathing has stopped even from here."

"No," Hanna says, shaking her head angrily. I'm shocked by the emotion in her voice. "You're wrong. This boy is a fighter, I can feel it. Heal him!"

"I've tried already. He was lost when we got here. This new chemical weapon works fast," Eclipse says. He sounds heartbroken, overwhelmed. "We haven't seen the humans use anything like this so far."

"It drifted this way in the desert winds. These people weren't even a target," Hanna says. Her voice is so quiet, but I can hear the rage beneath it. "And that's not all," Hanna says, shaking. She's still holding the dead goblin in her arms. "Over there."

Eclipse's face contorts with dread but he moves over to where Hanna is pointing, following the sand around the edge of the oasis. I go with him.

We come to a series of big wooden crosses planted deep in the sand. Imperial soldiers in violet armour are crucified on them, their helmets removed so their identities are clear. A sign stuck into the sand in front of them carries the sigil of a heart crossed with clawed gauntlets, and it reads in official violet paint:

DESERTERS ARE TRAITORS TO THE EMPIRE.

Some of the crucified soldiers look like they're only teenagers. Even in death, they look terrified.

"Empress Galvanize ordered that," Hanna says to Eclipse when we return. "It's an example for cowards who avoid the draft, or for citizens who don't chant her anthem enough times. She's insane. We're trapped between two evils now, all of us."

"We've got to keep going," Eclipse says bleakly. "Look, the sun is already going down, and you know how quick sunset is.

The cold of night will kill us even faster. Hanna, we have to find a new home for the survivors we have here. The Empire will be coming this way soon. I'm not in a state to fight them right now, and I can't fly on this injured wing."

"You should have saved some of that healing for yourself." But I can hear unspoken in Hanna's soft words what they both know. Neither of them would have been okay with anything other than trying to heal everyone here they possibly could. Eclipse's wound is minor in comparison.

"We have to go," he says gently.

"I know. I know!" Hanna responds. "Just... give me one more minute." Exhaling, she slowly closes the goblin's eyes.

But go where? The howling desert winds are rising and the sky is darkening. Eclipse staggers, the effort of healing clearly taking a greater toll on him than he realised. He's exhausted.

I'm left with the sight of the strange, beautiful oasis, of the silent dead and the body of the lifeless goblin still cradled in Hanna's arms. I'm left with the cruelty of both Empire and humans, a callous disregard that leaves Hanna shaking with rage. The desperation in Eclipse and Hanna is reflected in the wretchedness of their surroundings, in the unforgiving sand stretching on for all infinity.

I jerk out of the memory violently. Eclipse is still slumbering in his mammoth nest. He seems none the wiser about me tiptoeing through his most private thoughts. I stare at him. I'm realising I really don't have any inkling of what my Shadow has been through while he's been gone.

I lie awake for a long time. Then I slip away from Eclipse's side, making my way up to my quarters. But I don't go all the way. Instead I stop in the corridor before I hit my room, and check the coast is clear.

Then I bend down beside the hatch next to the wall and

pull it open. I have to heave it. Crimson light spills out from the engines below, the engines which keep our power on. The heat billows out from them in the form of ghostly, hissing clouds of steam. My feet blindly feel their way down to the ladder.

Closing the hatch above me, I descend into the hellish glow below.

"Please come now, I think I'm falling, I'm holding on to all I think is safe..."

The melancholic notes full of angst wake me. I'm disorientated for a moment. Suddenly I realise where I am. Eclipse's quarters. The lights are slowly come up on where the tanks are beyond Eclipse's glass windows, simulating morning.

I'm surprised by a sudden rush of joy, treacherous, like a forbidden treasure. Rolling over slowly in the loft I lean over the edge to drink in the sight of the giant dragon-parrot slumbering below me. It's like I'm a kid sneaking a glimpse of presents before Christmas.

The song playing right now is Eclipse's favourite from some of the tunes I played for him last night. It turns out he has a penchant for post-grunge alternative hard rock from the noughties. I must have set it as the new tone for my phone alarm.

I blink sleep from my eyes. I'm surprised I got any at all after my night-time stroll.

Eclipse's wings are outstretched. He looks proud and defiant, even in his sleep. I watch as he stirs at the brightness through the windows, his crest slowly rising in response. He sends a smouldering glare at the lights, as if it's personal. Then, seemingly unable to resist, he lifts his head back and booms a series of notes to greet the artificial morning.

I laugh, then catch myself. It just reminds me of how Cirrus would sing annoyingly early in the morning to greet a new day. Watching Eclipse, it's impossible not to recognise my Shadow as who he once was... to recognise who he still is. I feel a sharp pang in my chest.

Get it together, Griffin.

Even with the less than ideal circumstances of our reunion, having a sleepover like this feels big. It's like we've grown up. This is what it would be like if we'd had a chance to share a dorm at university. Instead of... the lives we got.

I'm human, Eclipse is a Shadow. A normal life was never on the cards for us, I remind myself, no matter how much our Mum wanted it to be.

I watch as Eclipse quietly rises from the floor and makes his way to the doorway, trying not to wake me.

"Morning," I say. Slowly, he turns and shuffles back, extending his neck so that his head rises just above the edge of the loft. He studies my sleeping space curiously, but I see a look of uncertainty flit across his face, as if he's wondering why I didn't sleep down beside him.

"Where are you sneaking off to?" I ask, distracting him. I subtly probe his consciousness, but I don't sense anything suspect in his thoughts. Instead, I'm surprised to sense a shade of embarrassed scarlet emanating from him.

"I... um..." Eclipse ruffles his feathers awkwardly. "I'm just going for a walk."

"Didn't you want me to give you the grand tour?" I smile at him easily, but secretly I'm highly alert, tracking each nuance of thought bubbling through his mind.

"Later, perhaps." Eclipse hesitates. "There's someone I really need to speak with, one-on-one."

"Speak with who?" I say casually, hiding my intense curiosity. "Zephyr?"

Eclipse coughs. My ears prick up.

"What was that?"

"Ember," he mutters.

I blink.

"*Ember*?" I repeat. Suddenly, my conspiracy theory about Eclipse being the one keeping Ember imprisoned seems a lot less likely.

"Why do you say it like that?" He raises a feathery eyebrow nonchalantly, but he sounds defensive.

"What? Nothing. I mean... wait. Are you and Ember a *thing*?"

"No! We haven't spoken since... it's just... it's complicated."

"Is that your Facebook status too?" I say, as amused as I am bewildered.

"My what?"

"Never mind." The thought is so weird that I can't help grinning.

"Oh, don't get me started on you and Phoebe," he retaliates teasingly.

I flush.

"What? Whaddya mean?" I splutter.

"I remember how you two were in the Underworld," Eclipse says knowingly. "And I can see Phoebe in your thoughts. You really still haven't acted on that?"

"I really don't want to get into it," I say. There's a beat. "Didn't Ember throw you in a cage?" I wonder aloud.

"Silence," he commands.

"Didn't you and Ember *fight* each other?"

Eclipse storms toward the exit. Well, 'storms' as much as he can, with that weird bird shuffle of his.

"Okay, good luck with that," I call, reclining. "Hashtag relationship goals."

His long, snake-like tail whips upward, slapping me. I fall backward in the loft, letting out a shout of protest. The tip of his tail is split into giant tail feathers, which smother me. I roll back and forth wildly, trying to kick it away.

"Argh!" I protest dramatically. "I'm trapped! NO, please…" I laugh, coughing as he pins me down. "Oxygen!" I gasp.

Eclipse finally frees me. I call out as he makes to leave.

"Um, Eclipse?"

The lumbering giant turns to survey me with his fearsome gaze.

"Uh… the Gardens could be good? You could take Ember there. Our training area has some nice garden paths around it we tried to decorate with edible plants. That's probably the most scenic part of the ship. Plus it's a big space, so you won't feel claustrophobic."

"The Gardens," Eclipse says to himself under his breath. "Understood."

Tentatively, I reach out to him and show him a visual tour of how to get there from our room. He doesn't pull away from the contact, and I feel a glow of gratitude from him. It feels strange to be giving him tips for his date.

"Of course," I add slyly, "if you two want this place to yourselves, I can clear out. Just say the word. I don't want to be here if you two are… you know."

"*Griffin!*"

"Are you seriously blushing right now?" I say, entertained. "Oh… also, everyone in the base is pretty curious about you since you arrived. I'm just warning you. You might get swamped on the way to your date."

"It's not a date," Eclipse says, nervous.

"You sure you don't want me to come with you?"

"I'm sure. Just… what do the people in this base know about me, exactly? About what happened?"

My laughter fades instantly. What he's really asking is: did I tell them the full story?

"You're my Shadow," I say finally. "That alone makes you a celebrity here, okay? What's past is past."

I detect a flicker of something from Eclipse's mind, a shred of thought. Something that slips past his defences, that he didn't want me to see. It's not much, but I glean one thing from it in that moment.

Sometime in the night, when I was asleep, Eclipse snuck out.

Crap! Where did he go? What did he do? I shouldn't have fallen asleep. I should have kept watch.

I clamber down from the loft, determined to follow Eclipse and keep better track of him this time…

Just short of the archway I come to a stop, smacked dumb.

The long table in the adjoining space has been covered in a fancy midnight-blue tablecloth. Two plates and two sets of cutlery are laid out neatly opposite each other. A simple selection of cheeses and fruit is laid out that Eclipse must have picked up from the kitchen during the night. Oh. *This* is why he stepped out.

"Eclipse?" I say slowly. "What is this?"

He grins, slyly.

"I woke up early and couldn't get back to sleep, so I decided I wanted to do something nice for you."

"Something nice?" I say, puzzled. His tone makes me suspicious. "What do you mean?"

Eclipse slinks out toward the door. It's hard to be subtle or stealthy when you're, well, him.

"You should get dressed," he says encouragingly over his shoulder. "Wear something smooth."

"Eclipse," I say loudly, dangerously, "What did you do?"

But he's escaped out the archway already. I prepare to rush out after him, then hesitate, taking one more look at the set-up. I don't know how Eclipse did everything so immaculately when he has talons the size of didgeridoos. Candles illuminate the space with a low, flickering light.

Weird. Eclipse gave me a solo romantic breakfast. I guess Shadows just show friendship in strange ways?

I hear footsteps entering the oversized room behind me.

"Morning!" a voice calls brightly.

I turn dumbly to see Phoebe, who has come to a dead stop. Her eyes widen, and she stands there frozen, taking in the scene before her. I'm framed by the ridiculously overly-romantic breakfast set-up.

"Um…" I say.

Phoebe looks beautiful. Okay, she's wearing what she basically always wears, her customary leather jacket in pride of place, and she does look like she just woke up. But I'm knocked over silly by the sight of her, every single time.

Self-consciously, I realise that I'm still wearing my pyjamas with stars and comets on them.

I'm going to kill Eclipse, I decide.

But it's not his fault. Well, it is. But it's also my fault that I'd sort of avoided telling him the girl that I like is dating Calvin. Eclipse doesn't get this is too complicated to be messing with.

Phoebe is still standing there, looking slightly petrified.

"Sorry," I say, embarrassed. "This was... this is all Eclipse."

"Oh," she says, relaxing slightly. She grins. "Is this his equivalent of making you breakfast in bed?'

"We've been listening through all of Ember's old punk favourites," Phoebe says, tossing another grape into her mouth from the magnificent spread. "Apparently that was one of the top things she missed about our world, apart from me. To be honest, I think she just might be full-on regressing back to her brooding teenager phase."

The breakfast food is just what would normally be served upstairs in the cafeteria but it does seem to taste ten times better when given such fancy presentation.

My gaze subtly traces the burn scars across Phoebe's face. They're waxy and ghostly white. I know them better than my own hands.

Okay, stop it Grif. You're being creepy.

Sitting there quietly with Phoebe at the corner of the breakfast table, just talking, feels so... *natural.* It fills me with a happy bubbling sensation. I've missed her laugh. Since her and Calvin became a thing, since everything hit the fan, we haven't had as much time with just *us.* Maybe that's my fault. She was right about that. When we were journeying to connect the worlds together, everything was so much more intense. Just the two of us against all the forces of the worlds who wanted to stop us. It's been hard going from that to being the eternal third wheel.

Thanks, Eclipse. I'm seriously grateful to him for giving us this one moment to be Phoebe and Griffin again.

"Does Eclipse have any news yet?" Phoebe asks. "Any stories on what's happening with the Empire?"

"He says he was stuck in the desert. That he's been off the grid, and doesn't know anything about what's happening over there, why everything's gone so quiet."

"And what do you think?"

"I think he's seen more than he's letting on," I say, and I shiver as I recall the haunting memory of the oasis.

"Are you enjoying yourself though?" Phoebe says, teasingly.

"I'm getting answers," I say, giving her a look. "That's all."

"Really? You're not having fun at all?" She acts impressed. "Well then. The Oscar for Best Actor goes to..."

I narrow my eyes. Phoebe grins.

"Did Ember stay in your bed last night?" I say, in an attempt to segue the conversation to a safer topic.

Phoebe laughs, the candlelight dancing in her eyes.

"You should have heard her. *'Phoebe, I love you, but I was the commander of Winghold. I led the Resistance into battle and ruled over vast areas of the Shadow world. What would everyone think if I nestled on your bed all night like some kind of obedient pet?'*"

"And?"

"Ember fell asleep in my bed before I did." Phoebe sips her morning coffee with a grin. "She ended up spooning me the whole night."

"I didn't know birds could even spoon," I comment. "They don't even sleep on their sides."

"Yeah, well it was really more of a mind-over-matter

type thing. Like, this bird was really determined to cuddle." Phoebe brushes a flaming lock behind her ear. "Come here," she says.

"Huh?"

"Come here," she says, taking my arm playfully. Sidling her chair around the table into me, she reaches across to pull me tightly into a hug. She's warm, like always.

"Thank you so much for bringing her back to me," Phoebe whispers into my ear. "I... I don't know what to say, or how to make it up to you. But I'll never forget it." She starts to pull away, before she hesitates. Her eyes catch mine.

I don't know if I'm imagining it. Maybe I am imagining it. Okay, I'm *probably* imagining it. But for a moment... I don't think I'm the only one who's not breathing.

There's the sudden sound of voices, and I jerk away like a scared bird taking flight.

Calvin and Zephyr enter through the archway, laughing. They sidle up to the table where I'm sitting with Phoebe over our candlelit breakfast. Neither of them bat an eyelash.

"Hey guys, sorry we're late," Calvin says apologetically. He's carrying more takeaway boxes, presumably with food from upstairs. "We only just got away."

"*Late?*" I say, boggled. "Am I the only one who didn't get an invite to whatever this is?"

Calvin and Zephyr pull up seats at the table. Calvin slides his around to be beside Phoebe, with her sandwiched between us.

I try to edge my seat away from them. It squeaks.

"This is just outstanding," Calvin says emphatically,

picking up his cutlery. "When Phoebe suggested a family breakfast, I wondered: '*why don't we do this more often?*'"

"No idea," I say. Edgily, I look to Phoebe.

"I hope you don't mind," she whispers to me. "I just thought it would be fun for us all to spend time together."

"*Super* fun," I say. I focus on trying to hack some cheese off a cheese wheel. Calvin is wearing his blazer, exuding professionalism and charisma. I'm very aware that I'm still in my baggy space pyjamas. It doesn't exactly scream: 'Leader of the GSA.'

Griffin!

Everyone jumps as a towering golden dragon-parrot comes charging through the open archway.

Calvin and Zephyr are coming! he explodes desperately. *If you and Phoebe are doing anything indecent...* He sees all of us seated at the table. "Oh, hello Calvin!"

I stare at Eclipse, raising an eyebrow.

Calvin's here, Eclipse tells me primly.

Thank you, I say scathingly. *Now please don't mention anything about my crush on Phoebe to anyone. That would be bad.*

He's back so fast, I wonder if he even made it to his own date, or if he chickened out.

"I was just about to tell Griffin that you were coming for breakfast too!" Eclipse explains to everyone, gesturing at them with his massive wings. "Which I just found out, and here you are." He grins awkwardly at me. "Splendid."

"Cirrus!" Calvin stands in welcome. He stares up at Eclipse, awed. Apparently he forgot how formidable Eclipse is in person. "It's very good to see you," Calvin smiles encouragingly. "I'm sorry that last time we didn't meet in the best circumstances... it wasn't exactly..." He clears his throat. "I'm glad to see my brother's Shadow is back home, and safe."

"Thanks. I, uh, I go by Eclipse now."

"Right, of course." Calvin looks embarrassed. "I just wasn't sure since you were still Cirrus, but Eclipse is the name you go by now, correct? That's your... um... that's your choice?"

"Calvin, we talked about this," Zephyr hisses.

"I know, I just wanted to be clear..."

"*Sssh.*" Shutting Calvin up, Zephyr stands too. He displays his fangs as he nervously smiles up at his 'little' brother, who looms above us all. "It's good to see you up and about, Eclipse," Zephyr says enthusiastically. "Welcome to the GSA. Welcome home."

"Thanks, Zeph," Eclipse says awkwardly. "But I, uh, I'm not sure how long I'm staying. This was sort of an impromptu..." But he doesn't get a chance to finish. Phoebe is striding toward him, grinning widely.

"Eclipse!" Phoebe greets him, then stretches upward to give Eclipse a giant hug. It looks kind of silly when she can barely reach his stomach. "I'm really glad you're okay," she says warmly.

Eclipse looks a little shocked, but then he bashfully bends down so she can hug him around his neck.

"I don't know what to say," he says, sounding surprisingly moved. "Only that I've missed you too, all of you."

I look away, feeling a confused tumble of emotions at seeing what good terms he's on with my friends and family. Before the war, all of this would have made me beam with happiness.

"How did you know Eclipse was a hugger?" I ask Phoebe quietly, as she sits back down beside me.

Phoebe smiles knowingly.

"I just had a sense that a hug, while unexpected, would not be entirely unwelcome."

That's when I see Ember standing in the archway of the room, staring up at the giant dragon-parrot between her and the breakfast table.

"Wow, so we're really all here now," I say. I wonder if I should excuse myself to get changed.

Eclipse turns. When he sees Ember, he goes still.

"Well, look who it is," Ember says, sauntering in. "Not even missiles can keep you down."

"Surprised?"

"Not really." She appraises Eclipse unashamedly, seemingly blind to the fact that the rest of us are sitting here watching the two of them. "I've had time in my cell to tally up my regrets," she says. "But one of the biggest was never telling you how sorry I am for what I did." I'm shocked to see her looking uncharacteristically emotional. "Phoebe told me that you're still Cirrus. That you've been him all along."

"That's what you suspected all along," Eclipse says. "Don't you remember locking me up in a prison cell for six months trying to remind me that I was him, not Eclipse?"

"Yes, but I shouldn't have!" Ember's feathers pulse with firelight. "I screwed up, damn it! I should have given you the choice of who to be, rather than thinking Eclipse was some..." her face contorts in disgust at herself, "...some *disease* to cure. You were right. I became just as bad as the Empire."

"You wish, you goodie-two-shoes," Eclipse says candidly. "You did me a favour. After my rebirth I hurt a lot of people. There was a certain... adjustment period. You did what was right, as you always do. Pull up a perch, join the party." He looks at me sheepishly. "It seems to be a family thing now anyhow."

Ember's gaze lasers into Zephyr.

"Break bread with *this* traitor?"

"Come on, join us," I insist, backing up Eclipse. "We're finally all back together for once. Can't we have a truce?"

"You do owe me for locking me in that cage," Eclipse reminds Ember with a smirk.

"Nothing sets the scene for a family breakfast like some emotional blackmail," Ember comments. But she fills the awkward silence by strutting past Eclipse around the table and seating herself beside me.

Calvin smiles around at everyone, nodding to himself, but he can't seem to think of anything to actually say. For a few minutes, there's nothing to punctuate the silence but the occasional squeaking of forks on plates and the sounds of chewing. I cast around for some topic which isn't about our work or the war. Nothing comes to mind. It's not like we get a whole lot of time to read the latest online celebrity gossip down here.

Ember and Eclipse are both silent. If a tumble weed had come rolling through our little breakfast party, I don't think it would have surprised anyone.

"Anyone in the mood for a lightning round of King of Tokyo?" I suggest.

"GO FOR ATTACKS! You can hit him with your Shrink Ray, he only has four hearts left anyway!"

"That's a lie!"

"Stop using Kraken to hide your points, Calvin, that's cheating!"

"Just roll!"

The dice clatter across the table.

"YES!"

The game quickly has the six of us laughing and shouting animatedly, eagerly surveying our cards and plotting our way to victory. I haven't grinned this much in a while. I don't think any of us have.

None of us here in the base have even really made any time to chill out. Or more likely they have, but I'm usually skulking in my room. Planning and brooding.

Once the game finishes and the others start tidying up the pieces though, it hits me that Phoebe and I still haven't told any of the others the biggest news. It shocks me for a moment that with all my fear and anxiety about Eclipse, I've ignored the threat I brought into this base which is possibly far bigger.

I look at Phoebe, and realise she's giving me a meaningful look. She always seems to be tuned into exactly what I'm thinking. We have the entire team together. There won't be a better opportunity then now, and the longer we hide it the more their reaction is going to snowball.

"Okay, team, listen up," I say, and everyone's attention swivels to me. Zephyr and Calvin. Phoebe and Ember. Even Eclipse, his head hovering up above us all. "There's something else that happened at Troy," I tell them. "Something that means... I don't know what it honestly means, but it's big. Huge. Also, please don't be mad at us not telling you sooner."

"What?" Calvin says, fixing me intensely with those storm-grey eyes.

"You *can't* get mad."

"We can get mad whenever we want," Zephyr scowls, annoyed at his personal freedoms being infringed upon.

"Okay, okay," Calvin says. "We won't get mad. What haven't you told us?"

"So there's the slightest chance, the teensiest possibility, that in a prison cell at Troy... I found Raven."

You could drop a teaspoon and the sound would probably shatter our eardrums.

"Also his Shadow, Winter," I add for good measure.

They're all staring at me, except for Phoebe. Ember's shock is radiating from her, but Calvin, Zephyr and Eclipse seem to be waiting for a '*psych*!'

"I don't get it," Zephyr says.

"Well, there's nothing to get, Zeph. It's the truth."

"Raven," Calvin repeats. "The one who betrayed our family. The one who started the war. The one who..."

"Yes, the one who created and controlled the entire Shadow Empire," I say rapidly. "He of many titles." I can't help the gallows humour. Raven being here is twisting my brain. At least now we're all experiencing the same sensation.

"So, if you found these two, where are they?"

"Well," I say, "unless Phoebe misplaced them en route..."

"They're in the De-escalation Area," Phoebe says calmly. "Chained up and locked in one of the cells."

Then the others seem to finally click that this isn't a prank. The mood in the room takes a dark turn.

"What the hell, Griffin!" Calvin explodes, rising to his feet. "You brought *him*..." He stabs the table with his finger in emphasis, "into our base, without even telling me?"

"It was both of us," Phoebe says, strangely angry that he's leaving her off the hook.

"There was a lot of other stuff going on..." I start.

"I'm your number two!" Calvin shouts, making me stop. "Just because you're running this show doesn't mean that you can keep me in the dark whenever you feel like it."

"Technically, there is no number two," Phoebe says, raising her hand. "Unless there's some secret boys' club that no one told me about."

"I'm sorry," I say, facing my big brother squarely. "You're right, everyone had a right to know. But, please. I'd just found Eclipse again. Phoebe just got Ember back."

"I understand it's a crazy time," Calvin says, his tone finally less jagged. "But this changes everything. We need to decide how we're going to handle this. How, in all the random complexity of the universe, did Raven end up sharing a prison with Ember?"

"I had no idea they were both there," Ember says. She looks just as enraged as Calvin and Zephyr at finding out who our new guests are. Her feathers spark dangerously.

"What has Raven said?" Zephyr demands. He's on his feet too. Raven has cost him as much as any of us.

"So far?" Phoebe says grimly. "Nothing." I see a flicker of trauma in her features, but she skilfully buries it. It's easy to forget that we're talking about the best friend who used to keep her alive on the streets. The one who betrayed her, who she'd banished to the Shadow world. I can't even imagine what it means for her, what it's like to have him here, the man she knew as Taylor, so close to where she sleeps.

"We need to question him," Calvin says.

"It's worth a shot," I say. "Eclipse?"

"Yes?"

"You've been quietly brooding. Did you hear anything while you were in the Shadow world about Raven being ousted?"

Most of the Empire is in complete denial that a human has been secretly running the show all of these years, that Empress Galvanize is still carrying out Raven's commands. Is there a chance that Galvanize had enough of him? I wonder. Or did she have no idea at all he was being held in that prison?

All of our attention is glued to Eclipse. He shakes his head awkwardly.

"Galvanize reveres Raven," he says, troubled. "He raised her up, gave her everything, just like how Raven played Hanna when he groomed her to be Empress. Galvanize is even more of a blind follower of Raven then Hanna was."

"I've heard equally zero," Ember says. "But then, I'd been locked up in there for a long while. Started to wonder what Galvanize was waiting for. Probably takes a while to plan a nice big execution, get the napkins matching with the table cloths, that sort of thing."

"Don't even joke about that," Phoebe says sharply. Then, to the rest of us: "The Shadow world has been oddly quiet. Something is brewing, but we don't know what." Phoebe's expression is grave. "The UN fears it means an attack is imminent, but it could be some other kind of shake-up over there."

"What matters right now is that we have Raven, and Galvanize doesn't," I point out.

"You know what Raven took from me," Calvin says, his voice like acid. "Unless Raven's returned to give us back Mum and Dad and the life we all should have lived together…" His face contorts with emotion. All of my life it's as if there's been this shard of glass in Calvin, this pain buried deep down which defined him. No matter how much he smiled or laughed and no matter how much he achieved, there was always a part of him which seemed to loathe the world. A part that had been born the night that his friend Taylor had betrayed him.

"That does leave a giant gaping question," I say. "What do we do with Raven long-term?"

"You searched him for bugs and trackers when you brought him in?" Calvin says suddenly to Phoebe.

"Yeah. Of course. They both came up clean."

"Did he try to talk to you, Phoebe?" I say quietly.

"No," she says. Her voice is stony but I can see she's troubled. "He didn't say anything. It's like he's… shell-shocked or something."

I think again about the note I'd found from Raven as we'd flown away from the island, as the portals opened and the war began.

'Your move.'

Something tells me that Raven turning up in a prison is his.

"We can't *not* take action because we're worried of taking a wrong step. I say we use him as a bargaining chip," Phoebe puts forth. "Let's see if the Shadow world will agree to peace. Empress Galvanize worships Raven, right? Enough for her to end the war if Raven ordered her to?"

"We don't know if Raven's still calling the shots. He should be taken back to the Shadow world," Eclipse says earnestly. I can feel him hoping that I'll side with him on this, but surely he knows there's no way I will.

"Have you taken leave of your senses?" Calvin says in disbelief, his nostrils flaring.

"Don't talk to my Shadow that way," I scold Calvin. "But yeah, Eclipse. What the hell?"

Eclipse stews for a moment.

"Raven has wronged my people even more than he has wronged yours," he says carefully, "and for far longer. Let me take him back. The people can hold him to account for his crimes."

"Yes, I can just see the Empire stepping aside and allowing everyone to take a vote," Zephyr says, trying to rein in his temper, clearly not wanting to clash with his younger brother. "If you march Raven back to the Shadow world he'll just be able to pull the Empire's strings all over again."

"The humans, then," Ember says with passion. "Hand Raven over to the UN. See what they make of him."

"The trouble is that Raven's too clever," Phoebe says, frustrated. "I can see him talking his way out of that somehow, can't you? All he needs to do is promise intelligence and resources to the UN to help them get an edge in the war and he'll be put up in a penthouse and have servants waiting on him without even having to click his fingers. What if you make one of your videos, Grif? We could interrogate Raven, stream it..."

"Not everyone will believe it," I say dully. "They'll say we're just feeding him lines. Hardly anybody would even recognise Raven anyway. That's how he's operated so well for so long, staying out of sight, off the radar. No. Even if Raven does confess his part in starting the war..." I swallow. The truth must haunt all of us, no matter how hard we want to escape it. "Raven's confession won't stop anything.

The worlds are both greedy, hungry for everything the other one has, still refusing to recognise that they each face extinction. So, we question Raven." I feel the adrenaline surging through my veins. "Let's head up there and get the answers we need. If he has any other nasty surprises in the pipeline for us, I'd rather find out now."

"We can't right now," Phoebe reminds me, looking at me like I'm a cretin. "We have responsibilities, duties. Jobs that can't wait. Jobs that you *gave* us. There are members in the field who need to check in. Lives that hang in the balance, all that jazz."

"Okay, fair point," I agree. "Let's check our schedules, find a time we can all do. Let's say midday or straight after? And remember!" I conduct them as we all say in a monotone chorus: "*It's probably a trap.*"

"Nice," I say. I look at them all, reflecting how much I care about each person in this room. What a miracle it is that after so much and so long, we're finally reunited.

"Let's do this together," I say. "We've all lost things we cared deeply about because of that man. None of us should have to face him alone."

9
OLD GRUDGES

On the screen before me, human soldiers fire at giant bees as they attack. The insectoid Shadows are descending from hives of multi-coloured crystals which glow in the night. A deep river of honey gushes beneath them. One of the hives is struck by a missile, exploding in lurid pink and green goo to the mournful cries of the Shadows.

I look away, moving my gaze to the next holographic screen beside it. Each display shows either a map with glowing red dots indicating troop distribution, or a video feed from our own drones or from military intelligence that we've hacked. Spread out before me are a mud-slicked battlefield in Europe, a live stream of the United Nations Security Council in session, a feed from the entrenched fighting in the Firenight Marshes... yet still we have so little knowledge of what the Empire is truly up to. They're keeping a tighter lock down on information than ever, including the civilian networks. Something's shifting over there, I can feel it. Something is coming. Something big.

It's second nature to me, taking in all of the data spread before me and making split-second decisions with it. It's just like playing one of the strategy games I was raised on. This is the one and only area where I could always beat Calvin and I believe it's one of the reasons I was given the opportunity to run this place over him. At least when it comes to understanding the game of war, I've always been king. It's a weird kind of bragging right.

Obviously what's tricky compared to the games I used to play is that the only way to win the game for us is to get the two armies to kiss and make up.

I try to hide the sinking feeling in me as I look at the data. I always channel my inner Calvin Cameron when the others in the bridge are looking at me, like Alexander the Great marshalling the troops. I learnt to lead, to inspire others, from watching my brother. But privately I can see that despite everything we're throwing at this war, we've still managed to be nothing but a nuisance to either side. The day where we bust out the Fanta celebrating the end of the war feels very far away.

I created this organisation, and now I feel powerless to alter our direction. It's like watching a boat slowly sinking. Calvin, Zephyr and Phoebe seem convinced that any day now we'll hit a turning point, but we need to be bolder. We need more ambition. I just wish the others could see it my way.

"Wow, you've got so many cool spy toys now," Eclipse says. I turn to see his head emerging from just inside the tunnel of the bridge. The tunnel is too small for him, and it's clearly taken some effort to worm his way into it. But as he hunches there, his eyes are dancing with amusement. He gestures with a wing at the set-up, nearly sending two people flying.

"Easy, BFG," I say, tearing off the gloves that let me operate the holo-screens. I notice Eclipse's gaze roaming across the displays and readings, and I feel abruptly uncomfortable with the amount of revealing information about our operations up there, and the movements of human troops.

"Keep at it, minions," I say absent-mindedly to Sien, Pixie and the others. "I'm going on break."

"Hey, everyone," Eclipse says, nodding to them. They're all staring at Eclipse with great interest. Some have their jaws hanging open as they take in his immense size.

"Come on numbskull," I say, prodding him so he'll back up down the tunnel. His giant, serpentine tail winds along the floor, nearly tripping me up on the way out. "Time to give you the official tour."

"Just trying to be supportive of your work," Eclipse says, smiling innocently.

"Yeah, well, be supportive from the outside, where you can't break million-dollar equipment when you sneeze."

It's stupid, after so long being cooped up in here detesting this place, but I still can't help feeling proud of it. I'm excited to show Eclipse each and every part of it, to share with someone what my life has been like for the last nine months, to share everything that we've built here... because I've dreamt of this moment. Even though I tried to stay angry at Eclipse during all this time, when I was suffering from insomnia in the dead of night, slaving away on my own in the bridge, I would imagine what it would be like if my Shadow came home. I fantasised about us getting our friendship back through some kind of miracle, even if I barely admitted it to myself... and now he's here.

I try hard to quash those excited feelings, knowing that they'll just end up hurting me. It's tricky though.

"Can I ask you something?" I say. We're making our way through the offices and strategy meeting rooms on the top floor. The passages are made for the tallest and widest of Shadows, but Eclipse's crest-feathers still brush the roof. I can't help but notice how keenly Eclipse studies each room we pass, catching glimpses of the screens in each one. "What is it that you see in Hanna?"

"You're still angry at her?" Eclipse says, unsettled.

"Angry at her?" I repeat in disbelief. "Hanna *stabbed* me, in the back. I was nearly killed by the girl, the Shadow, who I thought I was in love with."

Eclipse stares down at me intensely, and I can feel his mind automatically searching my feelings as well. I raise the barrier between us, uncomfortable.

"Do you hate her?" he asks me quietly.

I don't know what to say. In my mind I'm floating down an underground river again with Hanna and Cirrus, beneath a cavernous roof of glow-worms that shine like stars.

"Cirrus?" I'd whispered.

"Yeah?"

"You two are the only ones who care if I live or die. Thank you."

"Not just us, dude."

I fight the memory away before Eclipse catches a glimpse of it.

"How can you just forgive her like that," I say to him,

"after what she did to you?"

"We forgive for our own sake. What's that quote? *'Holding onto anger is like drinking poison and expecting the other person to die.'*" He pauses, troubled. "But it's more than that. I have to believe that when someone falls into darkness, that they can find their way back to the light. And she has. That gives me hope."

"I don't know if I believe someone like her can ever change."

"What if Hanna met her human?" Eclipse asks, as if he's testing me. "I thought you believed if a Shadow and human came together they'd each become the best versions of themselves, that it's just their loneliness that motivates them to do evil things."

"That was what we *both* used to believe."

"So you believe anyone can be redeemed except for Hanna? Because she put a knife in your back?"

"No," I say, "because she hurt *you*."

Eclipse doesn't know what to say for a moment.

With a flash I'm remembering New Redemption, and I know he is too. I remember my desperate hunt for Cirrus on the ship while I felt Hanna trying to break our connection. Then when she'd turned the contraption on me, I'd felt Hanna's own memories inside my head. Then I'd been freed, and I'd stood over Hanna, raising my sword...

I'd nearly killed her, but then Cirrus had screamed with pain and something had stalled me. But I'd felt that fury inside me. I know how close I came to doing it. I told myself I was doing it for Cirrus.

"Sometimes love leads to the worst kinds of violence," Eclipse says quietly, and I think he's seen my thoughts. "Hanna's appalled that she ever did what she did to me on

New Redemption. But think of what she's been through. As a child, she was kept locked in a basement, fed through a slot in the door. She was deprived of all human contact until Raven found her and rescued her. He was the only one she ever really knew, the only one who ever showed her something like love. He turned her into the Empress. Hanna saw the world through his eyes. When she met you, you showed her kindness, joy, and laughter for the first time ever. Only for you to reject her as your Shadow. The first person other than Raven who had ever showed her love had abandoned her. Suddenly she was that girl locked in the basement again: helpless, lonely, and determined to do anything to make it stop."

"That's not an excuse," I mutter, "that's just how she felt. You can always choose to be better. You can choose to not let your past define you."

"That's true, and finally she did choose. She betrayed Raven to rescue us and the prisoners in Aeyu. She threw away a chance to become the Empress again to become a refugee in the desert with me, starving and dying of thirst, hunted by her own kind and yours, saving anyone she could from suffering."

"You see something of yourself in her, don't you?" I accuse him fiercely. "Something broken. That's why you're drawn to her. But you're not broken, not like her."

"That's what we all say to comfort ourselves," Eclipse says humourlessly, and the words seem again to hint at things he hasn't shared with me. "Sometimes I think I'm the most broken of all. What I'm saying is, Hanna chose to be good, even when she had every reason not to."

"She'll betray you again," I say grimly. "She always does. I don't want to be in a position to say I told you so."

"That's enough," Eclipse snaps. I jump at the force of his response, shocked at his anger. We glare at each other. Jeez he's intimidating, but no way in hell am I going to look away.

"I wouldn't be alive if I hadn't had her," Eclipse says in a hush. "I hope you can at least be grateful to her for that."

Eclipse, what happened to you? I wonder, looking at him. Why are you really here?

"Grif?" he says. "Come here."

"Why?"

"I want to show you where I've been. What it's been like. Answers to all of the questions you have that you've been too afraid to ask."

Eclipse bends his head all the way down to my height, surprising me. I move to meet him and our foreheads touch, the bridge of my nose pressed against his beak. He breathes in and out, slowly and instinctively. I copy him. It reminds me of the traditional Māori hongi, where you welcome a visitor by sharing the breath of life with them. I'm welcoming Eclipse aboard our ship, letting him into the GSA's inner sanctum... and my own.

I'm in Eclipse's memories, but this time he's opening up to me, showing me one particular moment in time.

It's very familiar.

I'm back in the haunting oasis, surrounded by the desert sands. Eclipse has collapsed amongst the glowing fern fronds, exhausted from healing the survivors. The fronds sway back and forth, rippling in a non-existent wind. It's as if they're silently screaming a warning to the town that was never heard. A warning to the lifeless bodies lying among the ferns.

It's getting dark. Night is falling.

"Eclipse," Hanna says tensely. She softly places the body she's

been cradling onto the grass, freeing her arms for a fight. "We have company."

I watch as countless refugees start to make their way into the oasis. It's a stream of them. There are families of every kind of Shadow imaginable. I hear their cries of shock as they take in the dead Shadow's strewn across the oasis beneath the suspended homes, victims of chemical warfare.

Then their attention catches on Eclipse and Hanna. The refugees hiss and recoil at the sight of the golden dragon-parrot, slowly fanning out to surround them both.

"The Beast!" I hear some of them shouting back at the others. "It was the Beast who did this!"

In no time the refugees are throwing stones and handfuls of dirt at Eclipse. Some of them try to get close to kick him, fearful, snarling, even though he could end them effortlessly. They're torn between fear of him and their own loathing.

I feel my blood boil. They only suspect Eclipse because he's different, and because of whatever lies Empress Galvanize has been spreading about him, I suppose. But Eclipse is so exhausted, I can feel it, and he can barely lift his head from the effort of healing so many of those poisoned by the chemical gas. He doesn't even lift a talon to defend himself as a rock grazes the ridge of his right eye.

I want to step in, to shout at the violent refugees to back off, but instead Hanna lands between them and Eclipse. She stands defiantly in front of him, spreading her violet wings wide as if she can protect the giant with her human-sized frame.

There's whispering. The refugees recognise the Shadow who used to be their Empress, even if she is wearing rags, her face smeared with dirt.

"Listen to me!" Hanna cries out. She looks mad. Witnessing the dead all around them has left her with a very short fuse. "I *don't know what lies Galvanize has told you about Eclipse, but..."*

"We don't care what Galvanize says!" one of the refugees cries. "But that abomination you're protecting is just as bad as her... and so are you."

Someone throws another rock at Eclipse, but Hanna steps into its path. It strikes her in the cheek, leaving a deep cut. She doesn't flinch.

"Yes, I've done terrible things," Hanna says clearly, so all of them can hear her. Someone throws a dry clump of mud which hits Hanna, but still she keeps her chin upright. "I made my own choices but not in circumstances of my choosing. Raven manipulated me, just as he has Galvanize, just as he has all of us. But this Shadow, this one you're determined to call the Beast..." she gestures at Eclipse, emotional. "He's been using the powers he's been given to try and save as many of you as possible. When he was young, he suffered under the Empire and thought he just had to live with it, like all of you did. But now he's doing something to try and save you from that Empire and from the humans. You have no idea what he gave up so that he could be here protecting you. This wasn't him! He didn't hurt these people, he healed whoever he could. All so that you could throw rocks at him? Shame. Shame on all of you."

For a moment it looks like Hanna is getting through to them. Then a rock hits Eclipse in the face and he cries out in pain and surprise.

"He's trying to help you!" Hanna cries out, trembling with exhaustion and grief. "Why can't you see that? Take it out on me, but not him!"

I think that's all Eclipse meant to share with me, all that he meant for me to see, because the colours start to fade.

But I'm determined to watch it to the end, and I cling onto the memory, digging deeper...

I watch as all of the refugees go strangely silent. Some of them gasp.

New Shadows are emerging through the trees. The surviving Shadows of the oasis who Eclipse managed to heal. They surround Hanna and Eclipse in a protective circle, shielding them from the hostile refugees.

Then the villagers turn to face Eclipse, and drop to their knees. They prostrate themselves before Eclipse, who's so exhausted he's barely-conscious. He watches them puzzled through half-closed eyes. I see that some of those bowing to him are crying, and some I can hear sobbing for their friends and families who have fallen, but so many of them have people they love who are still alive. Because of Eclipse.

"You brought us back from the brink with a single touch of your claws," one of the villagers announces in awe, so that all the refugees watching can hear him clearly. "You are gifted, sir. Please, please be our protector. Save us from the human threat, save us from Galvanize. We will follow you wherever you want to go. You are our light."

Eclipse looks shocked, then oddly shy. Hanna has a hand over her mouth, which I notice is hiding a smile.

Then something happens that surprises me even more. Stunned and ashamed by what they've heard, all of the refugees begin to bow down too, even the ones who threw things at Eclipse.

As the countless desperate, disenfranchised Shadows bow down before Eclipse and his miraculous powers of healing, a cloud of butterflies streams through the oasis. They fly over the prostrated heads and past Eclipse, out across the desert sands, as if riding the winds of change.

Their golden wings glimmer in the dark.

During my tour with Eclipse, privacy is hard for us, due to him being, well, Eclipse. Some of the other members of the GSA have to squeeze awkwardly past him in the corridor. This makes it hard for them to hide the fact that they're ogling him. They're too nervous to wave or introduce themselves though, like they're afraid I'll growl at them or something. I guess in the past here I have been pretty prickly about discussing him.

I've got to admit though, it's kinda hard to ignore the pride I feel as the other humans stare at my magnificent counterpart and cast me almost jealous looks.

They're all staring at me, Eclipse says, perturbed.

Um... no? I don't think so.

I think back to Eclipse's memory. Not the part he showed me of Hanna standing up for him, but of the ending that I glimpsed. I'm not sure if he knows what I saw, if he felt me searching through his mind. His mental defences are strong, but I just have to hope that mine are stronger. There are things that I don't want him to know, things that he *can't* know, for all of our sakes.

When I witnessed the refugees offering their gratitude to Eclipse in the oasis, I knew it signalled something, I'm just not entirely sure what. His mind is still a puzzle, its interlocking layers taunting my curiosity.

As we walk, I realise that Eclipse's attention isn't so much on the layout of the ship as it is on the pairs of Shadows and humans we pass in the corridors.

"So, is this all the GSA focuses on?" Eclipse asks quietly.

"Minimising the casualties in the war while pushing for the human leaders to agree to a ceasefire?"

"Yeah," I say. "It's a breeze."

"You know Empress Galvanize will never agree to that."

"This war is costing her just as much," I disagree. "Even a deranged wasp like herself will realise it's a choice between peace and mutual extinction."

"If you say so," Eclipse says. "And then I suppose she'll be just fine with the idea of Shadows and humans all coming together as counterparts like you want?"

"Well... we'll worry about that when we get there."

Eclipse looks hesitant.

"So... you really haven't been working on anything else?"

"Like what?" I say, my suspicion suddenly triggered. I'm instantly alert.

"I'm not sure. Just with all of your talents... you, Calvin, Zephyr and Phoebe working together... I thought there might be something else, another project that the GSA is working on, another way to end the war."

Now it's my turn to hesitate. If it was up to me as the leader, there would be.

There's only one hope for us now, and that's what burns at my core. That's the conviction that keeps me going.

But I can't share that with Eclipse. As much as I've missed him, nothing could be more dangerous to share with him. That's what's changed from the old us. We have secrets now.

"Nope. Sorry to disappoint. What would you do if there was?" I say casually, trying not to sound too invested in his answer. "I mean... can you still really think that bringing humans and Shadows together is so bad after all that's happened in this war? Don't you at least think that would be a lesser evil?"

My voice doesn't break, and I'm glad. It was close.

Eclipse seems unable to speak for a minute.

"I like this place," he manages, dodging the real thrust of my question. "I like what you've made here."

"You do?" I say, heart beating loudly.

"It reminds me of Winghold. Shadows and humans getting to live together." He says it sadly, nostalgically. His smile is almost bittersweet. "To be free."

"It could have been even better if we'd built it together," I say, surprising even myself. He doesn't respond. I turn red in the face and look quickly away. "I hadn't... I didn't mean to say that." Eclipse still hasn't answered my real question, but I decide not to push it for now. "Anyhow, come on, let's get to the cafeteria. I'm guessing you need more than the usual standard rations, I don't think a single microwave meal would be enough for you. How many calories do you take?"

"Eat your peas before you have seconds, okay?" I tell Eclipse. "They're good for you."

"They're infinitesimally tiny," he broods, prodding the green orbs with the tip of a talon.

The stack of microwaved meals piled on Eclipse's side of the table is about two metres high. Man, we really need to source some new rations after this.

"So why are you so curious about operations here, anyway?" I say.

"Why wouldn't I be?"

"I'm just wondering why you asked if we have anything else we're working on here." I'm speaking casually, but I keep a careful watch on the colours of his mind, searching for any anomalies. "Why, did you hear something from someone here?"

Eclipse hesitates. I don't need to read him to know he's wondering if he should trust me.

"Something just rubbed me up the wrong way about my conversation with Zephyr when he was healing me," he says, surprising me. "I got a strange vibe from him." Eclipse's voice grows soft. There's raw emotion in it. "It was very good to see him again, but I could tell there was something that Zephyr wasn't telling me. Something was weighing on him. It just made me wonder... I know I'm just a visitor. I know I don't have any right to ask how this place works, that I gave up that right when I left. If there's anything else going on here though, something big which your core team isn't telling me about... I'd like to know, even if I haven't earned that right."

I frown, feeling uneasy.

"No. Nothing that... nothing that I know about."

"So that's a no," Eclipse says.

"Yes."

"Because you run the place, so you would know."

"Precisely." We look at each other. The pause stretches out. "There's something else you're not telling me, isn't there?" I ask knowingly.

Eclipse hesitates.

"It's Calvin. He's been... very, very nice."

I scowl.

"He was being nice again? That arsehole. Yeah, it's his new thing. Don't worry, I'm pretty sure it's just a phase."

"I'm not joking. He's been very welcoming, but I have caught him staring at me a few times. It's as if…"

"As if what?" I say quietly.

"It's as if he's weighing me up. Whatever it is, Zephyr is in on it. I'm sure."

I don't know what to make of that. I put down my cutlery with a clang, making sure that no one else is close enough to listen in.

"It feels like Calvin is judging my every move behind that smile," I say quietly. "I'm afraid any failure of mine might be an opportunity for him to go for the jugular and take charge."

"That doesn't sound healthy."

"What can I say? I've always pushed myself to be better to avoid disappointing him. It's been a valid and effective parenting strategy." I think the sarcasm is clear enough that I don't have to spell that out for Eclipse.

"Can't you accept that maybe he has changed since he became a Majestic with Zephyr? That this nice Calvin isn't a phase? It looks like he's really trying with you."

I shrug uncomfortably.

"He acted all chummy when I came back from the Shadow world the first time. It turned out he was just using me to hack the Oracle for him so he could get his moment in the limelight. I love him, and he definitely *seems* more laid back, happy even. But I don't know if he's capable of truly changing."

"What matters is that we try to be better than them," Eclipse muses softly, "that we try to learn from their mistakes, and the harm that they did to us. Zephyr did change though. He found his way back to the right path.

Have faith in your brother like I do in mine. They share the same soul."

He catches me looking at him.

"What?"

"I want you with me when I interrogate Raven," I say.

Eclipse stares. I've surprised myself too.

"Are you sure?" Eclipse says uncertainly.

I weigh him up, considering the unknown parts of his mind that I haven't yet mapped out. He's my best friend. But is it really smart to take an all-powerful Shadow who's opposed to what we're doing and put him in a room with an asset as valuable as Raven?

It's worth the risk if I use this as a test. I can use this as a way to try and get a reaction out of Eclipse, to discover his true motives.

"I'm sure," I say.

"Okay," Eclipse says, playing it breezy. He looks touched though, a strange amount of emotion passing over his feathered features. His crest of feathers stands upright like a Mohawk.

"You had a point, this concerns your world too. Also, we should be spending all the time together that we can while you're here, right?" I say glibly. "Nothing says bonding like interrogating a murderous dictator."

Also, I really don't want to go in there on my own. The thought of talking to Raven face-to-face is as scary as it is disturbingly tempting.

"Grif, why aren't we sitting with them?" Eclipse asks curiously. His gaze has strayed to where Sophie and her group of friends are hanging out at the table near ours.

"Sssh!" I hiss. Eclipse's voice is deep, and it carries. But

Eclipse just looks at me, perplexed by the social complexities of humans.

"But they are over there," he repeats slowly, as if I'm clueless. "Do you really think they haven't already noticed us?"

I consider this. Eclipse's crest feathers nearly touch the roof, and he's awkwardly stooped over the tiny little table that we share. Everyone else eating in here is clustered at the other side of the cafeteria, staring at the two of us.

"I think we're good," I say.

"Don't you wish to sit with your friends?"

Come on man, shut up already! I've just... I shuffle in my seat awkwardly, fixing my attention on my lasagne. *I've just got this lone wolf thing going on, okay?*

Right, Eclipse says in amusement, looking down at me. *Because you're so dark and twisted.*

Exactly.

After our lunch I tell Eclipse I have a few tasks to do. But instead of heading to the bridge, I find myself drawn to another part of the ship.

Troubled, I look around me, checking the coast is clear. A million thoughts and desires clash inside of me.

The darkness in the corridor before me is calling to me. It leads to what we officially call the *'De-escalation Area.'* But most of the GSA secretly call it something else under their breath.

The Asylum.

The things we've seen in the field can leave a scar. I know I'll be having nightmares about Troy for the rest of my natural life. Some of our members have been placed in the Asylum when it seemed they'd be a danger to themselves. We've also rescued soldiers who've broken mentally after coming face to face with their Shadows in the battlefield. Something about trying to shoot the other part of yourself seems to cause a particularly potent form of PTSD. This place was originally built into the ship because we thought some people may be distressed at hearing their counterparts thoughts for the first time. The facilities have since come in handy.

Now they're also home to the man whose life has been entwined with mine since I was a kid; the man who pushed the worlds into war and used me as a tool to achieve it.

No, I can't do this. We all agreed we'd do it together. Eclipse and I are going to question him soon with the others observing, united as a family seeking justice. Everything will go on the record.

Except... I remember the acid in Calvin's voice, his loathing for the man who had once been his close friend, the man who had babysat Cirrus and me when we were just kids. But Calvin's loathing is something that I can't find in myself.

I ought to hate Raven. I know it. I know it as a fact. But I can't.

The first time I'd faced Raven in the Shadow world, he'd seemed every inch the devil I'd imagined who had killed my Mum: hooded and full of contempt. He had a monstrosity stitched together from other people's Shadows, forced to serve him as if it was his own. He'd slashed me open with a knife. I still remember the pain. I almost bled out and died. The only things that had saved me were Eclipse and the desire to make it home to complete Mum's mission.

But the second time we encountered each other, everything had changed. Raven had just been... Taylor. I'd seen in him the teenager he used to be, before his best friend had banished him to a strange world full of monsters where he was completely alone. In his lonely and formidable palace of Aeyu he'd made me pancakes.

It was like remembering a big brother I'd lost a long time ago, and that was enough to mess me up at a seriously deep level. What made it even harder is that my worst enemy had been more honest with me than Calvin ever had. Calvin had never told me that my Dad had stolen away Taylor's Shadow, Winter, when Taylor was just a child. My Dad had been... confused. He wasn't right in the head, and he did something terrible. He came to believe that Winter was his own Shadow and stole him from Taylor. Taylor had killed my Dad in revenge, but considering the trauma he was put through... it's not as clear cut as I'd believed.

I don't know how I feel about any of it. It's too painful and complicated to even start to digest.

Raven had known for his whole childhood that something precious had been stolen from him, but he had never understood what that precious something had been. In that way, our childhoods were very similar. I had to grow up without Cirrus too.

The pain is still fresh that my Dad could do something so awful. Eclipse was right when he talked about Hanna's motivations for following Raven. Love does make people do the most terrible things.

Also, I know now that my Mum's death was an accident. Taylor had freaked out and Mum had fallen and hit her head as a result. It was still Taylor's fault, but the burning quest I'd defined myself by growing up, to find the mysterious killer who'd murdered Melissa Cameron... well, the truth is much more complex.

That doesn't change the fact that as Raven, Taylor truly became someone capable of monstrous acts at a global scale. Or that he fused Zephyr and Calvin into a freakish instrument of death who then lost control and tried to off us.

But all the same, I seem to find my feet pulling me of their own accord, walking me into that dark. I just want answers, both from Raven the dark dictator and from Taylor himself.

He'd said that he wanted to be a family again, that together we were capable of great things. Of course I'd assumed it was all crap. Then he saved my life in the Underworld. I need to ask him why.

The Asylum is softly lit, the doors to the padded cells passing me on both sides. But I only have eyes for the cell at the far end of the passage.

Before I know it the door to Raven's cell is in front of me, and I watch as my hand reaches toward the handle.

But my hand stops mid-air.

It's wrong to do this without all the others. But there's a longing in my chest, this... this *need*. What is it?

It's stupid and I can't even admit it to myself. I close my eyes, thinking back to that perverse moment in the palace kitchen, when Raven had placed a pancake onto my plate shaped like Cirrus. When he'd told me what he'd always seen in me, with something in his voice like pride. Like love. Something I never remembered hearing from Calvin.

I can't help thinking if Taylor had never become Raven, if Mum had never died... Taylor would have been my big brother, just as much as Gecko; someone to teach me about what it was to be an adult, about how to *be* in this world. Someone to look up to who actually showed he cared about me.

I turn away from the door, ashamed.

It's ridiculous, a bizarre delusion. I don't know how I think I can look into the face of that mass-killer and expect to see this alternate, parallel version of the Taylor who could have been, staring back at me. But part of me desperately wants to. Part of me needs it.

Eclipse believes anyone can find their way back to the light. Executing Raven achieves nothing. But making him realise his mistakes? Helping him realise and repent the true horror of who he's become?

Now that would be justice for my parents.

That's when I hear it. A muffled shout comes from the other side of the door.

I jerk on the handle and the door swings open. I realise it was already unlocked.

The cell is huge, the size of Eclipse's quarters downstairs. Like those, this place was also built to accommodate the largest of Shadows. For the most part, it's eerily empty. In the centre of it, Raven and Winter are bound in chains. Winter is huddled on the floor. He's a skeletal mess of black feathers, shrunken in on himself. Raven has been knocked off his chair. He lies on the floor in the dark, flinching, his body curled inward to protect himself.

An assailant is kneeling on top of him, holding Raven down. The intruder's bare hands are fastened around Raven's throat, choking the life out of him. I can barely believe what I'm seeing.

"Calvin, no!" I scream.

10

I'M STILL HERE

I lunge. Grabbing hold of my brother's strong shoulders I try to pull him back but it's as if he's carved from iron. For a moment I'm scared I won't be able to stop him from killing the defenceless man writhing on the ground.

All of this time Winter is crying, his haunted warbling deafening. But he's chained to the ground, his wings clamped. Frost gathers on his feathers but without his wings he can't direct it. Winter strains at his bonds to try and stop Calvin but he's forced to watch as the life slowly leaves his human.

"I said *NO!*" Finally I wrench Calvin backward. He's shaking, like he's possessed by some twisted demon, his face totally unrecognisable. Then I'm bundling him out of the door, slamming it shut. I hear a clunk as it locks behind us.

Calvin collapses against the door, sobbing helplessly. I fall to my knees beside him.

"Calvin," I say, stunned. "What did you do?"

"I want to kill him," he cries.

"I can see that. So what, you lied earlier? You were always planning on coming here alone?"

"I tried to fight it." He's still crying. It's like I'm not looking at Calvin Cameron anymore but the scarred, demented boy from all those years before. I'm seeing the shell that Raven left. "I'm supposed to be an example to you," Calvin says, shame-faced. He's not meeting my eyes, as if he can't stand to look at me. "I'm your big brother."

"Calvin..." I say, taken aback.

"It's too late to be a good role model for you, huh?" he laughs. "Yeah. I figured." He buries his face in his hands. "He took everything from us."

"I know." Clumsily I reach out, putting a hand on Calvin's shoulder to comfort him. "I know."

"Because of him, you didn't have Cirrus. Because of him... you had to..." Calvin grapples at me, pulling me closer by the front of my jacket. It's not a hug, more a desperate need to be connected to something. It's like he's staring into the terrifying eye of the past, of a night that only he can see.

"You have Zephyr now," I say quietly, but I'm unable to keep the edge out of my voice. "You have Phoebe. You should be happy. It's time to let the past go."

"And you have Eclipse," Calvin emphasises, staring at me as if he detects something off in my tone.

"Yeah," I say, breaking a little inside. I wish I could be as sure as Calvin sounds.

"I'm going to lose you all over again," he says.

"That's not true."

"Raven's here just to watch, can't you see that? He's here to watch as I lose you, and Phoebe, and Zephyr, and he's going to enjoy it. I've tried so hard to change, to be the *me* that you all miss. I've always envied Taylor, always wanted to be him. Now I'm trying to remember what it used to be like to be the good guy. That used to be what I was best at."

Were you being the good guy when you blocked my idea for the amplifier, the one idea that could have saved all of us? I want to challenge him. *Or was that just you wanting to keep your hands clean?* When Calvin was raising me I wish he'd made an effort to be the good guy. Right now though, we need his killer instinct. *I* need it. I need his take-no-prisoners attitude and his genius. Instead I'm stuck trying to comfort the crying brother who didn't raise me to be good with emotions.

"What would you give in order for everyone to survive," Calvin says, sounding conflicted, "for an end to all the killing?"

I pull away to look him dead in the eye.

"Anything," I say, almost as a challenge.

"Even if it cost you who you are?" Calvin whispers.

"I've been willing to give my life to Mum's mission ever since I learnt the truth," I say with complete honesty. "What would *you* give?"

Then the moment passes; my bottled-up anger falls away, and suddenly I'm as sad and exhausted as my brother. I press my back against the wall beside him, and shut my eyes.

"I have something to confess," Calvin says. "It's about Raven's tech that Phoebe brought back from Auckland."

"You've finally figured out what it is?"

"Most of it is just an odd assortment of weapons and devices Raven engineered over the last ten years I'd say.

There's no joint purpose to it all, it's just a collection of sorts. Every item is genius, of course," Calvin concedes bitterly. "However the silver cube, the massive one they brought back.... I've known what that was since I ran my preliminary tests on it, months back."

"And?" I press him intensely.

"It's a Majestic machine."

I stare. Then I laugh, a borderline hysterical sound.

"Griffin?" Calvin says, worried.

"You *hid* that from all of us?" I shake my head, overwhelmed. For a moment, I don't feel sane. "Why the hell didn't you just destroy it?"

"I'm sorry, I shouldn't have hidden it from you. You're our leader, Grif. But I thought if I could analyse all of the tech, figure out what each one did, I could get insight into Raven's head. I thought I could learn more about how he thinks, what his mental processes are. I was trying to find Raven's Achilles heel so we could exploit it."

For just once, he wanted a chance to be the one who brought Raven down. I can understand that much.

"Griffin?" Calvin says hesitantly. "I've been wondering... I've been meaning to ask you... if there's anything you want to talk to me about."

"What do you mean?" I say, keeping my face carefully blank, betraying no sign that my pulse is skyrocketing. I'm thinking of when he walked in on my breakfast with Phoebe this morning.

"I just... I feel like we never get to catch up any more. What's been going on with you? Are things going okay with Eclipse? Are there any, you know..." Calvin fidgets, clearly in unfamiliar territory. "Is there anyone you've been seeing, romantically? Or casually. Whatever you're into."

I stare at him. It sounds like... like he's trying to bond with me? *Now?*

"We don't need to talk about this," I say awkwardly.

"No," Calvin reassures me quickly, "I want to."

"Well, it's not always about what you want." I wince as the words escape me.

I expect a sharp *"Griffin,"* from him in reprimand, as I did a thousand times growing up if I didn't keep to the strict boundaries and expectations Calvin set for me, but one doesn't come this time.

"That was unkind," he says instead.

"Sorry. But really, do I have to say out loud why we don't have catch ups and heart to hearts, why that might feel weird for me still?" I tick them off on my fingers. "There's lying to me about how our parents died. There's how you had Mr Falco pose as an actual therapist to convince me that Shadows weren't real and that I was crazy. You made sure he convinced me that Cirrus was just an imaginary friend I should have grown out of sooner."

"I've apologised for that, again and again..."

"When?" I ask pointedly. "Oh, here's another one: when you hit me after I first discovered that portal in our company's basement. Or there's the moment after I brought you back your Shadow, when you acted like we were partners, only to throw me aside after I hacked the Oracle for you, just so that you could have the spotlight to yourself. You nearly wrenched my arm out of my socket trying to use my hand to activate the portals. Like I was just some... *object.* Your tool." I'm about to mention down in the Underworld, how Calvin's Majestic bearing down at me, the darkness and murderous hatred in his eyes as he came to kill me, and the traumatic dreams I've had ever since. But I know that's not fair. Calvin wasn't in control. I've said enough already.

I remember how I managed to break through to him in the temple. I remember how even Raven's dark experiments on him couldn't defeat the love that still exists between me and Calvin at some level. But that doesn't mean that it's still not hard.

Calvin looks pale, stricken.

"I'm just here to listen," he says honestly, not refuting any of it.

I regard him for a moment. My big brother seems smaller than I remember, not the titan who dominated the world I lived in as a kid. He sounds like he really means it. But I feel a squirming in my stomach as I think of Phoebe, and of all the unspoken weirdness that lies there which Calvin seems completely unaware of. I can't bring myself to talk about it with him. They're just feelings anyway. Feelings that won't shut up and are with me every single minute of every day, but you know. Just feelings.

"I promise not to judge," Calvin says softly. "I won't even talk if you don't want me to. I just want to know what's going on in your life. I want to know what I've missed."

I'm dumbfounded. Something about his face is so unlike the person I thought I know. More like the brother I'd always wished I had.

"Whatever it is," he says, "we can work through it."

For a moment, I ache with wanting to believe him. The little kid in me rises to the murky surface, and I want to tell my brother all of it, every last piece. He's just sitting there patiently, not judging. I want so badly not to keep all of my secrets bottled up anymore, because sometimes I feel like they're killing me.

Have I really been unfair to him? I've suspected something was off about Calvin since we left the Underworld, but maybe, just maybe, I could have been wrong.

Maybe it was just paranoia after all.

I want to tell him about Phoebe, about how close we became on our journey to the secret station, how much just the sight of her makes me feel like my entire body is humming with light and how much it hurts when I watch her with him. I want to tell him about Eclipse, how even though I finally have him back, something tells me to listen to my instincts: that Eclipse being here is no accident. I want to tell him about...

No. No, I can't, he'd never understand.

"You can tell me," Calvin says gently.

"I CAN'T!"

I thought the scream was internal until I realise that I'm standing and Calvin is staring up at me, shocked by the force of my cry.

"Let's go round up the others," I say, looking away. "It's time to get our answers."

"How did you end up in that prison?" I ask Raven. My voice is loud in the spacious padded cell.

I'm standing before Raven and Winter. Zephyr has tended to Raven, and the man is now back upright on his chair. Winter's wings are still restrained so that they can't unleash his power, the frost to Ember's fire.

Eclipse stalks the perimeter of the big cell, circling around Raven and Winter, intimidating them with his hulking presence. I have to admit, at times like this I'm pretty grateful he's on my side.

Phoebe, Ember, Calvin and Zephyr are silently watching via the feed from the cameras positioned around the room. Eclipse and I are left to imagine their reactions.

"How did you end up in the prison at Troy?" I repeat. I feel anger. I feel loathing. But more than those, I feel awkward. This isn't what I expected. Raven's hair has grown long and lank, dark greasy locks covering his face. His scruffy beard masks his features too. His frosty irises stare blankly into nothing. He looks like a stray dog you'd take pity on. This is the moment that's been coming for so long. We finally have this man at our mercy. Our family is at last confronting him for his crimes against us. So why does it feel so anti-climactic?

I realise that though Raven might be still, his eyes are moving, fixated on Eclipse. I feel a creeping sensation.

Did he have his mental state assessed when he arrived? Eclipse mutters, just so that the two of us can hear. Eclipse seems just as taken aback as I am at Raven's state.

No, actually. But I'm beginning to think that may not be such a bad idea.

"Okay, what move of yours is this?" I ask, masking my real emotions with impatience. Raven still doesn't respond. "You like games, don't you? That's what this war is to you. Everyone is just a piece on the board. Humans and Shadows, dying in the millions. All part of your plan?"

Nothing. I look at Winter. The very sight of the humanoid crow is unnerving, bringing up murky nightmares that have haunted me for years. Remnants from the night that Raven sent Winter to bring Cirrus and me down to him when we were just children. Raven hadn't meant for Winter to try to hurt us, but he had. Winter had been twistedly and misguidedly trying to please his counterpart.

Winter looks more pitiful than Raven even. There are permanent tears in his widened eyes. He's a shattered reflection of the terrifying being who'd entered our room that night. Winter has shrunk down like his human to take up as little space as possible. Now and then he makes small little cheeps like a sad baby chick.

"What's to stop us from executing you both right now?" I ask them, my mouth dry as I say it.

Silence. Then:

"Nothing," Raven croaks. I shudder, and Eclipse does too. It's the first time Raven's spoken, and the sound is like dry wood cracking. His eyes are dead and unseeing.

I shoot a look at Eclipse.

"Are you saying you no longer care what we do to you?" Eclipse probes him.

"I didn't care," Raven says, and he surprises me by smiling wryly up at Eclipse. As if there's some secret under-standing between the two of them. "I didn't care for such a long time."

"Look, arsehole," I say, a storm brewing inside me. "You don't get to just quit. After all you've done, you don't get to just..." I trail off, bewildered. Wait, what am I doing, giving the master of evil a motivational talk? That's not my job.

"The things we do to each other, eh?" Raven mutters, more to himself than anyone else. "We grasp for power so that we will be loved. We seek even more of it so that we never have to rely on love again. We kill for love and we kill to escape it."

Eclipse stirs slightly, like Raven's claptrap actually

means something to him. I feel the shifting shades of gold in his head change to murky, bloody brown.

Did something just pass between Eclipse and Raven that I missed? Did Raven just cryptically convey something to Eclipse which I didn't see?

Are you getting any kind of a read off of him, partner? I ask Eclipse.

Apart from how he's clearly going through some kind of super-villain quarter-life crisis? Eclipse asks dryly. *Negative.*

"It's a relief to see you here," Raven says to Eclipse. His expression is strange. It's... peaceful. "Alive."

"Alive?" I snap. I look between the two of them, unnerved. "Why wouldn't Eclipse be alive?"

"He's just trying to get under our skin," Eclipse says, apparently unmoved. There's only scorn in him as he looks at the chained man in the chair.

Winter anxiously shuffles over to where Raven is bound to his chair. We've extended his chain, so Winter can at least touch his human counterpart. It seems to have calmed him after what Calvin did to Raven. Winter peers down at Raven's neck and lets out a croak of distress. Tenderly, Winter rests one of his hands on Raven's arm.

Raven yells suddenly. He lashes out with his legs, managing to kick Winter in the abdomen.

I scream. Eclipse roars in shock. I've never seen anything like it. A human hurting his own counterpart, wounding his Shadow purely out of spite. It makes me feel sick, like I might throw up. I can only imagine the reactions of the others who are watching.

I haul Winter away from Raven, shivering with revulsion as I touch that moulting, feathered skin. It's like someone crossed a crow with a human but got it terribly wrong. I let go of Winter as quickly as I can, even though I find myself feeling sorry for him for the first time ever.

Eclipse bends down like he's prepared to crush Raven's head in his beak. Raven looks between me and Eclipse blearily, as if seeing us for the first time. His features slowly light up. It's like a rare beam of happiness entering a dark, subterranean chamber that hasn't seen sunlight for aeons.

"Griffin," Raven says. His voice is still rough and uneven, but there's softness to it. "Eclipse. I can't believe we're all together at last."

"Haven't you hurt enough Shadows?" Eclipse says. I can hear how much he despises the man before us.

"Why did you do that?" I explode at Raven. "Winter's worried about you! He's just trying to help you!"

"I don't want him touching me," Raven mutters, shivering. He seems to be starting to come out of his weird comatose state. His voice is sounding more like Taylor, less like the dark mastermind with a penchant for evil monologues.

"Winter's your *Shadow*," I say.

"I wanted my Shadow more than anything, you know," Raven says, smiling sadly. "I thought it might be Ember, until we realised that she was Phoebe's Shadow. Then when we found Winter, crouching in that basement, and Phoebe told me he was mine..." Raven keeps his gaze averted from the cowering misery that is his Shadow. "I felt nothing. I knew *that* couldn't be me. Winter couldn't be my other half, after all of my searching."

"It's because Winter was taken from you," I say, my voice cracking as I think of Cirrus, "and he shouldn't have been. But it wasn't Winter's fault. He wanted to come back to you."

"I made it my mission once I arrived in the Shadow world to find the one who'd complete me," Raven says, as if not really hearing me. "There were so many to choose from, so many to search through. Billions. For each Shadow I thought might be the one, there was always another that I seemed to like more, that seemed to be more *me*. Still, none of them filled that hole inside me."

"That's why you made Ammut," Eclipse says with sudden understanding. I recall the howling monstrosity of black smoke composed of different Shadows, its multiple pairs of eyes gleaming from within with crimson light. "You made him so that you could have a Shadow greater than Winter who would be worthy of you," Eclipse says coldly. "Even while Winter was obediently staying by your side that entire time, wondering what he was doing wrong."

I'm reminded suddenly of my childhood with Calvin, and quickly wave away the disturbing comparison.

"Where is Ammut now?" I say, wondering why a terrifying entity with that kind of power has been suspiciously absent.

"Dead," Raven says, his mouth twitching. It's a spasm that's easy to miss. "Ammut was an experiment, but he was too temperamental. I was wrong to create him in the first place; so I put him out of his misery."

"You put him..." Eclipse is wordless with shock.

"He wasn't just a sick cat," I say, incredulous. Still, at least those poor Shadows who were absorbed as part of that monstrosity are now at peace.

Raven looks between me and Eclipse.

"You two are together again," he says, smiling sadly. "Even though I told you that you're not meant to be."

"Hey, screw you!" I say.

"Yeah," Eclipse agrees.

Huh. Maybe what we needed all along to bring us together was a relationship counsellor we could loathe equally.

"The two of you aren't counterparts," Raven persists. "The telepathic link that you feel between you is a remnant, a leftover of the connection that ran between Cirrus and Griffin. Now that Cirrus has changed into Eclipse you two aren't destined for each other any longer."

"You're delusional," I sneer, swallowing past the lump in my throat. I guess part of me has always been scared that maybe Eclipse wouldn't have left for his own world if he'd had another human he truly felt commanded his respect. I've been afraid that I'm... not enough.

I walk over to Eclipse to stand beside him. His head looms above me, glaring down at Raven.

"Griffin is mine," Eclipse hisses, with awe-inspiring fury, "and I am his."

I feel a little swoop in my chest to hear him say that.

"Sweet," Raven comments sadly, "and mistaken. But I've been fooled too in the past, so I'm hardly the one to talk. When you see your true Shadow, Griffin, you'll know it." He's talking to us comfortingly, like he's doing us a service, like he's looking out for us.

"Who do you think you are to tell us who we love or who we are?" Eclipse demands.

Raven's wrong. He must be. Raven's clearly delusional about Winter not being his Shadow. But another part of me, at the back of my mind, reminds me that Raven is also the biggest expert on the human-Shadow connection across both worlds. He ran experiments on New Redemption researching the nature of the links between counterparts. He had unlimited resources and carried out experiments no other scientist would have been able to justify ethically. He's explored horizons which others don't dare explore. So who would know better the nature of my connection with Eclipse since he transformed from Cirrus?

I'm being stupid. I'm letting the paranoia get to me.

Then Eclipse throws a complete curveball which changes everything.

"Is it you who's been brainwashing Shadows in the last few months?" Eclipse asks Raven, his voice like thunder. "Have you been running experiments in my world again?"

I turn to look at Eclipse so sharply I nearly snap my neck. Even though he must feel my gaze on him, he ignores it, his attention fully fixed on Raven's response.

But if Raven knows what Eclipse is talking about, he has the best poker face I've ever seen. He looks just as clueless as me. So does Winter. I shoot a look toward the cameras, wondering at the expressions of the others staring in at us.

"I have absolutely no idea what you mean," Raven says, but it sounds like his interest is piqued.

"I don't believe you."

Eclipse, what the hell are you talking about? I think madly. *Could you not go off-script without clueing me in? I'm the one who agreed to let you be here.*

"It's a strange new outbreak which we're worried could turn into an epidemic," Eclipse answers out loud. He's looking at Raven accusingly. "Hanna and I heard rumours of a handful of Shadows in different corners of the Empire who have been acting bizarrely. Shadows who were claiming they had suddenly felt the voice of their human counterpart inside their heads. One moment they hate humans with all their heart, the next all they can talk about is finding their human on the other side, as if they're obsessed. Someone has been brainwashing them and I don't know why. I do know who has the means to do something like that though."

I feel Raven's gaze and avoid looking at him. Eclipse's words are crashing through me.

Shadows suddenly hearing their human counterpart inside them, even from an entire world away.

Could this possibly mean what I hope it does?

Worse than that... is *this* the real reason that Eclipse came here?

I seize control of my thoughts, hiding the storm inside me from my big-bird buddy-cop. This is why Eclipse hasn't told any of us about this until now, I realise. He wanted to see my reaction. Eclipse wants to know the GSA isn't behind these strange new cases. He hopes Raven is the one really at fault.

Eclipse is watching me right now closer than ever, I can feel it.

"It sounds ingenious, if what you're talking about is real," Raven says, sounding very interested. "I'm afraid I can't claim the credit this time around, though."

I have plenty more questions for Eclipse but now's not the time for that. I force myself to focus on Raven, even though everything has suddenly changed.

"So, what were your plans for all that tech that Phoebe found hidden under your old place in Auckland?" I say, switching the topic to safer territory.

"Oh, Phoebe found those, did she?" Raven smiles sadly. He shrugs, almost embarrassed. "All those pieces were just trophies. I won't lie, I'm proud of what I've created over the last decade. I wasn't always right, but I was a visionary. I designed things people in our world couldn't even have conceived."

"Why would you keep one of those foul Majestic machines as a memento? Are you still kidnapping innocent teens and using them as guinea pigs?"

Eclipse whips around to stare at me, shocked. I'm sure Phoebe looks the same way, if she hasn't killed Calvin yet for keeping that from us. I'd forgotten to tell them what Calvin told me, about the true nature of that silver cube.

"No," Raven says. "That's not me anymore. But can you blame me for being fascinated by Majestics? They're angels, Shadow and human made whole in a perfect synthesis. Compassionate, serene, seeing through all of time and space at once. I thought if I could create my own legion of them, control that power... the things we could build. But you saw what happened with Calvin and Zephyr: demented, full of rage... and so *weak*, only a shade of what a true Majestic really is. They weren't a God. No, I've abandoned that particular dream."

"So let's just say that you did end up in that prison cell at Troy by accident." My voice drips with scepticism. "Let's say that you didn't arrange to be brought here on purpose. And that you didn't feed me intelligence about Ember so we would come and find her in that prison and you as well. If that's true, then how do you explain Phoebe and me just *stumbling* upon you?"

"Destiny," Raven says, staring at me intently. A faint smile starts playing at the corner of his mouth. A smile of hope. "Just what Melissa and Silvaluna always believed in."

"You don't get to talk about them," Eclipse hisses, raising a massive claw threateningly. Stretching up, I place a hand on his claw, lowering it back down. He obeys, resentfully.

"Destiny brought you here to be executed?" I ask Raven ironically. His smile flickers, as I see the first shred of doubt in him.

Wait. Are you actually planning on executing him? Eclipse ponders, his flicking tail belying the fact that he's entertained by the thought.

What? No! I don't think we do that. I'm just being the bad cop.

Oh, Eclipse says. *I thought I was the bad cop?*

We can switch in a minute.

"Destiny brought me here to your base to finally reunite this family," Raven continues, "to complete what we began." Against my better judgement, I can feel my pulse quickening. "There's something I wanted to tell you back at Aeyu Palace," he confesses. "Something I was trying to work up to, before you opened the portals and accelerated things way quicker than I'd planned." Raven's gaze seems to stare into my soul. A suspicion starts to play inside me, but it's absurd.

I think of his entire change of character ever since our confrontation back in Sanctuary City. I remember his talk about family when I saw him in Aeyu Palace.

Raven's looking at me, meaningfully. I'm thinking quickly, pieces starting to move into place. I'm thinking of the note he left me. *'Your move.'* As if this was all a game.

"You've got to be kidding me," I say.

"What?" Eclipse demands. I'm hiding it from him, too embarrassed that I might be completely wrong. I'm contorted inside. It doesn't add up, it doesn't make sense.

Does it?

"What Griffin knows," Raven whispers heavily, "What part of him has known since we last met, is that we're not on different sides anymore."

"Oh, right," I say, rolling my eyes. "Of course. Oh, wait, what about that *army of Majestics* you were building to take over the worlds or something?"

"I wasn't building an army, I was learning more about what it meant to be Shadow and human. I was solidifying what I'd already begun to suspect. What I'd started to believe. I was wrong to turn Shadows against humans under the Empire."

Eclipse and I stare at our nemesis. There's complete silence.

"That was the greatest mistake of my life," Raven continues, wearing a broken smile. "At the time it was just an easy route to power: gaining control over the Shadows through their fear. Also, I was so, so angry at Melissa for being gone. Angry at the worlds. Angry at everything." For a moment I think I see a tear glint in his eye, but I must have imagined it. "I fought against Melissa and Silvaluna's vision for too long. But when I ran into the two of you in Sanctuary City, I began to realise how long I'd been on the wrong path. It forced me to start confronting the fact that the only way to set things right, to honour both of your mothers, was to invest everything I had in making their vision real. It's the only way for me to be redeemed. It's the only way for me to make all of this worth it."

"Liar," Eclipse hisses.

"They're not lies," Raven replies, looking up at him beseechingly. He smiles softly. "Listen. You both dreamt of a better universe, one of Shadows and humans living in symbiotic partnerships that brought out the very best in each other. But people are weak. They don't always choose what's best for them. The only way that the citizens of the worlds would ever accept such a radical new paradigm was if a more pressing threat of extinction drove them to it, if it really was a choice between paradise and oblivion."

I stare at him. It feels like the room is falling away around us.

"You started a war," says Eclipse slowly in disbelief, "an apocalyptic war that has driven both worlds to the brink... just so that they would be more willing to accept each other as counterparts? That was your logic?"

The way Raven talks about it is so black and white. It makes me think of the decision I'd made back at Winghold; submitting to the Empire in order to save lives. Ember had wanted to die for her beliefs. Without me, her people would all have died. It was one situation in which the ends had justified the means. What was it Raven had said to me back at Aeyu? *'Admit it. I just took your game and went pro.'*

Raven was always capable of viewing the worlds as a giant game board, of coldly doing whatever was necessary for the required result. What if this was inevitable? If we had to truly see the worst of people, the evil that lies in the hearts of humans and Shadows, before we could see the heaven that could be made from the ashes?

Your move, his note had read. But I had misunderstood. The game was never between me and Raven.

Raven had meant that it was me and him against the game. Impossible as it seems...

"You're saying we're on the same side now," I say, needing to hear it to gauge how insane it sounds.

"Yes. Just how it was always meant to be. Unfortunately, the ever-so-lovely Empress Galvanize deciphered what I was up to," Raven says with a trace of irony. "She figured out that I was moving the pieces into place for Shadows and humans to come together and live side by side, despite what the Empire had been preaching all these years. She didn't take it well and tried to have me executed. So I ran."

"You chose Galvanize as Empress and gave her the throne," I say, not believing him. "From everything we've heard she's utterly loyal to you."

"Yes. Well. She also takes being misled as a very personal betrayal. No one hates humans more than her." Raven barks with laughter but there's no amusement in it. "I was so easily removed from the Empire I'd built. I was careless. I went from unimaginable luxury to being homeless again, exactly where I started all those years ago. I was sleeping in ruins in the Shadow world, living off scraps."

"And now?" I say, feeling like I'm having an out-of-body experience. "What was your grand master plan of how we climb our way out of this mess?"

"You're the leader of this place," Raven says, gesturing around us at the walls. "'*Griffin's Shadow Academy*,' am I right?" He smiles. "I told you I always believed you were destined for a great purpose, Grif. I don't have a grand plan, not anymore. The next step is all yours. You're the leader of this dysfunctional family now; we're yours to command. So, you tell me. This is the endgame. What's our winning move to finish this once and for all?"

11

EVERY MOVE YOU MAKE

"What the heck was that about?" I explode, once Eclipse and I are back in the bottom of the ship.

"What?" Eclipse says.

"Oh, just you blindsiding me with the fact that some Shadows are suddenly hearing their human counterparts in their minds from a freaking *world away*?" I flap my arms around madly. "You thought you'd just, what, leave that out? Tell me everything, *now.*"

"There isn't much more to tell than that."

I pace between the glowing blue tanks, unable to stand still. My pulse is going into overdrive. Eclipse thinks that I'm angry about being kept in the dark, which I am, but I hide the true emotion from him that's swirling inside me.

A sense of complete soaring elation.

I can't show that to him though. Doing so would be dangerous. If what Eclipse says is true, then this is game-changing.

"When did this start happening? How many Shadows were affected?"

"I told you all I know," he says, shrugging his hefty wings. "All I'd heard were fables, until I saw it happen myself."

Something about the way he's looking at me is strange.

"Wait, is this why you were asking me if the GSA was working on any other projects? You thought we might be responsible for this?"

"Perhaps," Eclipse says, shifting his weight from one foot to the other with the slightest hint of discomfort.

"Eclipse?" I say accusingly. He looks at me, appropriately shame-faced.

"It's been nine months since we'd seen each other," he says. "So much has changed. I wasn't exactly sure what I could rule out."

It's a punch to the gut that Eclipse was hiding this, that he sees this new phenomena in his world as something sinister that has to be stopped. It's a powerful reminder that we still don't see the worlds in the same way. The gap between us is wider and deeper than I'd feared. At least now I know that this is Eclipse's big dark secret, not that he came to destroy all of us and bring down the organisation. He'll establish that we're not behind these unique cases, and that Raven isn't behind them, and then he'll be on his way.

Then Eclipse will leave.

"You could have come out and told me straight away," I say reproachfully, "instead of trying to be all ninja about it."

"Even if Raven isn't behind this strange outbreak in the Shadow world..."

"This miracle," I interject. "These Shadows aren't being

hurt, are they? They're just spontaneously becoming aware of their other half. They're waking up."

Eclipse ruffles his wings.

"My point is that Raven's still playing with us. It's just games on top of games."

"It's a weird game," I say, contemplating. "If Raven really is playing with us then what does he stand to gain by this? Maybe he really has had a change of heart. Phoebe always said that he really did care for my Mum. She was his mentor, the parent that he'd never really had."

"Would you want someone as evil as Raven on your team, even if he has had a change of world view? Why are you so against Hanna but Raven gets a free pass?"

"I never said a free pass, I'm not insane. Just trying to figure him out."

"Also..." Eclipse frowns, troubled. "I've been meaning to tell you that when I was at Aeyu, before I found you, Raven tried to court me to come over to his side."

"He... what?"

"He gave me these fancy chambers at the top of the palace, tried to convince me that we would work better together. I just didn't have any idea that this is what he meant."

"Would you have believed Raven if he'd told you then?" I say. "That he wanted Shadows and humans to live together?"

"Even if I had, I wouldn't have supported starting a war of mass death thinking that would somehow bring coun-terparts together," Eclipse snorts.

There's an awkward silence between the two of us. Eclipse seems to realise he's stepped into difficult territory.

"Griffin..." he says, sounding anxious. "I want you to know that I didn't mean everything I said, in the station."

I jerk my neck violently to look up at him.

"I said that to hold you too tightly was for both of us to burn. That's not true. I've gotten so much from knowing you. You've made me stronger and happier in so many ways. Even if I still believe that humans and Shadows are better off in their own worlds... I'll never regret knowing you. I'm glad we've got this chance, here in this place, to hang out more."

I don't say anything. I know it's not his intention, but the way Eclipse says it sounds like he's dangling the possibility in front of me that he may still have a change of heart and decide to stay. I don't like having my feelings toyed with, even if he isn't aware that he's doing it.

"You don't know what it's been like," I say vulnerably, "being constantly reminded that I'm one of the only ones here without my own Shadow."

"I'm sorry. But there are still other people here who care about you. You could have more friends in here if you let yourself open up more."

"I don't want other friends," I say without thinking.

"Oh, please!" I jump. Eclipse's tone is scathing. "You used to go and shoot lasers at strangers in the arcade on weekends because you didn't have any real friends. Do you know how *happy* little Griffin would be to have a home like this, even with the war going on? You have friends here, a team of people who trust you and love you and will follow you anywhere! And you're pushing them away, when they're risking everything with you. You're choosing to push them away just because I left."

"You don't get to tell me how to live my life anymore."

"Yeah, I do. Because I'm your friend, even if you don't want me to be. And what makes someone a friend is that they believe you can be the best version of yourself. They hold you to that, even when you don't."

"I think that's pretty rich coming from you," I say. "Considering how much you've turned your back on everything you used to stand for."

I storm off toward my loft, clambering up the ladder. Then I lie awake, hearing Eclipse madly rustling around down in his nest. I can feel his temper radiating from him, more than matching my own.

Sooner or later though, the red in his mind darkens into sleep, and the noises from below me fall quiet, replaced by heavy breathing. Sleep definitely doesn't come for me as easily. It doesn't come at all. Too many thoughts are crowding in, taunting me as I stare up at the high vaulted roof of the room we share.

In Aeyu Palace Raven had suggested I'm capable of more than I've given myself credit for. Whether or not that's true, since Aeyu I definitely started applying myself more than ever before. Back when I was growing up, I'd always felt overwhelmed and defeated before I even attempted anything, in school or at my brother's work. It was like I already thought I was going to fail, that I already knew I'd fall short of my great brother's reputation as a genius. But after Aeyu, I started to believe I really had what it took to change things. Now more than ever, the success of this organisation, the lives of its members and the lives of billions of humans and Shadows rest squarely on my shoulders.

So, you tell me. This is the endgame. What's our winning move to finish this once and for all?

I know what's needed for us to win. I do. I just don't know if I can bring myself to do what's required.

I'm not sure how many hours I've been turning it over in my head, alone with the darkness, before a hot, prickly itching spreads across my right arm. Squinting as my pupils adjust to the dark, I lift my arm up, investigating it.

Small dark growths are pushing out from my arm, like needles. They press through the skin, expanding like feathered arrow heads, like a dark green fungus consuming my arm. With a sickening crunch my finger bones condense into each other, the finger tips curving into twisted talons...

I scream, and jerk upright. Panting, I look down at my arm. I can't see, it's too dark. My pupils have to adjust to the dark again.

Of course they do, it was a nightmare. I must have drifted off. When I can finally make out my arm it looks normal; the skin's smooth and unmarked.

A crash from down below the loft makes me jump. I scramble to the edge of the loft and look down to see Eclipse thrashing, his tail and wings jerking, as he mutters to himself, his eyes still jammed shut. That's when it hits me. It wasn't my nightmare, it was his. And he's still trapped within it.

I swing myself down onto the ladder, making my way down it as I reach out for his mind with mine...

I see Eclipse standing in the chapel on New Redemption. There are bodies around his feet, countless bodies crammed into piles in the aisles between the pews. I can make out Zephyr and Hanna among them, lifeless and still. My insides twist as I recognise a third familiar face. I'm there too, among the dead.

"You must save them," a voice whispers seditiously to Eclipse. It's an ancient, timeless voice that reverberates

through everything, a voice from an entity who's all-seeing and all-knowing. "They will die without your sacrifice. You really thought this gift was yours to keep? Everything goes back into the box. As it was in the end, as it was in the beginning."

Eclipse's prodigious wings are shrinking, his feathers turning green, receding into himself. He's turning back into who he was before, I realise. Into Cirrus. I can feel what he does: his personality, his mind, the very fabric of himself altering.

"Please," he cries to the all-knowing voice. "Please, don't make me do this! You can't, you can't ask this of me!"

I pull back from Eclipse's nightmare, gasping. Cold sweat is turning my forehead into a swamp. It didn't even feel like a nightmare. It was so vivid, the pull of it so strong... it felt more like a vision.

"No," Eclipse is shrieking in his sleep, crying out into the night. He sounds wretched. "No, I'm me! I'm *me!*"

His tail lashes out, nearly cracking the ladder in two. I drop down, then duck under his tail as it swings overhead again.

You're okay, I say shakily, trying to get closer to him. *You're okay.*

I visualize a sunset in soothing pink and orange pastels above an ocean as smooth as glass.

Eclipse thrashes out with a foot, missing me by a metre. If it had connected with me, it would have killed me with a single blow. Instead his talons just tear a chunk from the wall behind me.

My bolt of fear just distresses him more, feeding the nightmare. I get to my feet, but in his restless, upright sleep he's shuffled to block the ladder from me, and escape from our room is obstructed by his whipping tail.

I shut my eyes, searching for anything happy to get through to Eclipse. Something better than a sunset.

And for some reason the first thing that comes to me is the heart-to-heart I had with Calvin in the Asylum. When he said he wanted to fix things. That all he wanted to do is to listen, to know more about my life.

I show the memory of the conversation to Eclipse, and something about the shift in my emotions seems to get through to him.

Calvin was different with me, Eclipse, I think. *Maybe... maybe I've been too hard on him. We've just been through so much. But he's still my brother. I really did feel that Calvin honestly wants us to be closer. In the same way that Zephyr cares about you and wants to know you better. You mean the world to him, Eclipse. You really do.*

Eclipse's spasms slow slightly.

You know, I say to him nostalgically, *I remember running through the trees of Kashlak with Hanna and you, breathless, just the three of us beneath the stars. I remember the safety of Winghold, how beautiful that place was, and the moment there that Ember told me what it meant to have you as my other half. I was apart from you for so long... until I finally saw you again down in the Underworld. I'll never forget that, how you summoned a burning wall of flame to protect me from Raven's army. 'No one harms my human.' That's what you said. That's who I am. I'm your human, Eclipse.*

Eclipse stops his thrashing movements. His creased face relaxes as the nightmare breaks. I can feel him slowly slipping back into a world of quieter, more contented dreams.

I tremble. Then I slowly crawl under his wing and curl up there in the foetal position. I listen to his inhalations and exhalations like gentle, rolling thunder all around me, the sound of it the only thing that keeps me from feeling totally lost.

I lie there, agonising. I need to decide exactly what I should do. I don't want to make the wrong choice, but all of the paths in front of me look so murky.

Raven's words from our interrogation are running in circles through my head. I imagine him and Winter locked in their cell. They looked so weary and beaten down. Being betrayed by Galvanize and hunted by the Empire has shaken them both. Especially Raven. He has one of the brightest minds in the universe. Could he really help us end the war?

And if it is a trap, am I smart enough to play him better than he plays me?

I pull open the door to the Pandora's Box, hoping I've come far enough to be able to control what I'm about to unleash from it.

Raven is sleeping on the floor of the cell in his chains, no longer bound to the chair. He jerks awake as I come in, looking around in terror. Winter has crawled closer to Raven as he slept, but now he hobbles away from his counterpart in trepidation, out of striking distance. Raven looks up toward me in surprise, shielding his eyes from the unexpected brightness behind me.

"Raven?" I say grimly. "We have work to do."

12

ALLIANCE

I escort Raven and Winter down the eerily silent corridor. Heart thudding, I flick through the surveillance feeds on my phone to check that the coast is clear at each turn within the ship. With my other hand I keep a gun trained on the prisoners' backs.

I can't believe I'm doing this. If we get found out, this is all going to be over before it's begun.

I lead them to the innocuous metal hatch near my own quarters and heave it open. The bloody glow spills out from the engine room along with trails of steam.

"After you," I say determinedly.

The hum is loud down amongst the engines, the heat overwhelming. I shepherd Raven and Winter along the track of metal between the giant cylinders, navigating toward the back wall where the hidden door is concealed. A door only I know about. I had this space converted a little while back. We'd been having some work done on the engines, just in case we ever need to actually fly this thing, and that provided a cover for some secret renovations.

I make my way toward the door, haul it open, and gesture for them to enter. I follow in after them, closing the exit behind me.

Inside it looks like a frenzied laboratory. Sketches on sheets of paper litter the desks, the floor and the pin boards arranged around the walls. There are blueprints and schematics, mathematical workings... Several monitors are sitting on tables, humming, displaying audio wavelengths or MRI scans of human and Shadow brains.

Raven moves slowly, as if in a trance, tracing his hand along the sketches papering the walls. I try hard to keep my cool and impassive expression in place. Raven is a genius, the only one who could outsmart my brother every single time. I'm sure my workings look like child's play to him.

"You did this?" Raven whispers.

"Yeah," I say defensively. "Well, I've been trying to hone it. It's in the final stages. I call it the *Siren*. The thought behind it, or at least the idea..."

"It's a catalyst to amplify the Shadow-human telepathic connection. Information encoded into visual and audio input. A single viral video clip," Raven states, examining the schematics.

"Exactly," I say. I'm surprised, maybe even a little put out, at how quickly he's gained the measure of what I'm trying to do. "I've been running tonnes of experiments here in the base with our members, seeing how far Shadow and human counterparts can be apart and still psychically communicate. I put some of them in the water tanks downstairs, loaded them with salt and blacked out the glass to make sensory deprivation floatation tanks. That helped us to increase the strength of those telepathic connections and learn more about what enhances them and what doesn't. I wanted to know what was unique about each counterpart's connection, and what they all shared. Phoebe and the others think this was all just research to get a better understanding of what it means to be Shadow and human..."

"...but it was really to let you create this," Raven interjects with a fascinated smile. "To amplify what's been suppressed in humans and Shadows and tap into the link that's tied them together since birth."

"Exactly," I say, unable to hide my enthusiasm. "It can be viewed on TV, or go viral all over the web like my video on the truth about Shadows did. When somebody watches and hears this video clip, it will tap into that primal part of them, and help bring it to the surface. Suddenly they'll hear their counterpart, even if they're an entire world away. All of the soldiers would refuse to fight. Even the politicians and commanders would be afraid of hurting their counterpart in the other world. They'll all be forced to confront the fact they're interconnected. Thanks to the Siren, the war will end. The worlds will be united, as Mum always wanted."

"All with the press of a single button," Raven murmurs. He looks at me, and I'm shocked to see what looks like real pride in his eyes. I look away, feigning difference. Trying to pretend it doesn't mean anything to me.

It really shouldn't.

"Griffin, all of this... I can't believe I didn't think of it. It's ingeniously efficient. The minimum effective dose to achieve our aims."

"It's a work in progress," I mutter, looking at my feet.

"It's beautiful. Elegant. I can see your coding background and its influence on your process. With Melissa, Calvin, even me, it was always about hardware... go bigger, go bolder. Gargantuan portals, bulky Majestic fusion units… this is subtle. Precise."

He's just trying to play me with his flattery, I remind myself. He'll have to do better than that.

The truth is, a year ago I would never have thought that making something like this was within my capabilities. Not in a million years. When I was a kid I used to love building computers from parts and writing new programmes. But none of them ever seemed to be enough to impress Calvin and none of it seemed nearly as amazing as the things he created for our company. So I guess I just… stopped. I think I'd developed something of an inferiority complex.

For some reason, after I talked with Raven in Aeyu Palace, I felt that urge to start making things again. As much as I hate to admit it, something about our conversation had stayed with me and when Calvin and the others blocked me on this amplifier I knew that it was up to me to make it a reality, even if it tested me like nothing else.

"The others think it's wrong," I swallow. "That's why I haven't told them about this. They thought it was like I was suggesting that we should brainwash everyone and take away their free will, but it's just helping everyone to access part of their brain that's already there. And yes, not everyone takes well to meeting their Shadow…" I avoid looking too pointedly at Raven and the forlorn Winter who's moping about, "…but really, could their reaction be any worse than this apocalyptic war and the crazy death tolls? This is the only way. I've tried transmitting the signal a few times in test areas, but I thought nothing was working, that I'd hit a wall. Then Eclipse revealed what's been happening on the other side…"

"That was you, those isolated cases he talked about. It

means that your Siren is working." Raven looks at me, awed. "Who's been helping you?"

"No one. No one knows about this place but you two."

"Not even Eclipse?" Raven asks softly.

I don't answer.

"Or Phoebe?"

"Don't say her name."

"Please," Raven smiles wryly, but his voice is sad. Resigned. "I think I got a measure of her real feelings after she ran from me last time. You'd think that Phoebe banishing me to the Shadow world would have taught me that lesson the first time around. No, I've given up on that. I was looking for acceptance in the wrong places. I am who I am. Phoebe couldn't accept that but I have to. Now I'm just focused on ending this war and on building Melissa and Silvaluna's utopia, as I should have all along. As are you," he breathes, approaching the device resting on a pedestal in the centre of the room, the heart of the entire operation. Wires and circuits slither from all of the monitors and hard drives connected to it. "May I?"

I've holstered my gun, but my fingers trace the grip for a moment before I take my hand away.

"Yeah," I say. "Sure."

Raven picks it up delicately in his hands. A small hand-held device like a smartphone, its body ovular with a talon-like appendage curving from each end.

"You modelled it on the shape of the Oracle you stole from me," Raven whispers, fascinated. "But this isn't it... is it?"

"No. Your Oracle was destroyed when Cameron Technologies fell, thanks to you." I feel another squirming inside me, remembering all those lives snuffed out, and how this unassuming man in front of me was the architect of it all. "This is built from scratch, but I copied the look of the Oracle. I thought it seemed fitting, you know."

Raven examines it. The plastic casing around the screen is gold instead of the black that the Oracle had been.

"The light to the darkness," Raven murmurs, examining it. He smiles. "Alpha and Omega. So what do you need me for? You seem to have done pretty formidably well by yourself."

"I need to fine-tune what I have, figure out why it's working and what can still be improved," I say. "I need to run another trial, see if I can replicate it at a larger scale. Trust me, I hate to admit it, but no one knows the science of the connection between counterparts better than you do. You're the expert. You conducted experiments on New Redemption that were unspeakable, but at least maybe now the suffering of all those subjects won't be for nothing. Help me fill in the gaps and figure out what parts of this are working and why. Even with all the evil you've done, I know that you loved my Mum like she was your own. So this is how you redeem yourself, Taylor. Help me to cure the madness that you started."

"Well, then," Raven smiles. A light tentatively flickers to life in those dim eyes. "Where should we begin, Mr Cameron?"

"Come with me," I say to Eclipse the next day after work. I've had zero sleep.

The deadly vapour from the Empire is still hanging above the base, almost like a conscious sinister entity, waiting to eat through anything organic or inorganic. It still hasn't rained.

It's been two days since Eclipse arrived.

Eclipse follows me obediently. We find Sophie and her friends on the bean bags in the lounge. Since arriving here Sophie has clearly established herself as the ringleader of a gang which includes Molly, Grindelbark and Blanca among their numbers. Sophie flicks a lock of hair behind an ear animatedly as she talks, but I notice her attention lingering on each of the Shadows in the group. I can still see in her that ever present longing for her own counterpart which she carefully disguises. I imagine it's not easy being the only one in the base apart from Blanca without a counterpart, especially since Phoebe and I have ours now.

I swallow my pride, and take a deep breath. This is my way of making peace with Eclipse, by showing him that I've listened to him about making other friends here in the ship. But as I'm getting ready to saunter over to them, I realise I hadn't counted on the amount of sheer terror I'd suddenly feel.

I don't remember how to be a normal teenager, Eclipse, I think, suddenly frightened. *I just don't.*

You'll be fine, Griffin.

What am I meant to talk to them about? I have no social life. All of my time is spent working.

It's the same with them. So just talk about something else for a change. Anything. I know how much you care about them, how protective you are. But sometimes spending time with them is the best way to show them *that.*

Obviously by this time Sophie's gang have noticed there's some mental bickering going on between a young man and his oversized dragon-cockatoo. I stick my hands into my pockets and saunter over.

"Hey, folks. Wassup?" I ask casually.

"We're not slacking," Celeste, the pink-feathered meerkat, says in alarm. I see her trying to awkwardly hide some fashion magazines between the beanbags.

"I didn't say…"

"We can get back to work, if you want us to."

"I didn't come over here just…" I think I'm sweating. "I did it because…"

They all look at me quizzically, as if they're trying to figure out a riddle.

"Do you… um…" I struggle internally, embarrassed. "Do you mind if we join in?"

They all stare at me. Only for a moment.

"Oh my gosh," Sophie says delightedly, a gleam in her eye. "Are you wanting to join us for a *slumber* party?"

"Ummm…"

"Hey, Eclipse?" Sophie calls. Eclipse is doing a terrible job of trying to hide. He's snuck back into the corridor, but he's peeking in at us, his upright crest feathers give him away spectacularly.

"Oh, hello," he says.

"Hey!" Sophie says. "Do you want to join us too?"

Eclipse smiles.

"I'd like that."

We join in with Sophie and the others for two rounds of the board game Catan, backstabbing each other over sheep and wheat supplies for our fledgling island nations, and making a lot of inappropriate jokes about which players have wood.

The Catan board is just a meeting place it seems for incredible amounts of gossip about the surprisingly active personal lives of every single member in the base. Sophie and the others even start trying to draw a diagram for us of all the romantic entanglements in the base, with helpful lines and arrows. Meanwhile Little Marty, giggling delightedly, uses Eclipse as a slide, slithering right down his long scaled tail.

I have to leave to get some work done, but we regroup in the lounge a few hours later and turn down the lights to watch an old horror movie, using Eclipse as our ginormous bean bag couch. Zephyr joins us too. The movie is about alien abductions, and it has the recurring motif of an owl with haunting dark markings in the place of its eyes. Zephyr, surprising us all, turns out to be particularly scare-prone, and has to leave part way through when someone drops a spoon and gives him a minor heart attack.

Later that night we gleefully draw a cut-out owl with big dark eyes on a piece of A4 paper, and hide it at the end Zephyr's bed to see when he wakes up in the morning. I know. We're terrible.

In one day I feel like I've spent more time with the others here then I have in months. Spending this much time with Eclipse too feels more magical than I could have wished for. It's like... it's like this day of movies and games is a precious example of the quiet life we could have lead together in another existence.

Sophie lies down on the couch with her legs dangling as she dramatically reads off the menu for the catering the next day. There are cheers for the butterscotch slice and groans for the meals consisting of a single piece of toast or one lonely fruit smoothie.

Keen for one final movie, we throw on The Lion King. Eclipse seems hypnotised by it the entire way through. He even starts singing along with *'Hakuna Matata'* under his breath.

"But he had to go back," I hear Eclipse muttering to himself near the end of the movie. "Otherwise he never would have faced Scar. The Pridelands would never have been freed."

I feel a strange stirring in my heart. Eclipse keeps saying he has to go back to his own people. But I can feel how torn he is. I realise for the first time that part of him desperately wants to stay with us, but he can't. I try to push down the hope in me that's too quick to flame to life. The hope that I can make him stay.

Our base is becoming Eclipse's safe place, away from the grief of the war and the responsibility he feels to the Shadow world. The GSA is his Hakuna Matata.

Sophie and the others start clamouring for Eclipse to show off his special power to the rest of them, so we all make our way down to the training field we have in the ship. As we do a surprising amount of GSA members join in with us, word spreading like rapid fire.

"All right," Eclipse says with surprising dramatic flair, "who's up first?"

Pouncer is the first to volunteer his power. Eclipse presses his claw gently against the dragon-dog, then summons a miniature storm. Everyone exclaims with excitement at the indoor fireworks show, lightning lashing over our heads.

Everyone eagerly clusters in at Eclipse. The next he chooses is Islandia, who closely resembles an Alpine Marmot.

Before long miniature mountains are surging up out of the ground of the training room, whisking some members up toward the roof, shrieking and giggling. The mountains are carpeted in lush green grass with patches of wildflowers on their slopes, and the air smells fresh; for one moment it feels like all of us are finally outside again, and that the artificial lights above are actually the sun, radiating down on our faces.

Humans and Shadows slide down the green slopes, tumbling and whooping, with more and more rushing down through the ship to join us as word spreads. Soon the miniature mountain range is filled with shouts of joy, a sound our base hasn't heard in a long, long time. Eclipse turns to grin at me with a face so full of joy that I start to wonder if he really is having a change of heart. I smile back.

Maybe, after all of this... he's actually going to stay. Maybe he knows that this is his home.

"Thank you for doing this for them," I say to Eclipse. We're lying on the grass amongst the flowers, staring up at the dark roof. It's night time and the lights are off, but all the members in the base have elected to have a mass-sleep out in the new temporary mountain range. I feel like we're Simba and his friends, musing on the meaning of the stars beneath a night's sky. "They really needed it."

"So," Eclipse says softly, "you know one question which you didn't answer in that gossip session?" He grins at me. "Who do you *like*?"

Mind your own business, I think, blushing. I'm very aware of the listening ears all around us, even if they're pretending to be asleep.

Come on, I'm serious. What's really happening with you and Phoebe? I was going to let you bring it up, but you haven't talked about it, once.

I bite my lip. I don't want to say anything, but the noise inside me wells up to such intensity I think I might burst.

I... I like her, I whisper between our minds. *But it's not meant to be.*

Oh. I'm sorry, Eclipse says apologetically. *It's just that it's kind of impossible not to hear it really. Your mind is constantly screaming it.*

I swallow. I'd barely admitted it to myself, trying to fight the truth down. Knowing it's that obvious makes my face burn.

Oh, I say, embarrassed. *Is that why you tried to organise that date for us?*

Yes. My bad. So you've got a thing for Ember's human, and I have a thing for Phoebe's Shadow, Eclipse says wryly. *Is that a thing, do you think, that feelings will always be mirrored like that? If I fall for anyone, will you always fall for their human too?*

I don't know, I say, thinking about the crushes and small romances that have sprouted up in the base amongst the members here. It can feel a tiny bit incestuous. *Sometimes, but it's not a rule. You could have had girlfriends over in the Shadow world without me feeling the need to date them over here. But I do think there's something about feeling part of your soul and part of someone else's soul fall in love which makes it hard not to experience the same feelings.*

You're both so cute together, Eclipse grins. *You and Phoebe.*
Oh, stop.
I ship you both, times ten thousand.

She's dating my brother, I burst out. The confession is wrenched from deep inside me.

Eclipse's beak drops open.

She's what?

Phoebe and Calvin are dating. You know, they used to be a thing back before she was frozen in stone, and I guess they've been trying to pick up where they left off...

"Why didn't you tell me this?" Eclipse exclaims out loud.

Can you keep your voice down? I cringe.

This means... oh, that is terrible. I can't believe... wow. That date I set up for the two of you must have been really awkward then!

I roll my eyes, but smile.

Don't worry, Griffin. It just means that we'll have to be more smart in how we tackle this.

Eclipse? I warn him. *No. What it means is nothing can ever happen, even if Phoebe did ever get feelings for me too.*

I'm not an expert on romance, Eclipse confesses. *I've been stuck in a desert. But I do know that ignoring feelings never ends well.*

Staring up at the roof, I shake my head.

You love her, Eclipse says softly.

I roll my eyes at him.

I don't love her, I mutter, flushing.

Yes, you do. You have since you broke into Cameron Technologies in New York together to find the coordinates for the station. That's why you risked your life for hers in the forest when the Majestic was hunting you. It's why it meant everything when she risked facing Raven in the palace to save you. She's your happy place.

I feel tears burning, knowing that Eclipse isn't just

making this up. He must have seen all of this in my memories when we were last together. He saw the truth in me more clearly than I have myself.

I'm in love with Phoebe, I think.

I'm in love with someone I can never possibly be with.

"Eclipse," I say, looking down at my hands.

"Yes?"

Why did you do it? Aching, I turn to look across at him. *Why did you try and destroy the portal station on the island? Why did you leave me for the Shadow world?*

I wait for a moment. There's only his stunned silence.

"I've been thinking about it," I say quietly, looking back up at the roof. "I've been turning it over and over again in my mind. Looking for signs I might have missed. Maybe I could have stopped it from happening, maybe I could have looked out for you more. Maybe if I hadn't left you in the Shadow world when I returned with the Oracle things could have been different. But... it just seemed to come out of nowhere. That was the worst part of it: the shock. I couldn't sleep at night, wondering how long had it been growing in your mind? I feel like you were always just as passionate as I was about finishing what our Mums started. Then you spend a little time with Hanna journeying through the Shadow world... and suddenly you're all about Shadows being independent. Suddenly humans are too corrupting for Shadows. And it's like everything we ever talked about, every single part of our lives leading to that moment in the station's control room just didn't matter to you anymore."

I wait. Still silence.

"I'm not angry," I say, closing my eyes. "Well, not now. I just want to know the truth. What was going through your head? Losing you is impossible without knowing why. Just let me know that, and maybe I'll be able to try to let you go."

"I don't want you to let me go," Eclipse murmurs.

"But you're still going home after this vapour clears, aren't you? Then we'll be on opposite sides of a war again. Not Eclipse and Griffin. Just a Shadow and a human."

"Grif," he says, tortured. "When I was growing up without you, all I ever wanted was to find you again. Even when the Empire started telling everyone that humans were diseased, even when my own brother started helping them burn anything to do with humans... I never gave up on finding you. I remembered humans as these gentle, beautiful things. In my head they seemed like guardian angels, because I was only a little kid when I left the human world. Then when I travelled with Hanna to those islands, she showed me everything that was wrong about how the Empire worked. But she also showed me all of the good things about the Shadow world, things that I'd never had a chance to see. I'd always liked my world, I always wanted to explore it with you one day, but this was something *deeper*. Hanna helped me learn to love my world again, to love my own kind. She helped me to see everything that Shadows could be, if a certain human hadn't arrived in our world and created the Empire, if Raven hadn't twisted the meaning of what it was to be a Shadow.

'Finding out a human was behind the Empire who'd made my childhood a hell was hard enough for me to swallow, but then humans came through a Rip in Sanctuary City. I was so excited to see them, so glad that the humans had finally come to save us all. But they bombed my home, Grif. They shot at me. I told myself that was because they were like Raven. There are some bad humans, just like how some Shadows are bad. Then I saw human soldiers slaughter innocent Shadow refugees in the Islands of Sun and Moon. I watched as they tried to hurt Hanna, who somehow had become the only Shadow who understood me. I lost it, Grif. I just..." Eclipse shudders. *I killed the soldiers,* he thinks sadly. *And as soon as I did, I was sick at the thought of how you'd look at me. I watched as Raven fused human and Shadow counterparts into hideous demons. Hanna and I rescued those humans from the palace and as thanks that human girl April tried to shoot me just because of what I looked like. Hanna nearly died taking the bullets for me. It was all too much. Everything I believed had been challenged but that was the moment that I just felt it. Somehow I knew that forcing our worlds to come together would end badly. It was like I could sense this war coming.* He swallows. When he speaks again, it's out loud, his voice soft. "As Shadows, we've never been able to explore what we could really be. We've been defined by humans for years, even when we didn't know it. We were controlled by our blind love of humans or our blind hate. So when you and I got to that control room, I just knew that I couldn't do it. The Empire had made me miserable my whole life. It was time to try and fix it. To finally try and be proud of what it meant to be a Shadow. So that no Shadows had to suffer the way that poor little Cirrus had suffered. I had to stop those portals opening."

"But you failed," I say, a lump in my throat. "And we started a war. You were right."

"That was little comfort on all the lonely nights after that," Eclipse whispers, "when all I could see was the look on your face when I betrayed you."

I wipe some snot away. I don't know what else to say.

The air is so heavy. All I know is that feelings for my Shadow which I thought I'd pushed far down are rising to the surface, reminding me that they were there all along. They never died. I'm scared to say anything that might ruin this moment, but I know now that I have to do whatever it takes to convince Eclipse not to return to his own world. He's my best friend, he always has been. And it's our destiny to fulfil our Mums dream together.

Somehow, I have to convince him that our worlds can still make each other better. I have to somehow make Eclipse see that the Siren is our only chance.

13

MY SILVER LINING

As Eclipse slumbers with the other GSA members in the miniature mountain range, it's straight into work for me and Raven. I slip out as soon as I'm sure Eclipse is asleep, retrieving Raven from his cell. When we reach the Siren room, we don't waste one second.

Having Raven as my lab partner is still somewhat unthinkable. I never would have imagined we'd ever be in this situation, not in a thousand years. Yet we pick up just where we left off from our previous session, trading ideas, bouncing off each other. If at times I'm lost in the work I shout for a cheese scone and he'll chuck one across the room to me which I catch without looking up. Already we're deeply and weirdly in sync.

Meanwhile Winter is handling data entry and general manual labour. He's hardworking, he just doesn't quite share the intelligence of his human counterpart. Still, kudos to the creepy bird-man for loyally and diligently helping us in our task. Honestly, he just seems pleased to be doing something useful for us. I'm becoming more used to his presence. I get less heebie-jeebies now from that skeletal frame and from those beady eyes. I still keep the gun on me at all times when we're working, and Winter's wings are bound so that he can't freeze me with a blizzard from his wings. But I think now I just feel more pity, more sympathy for Winter than anything else.

I've realised that despite Raven's investment in our project, he's avoided watching the video that enables the viewer to hear their counterpart's voice. I wonder if that's because he's scared of hearing Winter more clearly, what with their troubled relationship, or if he's more afraid of watching the video and hearing nothing at all... of confirming his suspicions that Winter isn't truly meant for him.

We're trying to replicate and perfect what the Siren achieved during my last trials, building toward testing it on a wider scale. Every minute we don't figure this out is another minute that cities burn.

It may be strange, but it feels at this moment that all three of us are exactly where we are meant to be. None of us are running anymore. Now we have a clear goal: stopping this war that Raven and I helped to start, before the two sides... you know... successfully eradicate all intelligent life in the universe.

I'm shooting off some work in the bridge the next morning, getting the bare minimum of daily tasks done as head-honcho of the GSA before I can risk vanishing back down to the Siren room. I wish I could keep Raven and Winter working down there 24/7, but I have to keep sneaking them back to their cell in case anyone decides to check in on them. I suspect that there may be the slightest panic if people think Raven and Winter have broken out.

I don't know how I'm still operating on next to zero sleep. The only shut-eye I've had has been the odd power nap at my desk. In each one of those I've had the strangest vivid dreams. Whenever I don't dream of the Siren... I dream of Eclipse.

The Siren is the one burning thing that I can't share with him. It's the secret that's keeping us apart, a ticking time-bomb. Every time I'm around Eclipse, I feel like I'm living a lie, that I'm deceiving the other half of me as well as myself. I know what he believes now. I know that he's going to be furious when he learns that I'm responsible for the Shadows who have been glimpsing their counterparts over in his world. But I still want to share this with him so badly it's erasing almost everything else.

There *has* to be some way to get through to him.

Sitting at my desk, I hesitate. Then I press my forefingers against my temples. I find this helps me to turn my gaze inward to my link with Eclipse, and to block out the real world around me. I focus, trying to sense where Eclipse is, my consciousness stealthily probing the borders of his own.

Finally I figure out whereabouts in the ship Eclipse is, and I freak out. He's making his way down the corridor where the hatch is that leads down to the hidden Siren room.

Did Eclipse follow me? Has he been watching me? If he's managed to spy through me as I am through him right now, this could all be over.

If he finds that hidden room, the game is up. But there's

no way Eclipse can fit down there, unless he starts shredding the metal floor of the corridor apart with his talons...

Then Eclipse slowly shuffles past the hatch, as if scouring the corridor for clues, and I breathe a sigh of relief. He's like a giant Pac-Man making his way through the maze. What's he hunting for though, if it's not cute fruit made from pixels?

I watch him through our connection as he walks systematically through the base, exploring each corridor as if he's checking them off. Like a bloodhound searching for a scent.

Slowly, I start to delve into the deeper fabric of his consciousness... but then I pull back, growling with disgust at myself.

What am I doing? How do I know that this whole theory about Eclipse isn't just in my head, isn't just a symptom of being cooped up down here too long like Phoebe suggested? I've pushed Phoebe away; I've been clearly misreading Calvin and keeping him out all this time. I'm suspecting the other half of me, my best friend since birth, of being a double agent. Eclipse has shown me nothing but kindness and compassion, despite all of my own failings.

When I thought Cirrus had died in my arms on New Redemption, I never would have imagined that, if there was a miracle and I got him back, I could end up treating him as my enemy. But here I am, using the sacred link between us to spy on his deeper secrets while acting like his old friend the entire time.

I want to trust him, I realise, grief spreading through my heart like a weed. I want to trust Eclipse more than anything. I want my buddy back. Someone who I'll never truly lose, who knows me better than I know myself, who can keep me in check when I stray too far from who I am. I'm sick and tired of sparring with the scars of past traumas that keep me in this cage.

I need answers though. This isn't just about me. It's about the others down here. It's about billions of other lives.

Agonised, I force myself to reconnect with Eclipse's mind. Fighting the guilt, I delve into the dream-like realm of Eclipse's subconscious one more time...

Eclipse is standing in a great war-tent amongst the desert dunes, surrounded by advisors in tattered clothes who look more like farmers or refugees. Hanna is lithely perched on the end of a table, eating an apple. As always, it's hard for me, seeing her again. I'd forgotten how ethereally beautiful she is. But now instead of hurting me, it just leaves me feeling a deep ache for what we lost.

The table is covered with a map. A few gold objects resembling chess pieces mark the movements of troops, surrounded by opposing pieces in violet.

I leave that memory, and move onto another: I'm watching Eclipse standing on a grand, underground stage. A host of nerves is roaring inside him, almost as loud as the roar of the crowd. I can hear him thinking about how big this audience is, which has gathered in secret from all the corners of the Empire. They're here in this subterranean cavern beneath the sands to see him, to see his power for themselves. They're here to listen to the Eclipse they've heard of only in hushed, treasonous whispers.

"The humans aren't evil," I hear Eclipse insist passionately to the enormous crowd before him. "They aren't a disease like Galvanize wants you to believe, but they're not our salvation either. We are our own salvation! Together, we can rise up to

take on Galvanize. Together, we can close the portals and take back control of our world. Together, we can build a better future for all Shadows, no matter the circumstances that they're born into or what unique power they're born with!"

The cheering of the crowd is so loud in the confined space I think my eardrums will burst. I'm still reeling from what I've seen but the memory is dissolving again...

Now I'm watching Eclipse in the midst of a battle between humans and Shadows at a small desert outpost. Eclipse is trying to heal a wounded Imperial soldier who looks up at Eclipse, his bovine mouth curving up in a fanatical smile.

"I can hear him," the solder whispers, his expression extraordinarily blissful.

Eclipse shivers. For some reason, he can't help himself.

"What?" he asks uncertainly.

"My human," the soldier says with wonder, his eyes glowing strangely. "It's really him."

My heart rate accelerates, and I desperately want to see more, to know more about the soldier who's wearing an expression of sheer joy. But I'm no longer in control of what I see, instead moving on to the memories Eclipse himself is revisiting at this very moment...

I see a camp in the desert sands, set up in the shelter of some great ruined temples. There's the boom of thunder as rain sweeps down across the sand and stones.

Eclipse is backing away, leaping up the steps outside one of the pyramid-shaped temples. Surging up after him are Shadows in rags, clamouring, reaching for him.

"Heal us!" they cry.

"Bless us, touch us!"

But the golden giant keeps backing away, talons fastening on rain-slicked stone.

"I can't," he mutters, afraid. He's panting heavily and his eyes look unfocused. Delirious. "I need rest... I can barely..."

"Help us! Golden one!"

Eclipse stumbles backward, nearly tripping over a step. Then he staggers out of the dark rain through the temple entrance.

Deep within the cool dark of the pyramid, Eclipse makes his way over to a hollow space, what once may have been an ancient swimming pool. He clambers into it, shivering. Thunder rumbles overhead. Eclipse's eyes have an eerie look, as if seeing threats not of the physical world. He looks somehow small in there.

There's the flutter of wings through the dark, and Hanna lights on the stone rim of the empty pool. She's human-sized, so her legs dangle over the edge as she looks up at the quivering dragon-parrot.

"Do you want to talk about what just happened?" she asks conversationally.

"I couldn't take it," Eclipse mutters, feverish. "There are so many of them... they want me to be enough for all of them, but I'm not. There's some seriously end-times crap going on. They want me to tell them that we're going to win, but I don't know that. We're just making it up as we go along."

"I know," Hanna says quietly.

"Not to mention that I just turned on one of my own advisors, someone who was meant to be one of us."

"That advisor was trying to sell us out to the Empire, and then all of the people here would have been butchered in their sleep," Hanna says. "You did what you did to save the lives of everyone here who's relying on you."

"This uprising is meant to be about peace," Eclipse whispers, looking unhinged. "How could I do that?"

"We're not as bad as the Empire."

He snorts.

"So we're not forcing Shadows into slave labour to make our weapons or drafting children as soon as they're old enough to hold a sword? That's a low bar. The two of us were addicts to the dark side. Once an addict..."

"Does it matter if we walk in the darkness, as long as it lets us protect those in the light?" she counters softly.

"Hanna... are we doing the right thing?"

"It's a little late to ask that now. There's that small matter of the army we've amassed downstairs to march on Empress Galvanize."

"I don't mean taking on the Empire, I mean teaching everyone that humans aren't the answer."

"Are you having a late-teens crisis?" Hanna smiles at him. "My faith gets tested too, you know. Look, even if we were selling friendship between the worlds, nobody's buying. The Resistance's support utterly crumbled once the humans started attacking. We're doing the best that we can."

"I wonder where Ember is," Eclipse whispers. His voice is troubled. "If she had to go on the run or if Galvanize has her."

I catch a flash of something like hurt across Hanna's face. But she forces another smile. One that seems more for his benefit than hers.

"Someone has a serious case of Stockholm Syndrome," she says, teasingly. Then, in a kind voice: "I'm sure Ember's fine. She'll have gotten away. That's one Shadow who can handle herself."

"Are you really okay with never meeting your human?" Eclipse asks Hanna. He seems curious, like she's a complex mystery. "It's the one thing you always wanted more than anything. Now you'll never even see her face."

Hanna hesitates, and I see a tortured look in her just for a moment.

"Yes, more than anything," she admits, "but this isn't just about me anymore, is it? This is about putting the survival of our species first. If I never get to see my counterpart, but the Shadow world is somehow better off because of what you and me are doing... then that will be enough for me. Even if I only ever see her face in my dreams." Hanna takes a breath. "At Aeyu, when you found out I was still working for Raven, I felt sick. I couldn't take how you looked at me. I felt that I'd lost the part of myself that you helped bring out. I might as well have been back locked in that basement again." She shudders. Eclipse watches her. Even in his rattled state, Hanna seems to have got through to him. I'm guessing that he doesn't often hear her talk this openly about her childhood. "My adoptive parents feared me because the blood of an ancient, royal and let's face it, psychotic line ran through my six-year-old veins." Hanna snorts. "Raven only liberated me from that place because he believed that big-name royal heritage would make me more palatable as an Empress to the people. Either way, he only saw my value in my blood-line, not in me. He was just like my so-called parents.

'You know, ever since the war broke out, I've felt like I was just waiting to die. Like my only hope for redemption was to save as many lives as I could before I got shot. But now we have a chance to really screw with the system! To fix the evil Empire that I helped build." I see tears in Hanna's eyes as she smiles. "We're doing this for all the little Hannas and Cirruses out there, so that they won't have their childhoods messed up by the Empire anymore. No Shadow should have to hide who they are, or be afraid that the wrong word could get them locked away."

I see something in Hanna then, something that changes me. Something that makes me feel completely confused.

It's the selfless love in her voice as she soothes my Shadow... and how Eclipse seems completely oblivious to it.

"Griffin, Griffin!"

The hushed whispering tears me out of Eclipse's memory, and suddenly I'm no longer in a ruined desert temple under a stormy night sky in the Shadow world. Instead I'm lying on the floor of the tunnel leading from the ship's bridge. I look around, disorientated, wondering how on earth I got here.

Someone is clutching me. It's Calvin.

Shocked, I realise I somehow wandered down here while I was lost in Eclipse's thoughts. Like... sleepwalking?

"What... what happened?" I say. A strange giggle of hysteria escapes from me.

"You were muttering to yourself, like you couldn't even hear me," Calvin says, worried. He looks down the tunnel, checking that no one has seen me in this state. "Then you wouldn't stop laughing."

I swallow, unnerved. I definitely feel... *wrong,* somehow.

"What happened? Grif, tell me, what's happening to you?"

My brother's desperate voice, breaking with his concern for me, is my only anchor.

"I was hunting through Eclipse's memories..." I say, shuddering, "looking for anything he's hiding from us..."

I put my head in my hands. My forehead feels cold, but it's slicked with sweat as if I have a high fever.

"You need to stop this," Calvin is saying. He sounds afraid. His hand is on my shoulder. "*Spying* on Eclipse? You can't keep fighting the other half of yourself, it's tearing you in two. Being at odds with him is killing you. You're losing your grip on reality, Grif. Look, I get that it's hard. It was for me and Zephyr too when you brought him back for me. But you have to start trusting that Eclipse isn't hiding anything from you."

But Eclipse *has* hidden things. He gathered together an army of citizens and refugees ready to try and take on Empress Galvanize before I ran into him at Troy. He built a movement to challenge the Empire, a movement that didn't believe humans were an evil sickness to be eradicated, but instead believed the portals should be closed, the worlds remaining separate.

Suddenly I realise how far apart Eclipse and I really are in terms of what we think is best for everybody. How unlikely it is that he would ever want to be my partner in making the Siren work.

"I have to go," I say, my mouth dry, pushing myself to my feet.

"Griffin, you should at least let Zephyr check you out... maybe do a psych eval..."

"No. You're right. It's time to get everything with Eclipse out in the open."

When I reach Eclipse he's skulking in a corridor near the quarters of the leadership team, near the room I used to sleep in before we started bunking together.

"Griffin?" he says in surprise as I charge toward him. "What's going on?"

"What are you doing here?" I demand, gesturing wildly. "What in the blazes are you looking for?"

My carefully laid stratagems are all going down in flames. Now I'm just operating from pure emotion. I know it even as I'm doing it, but I can't stop myself.

"I'm not looking for anything," Eclipse says tightly. "I

love being here with our family, but this place... I feel like a tiger in a cage. I need to stretch my legs, so I pace the place, going in circles. My wings miss the open sky."

"What did you plan to do here, Eclipse?" I challenge him, shaking.

"What?"

"Why are you here?" I demand. "What do you want?"

"I... I don't know," he confesses.

"I don't believe you. You moved an ocean with your mind to end the battle at Troy just to get our attention."

"I don't know. I want to eat ice cream. Watch bad vampire movies. Do... friend stuff."

"How can we just snap back to being friends, after what you did? After what you've done?" I laugh at him, but there's no warmth in it.

"What have I done, Grif?"

"When I ran into you as Cirrus in Sanctuary City," I say, ignoring him, "we were just two strangers wanting someone to magically fix our lives. Then when you sabotaged the station and left, I realised I had to look out for myself. It was hard, Eclipse. It's even harder with you acting like nothing has to change, when everything has."

Eclipse stares at me, wounded.

"You haven't really forgiven me, have you?" he asks, smiling wryly.

"Next question," I shoot at him. "Why did you abandon me and try to destroy our dream, really? How long before we entered the core of that facility had you already made your choice?"

"Griffin, I'm so sorry about... you know why I did what I did." Emotion creeps into Eclipse's voice. "I felt something terrible was going to happen if those portals opened. I know it doesn't matter if it did or not, I know that the point is... I hurt you. I tricked you and I left you behind. But at the time, it felt like the only right thing to do. It felt like doing anything else would be losing *me*, when I'd only just found out who *me* was."

"So you just left Phoebe and me to drown?"

"What?" Eclipse seems genuinely aghast. "What the heck do you... the self-destruct," he realises. "But you had the elevator to the surface..."

"All the doors automatically locked to contain the water. The only way to survive was to start up the portal process again. If we hadn't figured that out, we'd have been goners."

"I had..." There are tears in Eclipse's eyes. He's trembling, and shakes his head as if he can deny it. "Griffin... I had no idea. I never meant to hurt you."

"Right," I say, crossing my arms. "Because if I drowned, you'd be dead too, right?"

"Don't even say that. You know that's not it."

"I've seen your memories. You told me you were in the Shadow world alone, just you and Hanna. You didn't tell me you'd started recruiting followers or that you were building a new movement to take on the Empire. Why did you hide that from me?"

Eclipse's eyes spark, and I feel his fury like a solar flare.

"You've been spying on me?" he says dangerously.

For a moment, I really think Eclipse is going to kill me. The way he *looks* at me.

Then, strangely, he turns to leave.

"You're insane," Eclipse says without looking at me. "I should have known that it was a mistake to come here. You've lost it."

"Don't tell me I'm making this up! I know what I saw!"

I rush after him. It's irrational, when the threat I was worried might kill me is suddenly leaving of his own free will. But there's something I missed. I know it. If I let him off the hook now, I might never find the answers I need.

So I follow after Eclipse and I give it everything I have. I drill deep into his mind with the full force of mine, searching for the memories I've missed, searching for proof of his intent...

"Stop it!" Eclipse hisses. His own mind is battling against mine as if our duelling consciousnesses are weapons. The two of us are locked in a mental battle, projecting phantasms into each other's head to war with each other, clashing with the ferocity of a storm. Vying for control, I fight even harder. Finally I gain a foothold, and images that were locked deep down inside Eclipse's psyche are suddenly flooding through my mind. I feed on them hungrily, aching for the whole truth...

Eclipse is flying across the endless desert sands beneath the stars. His wings are aching, and the cold night air bites at his scales. I see the dunes pass down below and it's as if I'm sitting on Eclipse's back, riding high above the world.

"Hey, Griffin," I hear Eclipse say. I start, but then realise he's not talking to the Griffin who's spying on this memory right now. Instead Eclipse is speaking softly up at the stars as he flies. He cranes his neck up to look at them, burning bright in the black velvet. "It's me again. Empress Galvanize has been hunting us, and I can't see any way out. I've never wished more that you were here with me. We have such an impossible choice, Grif. Do we give up and run or do we take the fight to her? No matter what I do, people I love are going to suffer. No matter what I do, something tells me that it's going to cost me my life.

'I think my only hope is that I can kill Galvanize somehow. I know you taught me that killing is wrong, but at least that will end this. At least she'll stop making the Shadow world so toxic, and I might have done something good, one single meaningful thing with my life before my light goes out.

'I don't know why I'm saying this. I know that you can't hear me, that most likely I'll never see you again. I know that you're probably still furious at me for how I left you. The thought of you hating me, the thought that that was your last memory of us, that's what hurts most of all. I didn't even stop this war. I did that to you for nothing, and war still came.

'Do you remember when we met again in Sanctuary, after all those years apart? I think about it every day. You were so strange. Funny. You'd become more you since I'd last seen you. I like to imagine what it would have been like if I'd stayed with you. I imagine if the war hadn't broken out where we would live: in my world or yours? I wonder what our home would be like.

'I'm not sure how much longer I'll be alive. I'm afraid of death, but I'm ready to face it if I have to... except that it means you'll die too. That's something that I'll never be okay with, the thought of your spark going out in the universe because I failed.

'I'm scared for you, Grif. I'm really scared. But if it's okay with you, I'll keep pretending you're here with me, just like I have been. Even if we wanted different things in the end, you always made me feel like I mattered. You always made me feel like my happiness mattered, even in the uncaring darkness of the universe. I'd give anything in the worlds to have you here with me. I hope wherever you are that you're safe.

'I wish you could see this place. It's just a wasteland in the day, but I like the hot winds under my wings, and in the evenings like this one the moon hangs above the dunes and the stars are so bright. I'd like to fly here with you, to see how high

we could go, until you could reach up and almost touch the stars with your hand.

'If I die, if we die, I hope that we will be together again. I hope that our souls join back together as they're meant to be and we live on as a Majestic. Like our Mums. I believe we will. I believe that even if this war takes everything, we'll be with each other again."

I gasp, and now the moonlit desert is gone. Now I'm with Eclipse as he flies high over the city of Troy as it falls to the human siege. Death and fire are everywhere we look. But I'm not just a spectator anymore. Now it's like I'm Eclipse himself, seeing what he sees, thinking as he thinks.

The humans came from nowhere, their ships blotting out the horizon. I see the humans and Shadows dying en masse on the beach and in the hills, and despair.

As I wheel through the sky, I sense you. Slowly and then all at once.

Griffin. You're here.

I plunge forth from the smoke cloud, my tail whipping through the air behind me, and then I'm clear of it. I see the human ships' cannons as they rotate swiftly toward your helicopter.

Without thinking I bend matter to my will. I pull on all the power I can find inside of me and unleash it. I watch the oceans turn the ships aside, something I've never achieved even to save my own people. Something I barely believe is coming from inside me. I alter the fabric of reality so that your heart will keep on beating.

If there's one thing I can wish for in this war, it's that no harm will ever, ever come to you. I wish for a life for you after all of this, one where you're happy, and free.

Then I can see you in the helicopter, just for a moment. I lock eyes on you fleetingly over the battlefield. I've missed your face, even though I see it every night in my dreams.

Then all the light in the world is snuffed out like a candle flame.

The last image that passes through my mind is a memory: two small children flying joyfully together around the hallways of Cameron Technologies.

The memory breaks apart. I blink, returning to my own senses. I'm standing facing Eclipse, in the hallway of the ship.

I look away from Eclipse, finally at a loss for words. The fierce pride and hot-blooded anger at the injustice is gone. As it breaks, the only thing left is fear.

Fear that Eclipse won't forgive me for breaking our trust. Fear that I'm now on the outside of the person I love.

I try to fight back the tears. They hurt.

What I'd thought were instincts was just paranoia, like Phoebe had been trying to tell me all along. Eclipse really did come here just to reconnect with me. He came here to see the friend he was afraid he would never see again.

I messed up the one true chance to fix things with my Shadow.

Oh no. I cover my mouth, heartbroken at how badly I've messed up. Oh no. I am so sorry.

What's he thinking right now? How badly have I hurt him? I can't tell. Eclipse's mind and heart are closed off to me completely now. And no matter how badly I want to know what he's thinking, I won't ever try to betray his trust again by breaching that wall. Never again.

"I didn't come here to hurt you, Griffin," Eclipse says darkly. "You have every right to hate me for what I did to you..."

"Hate you?" I shout at him, sobbing. "I can't hate you, because the one I'm really angry at, the one who broke the worlds... is me. I bypassed the launch sequence that you broke. I gave the worlds the means to go to war with each other. You were in the right, and I was in the wrong. All these people who've died, all of those millions of lives lost for nothing."

I feel myself shaking. My vision seems blurry. I can just make him out, still staring at me like I'm the enemy.

"Eclipse," I choke, anguished. "I've screwed up. I was wrong. I shouldn't have doubted you, and after everything you've suffered... I know that you'd never turn on me."

But that's just the thing. I didn't know that, and I should have.

"I am so, so sorry," I whimper. "Ever since you left... I've been a mess. You're right. You were totally right. I alienate people. I push them away. The pain at losing you... it's become a crutch. I've defined myself by it, and I've been a coward. Just the sight of you has been enough to send me running, when I should have spent this time fighting to have you back."

He doesn't move. He doesn't even react.

"I really didn't want you to be a double agent," I say, my voice strangled. "I don't think I could have taken it. You're a really good Shadow."

Then, cautiously, Eclipse reaches out with one wing. The feathers of it brush against my arm tentatively. I fall into it, crying. Eclipse pulls me into a tight hug that nearly crushes me, as if he can shield us from the world.

"You must hate me," I cry into him.

"Never," he hisses with feeling.

"Listen," I say when he releases me, wiping my tears

away violently. "We're bigger than this war. Whatever it makes us do, whatever happens between us because of it. We're bigger then it. I won't let it break us."

Eclipse makes a low thrum which I know is agreement.

"I wish our futures were different," he says. "I wish that we could rewrite them somehow to spend them together."

"Me too."

"I miss when we escaped Sanctuary together," he says longingly. "Those were the good times."

"Despite the fact that the Empire was trying to kill us both?" I grin.

"I remember feeling free flying through the trees in Kashlak together, or how safe we felt when we'd just arrived at Winghold. Those were the times when everything made sense. Those are the last times I remember feeling really happy. I hid what was really going on with me when we met in the Underworld, because I didn't want you to see where my path was taking me."

"But I saw the indecision in you," I say intently. "You *know* that you might be wrong about keeping the worlds apart."

"You're right, I don't know!" I flinch as the words explode out of him. "But damn it, I've set something in motion, Grif, and I can't abandon it now!"

I think of the army Eclipse and Hanna were gathering before he came here, their movement made up of the disenfranchised and forgotten. Does it even count as an army if they're not properly trained? If it's just made up of ordinary, everyday people? I wonder if they can really win, even with Eclipse's power, against an all-powerful global Empire.

"What if we did find a way to end the war overnight, to

bring humans and Shadows together?" I say slowly. "Would you stay then? Would you work with us?"

"I have to leave tomorrow at dawn, Grif," Eclipse says, his voice breaking. It's like a kick to the gut.

"Tomorrow?" I burst out. "But... the vapour. There's no way to fly through it and come out alive."

"Haven't you heard?" Eclipse says softly. "It's been raining. By morning it will be safe enough for me to fly to the Brisbane portal. Zephyr's offered me his healing power for extra protection. There are people relying on me. No matter what happens, I made them a promise to look after them, and I won't abandon them."

"You wouldn't be you if you did," I whisper.

Tomorrow morning. It sucker-punches me and I can hardly breathe. The thought of losing him, and so soon.

We fall quiet, just standing there, listening to the sound of each other breathing. The colours of our minds dance out just how badly we want to stay with each other.

We need to treasure this, I tell myself. I need to take careful care and attention to remember every moment. This might be one of our last. I think about asking Eclipse what exact time in the morning he'll leave and how many hours we have left. I decide I don't want to know.

We were always fated by the stars to be on different sides. Eclipse for the independence of the Shadow world; me for the coexistence of our two kinds. No matter how much I wish this wasn't how things are, it's where our lives have always been sending us... since before I was born, when Cirrus was still growing inside his egg.

14

FORBIDDEN FEELINGS

"My God," I say, covering my mouth.

Raven and I stare wordlessly at the screen before us. We watch as human soldiers, hundreds of them, throw down their assault rifles, holding up their hands in protest. The weapons litter the ground. In the background, the Auckland portal shines brightly, an epic hovering sphere.

"*The soldiers have been refusing to enter the portal,*" the newsreader says intensely. "*Just an hour ago, they all reportedly started claiming that they could hear 'their' Shadows inside their heads, and disarmed in protest. The UN has expressed concerns that a new Shadow weapon may be responsible for the sudden change in behaviour. The UN has released a statement saying that the troops were watching a new combat training video when the signal was suddenly highjacked...*"

It's late afternoon. Raven and I stand there, hidden in the secret room concealed by the ship's engines, surrounded by walls of scribbled calculations and mathematics together like the works of two complete madmen.

My handwriting and his. We marvel at the sight unfolding on the screen of the human soldiers refusing to fight, their expressions joyous. I know that look. They just found out that they hadn't been alone their entire lives as they'd thought.

We did that.

"No freaking way," I whisper, hardly daring to believe it. "It works."

Then I laugh, high on endorphins. Jubilant, Raven claps me on the shoulder.

Remembering myself, I clear my throat, stepping away from him. I cross my arms self-consciously.

We've just done the impossible. Something Calvin, something my Mum even, never came up with. I can feel something good running through my veins.

Power.

We have the power to bring people the other half of themselves. The power to make them whole.

Everyone else in the two worlds is waiting.

"We're going to finish this, Melissa," Raven whispers. He looks like he's seeing his redemption with my Mum up on that screen. As if just for a moment, it's not me that's standing here jamming with him on a problem of universal importance, but her.

As for me? I think of Eclipse. I know I'm trying to make peace with him leaving tomorrow morning, but looking at those happy soldiers I feel a sudden rush of certainty that I don't want to take Eclipse leaving lying down. I want us to fight this, together.

Just because destiny has led us to where we are that doesn't mean that our stars can't be rewritten.

It doesn't mean that I have to let him go.

· · ·

I hide in the darkness with the other members of the GSA, barely breathing. Phoebe's near my right. Concealed out of sight, we watch as Eclipse enters the cafeteria. I'm careful to shield my mind. Unless he reaches for it, unless he tries to sense where I am, he shouldn't be able to detect me lying in wait in the dark.

By the time he detects the carefully laid trap that we're waiting to spring, it will be too late.

We watch, secretly surrounding him from all vantage points as Eclipse makes his way stealthily into the cafeteria. It's not usual for the lights to be switched off in here, and there's no sound of GSA members or signs of activity. He's clearly suspicious. I watch Eclipse's crest feathers twitch, flattened into his head in apprehension.

We wait for the perfect moment to strike.

Eclipse comes to a stop, one foot half-raised. He's sensed the strange objects lying in wait in the dark, hovering innocently, their tendrils trailing down to the ground.

Suspicious, Eclipse boops a balloon with his foot. One of his hooked claws accidentally pops it. He hisses.

"SURPRISE!" we shout, launching to our feet.

Eclipse roars, the vibration reverberating through the ship around us. There's a rumbling through the cafeteria, as if miniature mountains are about to start crashing through the floor beneath us. People scream.

"Okay, bad idea guys! Bad idea!" I shout hastily, waving my hands frantically. I hadn't expected a surprise party ending in Eclipse accidentally killing everyone. "I should have thought this through!"

Eclipse's eyes are still wild. His long tail whips dangerously over our heads. Then the lights are coming up, and he's taking in the gold and blue balloons and all the traumatised members of the GSA with their party hats on. Party hooters drop from pale lips as they stare at him, aghast.

"What is this, Griffin?" Eclipse commands, momentarily terrifying.

"Your surprise goodbye party!" I cheer weakly, spreading my arms festively. I point toward the giant banner hanging on one side of the cafeteria. It reads: '*WE'LL MISS YOU, ECLIPSE!*'

Finally, the penny drops.

"I'm sorry," Eclipse says, embarrassed, looking around at everybody. He sees the fear in some people's faces and looks totally mortified. "Oh, I am so sorry. This is… this is really nice."

Clambering up on one of the tables, I hold something out toward Eclipse. He stalks slowly over to me, leaning in to examine it. It's a medal in the shape of two world globes, bound by a blue ribbon that weaves in an infinity symbol around them.

He sees what it is, and his emotions strike me like a sledgehammer.

"Eclipse," I intone formally, "I'd like to officially induct you as a member of the GSA."

He looks dumbly from me, to the others, then back to the medal. I can feel the feelings restlessly turning inside of him, like a typhoon. I've never seen someone so unstoppable seem so lost. I can feel him being torn between the love of me and our family, and his loyalty to the Shadow world. He's still questioning his beliefs about what's right for both of the worlds, I just know it. Maybe this is enough to remind him where his real home is. Maybe, I hope desperately, this is enough to make him choose us.

"When I came here, I wasn't sure what I'd find," Eclipse says to all of us, stumbling over the words. "But you showed me so much, you all have... this place is special." He hesitates, then bows, overwhelmed. "I'm honoured," Eclipse says. He takes a step closer, and then another, leaning down so I can pin the medal loosely to a bunch of his feathers. I didn't think about how small it would look on him, but I can tell from the pleasure and confusion emanating from him that it means more to him then I could have imagined.

"I know you think you have to go back," I whisper so the others can't hear, flushing. I'm nervous about his reaction. "But you have a home here. And I know you think that to stay would be going back on everything you said, I know that you're still not sure whether Shadows and humans really belong together. Look at Zephyr, though. He changed from our side to the Empire when he believed humans were dangerous, and then back again. That doesn't make him disloyal, it means that he's not afraid to change his stance when the evidence changes. Coming back to us wouldn't make you weak and it doesn't mean you're betraying anyone either. You can help them from here."

I can sense so much conflict in him, so much pain mixed in with the joy. It's like he's being torn in half.

"Getting to know you better the last few days has been the only good to come out of all of the rottenness of this war," I confess. I look up from the medal to meet those knowing eyes. I smile painfully. "You're my silver lining."

Eclipse seems weirdly disorientated for a moment. Not quite... right.

Eclipse? I lean closer to examine him, concerned. I take his bowed head in my hands as if I can steady him all on my own. *Are you okay?*

He looks at me, wretchedly, at a loss for words. Tears are burning in his eyes. I frown at the wordless agony in them.

Eclipse, I say uncertainly, with the slightest ringing at the back of my mind. *Is there something... is there something you want to tell me?*

He looks at me, those dark eyes beseeching.

Then all the party poppers go off with a BANG, making us both jump. Suddenly the party is bursting into life all around us, consuming us in a mad fit of colour and revelry. It's like a wild act of rebellion to celebrate the life that still crackles and burns down here, even in this dark pit in the most hopeless of times.

I don't know what choice Eclipse is going to make. I don't know if I can make him accept that what I'm doing with the Siren is good, when even Phoebe and Calvin won't side with me on it.

But no matter what happens, if Eclipse leaves tomorrow or if he stays... at least we have tonight.

I have tonight and I have my Shadow. And that will have to be enough.

For now.

The party explodes out from the cafeteria, taking on an insane life of its own. A cup of possibly expired Fanta is shoved into my hand and everyone's toasting me all of a sudden. I see drinks of water and instant coffee being served in fancy crystal cocktail glasses, making the most of what's on offer. Celeste and her squad start up a Massage Train, and Little Marty and his scuttling Shadow decide to ignite a spontaneous Neuf-gun war throughout the base.

There's a lot of gossiping too, especially about the strange phenomena on the news. All of those soldiers putting down their guns, claiming to hear their Shadow's in their heads. The members of the GSA sound curious, excited even, as they debate what it means, their voices strangely hushed. They're all wondering what could be the cause. At one point I feel a prickling on my neck, and turn to see Calvin looking across at me. I wonder if that's suspicion I see in his eyes.

A little later on someone is struck by the inspiration of building a massive blanket fort. Before we know it the fort has started to spread through the base, consuming the various passages and rooms in fluffy, plush districts constructed from every single available blanket and pillow. This means at some points you have to get down on all fours and crawl just to collect your drink and come back the way you came. Unless you forgot which room you left it in and are consumed by the fluffy labyrinth forever.

"Griffin!" I hear Phoebe and Ember shout in warning. I turn, then jump out of the way just as a triceratops comes crashing and sliding down the main stairwell, surfing on a mattress through the spot where I was seconds before.

"This has gotten out of control," I gasp, joining Phoebe and Ember.

"Are we meant to do something about it?" Ember suggests.

"Just let them have this one," Phoebe says, grinning ruefully. "They've all earned it. And if one of them happens to break a limb or two... we have Zephyr somewhere." She takes another long sip of instant coffee from her cocktail glass.

Then Eclipse comes striding into the landing, everyone quailing before him. His scaled tail whips above his head, and I see that a mattress is bizarrely tied around the end of it.

Someone runs up behind him, wielding a pillow. Without looking Eclipse smacks them with his mattress-tail, sending them flying to crash into part of the blanket fort which collapses beneath them.

"This is the scariest pillow fight I've ever seen," I say.

"I will destroy them," Eclipse says to me with relish, his face lit up.

"I'm glad you're having a really good time," I grin.

Then Eclipse seems to spot Ember for the first time. He becomes awkwardly silent. He gulps.

Phoebe and I study the contents of our glasses.

"How have you been?" Eclipse asks Ember, oddly formally.

"Good, I don't know, why?" Ember delivers aggressively at rapid speed.

"No... reason."

"I hear you're leaving tomorrow. For good." She glares at him. Eclipse shifts his weight from one foot to another.

"Well, I guess we'll leave you two to catch up," Phoebe says cheerfully to Ember and Eclipse.

"Huh?" Ember blurts violently. I've never seen the founder of Winghold so flummoxed. "You'll go where? Why are you two going?"

Phoebe raises an eyebrow, then takes my arm and leads me away from them.

"You don't think... with those two..." I start, oddly self-conscious that I'm talking about our Shadows. I look sideways at Phoebe. "You don't think there's something going on with them, do you? Ember trapped him in a cell for half a year. Last time they saw each other, they fought each other."

"Ah, foreplay," Phoebe mutters.

"What?" I say, sure I misheard.

"Nothing. Only, I think those two are more alike than they'd care to admit. Let's just say that feelings aren't always convenient.

It's part-way through the party that I realise that Eclipse has disappeared.

At first I just notice a general absence of his tall, golden feathered self at the party. But then when I reach out to sense where he is, I feel nothing. Well, not *nothing*... I can tell that he's still in the base, obviously, but he's cloaking himself. Hiding. I shut my eyes and press my fingers against my temples to focus on the link between us... but no luck.

I start to get worried.

"Hey," I call to Frigga, grabbing her arm as she passes. "Have you seen Eclipse anywhere?"

"Nope, sorry."

"What about Ember? Phoebe?"

"I think Phoebe said she was grabbing something from her room?"

"Cool, thanks..."

I make my way up the stairs, diving aside as some more mattress surfers come crashing down them.

"Can we get Zephyr on stand-by here, please?" I shout to Mellowfluff. The white, fluffy wolf with bunny ears has a pocket watch dangling from her jaws, excitedly timing the mattress race.

I feel a mounting sickness in my gut. The whole reason for throwing this party was to make this place feel more like home to Eclipse and to show him the fun that we could have here together if he stayed. Where the hell has he vanished to?

Maybe it's nothing. Maybe Eclipse just needed some time alone to think and he can still change his mind about flying out in the morning. But I can't stop the hairs on the back of my neck standing up.

I continue up to Phoebe's room. The party's spread up here too. I have to navigate a blanketed corridor and be transported by a conveyer belt of sitting Shadows and humans before I can be passed down toward Phoebe's door.

"Pheebs," I say, smashing through Phoebe's door into her quarters. "Have you seen...?" I stop. A knife is pointing directly at my eyeball.

Phoebe exhales, relaxing. She shoves me in the chest as she stows the blade in her belt with the other hand. "Jeez, Grif. We've talked about this. You'll see me naked or you'll get stabbed in the face, either which could be avoided by simply knocking."

I try not to be distracted by the idea of Phoebe naked. It's hard. I flounder for a few excruciating seconds as she moves over to the bed and closes her laptop.

"I was just getting down some ideas for the next mission, now that this vapour has cleared up," she says, an excited light dancing in those sky-blue eyes. "I think this one could really help us move the needle. We're on the edge of a breakthrough, Grif. I can almost taste it."

"That's great," I say, forcing a smile.

She takes in my expression.

"What is it?"

"It's Eclipse," I say, uncomfortable suspicions squirming through me. "I can't feel him. It's like he's hiding, or something, and something was off earlier."

Phoebe looks at me. She opens her mouth, then shuts it. She blushes strangely.

"What?" I say, confused by the unexpected reaction.

"Yeah," she says. "Uh, Ember's vanished too."

"I don't..." Then I cringe like I've just got a lethal case of brain freeze. Eclipse just went from radio silence to mentally broadcasting on full volume. He's with Ember. The two of them are downstairs in his quarters, talking quietly.

It's strangely intimate, seeing everything from Eclipse's perspective. I feel I'm spying on something personal, but Eclipse's brain and emotions are loud, and I'm getting all of it transmitted directly into my head without him realising. The lines between him and I are blurring, until I can't tell if I'm here with Phoebe, or below with Ember. By the looks of Phoebe opposite me, she's experiencing the same strange sensation.

I hear Eclipse speaking

"When I first met you," Eclipse says, "I loathed you and I was drawn to you at the same time."

Ember smirks up at him.

"I think I was in the same place."

"I'm sorry that I stole your power, during that fight in Sanctuary."

I breathe a sigh of relief, feeling stupid. Eclipse just wanted to talk to Ember. There's nothing weird going on. But the moment is so clear, sharp and vivid in Eclipse's mind that I can't stop seeing it. Opposite me, Phoebe looks the same. I feel embarrassed, like I'm prying into something personal, but it won't stop.

"I was pissed too," Ember says. "But I'm glad having my power kept you warm and safe on your journey to the islands. Phoebe..." she pauses for a moment, "Phoebe told me what happened in the station. How you had the foresight to try and stop this war. Even though it meant going against your human, your entire family, against what you'd believed most of your life. I wouldn't have been that strong."

"You would have. You have a different kind of strength from me entirely."

"Irate stubbornness?" Ember half-laughs.

"Yes. It's part of what makes you so beautiful."

Ember goes quiet. Eclipse is scared, not knowing what that means. She's such a mystery to him. An enigma, an angry storm-cloud.

"How can you say things like that?" she says incredulously. "I imprisoned you. For months."

"I'm glad you did," Eclipse says with feeling. "I was lost before you put me in that cage. I did unspeakable things. When I became Eclipse, the power... I was unprepared for it. I lost myself in it. When I became Eclipse, I lost all sight of who I'd been as Cirrus. I was nothing but bloodlust, ego and rage, with an unquenchable thirst for power." Eclipse hesitates, almost sounding scared. "But those little talks, those conversations we had whenever you came to visit me visit me in my cell... Even if it was just for one of those stupid pizza visits, or when you came bearing a Christmas cracker... it was in those talks that I started to find myself. To find a way back from the Beast, to who I am now. You made the world make sense. But it wasn't until I realised you still wanted me to change back into Cirrus *that I knew. The hurt from that told me how much you meant to me."*

"I failed you," Ember cuts him off. She seems angry, furious that Eclipse isn't... madder with her. "I've failed everyone, don't you get that? Everyone who followed me is dead or was forced to serve the Empire. The citizens who trusted us are back under Galvanize's wicked thumb. But I kept fighting on to the end, just like I always do. I was determined to hold out, even when there were only a handful of us left. Do you know how I ended up in that prison? A lot of my people switched sides when they could see we were going to get ourselves killed. Someone I'd trusted gave the Empire my location. I was betrayed."

"I'm sorry," Eclipse says quietly, knowing that nothing could have felt more total and devastating to her. It must have felt like the end of everything.

"But this place... what Phoebe and the others are doing here? It gives me hope. I wish you could see that. You belong here, Eclipse. You know that you belong with Griffin. But I'm not going to tell you what to do, or who you are. I did that last time."

"I know, and I was angry at you for a long time. But there's something still between us, isn't there? Something that won't let go."

"I don't... I don't know how to deal with this," Ember whispers, sounding shocked by her own confession. "This isn't who I am. Lately, it feels like I just keep falling." She shakes her head, looking like she's almost afraid to speak. "The reason I struggled with trying to call you Cirrus is because I was falling for Eclipse. I felt guilty that maybe that meant I was betraying my old friend, the fact that part of me wanted so badly to hold onto Eclipse a little bit longer. I didn't understand it either. I was confused, I thought you were an unfeeling monster. But now I see the real Eclipse, the Eclipse who Cirrus was always going to *become. After what happened with Zephyr..." Ember laughs darkly. "I didn't let myself feel anything for anyone else. What I mean is..." she says, grasping. She looks at Eclipse, earnestly, helplessly. "He was the only person I've ever been close to in that way."*

"I never have," he whispers. "I've never been close to anyone. Not as Cirrus. Not as me."

"Eclipse," Ember says balefully, looking up at him. "I don't deserve this."

"There's a gap between us," Eclipse says, aggrieved, "and I don't know how to cross it. But maybe at least... we can help each other forget the outside world. We can forget our responsibilities and our failures. Maybe we can do that for each other. I don't know how, but I'd like to do that for you."

Eclipse moves into Ember, craning his neck down toward her. He hesitates, shy. Then, gently, he rubs his beak against her neck, nuzzling her.

Phoebe gasps. I think I do too. Eclipse and Ember's minds are sparking and intense. Everything feels so vivid, so larger than life for them, and that's being transmitted to us. We're feeling what they're feeling, and as Eclipse touches Ember, it feels like I'm nuzzling Phoebe, like it's my lips brushing against her neck instead... like the distance between Phoebe and myself is no distance at all... and it's like I can feel her swooning, her body responding to my touch... but no, that's *them*. That's Ember, not Phoebe. That's Eclipse, not me, but the four of us are so interlinked.

"Phoebe..." I whisper.

"...hmmm?" she says, blinking, breathless, as much under their sway as I am. Eclipse's feelings and mine are all fused together, muddled and indistinguishable.

Daringly, heart in my throat, I reach out and trace

Phoebe's cheek with my thumb. It's not the friendly clap on the shoulder of a comrade like we've done in the field, not a hug like we've done so many times before as close friends. It's crossing into a forbidden area allowed for lovers but never for us.

I brush a lock of fiery hair behind her ear.

"Griffin…" Phoebe says slowly… but she moves closer into me.

"Pheebs," I manage, my head swimming.

Ember and Eclipse are doing a *lot* more than nuzzling now, and the anatomy of that is all very confusing for me, and it's very overwhelming feeling Phoebe so close to me with all of our Shadows' hijinks running through our heads.

I can feel Phoebe's warmth against me. Then my hand is around the back of her neck and my lips are moving toward hers…

…which is when suddenly Phoebe comes to her senses, and shoves me, hard.

The feed of sensations from Eclipse and Ember goes dark, the sudden shove helping me break free from their hot-blooded influence.

Suddenly I realise where we are, and what I'm almost doing.

"Phoebe," I say, shocked.

Phoebe covers her mouth as I look at her, then she gives me a look like daggers and storms past me. I guess she's angry enough to storm out of her own room.

Oh God, no. What have I done? Just like we were under the influence of some euphoric drug, the fog is beginning to lift, and I'm realising the consequences of what I've just done.

Oh, Calvin. Oh no.

I feel like being sick.

How... how could I? What just happened? Did I really just try to kiss my brother's girlfriend?

"Phoebe, wait!" I cry, running out of the room after her. "Phoebe!"

She's one of the few people who really matter to me anymore. Having her walking away from me and treating me like I'm invisible hurts more than any angry shouting from her ever could.

Running after her, I squeeze through the crowd of party-goers. I run into a black wolf as he emerges from a blanket fort tunnel and nearly trip over him. He quickly morphs into his opossum form, glaring sulkily up at me.

"Sorry, Tovii..."

I catch up with Phoebe in one of the quieter corridors further from the commotion. I take hold of her arm, and she whirls on me, looking fearsome. I quiver under that look. She tears her arm from my loose grip.

"I don't know what you thought that was," Phoebe says. I can't really say what the emotion is in her voice. Is she hurt, confused, betrayed or all three? "But we aren't our Shadows. Ember is the other half of me, she can do what she wants, but we don't have to be a thing just because they are."

"I never said that!" I shoot back at her, shocked.

"Also, just because Zephyr and Ember hate each other's guts, that doesn't mean that things can't work between Calvin and me," Phoebe says in a rush.

I stare at her, aghast. I didn't know that's something that had been going through her mind.

"I just don't know why you'd do that," Phoebe mutters.

"Hey, this isn't some whim," I say, angry.

"Then what is it?" she challenges me.

I look at her, and for a long time I'm not sure if I'm going to say it.

"I love you," I say honestly. I swallow. "I think... I think I have ever since we broke into Cameron Technologies in New York together."

It's the scariest thing I've ever done. It feels like the moment after leaping from a cliff when you're still hurtling through empty air, when the trajectory of your fall is no longer under your control.

Her face is so unreactive that I wonder if she actually heard me.

"Why would you say that?" Phoebe says finally. "What am I supposed to do with that?"

Her words puncture me. There are tears in her eyes.

"I can't be the only one who remembers what happened down in the station," I say, not without a little resentment. "Did you somehow forget?"

Phoebe's gaze is so intense it's like she might burn a hole through the wall.

"No, of course I haven't forgotten."

"Oh good, because I was starting to worry that was a hallucination," I say. "What with all the flames, and that rocket launching, and, oh, us kissing..."

"When was I meant to tell Calvin that I made out with his younger brother?" she hisses. "Oh, was I meant to mention it in the few minutes on the beach when Calvin was confessing his never-ending love for me, or after that, when the three of us were building a guerrilla anti-war organisation together?"

"I don't know. Somewhere in-between?" I suggest.

She gives me a look.

"We never talked about the kiss," I say, my voice falling. "You never even brought it up, as if it never even happened."

"You know what?" Phoebe breathes, more softly. "You didn't bring it up either."

I can't think of what to say to that. She's right.

"So you didn't feel anything for me in... that way?" I ask, trying to harden my heart against the answer. "Are you saying it only happened because of our near-death experience?"

"It doesn't matter now."

"It matters to me," I whisper.

"You don't get to ask me that," Phoebe tells me. "Calvin's my boyfriend."

"He's ten years older than you."

"Okay, now that's definitely not relevant to this conversation. Also, can I ask: how is it fair that you choose to tell me how you really feel *now*? How did you even think this would work? This same thing happened with Taylor too. Why can't a friendship just be a friendship?"

"You're really comparing me to Raven?" I say, arching an eyebrow. "Do I have to start worrying about being banished by you from my own world?"

"How can you even joke about that? Grif, I'd never hurt you," she says, with genuine feeling. "I want to give you anything in the universe that you want. You brought me my Shadow. You saved my life, you basically brought me back from the dead and you kept me going when all I could see was darkness. But this is the one thing I can't give you."

"You really love him," I say, smiling tightly.

"I do," Phoebe says, and as she stares at me it looks as if she's realising that for the first time. "I love him."

I take in her words slowly. I feel drained and so totally lost.

"Grif, you're still my best friend. Our work here needs us to be partners. We can't end the war if we're not in sync."

"End the war?" I explode, incredulous. "Don't you get it? Our work here is a lost cause, Pheebs."

She looks shocked. Like she's somehow blind-sided by this revelation.

"What do you mean? We're getting closer to negotiating a ceasefire..."

"This war's never going to stop! It might even already have destroyed so much that whether or not it ends hardly even matters, don't you see that? It's eaten everything. When we started this place we believed we could make a difference, but we had no idea of the forces we were up against. The more they blow each other into pieces, the more it seems like this whole war is some twisted act of self-hate, like they're all so eager to set themselves on fire and end everything, like neither side will stop trying until they're ashes." I take in a shaky breath. "I love you, Phoebe, and I love your determination. But nobody here is prepared to do what has to be done. I love that you're teaching the others how to be good, how to be heroes. I love that you're making them believe again that all of this has some meaning, that the *way* that we win matters. But it doesn't. This is all just a fairy tale."

It's too late to take it back: the truth that I've been fighting saying out loud all this time. Phoebe folds her arms, clearly rocked. When she meets my gaze though, she's all steel.

"So that's all this place is to you, a fairy tale? Sometimes you have to do what's right, even if you can't see the path, even if failure seems certain. We've been working so hard to make something happy here. A family. Do you not care about that?" Her voice breaks.

"Of course I do."

"Having a mission, having a family... that wasn't enough for Taylor, in the end. That's why I lost him. I don't want to lose you too."

15

DANGEROUS LIES

When I wake, Eclipse's tail is coiled around me, keeping me close to his feathered side. He's still asleep. When I move he shifts his wing back over me instinctively, as if to protect me. I smile.

It takes a moment for me to remember that this is our final morning.

Swallowing, I run a hand through Eclipse's feathers tenderly, as if I'll never let him go.

I was stupid to think that I could change his mind about going back just with that one party. It didn't change a thing. I even thought maybe last night with Ember would have given him another reason to stay, but I feel like that was really them saying their last goodbye.

Eclipse feels he owes the Shadow world something, and I don't think anything I can say will change that.

Ember went back to sleep in her and Phoebe's room last night, so I didn't have to awkwardly third wheel or return to my lonely room upstairs. Not that I would have minded, if it made Eclipse happy. But I'm glad we get one last sleepover together. It gave me a chance to talk to him about what happened with Phoebe too, grieving under the safety of his wing before sleep claimed me.

Now I'm just trying not to think too much about what him and Ember got up to in this nest.

I look around at our walls, my chest feeling heavy. Me and Eclipse decorated them together last night before we fell asleep. We took selfies together around the base, goofing around, and now the printed photos plaster the walls. I printed off a big poster of *Creed*, the band that Eclipse has been obsessed with since I introduced him to their music. There's a big sheet of paper with my hand and Eclipse's massive claw print side by side. We used it to cover over a deep cut in the wall that Eclipse made when he had his nightmare. We put up silly drawings too. Our room finally looks like a home. It was our way of dealing with the fact that he's going, I guess. To memorialise this space so that no matter what happens, this oversized room on this ship exists as a memento to our friendship.

I feel like Eclipse will be upset with me for not waking him earlier on our final morning together, but I can't stand to when he looks so peaceful. I felt snippets of his dreams while I was asleep: dreams where he's living in this base with me and he calls this place home. Or maybe those were my dreams.

But as much as I want to spend every last minute with Eclipse that I can, what happened with Phoebe is eating me up inside. I need to do something about it. Part of me wants to go running to Calvin about it as if I was a little kid and talk to my big brother about my girl trouble, except telling him about this particular girl would destroy him. Ashamed, I wonder if Phoebe's planning to tell Calvin, or if she already has. He deserves to know. He's my brother and, he's her boyfriend. It's gone too far now and it's my fault.

I fell for the love of my brother's life.

Great plan, Griffin, I chide myself. You really picked a doozy, you and your insatiable hunger for drama.

I feel like a stain on the universe and wish for a moment that the floor would swallow me whole. It's strange to have my feelings for Phoebe feel like a curse, when at the same time my love for her feels so beautiful.

Calvin raised me. No matter how many times we've sparred over the years, all I can think of now is the best times, the ones when he wasn't my antagonist. Growing up, he was my entire world. My hero.

Now he's finally got this happiness, in the middle of all this darkness: Zephyr... and Phoebe. I won't let that be taken from him.

The last thing I want to do is leave Eclipse at a time like this but that's a personal sacrifice I'm just going to have to make. I'll be right back, I just need to make things right. I need to tell Calvin and apologise. The thought makes me feel faint but I have to fix this and do what's right.

So I leave my sleeping Shadow and go to see my brother.

Yes, part of what happened between me and Phoebe was due to the transfer of feelings from Ember and Eclipse and what they were getting up to, but still. I can't believe I would have dared to act on them if my own feelings toward Phoebe weren't already so overwhelming. The thought of seeing the betrayal that might be in Calvin's eyes as he looks at me scares me but I have to talk to him, even if it means the end of us. Even if it means Calvin doesn't want me in this base locked in with him and Phoebe for one second longer. I don't know what will happen then. But the Siren is so close to being ready. Whatever the fallout... we can sort that out after Raven and I save the worlds. I just hope the future we create is one where Calvin and Phoebe are both still part of my life in some way.

At least I won't have to carry the burden of this secret around with me anymore. It's so heavy.

I head to Calvin's office. It's still early in the morning, so I'm not sure if he'll be in. I knock on his door, feeling fairly nauseous.

There's no response.

"Calvin?" I ask timidly, pushing the door open slightly. "Calvin, are you in? We... we need to talk."

I enter, but it's clear pretty quickly that he's not in yet. The space is empty.

He's probably still napping, I think, trying to push away the thought of Phoebe dozing happily in his arms.

Stop torturing yourself with the mental images, Grif! That's not cool. That's their own business.

Still. I hope that bastard knows how lucky he is.

But as I head to leave, I suddenly hear voices approaching the office. One of them is Calvin's, and I recognise the other. Phoebe.

Seriously, you have to be kidding me.

Without thinking, in a fight or flight moment, I run from the door, vaulting over Calvin's desk and curling into the foetal position to hide from sight behind it. It's cowardly but it was my gut reaction.

Great one, Grif, I think, mortified. *I'm sure he didn't come into his office to use his own desk.*

I am so freaking dead.

The door pushes all the way open, and I hear Phoebe

and Calvin speaking in low voices. They don't seem to care that the door was partially open. From Phoebe's voice, it sounds like she's been crying.

The voices fall silent.

Fudge, fudge, fudge...

I can't hear their footfalls anymore. Swallowing, I peek ever so slightly, foolishly, around the corner of the desk. Just a single eyeball.

Phoebe is hugging Calvin tightly and he's encircling her in his embrace. She pulls away, and I can see the tears on her cheeks. I did that, I think, feeling her hurt as my own.

"What is it?" Calvin asks softly, stroking Phoebe's chin with a thumb. "Hey, what's wrong?"

She shakes her head, unable to speak for a moment.

"Nothing," she manages. "Just... I'm being stupid."

"That has never been a word I've associated with you."

She smiles, but it's a wonky smile.

"I have you," she says. "I have Ember back. I've got everything I could wish for."

So she hasn't told Calvin what happened. That only makes me guiltier. Phoebe's left him in the dark, carrying that all on her own. I'm the reason that the two of them have secrets between them now.

I hear footsteps getting closer, and my stomach flips. I'm about to explode out of my hiding place, confessing why I'm here, when I hear something being set down on the desk above me.

Bizarrely, music starts to play. Calvin must have placed his phone down, I realise, and the tune is playing through its speakers.

It takes me a moment to recognise the song. It's 'Drops of Jupiter' by Train.

There's the sound of careful footsteps. I peer ever so slightly around the side of the desk again, hypnotised. I'm unable to look away as Calvin gently takes Phoebe's hand in his left and her waist with his right.

She blinks away tears, apprehensive.

"What are you...?"

Calvin gently starts to dance. Phoebe is robotic at first, staring at him in tear-stained shock. Calvin looks dorky at first going at it alone, but then I see Phoebe laugh through her tears, and she starts to join in. As they both warm into it, it turns out Calvin has some moves.

Calvin and Phoebe's dance moves grow bigger, more energetic, and I watch as he suddenly spins her round. Phoebe swirls before she comes back together with him, breathless, pure joy etched on her face.

The moment is magic, and the two of them together... man, they can dance.

I realise I'm smiling, surprising me completely. I can't help it. Even with my longing and quiet envy, I can't help but smile at the love between these two people I care about. Seeing them here together joined in this secret dance, as Calvin helps Phoebe wash away her sadness for one blissful moment, I can see it for the first time. The two of them are made for each other.

That's when I know I'm done. That's when I know that any private hopes I might have held onto that one day in some way Phoebe and I might end up together instead of the two of them... it's over.

"Thank you," Phoebe whispers as the music fades.

"I love you," I hear Calvin tell her softly, and I hear them gently kiss.

Looking past Calvin, Phoebe's gaze shifts in my direction. I pull my head back behind the desk, blushing hard. My heart rate is through the roof. Well, this is a new low, I think. Please tell me she didn't see me.

After a few tense seconds, I hear more soft murmuring. I exhale as quietly as possible, ridiculously relieved. I don't think Phoebe saw me. I hear footfalls leaving, then the door opens and closes. I relax.

But just before I check if I can step out of my hiding place, the door opens again. I shrink back into my hiding place, gulping. I hear talons clattering on the floor.

Finally, I hear Calvin speak in a quiet voice.

"Any response yet?"

"They're still deliberating. It's a long shot, you know that." It's Zephyr. It must just be the two of them in here with me. From their tone, I can tell this is definitely not a conversation that the two of them would be happy to know I'm eavesdropping on.

Human and Shadow counterparts can communicate privately and silently through telepathy, which is a mix of thoughts and feelings as well as words. A lot of the counterparts in here though prefer verbal exchanges, as it makes it a lot easier to be exact about your true meaning.

It's also easier to eavesdrop on.

"I'm quietly confident," Calvin responds. "The war is worse than ever. It's making the worlds unliveable. They'll soon be prepared to go for options that would have been entirely unthinkable a month ago." Calvin hesitates. "You're having second thoughts."

"I was prepared to do whatever it took to finish this," Zephyr says, and I'm surprised by the emotion in his voice. "I know that blindly following any goal can lead to evil. I also know the importance of thinking outside of ourselves, even if it breaks me. I was ready before Eclipse came here. I was ready until I saw how happy him and Griffin are again and how perfect they still are for each other. It's like no time has passed at all since they were two little maniacs in Cameron Technologies."

"They're ready to say goodbye today," Calvin says quietly. "Eclipse is already leaving of his own free will. This isn't on us."

"You can't know that. You can't know the choices they'll make. They've only just gotten each other back and when Griffin finds out what you've done, what *we're* doing... this will kill him. Every single person in this place will blame us, even if they do understand."

I feel a strange creeping sensation up my back.

No. No, Calvin. I thought you'd changed. What are you up to?

"That's the price, you know that. We both do."

"But will we be able to live with it?"

Calvin doesn't answer.

"We should tell the others," Zephyr presses.

"They can't know," Calvin says under his breath, barely audible. His voice is strained. "Not yet. The time is coming, I can feel it."

"But what will happen to your efforts to bond with Griffin if you're successful," Zephyr hisses softly, "and you're the one who takes Eclipse away from him forever?"

16

SOMETHING YOU CAN'T HIDE

"Eclipse!" I shake him urgently. Even unconscious he's casually magnificent. He sleeps upright in his nest, hunched into its warmth, eyes shut. A warrior with scales like burnished armour beneath his feathers. *"Eclipse!"*

What I heard upstairs has left a chill deep inside me. I still can't believe it. I needed to tell someone to help me make sense of it, so I rushed back to our room as fast as I could. Eclipse will help. There's no problem that exists which Eclipse's courage and his prodigious powers can't overcome.

He shuffles, reaching out with one of his wings to trap me under it. His serpentine tail knocks me off my feet, sweeping me into his side.

"This is... not the time... for snuggling!" I say, annoyed, trying to wriggle free. I prod him. "Hey buddy, I need you pretty bad right now, okay? Our brothers are up to something messed up, and I know it's your last day but I need you." I'm jabbering. All the possibilities of what they could be up to are flying through my brain. I thought I was so smart, leader of the GSA, secretly working on a cure for the war which most couldn't comprehend. Calvin though was my Achilles heel, the one threat that I didn't see coming. What have Calvin and Zephyr been up to while I wasn't looking, while I was distracted with Eclipse instead?

After I overheard Calvin and Zephyr they took some files off the desk and thankfully left. Immediately I wanted to break into Calvin's computer to hunt for answers, but all of our computers require a boot password. Without knowing his password I couldn't even turn it on, and all of my guesses at it failed.

Eclipse is still asleep, but suddenly he spasms, alarming me. His peaceful expression distorts into fear. Before I know it, I'm being pulled into his dreams, trapped there. No... they're memories. They're so vivid this time that I can't escape them, even as I try and raise the barrier between us. They come flooding over it, submerging me...

"Oh no, come on, not again..." I groan. "This isn't the time Eclipse, we need to..."

I'm watching Hanna confront Eclipse in their grand war tent. It's just the two of them in here, but the whiff of defeat is thick in the air. The sound from the camp outside is oddly subdued.

"No. Don't you dare give up," Hanna tells Eclipse, tears of anger in her eyes.

"Galvanize's forces are moving in on us," he reminds her, despondent. There's a weight to his words that I've never heard before. He sounds like a man marching to his grave. "They outnumber us and when they make it here they'll slay every last one of our followers. We've lost."

"We can't have lost!" Hanna shouts. "Not now. Not after everything!"

Eclipse looks at her.

"We can't win, Hanna," he says softly, and in that moment I can feel the depth of his feelings for his friend. The last thing he wanted to do was let her down, when she had risked everything by trusting him.

"Then we go down fighting," Hanna swallows, "but ordering them to break up the camp and flee in separate directions..."

"This way we fight again another day."

"It sounds a lot like you're dismantling what we've built," she says witheringly, "like you're giving up. You're not allowed to, Eclipse. We're a team. This is a group decision, you hear me? We'll face the end together, the two of us, just how we started all of this."

The moment vanishes, shifting into another memory. Now Eclipse is standing forlornly in a garden surrounded by the desert. A moon hangs enormous and full up above him. The garden is mainly made up of a twisting spiral maze of plants, the curving paths that lead through it paved with crushed sea shells. I don't know what this place is, who maintains the garden or who would have gone to the effort to bring seashells all the way here across the desert sands. The space feels sacred and very ancient.

Eclipse also looks very alone. I search for the vague outline of his camp somewhere on the horizon, but I can't see it. I don't know where he is.

There's a sudden whispering, and I hear the subtle scraping of metal against leaves. Soldiers start to appear in the surreal garden, stepping out of the spiralling greenery to encircle

Eclipse. He looks down at them all, surveying them. They're all wearing the violet armour of the Empire.

Once the Imperial soldiers are all in position, their spears with wicked tips directed up at him, they surround Eclipse twenty to one. I'm sure he could still take them out with no trouble. But strangely he doesn't. He doesn't make any move at all.

I want to ask him what he's doing, I want to scream at him, but I can't. It's his memory. Whatever is happening, it's the past. The outcome here is already set in stone.

"Well, look who came to us," one of the soldiers taunts Eclipse. The speaker is a tyrannosaurus with deep purple scales, covered in something like warts. His lurid green pupils glow with amusement in the night.

Someone jabs Eclipse with their spear, and he flinches, but he doesn't act.

The circle of soldiers all laugh in camaraderie, delighted to have the most powerful Shadow in the world at their mercy.

"Remember," Eclipse says shakily. "I'm the one Galvanize..."

"Empress Galvanize!" the tyrannosaurus spits.

"I'm the one that Empress Galvanize wants. If I die, so does my uprising. I'm her prize."

Oh, Eclipse. No. No, what are you doing?

One of the guards raises a blow-pipe to his lips, aimed directly at Eclipse's chest.

"Hanna," I hear him whisper right at the moment before he's shot. "Griffin. I..."

Then he's struck by a dart, followed by two more. Seconds later the mighty dragon-parrot stumbles. Everything in the memory starts to blacken and curl around me. The last thing I feel is Eclipse's mind as he recognises what the dart contained. One of the few things that can bring him, the unstoppable titan, down.

Poison from Galvanize's own stingers. Eclipse's kryptonite.

He collapses, and the garden, the soldiers and the moonlit desert all fall into darkness.

A new memory follows, but it's distorted, and through it I feel Eclipse's fiery pain.

I can just make him out, his giant form strung up by unbreakable chains that pull his wings and his legs wide, like a Vitruvian Man. He's suspended from the ceiling of a musty, straw-laden cell as if he's a stuffed bird: his wings stretched for prime display. His head is hung low in shame and anguish. I can't imagine what the Empire has done to him, although the traces of blood in his feathers give me a clue. I feel sickened.

I sense Eclipse's murky thoughts as he wonders, just for a moment, what it will feel like to stop existing.

The name Eclipse will still mean something, *he thinks to himself.* I fought. I tried to help others. I know who I am now.

Eclipse hears the procession of feet, and he feels a familiar bolt of fear. A moan escapes him. When he looks up through bleary eyes, Empress Galvanize herself is standing in front of him.

I hear Eclipse dully reflecting how long it's been since he last saw the insane dictator in person, when he and Hanna escaped her clutches back in the city of Midnight Crafters. Galvanize looks just as hideous now as she did to him then. Her green insectoid face, the bulbous purple eyes and the mandibles fixing into her version of a wicked grin. Her flawless violet armour and the long cloak that billows after her do nothing to counter her demonic vibe.

She's so small, Eclipse muses. He could crush her with his foot, if he wasn't bound and rendered helpless. Galvanize looks up at him with mocking interest, as if she's examining a prehistoric leviathan at a museum.

"This is a sad sight," Galvanize says demurely. Eclipse feels exposed. Every part of him is laid bare. "No witty retorts? No smug superiority?"

"If you're going to kill me, just kill me already," Eclipse breathes, and closes his eyes. "Just let it end."

That darkness doesn't scare him. Not anymore.

I cry for him, but neither he nor Galvanize can see me. I want to break Eclipse out of there, but I know that I'm powerless to stop his pain.

"Oh, this won't end anytime soon, Eclipse," Galvanize whispers to him. She takes a step closer, smiling as if she knows something he doesn't. "Killing you would be such a waste. No. When my people are done with you, you'll beg to be my obedient pet... and the two worlds will finally be mine."

I surface in horror. I can still taste blood on the air. I come to my senses fully, becoming aware of Eclipse sleeping with his wing around me. He's still slumbering uneasily. His erratic breaths fill the air.

The truth of the terrible memory I just witnessed crashes through me. I swallow, shivering in nameless horror. Everything feels cold.

Slowly I push myself away from Eclipse's reptilian hide, as it expands and contracts with his breaths. Carefully I extricate myself from under Eclipse's wing. The nest of odd debris rustles noisily, and with every slight movement I make I'm terrified that I'll wake him.

For a moment I'm afraid that my legs will give out under me or that Eclipse will wake and see me escaping.

The Empire caught him. They held him prisoner for who knows how long, breaking him down, physically and mentally, burying these memories deep down where I'd struggle to find them, hiding them maybe even from Eclipse himself. Maybe part of Eclipse wanted me to see them and that's why he showed them to me. I hope that's the case. I hope my Eclipse is still in there.

Empress Galvanize brainwashed Eclipse to use him as her secret weapon. A Trojan horse, I realise, the irony too much to bear. And we brought him straight into our base: a ticking time bomb.

Now that the vapour has cleared outside Eclipse is free to tear this place apart. He can remove the GSA as a threat to the Empire and their war efforts, escaping back to the Shadow world to report to Empress Galvanize directly.

I remember the video threat that Empress Galvanize had broadcast through the human world three months back, the strange radio silence we've been getting from her side. We knew something was coming. I just hadn't anticipated that it was this.

No, no, no. Please, Eclipse, don't do this.

Does he know what's happening? Or has he been a sleeper agent all this time, waiting for some signal to be activated by Galvanize?

I'm scared that when Eclipse wakes, I'll find out.

Once I'm out of the nest, I quietly release my breath. I'm not sure how long I've been holding it for.

Then I tiptoe slowly over to the doorway, careful not to make a single sound. My whole body is shaking.

"Where are you going?"

I go still. Slowly, as if I'm moving in a nightmare, I turn to face Eclipse in the dim light spilling into the room. A smile is frozen on my face as I stare back at him in his nest. His own lopsided grin is so genuine. As I race to make up some excuse, Eclipse yawns and clambers out of the nest. My chest constricts. Eclipse struts around me, stretching his stiff legs... and comes to a stop.

Whether by accident or not, he's now standing between me and my only escape.

I force myself to think of anything but what I gleaned in his head, not wanting to give myself away. I think of Phoebe's grin and of the smell of Burger Max. I think of memories of my Mum tucking us into bed and kissing me goodnight.

"Morning, sleepyhead," I say to him.

"What time is it?"

"About ten? Sorry, I let you sleep in."

Eclipse blinks. He looks disappointed to realise how much of our morning we've already lost. That, at least, seems real.

"You doing a breakfast run?" Eclipse grins, recovering. "I'll have seven burgers and some blue cheese side dip. Also, two litres of black coffee." His tone is so warm, the light dancing in his eyes playfully. The nightmarish visions of his capture, torture and interrogation that I found buried in his psyche seem so far away. So impossible.

"I'll see what I can do," I answer him, smirking. "But I just need to head to the bridge for a quick sec."

"Has the vapour cleared away yet?" Eclipse says, stretching languorously. "Is it safe to leave the base?" I see a dangerous glint in his eye, his talons clattering on the steel floor. I take in that cool smile.

"That's why I was heading up there," I say, feeling my pulse accelerate. "I'm just going to check if it's safe for you to fly to the Brisbane portal."

Eclipse moves out of my way, circling back around me. I feel a flicker of hope.

"Great," he says. "Let's go."

My stomach tightens. Smiling, I nod. I leave our room, hearing his heavy footfalls trailing close behind me as we make our way out toward the glowing blue tanks and the stairs beyond them. I keep my breathing nice and slow. In and out. In and out.

Secretly, behind the inane images I'm putting up as a defence, I'm turning over in my head all of the events since Eclipse came back here. The intelligence that Ember was being held captive must have been leaked, I realise. I was meant to find that. Eclipse met us at Troy intentionally, and we brought him back here. All planned.

Surely there's some way to get through to him, to stop him from hurting everyone. I need to get to a place where I can operate the security controls for the base. Eclipse is near invincible and unstoppable. The best chance I have to incapacitate him is if I manage to shut some of the emergency gates in the ship, locking Eclipse into one of the passages and knocking him out with sleeping gas. It might be enough to stop him. Maybe. Last I checked he had the power to create jutting spikes of earth like miniature mountains wherever he wanted, but he easily could have picked up the power of any other Shadow in this base since then. The element of surprise is all I have over him.

When we're close enough to the bridge, I'm going to have to make a run for the controls. Whether Eclipse catches me or not will decide everything.

We make our way up through the floors of the base, getting smiles and morning greetings from Sophie, Blanca, Molly and Grindelbark on the way up. I want to communicate to them the terrible danger that we're all in, but I can't say anything without giving it away to Eclipse, so I just force a smile and nod.

I don't know if Eclipse is even conscious of his true reason for being here, if Galvanize really turned my Shadow or if he's just been brainwashed to act at a certain time. But I don't want to be the one that triggers Eclipse to annihilate this base without barely having to lift his tail.

I can do this. I *have* to do this.

I can feel the cold sweat drenching my body.

We're almost at the tunnel to the bridge when I suddenly see some of the GSA rushing between the rooms. There are raised voices and shouts. It's a suspicious frenzy of activity.

"What's that about?" Eclipse says warily, and I feel him readying himself for action.

"Don't know," I say, in what I hope is a disarmingly casual voice. My pulse quickens. The attack alarm hasn't sounded, so I can only think that they're all reacting to some new Intel that's come in. Could it be that they know what I know? Has the information leaked somehow that Eclipse is working for Galvanize?

"Don't you think we should check in?" Eclipse says pointedly. "Shouldn't we see what that's about?"

"They've got it covered," I say, firmer this time. "You're about to leave forever, Eclipse. I just want to check we can get you back home safely."

There. We're at the start of the tunnel. I stare down it to the entrance to the bridge: that's my goal. It's the only shot I've got. Obscuring my thoughts from Eclipse, I try to calculate what point down the corridor we can reach before I should make a break for it on my own, trying to seal the tunnel behind me in time. I need the best chance possible of reaching the controls in there before Eclipse can catch me.

There's a TV screen positioned in the hallway, and it's playing coverage from a 24/7 human news channel. Something pulls my gaze slowly toward that screen. I see the headline banner along the bottom of it.

EMPRESS GALVANIZE CONFIRMED DEAD, the headline reads.

Time seems to freeze.

I stare at the headline. It doesn't make any sense, and I'm so focused on the immediate threat of Eclipse, who I've established as Empress Galvanize's secret weapon, that my brain almost can't process another brain-quaking revelation.

Empress Galvanize is dead. The leader of the Shadow world has been killed.

The date they're displaying for her death was two days before the battle at Troy.

How can that be?

"Griffin?" Eclipse says suspiciously, noticing that I've stopped. He hasn't seen the TV yet.

Galvanize is dead. That doesn't mean the war is over though, part of me thinks inwardly, before my conscious mind can possibly grasp the implication.

Doesn't that at least mean that we're not in danger from Eclipse, or was her brainwashing influence already in place before she died?

Suspicions are starting to crawl through my mind. I'm reliving the last few days in my head since Eclipse arrived here, examining them from all angles. I'm piecing together the clues that were lying jumbled and locked away in Eclipse's mind, which I was too slow to put together.

I need to know. What's most likely to be the truth? What's the right thing to do strategically? Figuring out those answers is meant to be what I'm best at. It's my job. I can't distance myself from the situation though, I can't find that cool, calm trance which has helped me guide our members unscathed through war zones, because my heart *is* the war zone.

For a moment I'm not here. I'm back in the dark, rainy skies of Sanctuary City again, a city filled with violet banners. I'm flying up higher and higher, sharp claws digging into me as Cirrus hoists me up toward the Clock Tower above.

Empress Galvanize is dead.

Part of me knows what that means, but it's impossible. Unreal.

We're in more danger than we could ever have known.

My entire world changes and at the same time I feel I've always been heading to this moment, reading that headline on the screen as I stand beside my Shadow.

"What is it?" Eclipse asks, voice darkening. He cranes his neck to read the words on the screen to see why I'm suddenly stricken.

Now I know that there's only one thing I can do.

I bolt down the tunnel toward the bridge, knowing that I have to make it, and that the stakes are the future of two worlds.

There's silence behind me. Just for one moment.

Then Eclipse lunges after me.

I sprint down the tunnel, as I don't know how many kilos of muscle, talons and beak come striding after me.

If I so much as stumble I know that I'll have no hope. I feel a rush of air as talons clench shut right behind me, attempting to trap me. But the passage to the bridge is a fraction too small for Eclipse, slowing him down. Then I'm flying through the door to the bridge. There's no one here. I leap over the ramp, skid across to the desk and reach my keyboard.

I jam a combination of three keys at once. Luckily I don't have to sign in to access the base's security measures.

The circular entrance to the bridge seals shut, shards of indestructible glass sliding into place to lock it shut. The impact of Eclipse smashing into it is deafening. I'm scared the barrier will shatter from the force of it.

I quickly seal the other end of the tunnel leading to the bridge. Eclipse is trapped now, alone in the tunnel. He surveys me through the glass. His feathers are raised, his crest pressed back against his head. A low rumble escapes him as he glowers at me.

My fingers fly across the keys as I double-check that the ends of the tunnel are sealed. I select the confined area so that the nozzles concealed in the roof will release knockout gas into the chamber, and I rapidly calculate a dose that's likely to tranquilise Eclipse without causing any medical complications. My finger hovers over the final key to release the gas. Doing so will activate all of the emergency alarms in the base, bringing all of the GSA to attention. If my gas fails, they'll try to incapacitate Eclipse by any other means necessary.

Whatever we do to Eclipse, we do to me too, I realise, remembering how I passed out when he was struck by the missile. But I'll do whatever it takes to prevent him from hurting the people here.

The Siren too, I think, feeling another wave of fear. The

Siren has to survive. Raven and I are so close to fixing all of this. Why did this have to happen now?

My brow is slicked with sweat. My finger is still hovering over the final key.

Eclipse and I eye each other, facing off. I try not to show him how messed up I am.

This isn't him, I tell myself. He's still brainwashed. You'll get your Eclipse back.

The problem is that I'm not a hundred percent sure that I believe that anymore.

Eclipse is scanning the shut door, taking the measure of it, tracing a talon along the glass. I don't doubt he could make quick work of that door if he really tried, but he can see that I'll press the key before he gets a chance.

"Griffin, what is this?" Eclipse implores me, frustrated. "Why are you freaking out? Just talk to me."

His voice is familiar and hypnotically convincing.

But I don't trust it. My finger moves closer to the key that will gas him. I don't know why I'm hesitating.

"Do you really think that will even slow me down?" he says quietly. His voice is suddenly deadly.

"Only one way to find out," I tell him, my voice hard, disguising the trauma in my heart. I'm searching his eyes with my own, looking for proof of what I secretly suspect.

"Let me leave, Griffin," Eclipse says. He flexes his talons subconsciously, his eyes fixed on where my finger hovers. "You know that you're not going to push it."

The metal floor beneath the sealed door erupts. A slab of rock stabs upward, crushing and fracturing the sealed door instantly.

'Griffin?' Zephyr's voice crackles over my intercom. '*What the hell was that?*'

With a sucking sound, the miniature mountain slides back down out of existence, leaving only fragments of shattered door between me and Eclipse. He strides into the bridge, indomitable. There's nothing between us now.

"Griffin," he warns, "don't..."

Then my mind is wrestling with his, will against will, like two serpents twisting and undulating. Our psyches snap at each other as I try to get under and around his defences, reaching for the incriminating memories that he's buried the furthest down, the memories that have the answers I've been hunting for since he first arrived...

Eclipse is suspended in Galvanize's torture cell, hanging exhausted from the chains. He stirs as he hears shouts and cries, followed by the sounds of battle. He feels a flare of hope, despite how false and cruel that hope has begun to seem after all his time at the Empire's mercy.

Back in the bridge, Eclipse roars, his mind fighting me, struggling to step closer despite my mental onslaught...

The clashing and screams inside the Imperial city continue for what feels like an age but can't have lasted any meaningful length of time. Eclipse waits with dread, wondering who's dying on the other side of those walls, the limits of his universe.

Finally a battering ram smashes open the doors to his cell. A group of Shadows come stumbling in. Eclipse stares at them, confused.

Then Hanna flies over their heads. She hurtles at Eclipse and embraces him tightly around the neck, hovering there. A wound is spilling blood down her cheek.

"You're okay," she sobs. "You're okay, it's over."

"You're not real," he whispers at her, trembling.

"I am. This isn't a trick, Eclipse. Our people are taking Opal Towers. You're safe now."

Eclipse's mind fights back against mine and I cry out. Images flare through our shared consciousness. He drags from me the memory of standing over Raven and Winter in the cell at Troy. I see myself hauling Calvin off Raven in the Asylum. I see myself standing before the others months ago, about to pitch my new idea of a kind of amplification...

No. I can't let him see that. I can't let him figure out that I'm responsible. Maybe it doesn't matter now with us already facing off, but I don't want to give him any other reasons to see me as his enemy. I fight back harder, digging even deeper while defending my own memories...

I'm back in the Imperial city of Opal Towers, but for the first time I can see more of it than just the inside of Eclipse's interrogation chamber. The namesakes are what first draw my attention, the undulating towers like massive pillars cut from opal. They contain fierce flecks of rainbow colours that burn when they catch the sun. The streets of the city are decorated with beauty, with fountains and blossoming plants. Some of it is looking a bit worse for wear what with the battle being waged throughout the city.

Citizens and refugees are still clashing with the few Imperial soldiers who are stubbornly holding out. Limping out of his cell, Eclipse lashes out with his tail, sending some violet-armoured soldiers flying. Then he launches himself into the air. He's wounded, every part of him straining from disuse after being tied up and imprisoned. But he forces himself onward, flying high above the fray, all of his focus on one place: the highest tower of the Imperial Palace.

At last his talons grasp the rail of the stone balcony, and Eclipse squeezes himself through the grand windows, shredding the curtains as he enters the Empress' throne room. I can feel him trembling from all that he's suffered, but he stalks into the chamber anyway, determined to stop Empress Galvanize's cruelty forever. The hell won't be over until she lies dead.

He feels something wet beneath his talons. Eclipse blinks. He looks down to see a pool of blood running red through the throne room. He follows the blood to an insectoid body, lying prone amidst her violet robes.

"Galvanize?" Eclipse says uncertainly, moving toward her. This isn't what he expected. Suspiciously, he searches the room around him for where guards may be hiding, twitching at any possibility of a trap.

Galvanize coughs wetly, grinning up at him with blood smeared around her mandibles.

"How the mighty have fallen," she giggles. Then, her mandibles twitching in agony: "He was meant to love me!"

"Galvanize?" Eclipse asks hesitantly. "Who did this?"

But her body is still. The ruler of the Shadow world has drawn her final breath. Her murderer a mystery.

Eclipse tries to find something in him, to feel some emotion at the death of the Shadow who tortured him time and time again. But there's nothing. All he can hear is the wind as it billows the shredded curtains.

Empress Galvanize's mandibles are stiff with death. He can't tell if her last frozen expression is a laugh or a silent scream.

Eclipse lights upon the sandstone stage in the city square below, his people and the citizens of the Imperial City pressing in at all sides. He can feel the fear of the Imperials, but also their overwhelming curiosity. Eclipse stares out at his followers, the underdogs, the downtrodden and dispossessed who managed to bring down a global Empire. Out before him, more and more Shadows are clustering in. including violet-armoured imperial soldiers who look somewhat lost.

I can feel the terrible pain that Eclipse is in, his legs barely holding him upright after the days of interrogation by Galvanize's henchmen. He hides it well, though. He looks every inch a legend as he calmly surveys the people before him: the people he was ready to sacrifice his life to save.

Seeing Eclipse up there on the stage, I can't help but think of the Cirrus I grew up with, and how far he's come.

"Empress Galvanize is dead," Eclipse says, and hushed whispers ripple through the massive crowd. "The evil of Galvanize's reign is behind us. Now there is only forward. No more Shadows living in total fear of their rulers. No more Shadows believing that there's something wrong with them that requires 'treatment.' No. We stand united to create something better. Together, we'll reclaim our world and rebuild it, but first we have to defeat a far greater threat." Eclipse surveys them, and I can see the trauma in his eyes, and the courage too. "First we must drive back the human threat," he declares, "once and for all!"

The crowd ripples as all of the Shadows before him fall to one knee. Eclipse watches transfixed as the citizens of the Empire bow down before him.

"Long live," one of the violet-armoured soldiers cries, startling him, "Emperor Eclipse!"

17

FACE-OFF

I'm remembering Cirrus' lair in his secret haven above Sanctuary City, where he would hide his artfully foraged odd knick-knacks from the human world. That clock tower had been his getaway where he was safe from the Empire's prying eyes, and his brother who worked for them too.

I remember when Zephyr, choosing the Empire over his own flesh and blood, disowned Cirrus because of his connection to me.

Cirrus had been lost at the hands of the Empire who had tormented him knowingly and unknowingly his entire life. I wish I could have saved him from that.

Emperor Eclipse.

My Cirrus, now the ruler of an entire world. Innocent, kooky Cirrus with his debatable social skills.

Now he's the Emperor who has succeeded Galvanize and Hanna to the throne of the Shadow world. He's the commander of the war effort against the human world. As far as my world is concerned? He's Public Enemy Number One.

Eclipse must have come here for something. He's the head of the Empire now. He used our past history to get inside our base. I'd wondered if the Empire had brainwashed him somehow when he was in captivity, but the truth?

Eclipse *is* the Empire.

We look at each other through the glass, and we both know the truth. He knows that I know.

I'm not here to hurt anyone, Eclipse says softly. *I have to get back to my world.*

Of course he does. He knows that if he's captured and held hostage then his people could be strong-armed into submission by the capture of their new precious Emperor.

I just came here for answers, Eclipse says urgently. *Please, let me go home.*

"What would you have done to me before I sealed that door on you?" I challenge him. I'm pretty traumatised. The Emperor of the Shadow world has been sleeping beside me all this time, lying with his mind, his words and his heart. "You're my Shadow; you wouldn't hurt me, right? If you hurt me, you hurt yourself. If I die, we both do."

Griffin, I don't want to hurt you, Eclipse says, anguished. *I just... I want to make you listen.*

If we trap Eclipse here, it will give us a strong negotiating position with the Shadow world. We'd just have to convince the humans to agree to peace. Can I really let my family be torn in two, though? Could Zephyr really keep his own brother prisoner aboard this ship? What would that do to our family?

It's Eclipse who started this, I tell myself. He's the one

putting us in this position. Eclipse is the most dangerous half of me.

I trace the surface of the single keyboard key with my finger. I prepare to press it. Now that the door between the tunnel and the bridge has been shattered, it means I'll have to flood both the tunnel and this bridge with enough sleeping gas to incapacitate Eclipse. The only trouble is that the amount needed to knock him out might kill me, which would kill him as well.

I have to trust that I can take it. The main thing is stopping Eclipse. If I push this, at least the rest of the base will be alerted. They might be able to find a way to stop him if the gas doesn't work.

But looking at Eclipse, I hesitate, agonising.

He played me. He betrayed us. Eclipse pretended to be a nobody in the war going on, someone persecuted by the Empire, when really he came here to spy on us. Now he knows about our operations, our struggles and our logistics. Jeez, he's the Emperor of the same Empire that pledged to eradicate us from the universe. All of the battles going on throughout the worlds right now are happening because Eclipse allows them to.

My head is swimming.

He has the power to command his army to step down. He could make every single effort to create peace between our two worlds. So why won't he? Why are our worlds still at war?

Because he's the enemy. Humans are only dying at Shadow hands now because Eclipse is giving the orders.

My Cirrus... how could you become this? What happened to you?

There's been some kind of mistake, or... or maybe

there's some kind of crazy explanation for this which will make it all right. I have so many questions...

...but suddenly all of the chaos going through my head quietens. I recall Eclipse's memory of him flying alone in the desert night, talking to me for comfort even though I wasn't there. I remember two giggling toddlers watching movies in bed in Cameron Technologies, back before it was blown up in the event which started this whole hellish war.

Eclipse isn't the only one who's been lying about who he is. I've been hiding something from him that will change everything. Something that goes completely against the new Empire he's reshaping.

If things were reversed, and in a way they soon could be, I'd want Eclipse to forgive me. I'd want him to give me the benefit of the doubt right now.

'Griffin, do you read me?' Zephyr yells over the intercom again. Eclipse flinches at his brother's voice. *'The entrance to the bridge is locked. What are you two up to in there?'*

As soon as I press that key, there's no going back. Everything will be out in the open, and nothing may be the same between me and my Shadow ever again. No happy fairy tale ending of us eating Burger Max together.

I'm tired of only believing the worst in people. I get to decide what kind of a friend I want to be. The one thing I've learnt from the last few days is how incredibly much I've missed our friendship. I refuse to believe that was all fake. In fact, I think it might have almost been enough for Eclipse to give up his throne to an entire world.

Just not quite.

He's my Shadow, and I'd do anything for him.

A cheerful song suddenly starts to play from my computer, completely out of place.

"Bananaphone, Bananaphone, Bananaphone!"

I have the song set as the tone for my automatic news alert. What now, more information on Empress Galvanize's death?

My attention flicks to one of the bridge's displays. I'm staring at a new headline beneath a grandiose painting of Eclipse. I read the headline numbly.

ECLIPSE TO BE CROWNED EMPEROR FOLLOWING DEATH OF GALVANIZE.

When I see that, I know. There's no time to waste.

I lean into the microphone.

"We're fine, Zephyr," I say. "Sorry everyone. Eclipse and I were just messing around. Everyone back to your posts."

I strike a different key on the keyboard, and I hear a hiss from the other end of the tunnel. The door at the entrance to the bridge has unsealed.

Eclipse looks at me, taken aback, as I walk toward him. The news is out. My GSA family will realise any second now that the enemy is on the inside. I have a feeling that being their leader won't matter so much then.

Eclipse simply watches as I extend my hand up toward him.

"Hoist me up," I say, determined. "Let's get you home."

My friend looks down at me, and his thoughts are like storm clouds as he tries to puzzle whether or not this is a trap, and what it is which caused me to change so suddenly.

"Eclipse?" I repeat urgently. "We have to go. *Now.*"

He bends a leg, lowering his head too. Strangely, I think he's bowing to me. I scurry up onto his shoulders.

Then an alarm starts howling through the base, the lights switching to a pulsing crimson.

"Go!" I scream, and then we're off, charging through the base toward the exit.

The whole base knows. They've seen the news. They know that they have an Emperor on board.

Eclipse is in trouble.

Griffin, what's going on? Eclipse asks me tensely.

They know, I say. I'm holding myself in place with the thick layer of golden feathers around his neck. *They know that you're the new Emperor.*

I nearly choke getting the words out. Eclipse reacts with speechless shock, followed by a wave of guilt. Hearing it said out loud makes it more real for both of us. He knows now that I understand the extent of what he's been hiding. Eclipse reaches out to my mind, bringing up another memory to show me willingly this time. It's his kind of confession, I think: a memory that's been carefully buried like a precious gemstone.

I'm in Opal Towers again. The capital of the Empire is lit by morning light. I'm standing with Eclipse at the rear of the rather daunting Imperial Palace. He's crouched on the stone terrace, poised to launch himself into the sky.

"Eclipse!" Hanna is striding toward him from the direction of the palace, fuming. "You can't do this. You can't just go running off on random side-quests now that you're the Emperor."

"I have to, these new cases could be a deadly new threat for all we know. Either Raven or the GSA have to be behind it. Thanks for locating Ember."

Hanna crosses her arms.

"Griffin will have her location too now, thanks to my leak. Just like you asked. What is your grand plan here, exactly?"

"I'll meet Griffin at Troy and ask to visit his base. I'll be back in a matter of days, before the news of my... promotion breaks."

"Yeah, right. You think it's going to be that easy to just jump between worlds? We have no idea how far away the GSA base is."

"Just... just keep a lid on what happened here for as long as possible."

"That's going to be hard; whispers are spreading like rapid fire," Hanna comments. With a flutter her violet wings carry her up to hover above Eclipse's eye level so that he's forced to look up at her for a change. *"Even though we have total control of the Shadow world's media now, I can't guarantee that your cover won't be blown."* Hanna shakes her head, her voice accusatory. *"You know the danger you're placing yourself in. This is suicide. You know why you're really going. You're freaking out about everything. You just want to see him again."*

"Hanna, this is urgent for all of our people. What we've been seeing, these strange changes in the Shadows... if this grows, if it intensifies... it could threaten everything we've built. Someone or something is playing with the minds of Shadows, and I don't want to wait around to see what their objective is."

"What if we're wrong?" Hanna challenges Eclipse. *"What if the GSA hasn't started using brainwashing to end the war? This could be some new human tactic to make Shadows passive, to make us stop resisting. You can't be sure about this."*

"No. But I have to know. We have to be able to rule Griffin and the GSA out."

The vision of the two of them in the early morning light dissipates. I'm clinging to Eclipse's shoulders, charging down the corridor through the GSA base. His giant strides carry us right over the heads of a very startled April and

Celeste. It seems not everyone's gotten the memo just yet of who Eclipse really is.

Now you know all of it, Eclipse tells me.

So Troy was all a set-up? I ask him.

Eclipse's mind studies mine, wretched.

Yes.

You lied.

I know I did. But are you really going to pretend that I'm the only one with secrets?

I almost think of the Siren before I stop myself. He can't possibly know about that. He wouldn't be leaving here if that was the case. That's the entire reason he came here; if I told him about it now I'm sure he'd still destroy it before escaping. He's just doing what he believes is right for his world.

Did you know we were waltzing into a massacre at Troy? I ask him. There are so many pieces I'm trying to match to the rest of the puzzle. *Those were your Imperial soldiers in the city...*

No. Troy had being reoccupied by some devout followers of Galvanize who refused to accept me as leader, Eclipse explains. *I heard they had Ember captive and I knew that you would come for her. But I had no idea Raven was in there. I had no idea the humans were planning an attack or that it would be so dangerous for you. I didn't plan on getting hit by an airborne missile either,* he adds as an afterthought. *Listen, Grif. I was wrong in coming here; the GSA isn't responsible for the strange brainwashing in my world, or whatever it really is. I don't see any reason that Raven would have to lie to us about it being his work, and he's been in prison for a while now anyhow. Yet it's still happening, to both sides. I've seen the news. Despite how much I loathe Raven, I don't think he's the architect of this. The answers I needed aren't here. I knew when I came here that I had limited time, but I had to know, and I had to see you again.*

But what would you have done, my friend, I wonder bleakly to myself, if you'd discovered that I'm the enemy you're searching for after all?

My Siren works. No matter if Eclipse thinks what it's accomplishing is evil, it has the potential to break through the wall of fear in people's minds and let them love their counterparts. I have to prove to Eclipse that it's possible for us to live in peace.

As we're striding down the corridor a metal door starts to slide shut, locking off the route that leads toward the hatch, the only exit out of the ship.

Get down, Eclipse says, and I duck. I feel the impact through my entire body as Eclipse simply rams through the door, metal shredding and flying away around us. The alarm is still howling in our ears.

Eclipse, if you're the Emperor, why don't you end this? I plead, asking the question that's been bothering me most. *Why don't you just end the war now? You know it can't be won. You know that for every human that's killed one of your own will die too.*

"If you find a way to convince the humans that the universe is balancing our deaths on a cosmic scale, do let me know." I feel a flash of fury from him. "In the meantime, us Shadows can be intelligent about how we fight by focusing on gaining strategic footholds and forcing the humans back through the portals. Trying for as few casualties as possible on both sides."

"Why don't you shut down the portals that are under Shadow control, at least?"

"We can't afford to when the human ones are still open.

The human-controlled portals are sites where they can pour infinite military reinforcements into my world. We have to press our advantage. Nothing about this is straightforward, Griffin. You know better than anyone that there's no black and white anymore. I'm going to end this war decisively with as little bloodshed as possible."

I shake my head, despairing. For a moment, I just want to fly far away with Eclipse. I yearn for the open air and winds of the world above, as if they're calling me at a physical level.... at least the air that's not tainted by smoke, ash and chemical warfare. I want us to fly away together, just like Cirrus once asked me to do with him.

I should have said yes.

But we can't run anymore. I can't return to the Shadow world with the Emperor who's disavowed humans, no more than he can stay with me.

The only thing that matters to me now aside from Eclipse's immediate safety is finishing this fight. I have to end the suffering for good.

Finally we make it into the hangar bay where the GSA's two jets are stationed, plus the one commandeered helicopter. I get Eclipse to help me haul the rusty-coloured door closed, locking it behind us. Then I activate the hatch high above and it grinds slowly open, to reveal a cloudy sky backlit with morning sun.

It's beautiful.

I've been holding my breath instinctively in case there's lingering vapour, but the air tastes surprisingly fresh.

"This is it," I say to him, distraught. "You have to go. The Brisbane portal is just North-East of here. Once you're sighted I'm guessing the Shadows there will rush to help you in any way they can. They'll get you home safely."

"Zephyr and the others will know you helped me."

"I'll tell them I tried to stop you, that you knocked out the cameras, erased the footage and dragged me in here as a hostage," I say.

"That makes me sound awfully cunning." He smiles painfully. "Do you think they'll actually believe that?"

"That's my problem to worry about," I whisper softly. "Godspeed, my Emperor."

I can feel his love and his gratitude. It's beyond words, beyond his ability to communicate with the colours and images between our minds.

"Griffin," Eclipse says, "what you've shown me in this place... what I've felt living here for a few days... it's challenged everything I believe."

"Don't say that," I say, rubbing tears away fiercely. "Don't tell me that, and play with my hope, when you know that you're going back anyway. You've chosen what side you're on. So go lead it."

"I wanted to tell you the truth," Emperor Eclipse says. "So, so much." His mind searches mine, overcome. "Aren't you angry?"

"Of course I'm angry. I'm freaking furious, Eclipse." I shove him. He backs up a couple of steps, although I'm sure he barely felt it. "But we made a promise. Our friendship is bigger than this war. We'll do what we have to, but we'll never turn our back on each other. We're still part of each other."

"Griffin..." Eclipse says, emotional.

"You're a freaking Emperor, dude," I say.

"I know."

"That's craaaazy."

"Tell me about it," he gulps.

"You'll make a great ruler," I say, my voice fiercer now. "Undo everything Galvanize did. Make it right. All you have to do is not be crazy or evil and you'll automatically be an improvement on your predecessors. You've got a low bar there. The Shadows don't know how lucky they are yet."

I can feel how touched he is. I can barely stand the guilt tearing at me from the inside out.

Because this is also calculated. If I can get Eclipse out of here without him finding out about what I've been working on with Raven, then the Siren still has a shot at going ahead. If Eclipse was to find out about it, he would tear the engine room out of the ship with his bare talons and destroy the Siren. I have no doubt.

Maybe if I can fire up the Siren and get it to work, then there's still a future for us. I shield the desperate thought so that Eclipse can't hear it.

The only way for Shadows and humans to be together, for me to maybe have a future with Eclipse someday when he's forgiven me, is for me to say goodbye to the big, stupid, brilliant dragon-parrot.

Eclipse searches through me, and frowns.

"What?" I say. He has to leave, we're wasting too much time.

"Calvin and Zephyr's conversation that you overheard. I just saw that memory in your head. I don't know what they're up to, but try this password. It might get you into Calvin's computer."

Eclipse imprints eight glowing numbers into my mind, and I struggle to hold them, to commit them to memory with all the other chaos in my brain.

"How do you know the password to Calvin's computer?" I say suspiciously.

"It's just a hunch. And... I'm sorry about what happened with Phoebe," Eclipse whispers.

"That doesn't matter now," I say, closing my eyes. But that's a lie too. I see her and Calvin dancing together in the hallway, their moment of quiet, effervescent happiness. I don't know if I can bear it. I don't know if I can stand being around the two of them anymore. It was easier to take when I had Eclipse here.

"You've faced far worse and lived," Eclipse says. "You're strong enough for this."

He lowers his head toward me. Taking it in my hands, I stroke the side of his face. His crest rises proudly, quietly chuffed at being adored.

I smile sadly.

"I am so proud to have you as my Shadow, have I told you that?" I ask him gently, my voice breaking.

"I can't ever repay you for this," he whispers. He holds up one of his talons and I curl my fist around it. "Brothers," he promises, "forever."

If the Siren works across two worlds, I wonder silently, and every Shadow and human's consciousness is suddenly pulled toward each other, what does that mean for me and you?

But I don't ask him out loud. Just with my soul. *Our* soul.

There's a crashing sound against the hangar door, and I hear shouts from behind it. They've almost broken in. Took their time.

"Eclipse," I say desperately, the air from outside cold on my cheeks. "Whatever happens between our worlds when this war is over... please don't hate me."

"No hard feelings, no matter what," Eclipse agrees, a

smile quirking at the corner of his beak, "and I could never hate you," he adds softly. "You are truly unique, Griffin Cameron. You're the greatest person I have ever known."

Then I watch him fly upward toward the sun, guilt and pain and longing storming through me. I watch my Shadow leave, shrinking to a tiny dot and then vanishing from sight.

"Please, dude," I say softly. "Forgive me."

18

REMEDY

"We had the Emperor of the entire Shadow world right here in our base?" Calvin explodes, outraged. I guess the tea he drinks that he claims makes him all zen only goes so far. "We had the perfect opportunity to get the Empire to enter peace negotiations, to fulfil the very purpose this organisation was formed for... and we just let him slip right through our fingers!" Calvin stops pacing the bridge and turns to look at us, flabbergasted. "We're a joke. Why should our own members trust us to make the decisions any longer? Not to mention, if Eclipse reveals our location to his Empire, the GSA might as well be done for, along with any hope of us realising our goal. We need to move this ship."

"We're too close to the Brisbane portal," Zephyr says. "That's the problem with hiding under the Empire's noses. If we move a vessel this big, we'll be shot down."

"Then we evacuate everyone on the jets."

"Where to?"

"You know, I hate to say it, but... I did tell you so," I point out.

Zephyr and Phoebe are standing beside me. The floor of the bridge is still littered with shards of glass from when Eclipse broke in. I'm clutching a pile of papers tightly in my hands, not taking my eyes off of Calvin.

He meets my gaze, and some of the steam goes out of him.

"I shouldn't have expected you to choose your family, your organisation and your mission over what Eclipse wants, Griffin," Calvin confesses. "You thought you were protecting him. It would have been a hard decision for anyone."

"I didn't help him escape, if that's what you're suggesting," I lie, feigning outrage at the accusation. "I begged him to stay, but he wasn't having it." Luckily the security footage from the bridge doesn't have any audio. To anyone who watches it, it will hopefully seem that Eclipse ordered me to come with him as a hostage. "Besides," I point out. "What cage could really contain Eclipse for that long anyway?"

"Just wanting to say, speaking as someone who actually *did* keep Eclipse in a cage, that never goes well," Ember chips in sourly. She and Zephyr look rocked by the revelation that Eclipse is the Emperor. The two of them finally look united, in their grief and anger at what Eclipse was been hiding from them.

"I'm sure he wanted to tell you," I tell them, "but he had people who were relying on him. He couldn't risk it."

"Do you really expect us to believe you didn't know?" Zephyr growls. "You have a permanent link into his mind."

Jeez. I can see how Eclipse's lies have cut deep into

Zephyr. He'd finally thought him and his little brother were getting close again.

Still, I feel a wave of anger rising, but Phoebe cuts through him before I can.

"Griffin was worried since Eclipse got here that he could be a double agent working for the Empire. He tried to warn you both but you wouldn't listen," she says promptly. "Neither did I, really. Griffin isn't to blame here. We are."

I look at Phoebe gratefully. It's the first time we've locked gazes since what happened at the party.

Calvin's mouth opens and closes like a fish for a moment. He scratches his chin.

"I'm sorry, Griffin," he admits, embarrassed. "She's right. I didn't mean to take this out on you."

"Oh, I'm sure you can find a way to make it up to me," I say with a hard smile. "Like, I don't know, maybe by working on a secret treaty with Zephyr without consulting the rest of us?"

Calvin goes still. So does Zephyr. The bridge is quiet.

"I don't know what you mean," Calvin says blankly.

"Really? I thought that was pretty specific."

Phoebe looks between us.

"What secret treaty?" she says suspiciously.

I move to my desk and slam the pile of freshly printed documents on the table. Eclipse's hunch about Calvin's passcode had been right somehow. Phoebe and Ember come over to examine the papers.

"Zephyr and Calvin have been lobbying the UN Security Council to have this approved behind our backs," I tell Phoebe and Ember. "If they get the Council to approve it, they'd just need the Empire to ratify it."

"What's in this treaty?" Phoebe demands, her attention

fixed on me. She's not looking at Calvin. Maybe she's afraid to.

"They're calling it the Treaty of Total Separation," I say, smirking humourlessly. "It's proposing that the worlds close down the portals: all of them, forever. Every single Shadow and human would return to their own world. The two worlds will never interact again. The GSA members who are Shadows would have to voluntarily return to the Shadow world as an example for everyone else to follow. Ember and Zephyr would have to return to their world for the rest of their entire lives. We'd never see them again."

Phoebe and Ember look just as appalled as I feel. I can't believe that my own brother would do this and betray Mum and Silvaluna's mission. That mission used to be the only thing he cared about. Something he would have given his own life for.

I realise that this treaty is exactly what Eclipse wants to happen, which makes this all the harder. Eclipse wants an end to the war and an end to our two species interacting. He thinks the worlds should evolve separately from each other.

This base provided a safe place for all the members we brought here after uniting them with their counterparts. They have no idea that they're now at risk of losing the most important being in their lives thanks to Calvin and Zephyr, who they trust.

"How could you two just agree to give each other up?" Ember says, flabbergasted.

Calvin and Zephyr look at each other achingly.

"We can't stay with each other if it costs millions of lives," Zephyr answers, "or soon: billions."

They must know that everyone here won't go through

with it. No way in hell will Ember or Phoebe go through with any of this.

That doesn't mean I'm not furious. How could Calvin see this treaty as a lesser evil than my Siren? If the UN and the Empire do somehow agree to these terms, there will be nothing we can do to prevent it going ahead.

What kind of a world is worth living in without any Shadows? I just got my best friend back. Even if he's left for now, the idea that I'd never be able to see Eclipse again is intolerable.

The room is dangerously silent. Phoebe puts her head in her hands.

"Tell me this is some crass joke," she says, nearly inaudible.

"I'm sorry we kept this secret," Calvin murmurs, bringing himself to look at Phoebe. I can hear the pain in his voice. How long has he been planning this with Zephyr, the two of them trying to come to terms with it while we all sat in the dark? It makes it worse that the whole time Calvin has been acting like we're one of those perfect families from a breakfast commercial. "It was meant to be a last resort. At the moment we're just trying to find expressions of interest from the Security Council to gain enough support."

Ember is looking between Calvin and Zephyr incredulously.

"You've got to be kidding me," she says. Her feathers are sparking dangerously. "We didn't come this far for *this*. Otherwise, what did all those people die for?"

"They died for nothing," Zephyr says curtly. "You've all seen the direction this war is headed. You saw how the Resistance fell apart, Ember. Our people won't accept living side by side with the humans they've learned to hate and fear."

"Phoebe?" Ember says suddenly. I turn to see Phoebe staring at the ground, her expression haunted. I feel sick for a moment. Finally Phoebe looks at Ember, anguished.

"What if there's no other way?" Phoebe whispers. "What if I hold you to me as the world burns down around us?"

"I didn't watch the Resistance rise and fall, just to…" Ember shakes her head, angry tears in her eyes. Her expression is heart-wrenching. "Silvaluna and Melissa Cameron wouldn't have given up. They would have found a way." Ember storms out. Phoebe watches her go, looking miserable.

"Phoebe," I say quietly. "You can't possibly be considering this."

"Wasn't it you who told me that the GSA isn't accomplishing anything?" she points out. "Didn't you say that this war couldn't be stopped?"

My face burns as I feel Calvin and Zephyr looking at me. That's not exactly the quote I want to be remembered by as leader of the GSA.

"You just got Ember back," I say. "The other people in this base… we can't do this to them. What has all of this been for if we do?"

"I don't know, Grif," Phoebe says honestly. She looks like a broken person. "If this saves all those lives, what right do we have to put ourselves before all those people? We vowed to end the war, to bring peace. Maybe… maybe this is the only way."

I stare at her like she's betraying all of us, which she is.

Calvin, Zephyr, Phoebe. Everyone I counted on. They're faltering at the worst possible moment.

"Let's start thinking of new places we could move our base to. Just in case Eclipse sends people here to stop our operations," Calvin says quietly.

"What if we're seen?" Zephyr says, not liking the idea.

"We can't stay here. And we need to be on the look-out for any activity from the Brisbane portal."

"One thing's for sure," Zephyr mutters. "Treaty or not, we have to find some way for the GSA to make a stroke of progress. After Eclipse, we need a win or this place is finished."

Zephyr's not wrong. Over the next few days I sense that morale in the base has taken a definite turn for the worse. The revelation that Eclipse is now the leader of the Shadow's war effort has broken the heart of this place. Most of the members I pass by don't look at me, or they act supremely awkward, as if they have no idea what to say. I'm alone again. I feel as if that happy day when Eclipse made mountains in the training area was made-up. I even start sensing hostility from some of them. I guess they don't exactly believe I could have missed the fact that my Shadow was the new Emperor. I wouldn't be surprised if some of them think I'm a traitor to our cause like Eclipse, or that the only reason I'm still in charge is because I'm protected by my friendships with the rest of our leadership team.

No one's missed the fact either that the rations are getting scarce, or that the news coming in each day from the frontlines is getting bleaker and bleaker. The violet-armoured soldiers in the field are slowly being replaced with gold-armoured soldiers of the new Empire. Even though Emperor Eclipse's strategy for forcing back the humans involves less bloodshed, the humans are still hungry for blood and victory, and Eclipse can't change a war overnight. The two sides are still locked in a grisly conflict of attrition that neither can seem to escape from.

I deal with it by burying myself in my work with Raven, with a new energy that transcends all the levels of obsession I've had so far. We're perfecting preparations for the final trials and fleshing out our plan of attack for how we're going to distribute the Siren's video across every possible screen imaginable. It's now our only solution, and the clock is ticking.

I've created a solution and Raven has helped me to hone it, to prove that it works. It's time for us to unleash it before the worlds are destroyed or before they separate forever.

A darkness has settled over me since Eclipse left, this bone-deep loss. I'm worried that I'll drown in it. The thought of what he's doing, leading his own kind against mine, is some kind of horrible nightmare. The love and pain are impossible to separate.

Breathing out deeply, I lay myself down in the nest inside our giant quarters and curl up there, staring up at the arched roof. I imagine the presence of a mighty golden dragon-cockatoo beside me, his wing covering me, as if he never left. I smile suddenly at the ludicrous thought that all along I was having sleepovers with an Emperor without knowing it.

"Um... Griffin?"

I look up. Sophie is peering around the corner of the tall

arched doorway, flushed, as if she's embarrassed to be invading a personal moment.

"Hey, Sophie." It's strange seeing her, but also kind of comforting. It brings back memories of stuttering out my Burger Max order to her before I ever worked at that place, back in a normal time before any of this began.

"I'm sorry, I shouldn't have..."

"No, it's okay. Come in. I'm sorry we haven't talked much in the last few days. It's been..." I pause awkwardly. She knows the truth, as well as anyone here. "Well, you know."

Sophie comes in a little bit but then stands a distance from the nest, wringing her hands. She's frozen up like a possum in headlights.

"How did you know I'd be down here?" I ask.

"You miss him," she says simply. "I'd be the same way if I had to say goodbye to my Shadow."

I blink, worried that I'm going to choke up. She takes a breath. "Griffin, I need to talk to you."

"What is it?"

"I just..." Sophie wrings her hands. "I'm thankful for you giving me a home here. My family... I miss them, and I'm worried about them, but this is still where I need to be. I can feel it in my bones. I can protect them best from here. Protect everyone. But to do that... I want you to teach me. If you will."

"Teach you what?"

"Everything. I know I don't have my Shadow," she says, ashamed. "And that messes with me. I want one so bad. The classes that we have here don't all suit me because I don't have a counterpart. I can't be helpful on missions in the same way that some of the others can, but I want to help. I want to know everything you know about Shadows, about strategy and coordinating teams in the field... about anything that might help us end this war. I want to be a part of this, Griffin. I don't want to be waiting on the sidelines."

"So you're here to ask me for... tutoring lessons?"

"Yes." She holds up a finger sternly. "Strictly professional. I only want you to do this if you think I have the potential to be helpful to you, not just as some favour to me because we have a history together."

"You're saying that you could be... my *apprentice*," I say, savouring the word.

Sophie rolls her eyes, smiling.

"Don't let this go to your head."

Another thought has occurred to me as I look at her though. Suddenly my excitement is reaching all new levels.

This is it: the next step. This is what I did all of this for.

"Okay," Sophie says, perturbed by what I'm guessing is a strangely maniacal grin on my face. "Now you're freaking me out."

"What if I told you," I say slowly, "I could introduce you to your Shadow?"

"Don't... don't even joke about that." She frowns. "Griffin? Stop smiling."

I spring to my feet. Sophie looks confused.

"Wait here," I tell her, "and you can't tell *anyone* about what I'm going to show you."

"Are you ready?" I ask in anticipation. The golden device is resting in my hands. The Siren.

Sophie's sitting on the edge of Eclipse's nest. Her hands

can't seem to stay still. It's strange. We're the same age, but for some reason she looks so young to me.

"This isn't some kind of joke, right?" Sophie says rapidly, nervous. "Do you really think you can help me find my Shadow?"

"Yes. I'm about to show you something," I tell her. 'Something you have to keep secret from everyone."

Sophie's gaze shifts to the golden handset. She's fizzing with excitement.

"Do you think she'll like me? Sorry, that's a stupid question."

"What I'm about to show you, you can't tell anybody. That's the price. That's what you have to promise me. Nobody can know about it until it's time."

"Okay, now you're freaking me out more." She can't stop fidgeting.

"Do you accept?"

"To keep a giant secret of yours and hide the fact you've been up to no good somehow in exchange for my Shadow?" She hesitates, but barely. "Yes."

I nod. A smile plays at the corner of my mouth.

"Okay, Mister," Sophie says. "Tell me why you're so proud of this gizmo. What is it exactly?"

The Siren's sleek casing is cold in my hands. It's so small and seemingly insignificant.

"Every Shadow and human have a link between them, right? If both of the counterparts become aware of that link, they can start to listen to each other's thoughts and feel what the other is feeling. But even before they're aware of that connection it already exists, like a radio with the volume turned so low that it's basically on mute."

"Sometimes that's because of distance too, right?"

Sophie asks. "Counterparts can't hear each other if they're far away. There's no way that someone in this world might hear their Shadow's thoughts over in the Shadow world."

"Not necessarily. Sometimes our counterparts still show up in our dreams. Or we'll feel déjà vu, even though it's our Shadow who's lived a moment like this before, not us. This... this is an amplifier. It can allow you to hear your Shadow's thoughts, spoken directly into your head: their wishes, their dreams. It's as if they were right here beside you."

"You're pranking me," she says in wonder.

"I prank you not."

"That's impossible. How did you... how could you... this could end the war." Sophie is overwhelmed. "You *made* this?"

"Yeah."

"Griffin... if you're right about what you've got here, then this is the *answer*."

"The others think it's wrong to force people to hear the minds of their Shadows when they haven't consented and they might not be prepared for it. They believe Shadows and humans have to come to understand their connection slowly by being around each other and if we force it, it could be... traumatic."

"The war that's killing everyone is pretty traumatic too," Sophie points out. "This... this could stop it. It could save our families and friends back home. It could save everyone. Wait," she says suddenly in wonder. "So *you're* the one responsible for what's been happening on the news? Those soldiers who started claiming they could talk to their Shadows in their heads?"

I nod.

"So. Are you ready to meet your Shadow?"

Sophie brushes her finger against the casing of the Siren. Tenderly, as if it's the egg of her Shadow.

"Please," she whispers, like a prayer.

I press the button on the side of the Siren. The screen lights up. I select an icon, then pause.

"What will I feel?" Sophie asks, nervous.

"You'll just hear their voice. It might feel weird, scary even at first. Strange. But the two of you will make sense of it together. You'll feel where she is on the other side, and we're going to find a way to bring her to you, okay? Just like we will with everyone."

"Okay," she says, taking in a breath. "Okay."

I tap the last icon.

"Just look here," I say. I tilt the screen toward Sophie. I hear the strange music emanating from the device; I watch the lights and colours play across Sophie's cheeks as she gazes into the Siren's depths, forgetting to breathe.

I think about the tests I ran on every member of the GSA to learn what made each of their friendships with their counterpart unique, and also what special traits they shared. I remember attaching the electrodes to my own head too down in the engine room, and reliving every happy memory I have of Cirrus/Eclipse. All of that feeling and emotion, everything unique about my connection with my Shadow, is now a part of that video in the Siren. At least my friendship with my Shadow will let billions of others experience that same unbelievable happiness, if not me.

Sophie looks serene as she watches the video's dancing colours, listening to its beautiful music, waiting for that same happiness.

Then, without any warning, she starts screaming.

It's a hideous, terrible sound. Clutching her head, Sophie falls from the edge of the nest and I catch her, then lay her down. She starts to spasm, lashing out in her convulsions.

"Sophie?" I say in horror, dodging an arm before it strikes me in the face. "Sophie!" My eyes flash to the Siren where I've dropped it on the ground. It's still playing its video, the subtle colours shifting and pulsing, the strange hypnotic music still playing. I lunge for it and switch it off, the screen going black.

It doesn't help. Sophie's scream grows and grows, rising to a crescendo. Her eyes roll back into her head. Her body twists violently, jerking grotesquely as if she's possessed.

Then she stops, going completely limp. Her eyes stare unseeingly past me. Like she doesn't even recognise me anymore.

As if we've never even met.

"Sophie?" I whimper, more scared than I've been in my entire life. I check her pulse. She's still alive.

I wrestle my phone from my pocket and dial Zephyr. He answers.

"Sophie's hurt! I need you downstairs in Eclipse's quarters," I shout. "Now!"

Sophie's whispering, and I try to make out the words, but it's nonsense. It's like she's talking to herself, as if she doesn't even realise I'm here.

"Sophie, Zephyr's coming, okay? Everything's going to be okay. I'm so sorry." I sob, holding her hand. "I'm so sorry."

19
ASYLUM

Zephyr takes a breath and presses his claw against Sophie's skin. I watch desperately, catatonic with dread.

Nothing changes.

Clearly, something is very wrong.

We're in the ship's on-board lab which doubles as its medical bay. The sleek lab is massive, cavernous. As one of the largest areas on the ship it serves as storage for critical equipment as well as being set up for any on-board research that we'd thought might be required during the transition.

There are details about it which remind me of our family's old lab at Cameron Technologies, once Mum's pride and joy, but this one feels gleaming and new. Reborn.

The roof here is super high. On both sides are shelving racks that would be big enough to hold trucks, ascending upward. Amongst the various equipment stored up there, I can see Raven's technology which Phoebe recovered from Auckland. This is where Calvin has been spending all of his time, trying to decode the secrets hidden within Raven's contraptions. The back wall of the laboratory is glass, but through it all we can see is the blackness of our ship's underground hideaway.

Surgical equipment runs down from the roof of the lab to hang above us like tendrils, as well a bunch of screens, all currently blank.

As a medical facility this place was built to be state of the art, but with Zephyr able to heal most physical maladies it really hasn't been used much by him other than to hold occasional scheduled health check-ups.

I'm holding onto Sophie's hand, but I don't think she can tell. She's muttering fretfully to herself. From what I can hear some of it is paranoid ramblings, while some of it is incomprehensible nonsense. Now and then a little giggle will escape her, which oddly scares me more than anything else.

It reminds me of the moments when I've lost control myself in here. Like when I was going to meet Eclipse after he arrived and I had a hallucination of Cirrus. Or when Calvin found me in the tunnel from the bridge with no memory of how I got there, laughing hysterically.

Calvin had said it was being at war with the other half of me which had done that to me. When I used the Siren on Sophie, did I somehow fracture the part of her brain that connects her and her Shadow, causing her cognitive damage? Is that why instead of being happy and filled with awe at hearing her Shadow as she'd looked forward to, she's a gibbering shell of the Sophie I know? Or was it my connection with Eclipse which I used to hone the Siren, infecting her with the same volatility that's now in me?

Phoebe is sitting loyally beside me, like she's on vigil, a

personal guard who will lash out at anyone who tries to mess with me. She's reading my body language, she knows me that well. She doesn't try to touch me or hug me, even though I can tell she's desperately fighting her instincts to comfort me.

I wish she was miles away.

I can't look at her. I can't look at any of them, but especially her.

Calvin meanwhile is standing nearby, extremely uncomfortable. I can tell he wants to make things better, but he's unsure how to act around me. What to say or do.

"It's such a tragedy. Such a sad day," he mumbles, clearly at a loss. Hesitantly, he reaches for my shoulder with a hand, but I recoil.

"I don't want to talk right now," I mutter, wishing the floor would swallow me whole and stop me from having to live with this. "I just want to know she's going to be okay."

Finally, Zephyr pulls away from Sophie. His eyes betray just how bad it is.

"It's not good, Grif," he says heavily.

No. She can't be gone. Not forever. This isn't the end for her.

"Have you tried...?"

"The brain is a sensitive and complex organ. Healing it is often beyond the scope of my powers. The scans I ran haven't given us any clues, and my power still doesn't seem to be working."

"What happened to her?" Calvin asks me, hushed.

"I don't know." The guilt and shame that I feel keeps intensifying with every lie that passes my lips. "We were just in the room, talking, and then..." My throat closes up, and thankfully it won't let me say anymore.

Sophie had to be sedated when I brought her in. Zephyr had barely started trying to examine her when she started lashing out violently, going berserk like she was being attacked. Nam had helped me bring her down to the lab; he's going to have a black-eye and some nasty scratches tomorrow.

It was scary.

Now, at least, Sophie's serene. Her expression is vacant.

"I recommend we hold her in one of the rooms in the De-escalation Area for the moment," Zephyr says.

"The Asylum? You can't put her in there," I say fiercely.

"Don't call it that," Phoebe says sharply. "You know that nickname has all the wrong associations. She'll be okay there, Griffin. This is for her own wellbeing, so she can get better."

"I can't say for sure that there won't be more violent outbursts, so we need to keep her safe from herself as well for the meanwhile," Zephyr says. "We'll monitor her to see if there are any changes and keep assessing the situation."

"She was just scared," I mumble. "She's okay now, isn't she?"

"She nearly hurt herself, too, Grif," Calvin reminds me, uncomfortable. "She's not the first to have a psychological break at the state of the world."

"*No!*" I snap at him and he jerks in surprise. "That's not what this was. Sophie was strong, and dedicated. This isn't the life she was used to but she was changing and growing. She was so excited to make a difference with us." I feel a fresh tear streaking down my cheek. I was so reckless. I don't know how to live with this.

"You're going to be okay, Soph," I whisper to Sophie. I squeeze her hand. "It's just for a little while."

She doesn't even respond. She's singing under her breath, but it's too quiet for me to make out the lyrics. Her enigmatic smile is uncomprehending.

We all stand in the De-escalation Area, all of the members of the GSA, clustered around Sophie's room. They keep calling it a room, as if that makes it nicer, but really it's a padded cell. Like all of the other cells here, it has a reinforced glass panel fit into the door. The door is hanging open at the moment so Sophie can see that we're all here for her. She's sitting on a hospital-style bed, eyes gazing unseeingly.

People tend to be torn between deep sympathy for the lost people in here, and fear of ending up in this place themselves. There's no easy cure from being literally at war with the other half of yourself. It breaks people.

I know that all too well.

The lights are all turned off. Every GSA member carries a small lighted candle, like tiny stars fanned out around Sophie's cell in a silent vigil. Calvin is there, along with Zephyr and Ember, the phoenix's feathers softly glowing in tribute.

Phoebe steps forward from the crowd to turn and face everyone, standing to the side of the doorway so we can make out Sophie, unresponsive in the bed. Phoebe looks to me tentatively, as if inviting me to say some words of support. I cast my eyes downward, staring dully at the floor.

"Um, thanks for coming here everyone, in this show of support," Phoebe says. "I believe Sophie can still hear our voices and recognise them, and that this will mean a lot to her. I thought this would be a good way to show that we're here for her, and as a way to deal with all of our own confused feelings around what's happened to her."

If Sophie even realises we're here. She seems completely blind to the real world, only seeing things that aren't real; trapped inside her own tortured brain.

"Sophie's always seemed really sweet. Everyone keeps telling me that Sophie is just a really good person. I haven't gotten to know her as well as I want to, not yet at least," Phoebe says. She sounds awkward to start with, but she pushes through, determined. "I wish I had, before, because she's really important to Griffin, and he's my best friend," Phoebe says genuinely.

I shut my eyes.

"He has a giant heart and he's a great judge of character. So I feel like me and Sophie will really get along. Once she's better, count on way more movie night sleepovers everyone. You're all invited."

There are some tearful giggles, a ripple of levity around the candlelit circle.

"Sophie hasn't been able to meet her Shadow yet," Phoebe continues. "Her friends tell me that's something that she was really worried about. So I thought it would be sweet if everyone wanted to draw pictures of what they think Sophie's Shadow looks like. We can do sketches or even paintings if you want. Think about what Sophie meant to you, how you saw her and draw a Shadow which represents that to you. We hope you get better soon, Sophie," Phoebe finishes. "I really...."

I walk out right then. I just can't bear it a second longer. Phoebe's kindness is too much and I'm the last person who deserves it. The guilt is festering inside me like a black fungus.

Phoebe looks dismayed, wide-eyed, as I leave.

"Griffin," Calvin says softly, stepping out of the group as I pass him, "it's going to be…"

But I'm already running out of the Asylum, my hand covering my mouth like I'm going to be sick.

Back out in the corridor, I scream. I slam the wall of the ship with my hands, a beast trapped in a cage with no way out.

I hear Phoebe run out into the passage after me. Once I would have been embarrassed for her to see me like this. Now I don't even care.

"Grif," Phoebe says hotly, "you shouldn't be alone right now."

"Yes, I should," I say darkly. "It's safer for everyone that way. Bad things happen when people get close to me."

"What? That's a load of crap." Phoebe steps forward, taking my head in her hands. She forces me to meet her eyes. "You don't see the Griffin I do," Phoebe challenges me. "You have so much goodness and love inside of you. You feel so much, you feel things at this whole other level. But I know, and *you* know, that it also means these things with Eclipse and Sophie will tear you apart if you let them."

I wrestle away from her. I'm thinking of Sophie beaming at me over the counter at Burger Max, even though she probably barely remembered who I was. She was so full of life and hope.

"I can't do this anymore," I say to Phoebe, even though I don't know exactly what I mean. I can't do our friendship?

I leave her there in the corridor. I can still feel her troubled gaze on me as she watches me go.

I wish I could travel back in time one single day, before I tried giving Sophie her Shadow. At the very least I wish I had Eclipse with me right now. We should have flown away together, going off to explore uncharted skies in a far flung corner of his world, where the war can't touch us. I imagine feeling the wind and the rain on our faces. Feeling free.

The two of us could have found a cave to roost in high up a cliff face, with the terrain before us stretching out to the horizon, somewhere where our laughter would be the only sound in the peaceful quiet of dawn.

But Eclipse is gone now, and he's not coming back. There's no way for me to get word to him.

The only way of fixing this is to get back to the engine room straight away. I'm going to have to troubleshoot some seriously abominable bugs in the Siren if either of the worlds are to have a chance to survive.

Maybe, just maybe, there's a way to bring Sophie back.

With the groan of iron, I open the hidden door, crimson light and steam spilling through the opening until I shut it behind me.

Raven turns from the work toward me, still tapping out calculations on his tablet's screen.

"How's Sophie?" he asks vigorously. "I'm still trying to isolate what caused her adverse reaction. I've already made some adjustments to tone down the intensity. We can alter these final trials to test a range of different inputs..."

"What if more people end up like Sophie?" I say distantly. "How do we even justify risking that?"

"We're doing this so we can find a way to fix her too. There'll be an answer to what happened, Griffin. I always find it. Okay? This is my element, and it's yours too. We'll fix this together."

I look up at Raven, remembering all of the memories of Eclipse's that I witnessed when he was here. Something has been bothering me, and finally it clicks into place.

"Griffin? Are you okay?"

I'm staring at Raven, weighing up my new theory in my head. It holds water. Suddenly, somehow, I know that I'm right.

"Empress Galvanize," I say clearly. "It was you." The pieces have finally fallen into place, and I know that I should have seen the big picture sooner. "It was you in the throne room."

"Well, that was a change of topic," Raven says. "I'm not following."

"You killed Galvanize. When Eclipse found her dying, she said: *'He was meant to love me.'* She was talking about you. Galvanize stole the Empire from you that you built from the ground up," I say. "You went from being in control of the entire Shadow world to being homeless again, forced to live off scraps and wander the wilderness. So you found a way to sneak back into Opal Towers, even with all of the Empire hunting you, and you murdered Galvanize. You got your revenge.

'Then you ran. Eclipse became Emperor but you were caught and imprisoned by Imperials who were still loyal to the memory of Galvanize. If we hadn't found you when we did, if the humans hadn't overrun Troy... I bet Galvanize's followers had a grisly fate in store for you."

Raven considers me, then nods.

"Yes, it was me," he confesses quietly. "Are you here to

judge me, Griffin? I've done far worse than ending Galvanize's life."

I'm shaken slightly by his casual attitude to cold-blooded murder. It's dangerous to forget who my lab partner truly is just because we've shared some scones over late-night equations.

"Galvanize did terrible things to Eclipse," I muse aloud, clenching my hand into a fist. "She put him through so much pain. But I think if Eclipse had killed her in revenge that would have set him on an even darker path. Maybe it's for the best that her blood is on your hands, not his." Then I look at Raven sharply, scrutinising him. "You must have heard when you were on the run that Eclipse was the new Emperor. Surely you knew."

"I'd heard a rumour," Raven confesses lightly.

"You could have warned me," I say, furious. "Eclipse came here to learn if we were behind the Siren. He could have destroyed everything that we're working on here!"

"He didn't, though. When the Siren's video plays across the two worlds everything will work out exactly as it's meant to. I believe that."

"Oh, yeah? Where does this new faith of yours come from?" I shout. "You just think that all of this can be fixed like none of this ever happened? Do you think after the war all of us are just going to be able to forget what happened like it wasn't *us* who did these evil things?"

Then I break down. I fall to the ground, weeping.

Suddenly Raven is right there. He's knelt down beside me, and moves to hug me.

For a moment I'm still in shock. Then I feel a wave of hate, shuddering at his touch.

"No," I say vehemently, fighting him off.

"Grif."

"I can't..."

Then Raven wraps his arms around me, pinning mine to my sides. I cry out, fighting him, but he's too strong, and suddenly I can't break free...

"Let me go!" I yell, but it comes out as a choked sob.

Then, I don't know how it happens, but all of a sudden I'm clinging to him, like he's my only anchor to this world. Now I feel Raven tense in shock, going rigid. Winter shuffles from foot to foot as he watches us, agitated, as if feeling left out. Then Raven just hugs me tighter as my entire universe falls apart around me. His wordless understanding is the only real thing amongst the dust and the echoes. Calvin, Phoebe, Eclipse... none of them know the truth. Raven is the only one who won't judge me for the darkness inside of me. Unlike the others, I don't care if he sees my worst side.

"She's gone because of me," I whisper. "It's all my fault."

"No. I didn't see this coming either. I should have, I have far more experience. But we didn't have any reason to suspect that..." Raven sighs. "This isn't on you, Griffin."

"I wish Sophie never met me. All she wanted was to find her Shadow," I say into him, my voice muffled. "She just wanted to be happy and whole, like everybody else here."

"Hey... I know," Raven says, strangely emotional. He pulls me closer into him, tentatively, as if he can protect me from the world. "I know."

The Asylum is silent. It must be the middle of the night, I figure, dazed. I've cancelled everything from my schedule except the most critical items, spending every last minute I can working around the clock with Raven. We've made new adjustments to the Siren, fine-tuning the frequency to make it less intense.

Raven is fairly confident we've fixed it. He thinks, in layman's terms, that in targeting the part of Sophie's brain that connects her to her Shadow we put too much pressure on it and it... snapped. Raven doesn't think it had anything to do with Sophie and her Shadow in particular, that it was just bad luck. That's what's scary. That this could have happened to any of our subjects.

Raven says he's confident that what happened to Sophie won't happen again, but we can't know for sure. How can I bring myself to risk using the Siren again, even while knowing how crucial it is for our mutual survival?

I press my hand against the window in Sophie's door. She's sitting on the spongy floor, muttering vaguely to herself. It's good to see her more active, at least. Not catatonic.

I want to talk to her. I want to be the kind of friend who can go in there and sing songs to her and keep her company until she comes out of whatever this thing is. But the thought of going in there with her terrifies me all of a sudden.

I've never found the Asylum to be a particularly favourite place of mine. This place is meant to keep its occupants safe, even from themselves. That's what we say. Really, though, some of them never seem to get any better, no matter our best intentions. When you come here, you come here to be forgotten.

That's when I hear something.

I listen closely. Was that someone's voice? I listen again. Nothing. Maybe it's just the sleep deprivation talking.

Then, I feel it. A voice. A voice inside my own head.

Griffin? Eclipse's voice asks, super faint. *Griffin, are you there? I need you.*

Eclipse? I feel a jolt of adrenaline. No, it can't be. This must be another hallucination, like when I saw Cirrus in the bottom of the ship. Maybe after everything that's happened, it's all been too much for me. *Eclipse?* I repeat in the mental equivalent of a whisper. Slowly, I take another step forward, and then another. The low light makes it feel like I'm in a museum rather than a psychiatric ward. The squishy padded cells on both sides of me are like tiny, private bouncy castles, creating the illusion of miniature worlds where everything is comfy and safe, where the war doesn't exist.

I'm up on top of the hatch. Please, let me in. I need to see you.

Eclipse? I gasp. A wild joy erupts inside me. It's him. I'm not imagining this. His mind is distant, but somehow he's managing to project to me all the way down here.

I don't know how he got here, but he's back!

I take out my phone. After my last face-off with Eclipse I hooked up my personal phone to the ship's security systems, just in case. I open up the security display to open the ship's hatch for him... then hesitate.

I'm being incredibly foolish. For all we know, Eclipse has figured out finally that we're behind the Siren and returned with a host of Imperial soldiers. I should sound the alarm. That's the sensible, responsible thing to do as leader.

I trust Eclipse though. Why, after all the games we've

played with each other? But I do, and overpowering everything is that the feel of his mind in mine is so welcome, so needed in my darkest hour, that I long to let him in. I want him to wrap me in those enormous wings and send me colours that tell me everything is going to be okay.

On my phone screen I check the footage from the ship's external cameras. I can make out Eclipse as he carefully clambers past one of them, pausing only to ogle the lens with a large, dark eye. He's the only one visible anywhere near the hatch.

I can open the hatch just long enough for him to come in and no one else. Of course, Eclipse is perfectly capable of bringing down the place on his own what with his powers...

Just let him in, Grif. It's Eclipse for crying out loud. You trust Raven, but not him?

I helped Eclipse escape last time, he knows that. We trust each other now. We have to.

I need him.

Emotional, I hit the button to unlock the hatch.

I watch on the security feed as an oversized dragon-parrot makes his way down each passage. It's night time, so most of the corridors are empty, but I guide him with my mind, checking that his path is clear as he advances toward the Asylum. I can feel his mind approaching mine like a moth drawn irresistibly to flame.

I was right when I said our friendship is bigger than this war, I realise, spirits high. No matter what happens, we need each other. I'm scared to do anything more than stand here in case I jinx this.

How can he be here? I wonder, torn between longing

and disbelief. I want so desperately for this not to be a hallucination concocted by my traumatised, unravelling brain, but I'm not so sure anymore.

There's no way that Eclipse can be back here already. He left for the Shadow world only days ago.

Finally I see him. He emerges out of the dark, his head bowed as he walks toward me. He looks... broken. The grief pouring from him reflects my own.

It looks like Eclipse flew here in a hurry; his feathers are torn, bedraggled. He looks lost.

But it's him. It's really him.

"Eclipse!" I cry, and I'm running toward him. All of our past conflicts, his lies and mine from last time, are forgotten. I throw myself into him and he furls his wings around me. My own sobs fuse with his until I can't tell them apart; suddenly my grief isn't just mine to hold, it's shared.

"Griffin, I'm so lost," Eclipse says, his eyes welling up. Whatever's happened to him since I last saw him has destroyed him, and it hurts to see him like this. "I just needed... I needed to come here, but I shouldn't have left... so many people need me. But I couldn't bare it. I wasn't even thinking." He laughs, crookedly, wryly. "Some Emperor I am. I was barely back and then I left them again, hopping between worlds at the drop of a hat."

"I needed you too," I whisper. "I'm so glad you're here. I'm so sorry for everything that happened between us. It was stupid."

"At least now we can be stupid together," he mumbles. Patting his scaled leg, I laugh. It shocks me.

"A few minutes ago I didn't think I was ever going to laugh again. Then one moment with you and you have me going. How do you do that?" I ask softly.

"I just want it all to stop."

"I know," I confess. "I don't know if I can do it anymore. Are you okay? What's happened?"

But he doesn't answer. In a way, I'm a little relieved. If he asks me what's wrong with me, I don't know if I could lie to him about the Siren and Sophie. I don't think I can lie to him any longer. I'm sick of showing him someone who isn't me.

Strangely, as if drawn by a magnet, Eclipse moves past me. He stops in front of one of the cells as if drawn by an unseen force. It's Sophie's cell. Eclipse looks through the window, fixating on the girl inside with deep curiosity.

What drew him there? Did he see something inside me?

"That's Sophie," I say anxiously. "You remember her? She was one of the ones we hung out with when you were here. She was…"

"…your first big crush and your first girlfriend. You used to go to the same school. I know, Grif. I know you."

Eclipse is staring through the glass at Sophie, captivated. He stares at her like a man dying of thirst who has just glimpsed fresh water, after thinking he'd never see any again.

It makes me uneasy.

"Now that I see her again," Eclipse says strangely. "She looks so… familiar."

"Because you've hung out with her. Because you've seen her in my memories," I say. But that doesn't seem to be what he's getting at. I shuffle my weight between my feet. The longer he curiously regards Sophie, the more petrified I am. Afraid that he'll see through me.

"You're scared," Eclipse realises, finally tuning to train his gaze on me. "You're scared to look directly at her."

I force myself to move up beside him, staring in at Sophie with him. She's splayed in a corner of the cell. She's talking to herself feverishly. She looks pale, waif-like.

Slowly I trace the glass with my finger.

"Hello, you," I whisper softly.

Eclipse is silent for a moment. Then:

"What's wrong with her?"

My mental defences are too depressed, too fatigued; there are holes in them. I struggle to hold up the barrier, to keep my secrets secret, but parts of my mind's walls are crumbling faster than I can maintain them.

"Nobody knows. It just... it just happened." I smile at him painfully. "Phoebe brought Sophie to this base because of me. I wanted to protect her, and I let this happen to her on my watch."

"Nobody knows what's wrong with her, you say. So why do you blame yourself for not stopping it?"

He's not letting this go.

"I don't know what went wrong. I just feel powerless, that's what I mean."

"I feel calmer around her," Eclipse says, staring at Sophie. "I don't know why, but she makes things feel simpler, as if everything's going to be okay."

"Sophie was good at that," I say, sniffing.

"Have you done things you're ashamed of in this war, Griffin?" Eclipse whispers softly. "I know I have. Sometimes I just feel...so, so tired. The second-guessing my own orders, the weight of responsibility for the lives of the others who count on me... I wish it would all just stop. Sometimes I just want to run, and run, and never look back."

"Eclipse, I miss you so much," I say. "I'm so sorry. I get now that you didn't turn on me, back in the station. You left me, and that hurt, but you never turned your back on me. And I'll never turn mine on you again."

For a moment, I wonder if Eclipse even heard me. He's staring in at Sophie, fascinated, as if he's hypnotised by her.

"Why are you so interested in her, Eclipse? What's going on?"

"I just wanted to see her," he breathes. Then he shakes his head, confused. "I... I don't know why I said that."

I feel sick.

"What are you talking about?"

"What happened to her?" Eclipse asks again.

"Eclipse, I've told you. Please stop putting me through this." Pleadingly, I reach out to stroke his feathers.

"Why do I feel like you're lying?" he says.

Because I'm scared that you won't forgive me, I want to cry out. I'm scared that that the truth will break things forever between you and me.

Then I look up at him, anguished.

"Because I did it," I whisper out loud, finally confiding in him at long last. "Sophie is in there because of me."

He just looks at me.

"It was a mistake," I say, my voice hushed. "I was just trying to find a way to bring all of the humans and Shadows together like our Mum's always wanted... but what the GSA was doing wasn't working."

"No. No. What have you done?" Eclipse whispers.

"Eclipse..." I say in anguish, but I don't have any words to follow it.

"It was *you*," Eclipse says forlornly, sounding lost. He stumbles, as if the ground has tilted under him. "No, no, no." He shakes his head stubbornly. Eclipse sounds so young. His crest is flattened to his head, his feathers fluffed up in a protective, bristling cloud to hide behind. "It was you all along."

Everything is pouring out from me now into his mind in a flood, everything I've been hiding from him, from everyone. It's all there for him to see.

I can't lie to him anymore; this is my last gambit. I have to make him understand. I need him to. I can't go ahead without him.

Eclipse staggers away from me.

"Raven?" he exclaims. "You've been working with Raven on this? This was his idea?"

"No," I whisper. "It was mine. He only helped fill in the gaps that I'd been missing." It would be so easy to blame what happened with Sophie on Raven sabotaging the Siren somehow. I won't say it didn't cross my mind, but I know that's not true. I can't kid myself. All I have to blame here are my own shortcomings. "But there are humans and Shadows out there who can hear each other now because of the Siren I designed," I say with a surge of passion. "It was *working*, Eclipse. It can still heal everything. This... this is just a bug that can be fixed. I can cure Sophie, I know it."

"You know nothing," Eclipse cries. "Why? Why would you think this was okay?" The question punches through me, an arrow-head of accusation. The way he's speaking it's as if I'm killing him. "What could possibly bring you to do something this monstrous?"

"Don't say that!" I fight back ferociously. "Don't act like all those others who would let our worlds crumble into nothingness just so they can stick to some code that lets them sleep at night. You're not like that, Eclipse. You understand what I do, that there's this grey line between good and evil, and that line is where both you and I are walking right now. No one came up with this concept for the Siren except for me, not even Calvin. I'm not stealing anyone's free will, okay? I've created a cure for the war, a cure for the hole in every Shadow and human's heart. What's happened to Sophie is a tragedy, and if I don't fix whatever happened to her I'll never forgive myself, but don't let her suffering be in vain. Please, Eclipse. I'll happily be the bad guy if it saves everyone. If that's the job that's fallen at my feet, I accept. If they want to make me the villain for what I'm about to do, what I have to do for all of us, so be it. Just don't make me do it alone."

"Can't you hear yourself?" Eclipse cries. He's spiralling.

"You're the Emperor, Eclipse, the people look to you! You need to be there to guide them through this when the Siren streams its video across the worlds! Mum and Silvaluna would have wanted us working together."

"How would they have felt about what you did to Sophie?"

The words sting deep, and he knew that they would. But I don't rise to the bait.

"Sophie believed that I could do this," I insist, cheeks stained with tears, heart thudding, "she trusted me, and I'm not giving up when she's relying on me to make this right."

I move back to Sophie's door to look in at her. She's still tracing the pattern in her hand, singing to herself. I rest my hand against the glass between us.

Sophie stops suddenly, as if finally sensing the presence of someone other than herself. She looks up at the window. Her eyes fix on me for the first time since I used the Siren on her. I'm scared, expecting to see judgement, fear or fury in her, but it's as if I'm barely even real. I feel like I'm just a character in some TV show that's caught her attention.

I press the button for the speakers so we can hear each other.

"Sophie?" I say uncertainly.

"I loved you so much," Sophie whispers, her voice crackling through to us. "I mean… she did. I did. We both did." She giggles suddenly, and for the first time something about the quirk of her smile gives me an odd sense of déjà vu.

"You're just dreaming, Sophie," I say. My voice feels strangled. "You're stuck in a dream. But I'm going to make you better."

Sophie cocks her head to the side. Demurely, she extends a hand, draping it out toward me.

"Come join me, Griffin," she says shyly. "Let's lie here and go mad together."

I shiver. I force myself to turn and face Eclipse. He's rocking his head back and forth, muttering. He looks as broken and irretrievable as Sophie. All I can hear from his mind is tortured chaos and denial. For a moment I fear that I've pushed Eclipse too far, and now I'm losing him too.

"It was you," he repeats.

"Eclipse," I croak, stepping closer to him.

"It can't be. You wouldn't, it's… you're a part of me. We're the same person. We wouldn't hurt her like that."

"Eclipse, just… breathe. Talk to me. Please."

He's losing himself to his grief. I can feel his agony, his hopelessness spreading through him like a cancer.

What am I missing here? There's something more to this. I can feel it.

I take another step. Eclipse raises his head and I freeze.

He's fixing me with a gaze that burns with loathing. Something has shifted deep within Eclipse, fracturing and bubbling into an uncontrollable fury. I can feel it burning within him. It feels like molten gold pooling just behind his eyes, about to overflow.

Abruptly I realise what the Shadow before me reminds me of, as Eclipse rises up, the corner of his beak bending upward in a bloodthirsty leer.

I remember when he first became Eclipse, how he'd killed twelve of the most powerful Shadows in the world and laughed. I'm watching my Shadow slipping away, regressing back beyond the veil as he reverts to the violent monster he once was. Suddenly it's like the Shadow I love is gone, and it's as if he's who he was when I first met him on New Redemption. A titanic dark beast who was all ego and destruction... and now all of that primal rage is directed at one single person.

"Eclipse?" I whimper.

20

Eclipse towers over me, leering savagely.

I desperately search for some sign of my friend, but it's like he's gone. Even though he's my other half, even though he's my best friend, I listen to my instinct. And it saves my life.

I turn and run.

My shoes skid on the floor as I run from the Asylum. When I'm almost out at the exit I feel silly for being so paranoid. I'm being ridiculous.

But then I hear a lumbering sound as Eclipse starts to charge, and I know that the nightmare is real.

Eclipse's roar shakes the foundations of the ship. I feel him lunging after me, his talons closing in.

My heart is in my throat.

This is Eclipse. Why is he doing this? What's happening? Is this really *him?*

Other than the blind rage, all I can make out of Eclipse's thoughts are scattered shards of memory that are out of order and nonsensical. It's like having pieces of a puzzle without knowing what picture they make when fitted together.

I glimpse a grand stage before a roaring, infinite crowd; I see a dress of magnificent gold, the hem sweeping its way up carved stone steps.

Escaping the Asylum, I dive into one of the narrower passages that I know will slow Eclipse down. Behind me I hear the metal of the hallway crumple and shatter as Eclipse comes howling after me.

I grab my phone from my pocket. If I lure Eclipse to a part of the ship where I can lock him in and gas him as I'd planned before, I can buy some time.

The sound of shredding metal shoots up behind me, and I turn, hurling myself into a new corridor. I know I don't have enough time. Reacting immediately, I turn another corner, then kick the loose grill in the wall on my right, throwing myself into the vent. Belly-crawling my way in, I bring my phone up to my face to activate the security systems...

Except I don't have it. I stare at my shaking, empty hands. My phone must have slipped out when I clambered into the shaft.

I focus on thoughts of velvety transparency, trying to hide my mind from Eclipse as much as I can so that he can't reach out and find me through our connection. I can't hear any sound from him. Maybe he's headed off in a different direction. My phone must be lying just at the mouth of the shaft entrance, back in the corridor. Sliding back toward it, I eye that square of dim light I just crawled through. I hesitate, then start to edge back toward it...

A giant claw slams down in front of the vent. I jam my hand over my mouth to stop myself from screaming.

That will have shattered my phone for sure. I hope he didn't notice it. He's just standing there; I can hear his heavy breathing. He's an alpha predator, one beyond comprehension. I forgot how terrifying he was when we first met.

I try to understand what's happening to him. Are all the parts that I knew as Eclipse just *gone* now? Were those parts somehow just erased when I told him the truth?

I really don't think I can take any more guilt right now.

I'm too scared to keep shuffling down the shaft, in case he hears me. He's fallen terribly silent. Where the hell is everyone else in the base? They must be coming. Eclipse's roaring and path of destruction can't have gone unnoticed. I realise all that's happened has happened in merely seconds. It just feels like a lifetime.

Help will come, I just have to survive long enough for them to activate the ship's defences.

I wonder what power Eclipse has stored within himself right now. It can't be anything destructive like lightning bolts or plasma bursts, or I'd be a smoking pile of ashes right now.

I watch as slowly, very slowly, Eclipse raises his foot and reaches into the ventilation shaft. Blindly, the giant talons feel their way toward me, cold and unfeeling. In the dim light spilling into the shaft from the corridor the black-ened scales of his foot seem to glimmer with gold.

It's coming closer and closer. I try to slide myself back along the metal shaft without making any sound. I pray that my efforts to make my mind invisible to his are working.

I push myself further away, and feel my back hit what

feels like the end of the shaft. I panic, but then I realise I've just hit an elbow where the shaft turns to the right.

Eclipse's talons stretch open. A nightmarish claw of hooked talons reaches slowly until it's just inches from cutting my face to ribbons. If I move, if I make a sound, he'll end me.

I cover my mouth again. A sob threatens to break free. Even as I'm trying to keep my consciousness silent, I can feel his crackling wildly. I keep seeing flashes of memory; the stone steps, the hem of the golden dress... puzzle pieces that don't make any sense to me but they're recurring in Eclipse's head as if the same synapses are stuck on a loop, firing over and over.

Eclipse's claw stops, fully extended. It just can't reach me. His talons trace the air around my head, feeling for prey, as if he's considering whether to tear the shaft from the wall instead.

I scrunch up my face, trying to stay still, but the memories firing from Eclipse are like electric shocks coursing through my skull, and I almost moan with the pain. I try to fight them, to focus on survival, but suddenly I'm thrown into one of the recurring memories that Eclipse is trapped within, seeing through his eyes and ears, and I'm not Griffin anymore. I'm him.

When the cool dawn of morning comes, I find Hanna trying to sneak out of the palace.

The Imperial Palace is massive, one of the most ancient structures in the entire Shadow world. It had lain empty for a long time until Raven had brought back the tradition of Imperial rule under Hanna.

Now, with Galvanize dead, we've gone from sleeping in a war tent in the middle of the desert to far more luxurious digs.

I saunter out into the stone courtyard. Hanna and I slept in our own chambers, which feels strange; after working and fighting alongside her for so long, it's strange having her feel so far away. Not being able to hear her snoring in the night is... oddly lonely.

I follow quietly behind Hanna. She's carrying a packed travel bag, and she's wearing clothes similar to the ones that Griffin and I found her in when we met at Kashlak forest. They're the clothes of a lone hunter.

Hanna keeps a fast pace along the stone promenade, moving surprisingly silently as she makes her way down the steps. She stays low, moving in the direction of the city's exit.

"Going somewhere?" I say languorously, following after her.

Hanna freezes. She turns around, sheepish, scratching the back of her neck.

"Oh, hey."

"Hey."

"Did you sleep all right?"

"Awful. Too many pillows," I say wryly, and she grins. "Also, the journey home yesterday was fairly rough."

"Oh, you get jet-lag going between the worlds?"

"No, but that ship that brought me back to Opal Towers was like riding a bullet. Thought I was going to be sick."

Hanna snorts.

"It's the private transport of the Emperor. Enjoy the perks."

"It's a nightmare. Anyhow, what is this, you traitor? You're sneaking out with no goodbye, when we finally won the Shadow world?"

"You don't want me here, trust me," Hanna mutters. "I helped you fight, I helped you win the throne. But this is where my path ends, amigo."

"Where are you going?"

She shrugs.

"I... I don't know. I guess I'll find out. Somewhere where the grass is greener, maybe."

"I can't do this without you," I confess. "You think I have any idea of how to rule a world on my own? The economy will collapse in the next hour."

"This is exactly why I need to stay away. The throne corrupted me last time. I don't want to be anywhere near you. My advice isn't the advice that a ruler should have."

"It was Raven who corrupted you," I remind her. "You're not the Shadow you once were. You're stronger now."

"I see, so you want me to help do your new Empire's admin for you. Is that the only real reason you want me to stay?" she says ironically.

"Sure. Also, you're my only friend that's the same species as me."

"Special. We should get matching bracelets," Hanna comments. She turns to look out at the water. "Eclipse," she whispers suddenly. Turning, I follow her gaze out over the city wall to the river, the one that winds past Opal Towers. Even from here, the change is striking.

It's crimson.

"Is that... blood?" Hanna asks, uncharacteristically gingerly.

"An algae bloom," I say. "Must be."

"Must be," she repeats, as if wishing she had my certainty. She wraps her arms around herself tightly. "Eclipse, this is some doomsday shit going on. People are talking about the end times. Not exactly the good omen we were hoping for on the morning of your coronation."

"No, but at least there is a coronation," I say. Looking out at the bloody water, I wonder if this is a real omen of things to come. In the olden times of our world, Shadows were more in

touch with the land. They believed that a magic infused it and that they were made from that same magic. It does seem that the land is screaming at us. "Stay for the ceremony, please?" I beg her. "The people need some festivity, something to get happy about. Let's not let this ruin today. Okay? Today is a day of hope."

Hanna bites her lip. For a moment, I think she's still going to turn me down.

"Okay," Hanna relents. She looks up at me with a bitter-sweet smile. "Just for the ceremony, bird-brain."

I'm followed by a procession of Imperial Guards. They're now replaced with loyal followers from our own camp, familiar faces who have been fighting with Hanna and me since the oasis. The signature violet armour of the Empire, a relic from Hanna's own reign and back far before that, is now replaced by new gleaming armour. Hanna had the idea to have it forged while I was away infiltrating the GSA. Now my soldiers flanking me are clad in resplendent gold, and they seem to stand taller than any Imperial Guards have before. Of course, I may be biased.

I'm escorted to the stage. Citizens and their families cluster tightly, stretching out in an infinite sea. It's astounding. Intimidating.

A massive banner hangs down the back of the stage; it's of the imperial flaming crowned heart crossed with clawed gauntlets; but now the claws have talons in the form of my own, and the crest is gold instead of violet.

As I take to the stage there's a roar from the crowd that seems to lift the roofs off the houses around the city. I wonder how it is that not so long ago I would fly through the empty skies of Sanc-

tuary City to take refuge in my private clock tower, staying up late and getting a sugar rush from all those Fruit Loops.

When I found out what Zephyr really did for his job, I hated the Empire more than anything. I never thought it would be my Empire.

The Elder, a bearded snail with arms, shuffles over to cast red dust over me. He blows hot air from the flame of a torch, murmuring the chants old and immemorial.

Then, placing myself near centre of the stage, I turn as I see Hanna coming toward me, and strangely my breath catches in my throat. She's smiling at me, radiant, as if I'm the only one in the entire city.

She's been outfitted in a formal gown for the ceremony, shimmering and glorious. It reminds me of how she dressed when she used to be the Empress. It's a way that I haven't seen Hanna look for a very long time, the two of us having been on the road for so long. She looks... beautiful. It feels strange, using that word. Instead of violet, in line with the new rebranding she's wearing a gown of resplendent gold. It catches the sun, shimmering like pirate treasure. Hanna's holding out a wide velvet cushion. On it sits a bronze circlet, custom-made to fit the proportions of my own head. The small circlet worn by Hanna and Galvanize would never have fit.

I experience a strong wave of déjà vu as I think back to Griffin's GSA initiation he put together for me. There's a tugging in my chest. But I focus my vision forward to the tasks ahead.

"Posture," Hanna whispers.

"Oh." I straighten gratefully. "Thanks," I whisper.

We get to the part of the ceremony where I think I'm meant to bow down for the crowning, as crazy as that feels. But instead Hanna flies up into the air, her violet wings fluttering out the back of the boofy gold gown which cascades around her. She hauls the heavy crown up into the air, her wings punching the air determinedly as she bears it aloft... placing it securely onto my head.

"Long live Emperor Eclipse," she whispers to me, as if it's just the two of us in this entire world.

Then she repeats it in a carrying cry, a cry that is taken up by the people of the city, and by the Shadows who are watching all across the globe. Shadows who are seeing this and knowing that it's a turning point in their own history, in the meaning of what it is to be Shadows.

Hanna hovers beside me, revelling in the moment with me. I'm heavily aware of the weight of the metal circlet upon my head now. It's as if the crown is burning with the responsibility of what it means, of the promise to my people that it entails.

I turn to regard Hanna, smiling at my companion. When we met each other we were products of darkness; both of us hated and despised by all. Something about being around each other though encouraged us to bring each other fighting and screaming into the light. We challenged each other to be better, to hunt for some way to have a positive impact on our world.

I nod to the Elder. He was waiting for my signal. Now he slides toward us, beginning to chant in an ancient tongue. His eyes are glazed as if he's seeing past, present and future all at once.

"I have a surprise for you," I announce to Hanna. "A present."

She blinks. This wasn't planned, not to her knowledge.

The Elder is passed something by one of his acolytes. When he turns to me with a velvet pillow, I reach down and pluck it from the cushion with a talon. The small circlet gleams in the sunlight where it hangs, the diamonds of the tiara lit on fire by the sun.

I bring it around to hold it out to Hanna who's still hovering before me, the beats of her wings sending ripples through the golden train of her gown.

Hanna looks at the offered crown and then back to me, uncomprehending.

The Elder hurls a cloud of red dust up at her, triggering a coughing fit. He begins to hum the hymns of succession once again.

"I don't understand," she says, gasping for air. "What's happening?"

The confusion on her face tells me that this was the right choice. Even now, she doesn't expect it.

I hold out the circlet to her, what was once her own crown.

"This is a coronation, Empress," I remind her.

Her eyes madly search mine, glistening with tears of shock. "But..."

"For the first time, the Shadow world will have two leaders, ruling together. Emperor and Empress."

"You're proposing to me?" Hanna blanches.

"What? I... no!" I feel myself flush.

"Okay, okay! I was just asking. I'm really confused."

"I'm offering for you to rule with me as partners. Partners in... in ruling. Shared Custody."

"...of the world," she says, clearly thinking I've cracked.

"Look. I'll be making a lot of changes to how the Empire works, and that will be far easier with your experience as Empress. Past and future, working together. Some of my subjects still believe that you're the rightful ruler anyway. The ones who hate you... well, now you have a chance to change their minds."

"I.... Your Imperial Majesty, I can't," Hanna says, overwhelmed. She hovers even closer to me, looking afraid. "It's my

job to serve you," she whispers. "I've pledged myself to your vision, your plan of changing the world that I broke."

"You don't need another master to pledge yourself too, like you did with Raven," I say with feeling. "You've changed, I've seen it. You nearly died for me; you've risked your life to save innocent people who didn't even care for you. You're not the same Empress who found me and Griffin in Kashlak forest."

"But... how can you trust me, with that power?" Hanna asks, blinking back tears. She turns to look out at the sea of faces. "How can you?" she softly asks the silent crowd.

"Because I do," I say.

Looking at me, she smiles a gorgeous smile that I've never seen before, illuminated with joy.

I offer the crown to her, balancing it delicately off the tip of my talon. She takes her diamond studded crown and fits it onto her head once more. The past and future of the Shadow world made whole, for a new era of self-determination.

Thousands in the crowd cheer, but there are also many dark mutters, and a few spurning shouts. Hanna still has to win many of them over; but I know her. She will.

"Thank you," she whispers to me, and the way she looks at me makes me think I see something in her eyes, something that makes me feel like maybe...

The smile freezes. Hanna's pupils contract, her face becoming strangely pale.

"Hanna?" I hear myself say.

Then she starts screaming.

"HANNA!"

She falls to the floor of the stage, convulsing, like she's having a fit. The scream coming from her is one of pure terror; it feels as if nails are scraping down my spine.

"Help her!" I cry, shielding her from view with a wing.

There's shouting, orders to cut the cameras. I wish more than anything that I'd never erased Zephyr's healing power inside me for another. Making mountains isn't going to help Hanna. "Get a healer here, now!"

The Imperial guards have stepped into a tight circle around us, weapons out, as if that can save Hanna from whatever is happening to her. I can hear the commotion of the crowd. Finally a swarm of healers are permitted to pass through the line of guards, racing to tend to the newly reinstated Empress of the Shadow world.

I crane my head, watching the Healers tending to Hanna, starting to run preliminary checks to try and diagnose what's wrong. As Hanna spasms, she looks up at me for a moment.

"I can feel her, Eclipse," Hanna gasps. "She's real. She's real after all."

Then her face turns strange. For a minute I'm scared of the very worst, and I feel my entire world breaking apart. I can see the rise and fall of her chest, but suddenly her eyes stare straight through me, like she doesn't even recognise me anymore.

As if we've never even met.

Drowning in Eclipse's memory, I finally break the surface. I'm me again, Griffin, hiding in the back of the air vent.

No, no, no....

I remember laughing with Hanna beneath the branches of Kashlak. I recall her entrancing emerald eyes, of how it felt to fall in love for the first time. I remember a shared kiss in the dunes, of risking my life to try and save hers on the beach and then again at Winghold...

Hanna is gone. My Shadow's best friend. Now she's just as lost, just as irretrievable as a certain someone else I know.

No, no, no...

I recall Eclipse staring in at Sophie in her cell, recognising something in her that he hadn't seen before. He was seeing her for who she truly is.

"I loved you so much," Sophie had said. *"I mean... I did. She did. We both did."*

Finally the horrifying truth hits me; the pieces finally fall into place.

I did this to both of them.

Hanna is Sophie's Shadow.

21

COUNTERPARTS

Hanna is Sophie's Shadow. The two have been each other's counterparts all along. What I did to Sophie with the Siren, I did to Hanna too on the other side.

How could I have known? I had no idea that when I was suffering a huge crush on the cute girl from my school at Burger Max that I'd soon be running through a gargantuan forest in another world with her Shadow. I'd fallen hard for Hanna just as I had for her human.

The two of them are so very different, but somehow I was drawn to both of them. At some level, I must have sensed something of them in one another.

Back in Eclipse's world, Hanna must be just like Sophie: unresponsive, trapped in her own psyche. When I first met Hanna she'd told me that what she wanted more than anything was to find her own human. Now, if her and Sophie had a chance to meet in this state... would they even recognise each other for who they are?

No wonder Eclipse has lost his mind. My experiment is

the reason he's lost his best friend. His grief is mirrored by my own; I hurt my own Shadow by taking away something he treasured so deeply.

Eclipse, I say brokenly, crying. *I'm so sorry. I am so, so sorry.*

Eclipse's oversized claw freezes. He heard me. He knows where I am.

He hesitates, as if he's reconsidering. Then, gradually, he retracts his claw, pulling it back out of the vent.

I exhale. Feeling destroyed, I bury my face in my hands.

Then I swear I can hear the strangest buzzing sound. There's the rustling of feathers from the mouth of the shaft, as if Eclipse is unfurling his wings out in the corridor.

It's not over.

It strikes me what's happening, a moment too late... or just in the nick of time. Then I'm scampering off down the vent to my right, away from Eclipse, no longer worried about making a sound...

The buzzing is growing louder.

I know what power it is that Eclipse has in him right now. I've heard that buzzing sound before in Kashlak forest when Hanna rescued us from the Empire. I recall how she'd opened her wings, and we'd watched in fascination as real, living wasps had emerged from the undersides, swarming at the imperial soldiers.

Eclipse took Hanna's power before he left her. Of course he did. Eclipse is honouring Hanna by carrying a part of her inside of him.

I hear the giant, killer wasps from Eclipse's wings flying into the air vent. I can hear the cacophony of buzzing as they swarm toward me.

I scramble forward in a panic, bursting out the end of the vent. I slam hard into the landing of the stairwell. Leaping to my feet, I can see the cavernous dark of the ship's lowest level over the railing, where the room I shared with Eclipse lies abandoned. The only illumination comes from the faint blue glow of the water tanks below me.

I spin around just in time to see wasps engorged to the size of small dogs explode out of the ventilation shaft. Their exoskeletons are the colour of Eclipse's feathers, and they swarm out of the vent like a living nightmare.

There's no time for the stairs.

In less than a second, acting on life-preserving instinct, I clamber up onto the railing, kicking myself off into the abyss.

Then I'm falling, hurtling through the dark air of the ship, feet pedalling at empty space, terrified that I'll miss...

...before I crash into the cerulean water of the tank below.

I'm submerged. I have no idea if the wasps will dare to go into the water if they're willed to do so by their master. Fortunately, they don't. I sink slowly, unable to breathe, surrounded by glass walls. Up above, I'm sure the wasps will be hovering en masse, patiently waiting for me to surface.

I took Eclipse's closest friend away, the Shadow who meant the most to him in the worlds, even if I didn't mean to. Hanna and Eclipse had gone from mutual loathing to a dysfunctional partnership, to finally freeing an entire world thanks to their friendship. Now Eclipse has snapped. He's gone back to being the dark, tyrannical monster he was before he changed. Before him and Hanna had struggled together to find out how they could be better people.

If Eclipse kills me, his own life force will be snuffed out too. What happens to me happens to him, but right now he just doesn't seem to care. All the rational parts of him and all the parts of him that feel anything are buried deep inside him, in a far off place that I can't reach any longer.

As I fight to stay underwater, wondering why the rest of the GSA haven't rushed to try and rescue me yet, I suddenly realise that maybe I don't want them to.

Maybe I don't deserve that.

Without warning a massive claw plunges through the water, curling around me. I scream, a flurry of silvery bubbles speeding from my lips.

Then I'm being lifted upward, breaking the surface into the dark of the ship once again.

The buzzing of the wasps is gone. Maybe they've returned to the wings they were born from, absorbed back into him. I'm lifted toward Eclipse's fearsome beak. A beak that can snap through metal when it wants to, and can tear through flesh like tissue paper. He cranes his neck down toward me, leering. His savage eyes look hungry.

I struggle, fighting against Eclipse's grip, but then I give up, hanging limply.

"Eclipse," I whimper. "Please. It's me. It's Griffin."

The claw holding me slows to a halt. Eclipse studies me, practically salivating.

"It's *me*. Can't you see me? I'm so sorry. I never meant to hurt you this much, it was all a mistake. I just wanted to make everything better. But please don't kill me," I cry. "You wouldn't do that. That's not us. That's not our story. Is it?"

I hear nothing. Then:

"Griffin?" Eclipse whispers.

"That's enough!"

The voice cracks the air, blasting from all directions at once like the voice of God.

I hang there limply, drenched, as Eclipse looks up to the ceiling.

There's a whirring as the metal panels on the roof high above us slide away. A bristling armada of laser-guided tranquiliser guns and electrified net cannons unfurls from it, all aimed directly down at Eclipse... and me.

I look up to see Calvin staring down at us from the railing, his face etched with cold fury. It's a glimpse of the old Calvin Cameron, and I realise it was his voice over the speakers.

Members of the GSA spread out along the railing beside them: Rihäm and Archeon, Woo-min and Pouncer, Sam and Solace... all of them are aiming at Eclipse with bows, guns and Tasers.

"Put him down, little brother." It's Zephyr's voice now. Zephyr comes into sight beside Calvin, and I see his horror at what his younger brother is doing as he stares down at us.

Zephyr's voice seems to get through to Eclipse. I can feel Eclipse's speechless horror at finding me in his grip. He's disorientated, trying to figure out how we got down here.

Griffin? Eclipse thinks again, broken.

But I don't respond. I'm rigid, shivering from the water.

"Eclipse, put him down now!" Calvin snaps.

Horrified, Eclipse places me gently down on the floor beside the tank. I stay down on my hands and knees, staring at the patterning in the metal floor.

"Griffin," Calvin says to me over the speakers. "Griffin."

Slowly, still shaking, I look up at Calvin. He stares down at me imperiously from the landing above, his hands on the railing. "Are you all right?"

Am I all right? I stare up at him, dumbly. The question makes no sense. He's all out of focus, anyhow.

"Eclipse? *Emperor* Eclipse?" Zephyr says steadily. He swallows. "The GSA is placing you under citizen's arrest. You are one of us, one of our family, so please cooperate. You can stay here while we unravel all of this and figure out what course of action to take. Otherwise we'll be forced to incapacitate you. Trust me, this ship isn't without its defences."

But Eclipse just ignores him.

"Griffin?" Eclipse says again, his voice cracking.

I can't bring myself to look at the towering dragon-parrot. An ugly anger is tearing at my heart. I recall the fear of the chase, the buzz of those wasps.

The burning hatred in his eyes.

Eclipse spreads his wings wide, turning to face our brothers, the GSA members flanking them, and the array of neutralising firepower aimed at him from the roof.

"Oh, don't kid yourselves," Eclipse says, sounding destroyed. There's no malice in his voice, just weariness. "I can break out of here without getting a scratch on me. But I don't want to hurt anyone doing it."

I can see that his calm, his confidence in his own power, rocks the members up on the landing. I see the fear in them, but they still hold their ground at Calvin and Zephyr's side.

I gather myself, standing weakly upright. Everything feels blurred around me, as if I'm still underwater. Shakily, my feet carry me away from it all. I don't care about anything, not anymore... nothing other than setting this right. I just need to get back to the Siren. Raven and I can fix it somehow. We can figure out what went wrong, what cost Hanna and Sophie their sanity. We can bring everyone together still.

All of this can still be worth it. That's all that matters. I can give this last inch of myself to bring it home.

"Stop there, Griffin," Calvin says. "You're not going anywhere either."

I look back up at him dully. The way some of the others are looking down at me unsettles me.

"What is this?" I mutter.

"We heard you," Calvin says. His voice is steely, but I can hear the anger and grief behind his words. "I'd realised that someone had been tampering with surveillance, looping old footage. So I got an alert when you messed with the security system to let Eclipse in. We all saw what happened, we heard the conversation you two had."

"I don't…"

"We know you've been working on your Siren idea behind our backs. We know that it's what hurt Sophie. We know that you've been secretly collaborating with Raven, giving him access to resources and letting him out of his cell without us knowing. You were lying to everyone here, everyone who chose you as our leader, everyone here who trusted you!"

I don't answer.

"Do you have any idea what might have happened if you'd tried this half-brained Siren scheme on a global scale, if everyone had been afflicted in the same way as Sophie?"

"I can fix Sophie," I whisper. "I can fix Hanna. I can undo all of this. But the Siren *works*. I've seen it. You all have to listen to me. This is what the GSA has been waiting for.

This is the tool we need to finish this. You have to believe me." My voice cracks as I take in the faces on the balcony. The faces I care about. The faces I've sworn to protect. "All of you. I've led you this far. I can lead you to the other side. To pull back now, just because we don't believe that we're capable of this... *that* is what will cost us everything."

But meeting me is only deafening silence.

"Please," I say, "come on. Some of you have to believe me, you know I'm right. This is your organisation too. You've seen what's been happening on the news, the soldiers who are hearing their Shadows and putting down their weapons. You know that this works."

But no one raises a single word. I sense that the only image they have in their mind is Sophie, sitting quietly mad in her cell.

And anyhow, who would trust a guy whose own Shadow just tried to kill him?

"You're fixating on me?" I cry up at Calvin, incensed. "*Really?* Eclipse is the danger here." I point my finger at him accusingly, betrayed. Eclipse still hasn't moved; he looks aghast, unsure what direction to turn in. He tried to kill me, and his only friend back home doesn't recognise who he is anymore. I don't think he knows in that moment what to do. "Eclipse is the one who tried to kill me," I say clearly, anger pumping through my veins. "He's the Emperor of the entire Shadow world. He could stop this right *now* if he ever cared about any of us at all!"

I know I'm saying it out of hurt, out of guilt. The trauma is still fresh of thinking my own life was going to end at the hands of my other self. But I feel like my entire soul is breaking apart as I stand here in my drenched clothing, all alone against the family I've given everything to.

"This isn't just about Eclipse," Zephyr says hoarsely, and there's compassion in it. He sounds worried for me. "You know something hasn't been right with you, Griffin. It hasn't been for a while."

But then someone else emerges, pushing past Zephyr and stepping out in front of the others, flanked by her fiery Shadow. My breath is knocked out of me for a moment.

It's Phoebe.

"Please, Grif," she says, and I can see tears in her eyes.

I stare up at her, rocked. I don't know why, but for some reason it's the sight of her that gets through to me.

"Please," Phoebe pleads. "I'm worried about you. I know that you've been lying to me, but we can work through that. All I want right now is to know that you're okay. Just... just agree to follow the protocol for this kind of situation until we can sort all of this out. The protocol that *you* came up with."

"You want to lock me up too?" I say, feeling unreal. I slowly move my gaze between each and every member of the GSA at that railing. A few of them, perhaps the ones in the past who I've alienated more than others, stare back at me defiantly. Those I know well have the decency to look down at least, as if they're embarrassed or ashamed; but for them or me, I'm not sure.

My face burns. This is ludicrous. Ridiculous. Unacceptable.

Suddenly all of the emotions I've been keeping buried in all my time down in this place are rising to the surface. I want to scream and scream and never stop screaming. It all comes bubbling up, a kind of fury, a kind of incandescent madness, all of it with nowhere to go. This is all such a joke. It's all a stupid, ridiculous, terrible joke.

I realise I'm laughing. I just stand there, laughing and laughing up at them and I don't think I'm ever going to be able to stop. I can see their faces, I can see how freaked they all are by my reaction. Good. I want to scare them. I want to knock it into their skulls how trivial this all is, when the answer to ending this war is so close to being fixed. So close to perfection. So close to bringing Sophie and Hanna back.

None of the GSA up there would be here if it wasn't for me. They would never even have met their counterparts. Now Calvin thinks he can just turn them against me?

Someone tries to restrain me and I lash out, hearing them cry in pain. Then I feel hands grip me firmly, trying to guide me away. It's Calvin. I struggle against him, fighting viciously. I can feel that I'm descending into a kind of madness but I'm unable to stop myself. Like I'm watching from outside my own body.

"Griffin Cameron," I can hear Calvin saying, as if part of him is breaking. "We're relieving you of your role as leader of the GSA, until you can answer to the hiding of vital intelligence, subjecting others to dangerous untested experiments, for aiding and abetting a known terrorist and war criminal..."

I'm still laughing as they inject the sedative.

22

MY BODY IS A CAGE

I'm scared to leave my dreams behind. I'm afraid to recall what consequences lie in reality.

My surroundings are indistinct as I come to. I try and will them into focus. I feel a brief wave of nausea but it passes. Am I... drugged?

My brain has rebooted enough to recall the horrifying chase with Eclipse. I remember my breakdown in front of the others too and I feel a sharp rush of shame as well as fear. How had I lost control so totally like that?

Slowly, I try and raise myself up, but I can't. For some reason, my arms won't move.

My fingers slowly stroke the wall to the right of my bed, searching for clues. It feels squishy, rubbery to the touch. Like an old, leathery armchair.

I'm on a narrow cot, a bit like a hospital bed. My arms and legs are bound with straps to prevent any movement. The floor and walls are covered in an ugly, brown squishy padding. The room is even and cube shaped, like I'm trapped in a box. I stare directly in front of me, at the door with a small glass window fitted into it. With horror, I realise that somewhere out there, a familiar, blonde-haired girl sits in a cell very much like mine.

A deep dread settles into my bones, followed by an almost overwhelming bout of ferocious claustrophobia.

I'm in the Asylum.

I remember my continuous laughter down below and how unreal the world had felt around me. It had felt as if I was living in a parody of reality. I hope I didn't hurt anyone with my wild flailing before they'd knocked me out for their safety and mine. It was like I'd had a full on psychotic break.

I feel sick. Not from the sedative. Then I sense someone staring at me and nearly have a heart attack.

Phoebe is sitting on a small chair in the corner of my cell to my right. She's watching me silently, resting her mouth against her clasped hands. A silent sentinel.

In a burst of claustrophobia I start fighting against my bindings, straining at the straps holding my arms and legs to the bed.

"Hey! Hey, you're all right. Look, I'll get those for you, okay?" Phoebe moves over to me and starts to undo the straps. She studies me as if she can run a brain scan with her eyes. "How are you doing?"

"Oh, you know, I've had better days."

"Sorry about this. It's just you started convulsing, and we were worried you were going to hurt yourself. You weren't... *you*."

Looking at her, I start to open my mouth, then realise I have no idea what I can say to her. My face burns. She must know now too.

She knows that Sophie was my fault.

Phoebe speaks softly but I can hear her rising anger.

"What were you thinking, Griffin?"

"About which part?" I ask brokenly.

"I don't know, maybe projecting the voices of counterparts into billions of minds?"

Slowly, I sit up.

"I didn't like keeping you in the dark. I wanted you with me, working with me. But I knew how you felt about..."

"How could you really think that was an ethical solution to all this? Experimenting by messing with the minds of humans and Shadows, when a million things could have gone wrong, when they *did* go wrong...." Phoebe's going to say more, but stops herself. She seems to realise that I've already experienced the cost.

"I can't forgive myself for what I did to her," I croak. "But if Sophie's loss leads to fixing the Siren, if it leads to Shadows and humans living in harmony... then her sacrifice can still mean something. Then it won't be for nothing. And maybe, I can still bring her back."

Phoebe's silent for a moment.

"I understand that you thought it might be our only chance," she says, "but *Raven*, Grif. How could you hide it from me that you were working with him? You know my history with Taylor. You know the things he's done. How could you keep that from me?"

"Taylor saved my life down in the Underworld."

"That's it? That's your reasoning for trusting him? Griffin, you know the things he's done. He destroyed most of your life and took away your family."

"You defended him to me once."

"That was before I saw what he's become, before Aeyu Palace and the Underworld, before he pushed us into starting this horrendous war. You're saying that Raven saving your life once somehow undoes him taking away our family? Putting us through so much suffering?"

"There's some kind of link between him and me now," I confess, face burning with shame. "I don't know how to explain it, but I do believe that he can still be redeemed in some way. There's still good in him, Phoebe. He's still the Taylor you knew, deep, deep down."

"Oh, Griffin," Phoebe says softly, some of her fire dying. She shakes her head, in disbelief or wonder I'm not sure. Maybe both. "You're still such a dreamer."

"I'm doing what I need to do to end this war. Raven can help us, I know it. He's part of the puzzle. The only way we can end this is by working together."

"I didn't mean that in a bad way. You've got the biggest heart of anyone I know, even after everything you've been through. You can even empathise with the man who's caused you more pain than anyone else. How do you know he's not just playing you, like he always does? That's who he is."

"I'm not anybody's tool. Not anymore."

"Well, let's be fair, you've been a little bit of a tool," she says lightly, but without any real meanness.

"The Asylum, really?" I say grimly.

"Don't call it that."

"Let me guess. Calvin's idea to put me in here?"

"You scared me," Phoebe says tightly, her voice small. "You scared Calvin too. You were at risk of hurting yourself and others so we thought it couldn't hurt to hold you here until you could get checked out. You haven't been right for a while, Griffin. You know that."

"Whatever, I'm perfectly mentally sound," I say. "That's

what my therapist would say. Or at least, he would, if he hadn't been murdered in front of me."

"Griffin," Phoebe says in shock. She glowers fiercely at me. "Do you really still think this is a joke? I know you're scared but you don't have to be so cold and dark. Not with me."

"I don't know how to be with you."

"Wrong," she says quietly. "You've always known. I've always liked that about you." Suddenly she chokes, a sob exploding out of her. She hides her face in her hands, shaking her head. I feel more awful then I have in my entire life as I sit here, watching her crying.

"I'm sorry, Pheebs," I say in a weak voice. I sound pathetic. "I never meant for this to..."

"What, never meant to get caught?"

"Never meant for this to hurt you."

"Well too bad, arsehole, because you can't stop people caring about you. No matter if you try your damnedest." She looks adamant now. "Now we find a way to move past this. The others will forgive you too."

"You really think so?" I say sardonically, raising an eyebrow. "Even Calvin?"

"Don't be an idiot. He's your brother, he loves you."

Dizzy, I note the deeper, depressive slump of Phoebe's shoulders. Something else is broken in her, I realise, a deep sadness that somehow I don't think is all my doing.

"There's something you're not telling me, isn't there?" I ask, breathing in deeply. She doesn't speak. I have a sinking feeling it's about the topic that I've been trying desperately to avoid thinking about.

Eclipse.

Suddenly afraid, I take a breath and open my mind, sensing for him...

I can feel him. My stomach tightens. He's here, still on the ship.

I'm hurtling down the corridor again, metal shredding behind me as Eclipse hunts me through the ship, as if he wants to kill...

I close my eyes.

"What's happening with Eclipse?" I say, tortured. "Where's he being held?"

Phoebe bites her lip, as if deciding what to tell me.

"He's not," she finally says.

"He's not contained?" I say, panicking. "What happened?"

"No, Grif, you don't get it. He's..."

Her face screws up in utter grief, like she's collapsing in on herself.

"Phoebe? Phoebe, you're scaring me. Tell me. Just tell me."

Phoebe hands her tablet to me wordlessly. I take it from her in my freed hands, cradling the tablet carefully in my lap. I hold it with trepidation, like an explosive object.

Mutely, I watch, transfixed, trying to make sense of the images being shown to me. I quickly discover why Phoebe has that look on her face.

I'm looking at unrecognisable piles of rubble. The footage has runes and markings scrolling along the bottom, and I realise these must be shots taken from Shadow world news channels.

"The UN tried to suppress this at first and keep it off the human news," Phoebe says.

I can see Shadows in bright yellow hazmat suits scanning debris. This is intercut with high, zoomed out shots of two entire cities, levelled to the ground. It looks like something from a movie that must have been done with special effects. But when I try to imagine what once stood there...

I recognise what I'm looking at. We're being shown devastation from two separate major cities in the Shadow world. There's a sound like static in my ears.

"Founder's Square," I whisper. "The Quantum Rivers."

They're gone. Nuked, blasted away into piles of rubble. What were once magical, breathing societies of the most incredible beings have been incinerated instantly by human weaponry of mass destruction.

"The UN finally got desperate enough to use nuclear weapons," I say, swallowing. The static in my ears hasn't gone away. Looking at the wreckage, at the extent of lives that must have been lost, I'm reminded of Aeyu Palace. The very air there had seemed to sing with the haunting voices of the departed.

What will Eclipse feel when he sees this, and how will he retaliate against my world? If I didn't already think Eclipse and I have lost and broken the bond between us completely... staring at the images is deeper, harsher proof than ever that the extreme feud between our people will always remind us that we're from different sides.

"There must have been millions," I say numbly.

"Tens of millions," Phoebe says. Her voice is flat, dead. I can see how spent she is. She retrieves the tablet and quits out from the video to open another window. After a moment, she passes it back to me.

I watch the new video play. It's a news segment from YouTube. I'm staring at the streets of a major human city. Streets in broad daylight, with zero movement. Dark shapes lie across the ground, littering the pavements as far as the eye can see. All of the cars have stopped suddenly, at a standstill at green lights. It's as if an entire functioning city... suddenly stopped.

"Is that..." I swallow. "Is that... Cairo?"

"Yeah. Washington, D.C. too."

"What happened?" I ask, shattered. I try to analyse this through an impartial, emotionless lens. Not as Griffin but as the leader of the GSA, if that's still what I am. What does this mean for the war, for our worlds? "Is this another vapour attack from the Shadows?" I ask Phoebe.

"No. The UN thought so, at first. But everyone just... they just dropped dead, the moment the UN launched their nukes on the Shadow world. So far? It looks like all of the humans suffered heart attacks. Over ten million of them simultaneously."

Ten million.

"Some kind of Shadow world weapon that Raven designed for them before he was cast out, maybe," I say, my brain struggling to make sense of it. "That's why the humans haven't used nukes so far, they've suspected the Shadows have something just as terrible to retaliate and blow up the humans with..."

But Phoebe is shaking her head.

"That's not it," she whispers.

So many dead. Oh, God. Could I have done more? Could I have worked any faster to stop the onward march of slaughter, of insanity, of the end of all life? Watching the footage, it feels like seeing a personal failure.

Mum, I'm sorry. I've let you down.

"You know how so far the universe seems to have been keeping its scales balanced?" Phoebe continues. "A Shadow gets shot down in the field and his human partner dies in a car crash on the other side, or a platoon is wiped out in battle so an earthquake kills several in the other world. There's always a price to be paid, some universal scales that need to be kept balanced. But what if these attacks were just too much? Like..."

"... like a glitch in a PC game," I say.

"Exactly. The Shadow death count from the nukes was all too much. So their humans in the cities on the other side just died, instantaneously. No more sleight of hand, no more concealing the deaths in some other unrelated way. This is the result."

I can't look away from the dark, still bodies in those streets. Lovers and families, children and their parents.

The screen goes black. Phoebe takes it away. My breathing's erratic, and tears burn my eyes. I try to fight them back. What good are my feelings going to do? I failed to find a way to stop this. The Siren was our best shot but I didn't find a way to debug it in time. If I'd been smarter, perhaps if I'd been as smart as Calvin, then maybe Raven and I could have worked out a way to fix the Siren. We could have prevented this.

We still have to fix it. It's our only shot now.

Somehow, I have to convince the others, and if not, I need to break out of here and get to the equipment. I need time to figure out if the changes that Raven and I made have managed to perfect the Siren and fix exactly what part of it reacted so badly with Sophie and Hanna.

"At least it looks like the humans have finally woken up to the fact that they're intrinsically linked to Shadows," Phoebe says bitterly. "Twenty million dead is all it took."

I look at her, surprised.

"Well, that's something, right?" I say, wretched. "At least something came out of all the deaths. This ends things. They can't continue the war now that they accept the connection between the worlds."

Phoebe doesn't seem as in agreement as I'd hoped her to be.

"Phoebe," I say, keeping my voice steady. "What else?"

Phoebe hesitates.

"A lot happened when you were unconscious," she says as she finds another video and hands the tablet back. I'm watching more footage taken from the Shadow world, this time from what I recognise as Sanctuary City. I watch as Imperial citizens gather in the streets of the floating city, staring up at the big crystal orbs that serve as electronic billboards in the main streets and squares. Instead of flashing up commercials and Imperial propaganda like they were the first time I was there, they're all showing the face of one Shadow.

Down in the streets, the people get on their knees and prostrate themselves before the Shadow's image. Billions of Shadows, all welcoming in the newest Emperor.

Who would have thought that one day little Cirrus would finally rise to take the position of Emperor, his face plastered right across the city of his childhood?

"I'm confused," I say, unsettled in the extreme. "Was this taken when Eclipse was last over there?"

"No, we let him broadcast this from our own studio. He hasn't left for the Shadow world yet, Grif, he's still here."

"I know, I can feel him. Wait, you let him...?" I'm starting to get angry. "After what happened? Okay, I'm going to need some answers, Phoebe, because everything's really screwed up right now, and my own Shadow just tried to kill me, and..."

"Eclipse didn't try to kill you."

"It felt suspiciously like that," I mutter. "You should have seen him. He was berserk. He was out of control..."

"Exactly. He wasn't in control. That wasn't him, Grif. He's always had some darker instincts, right? As Cirrus, as Eclipse... but he learnt to tame them. The good in him always won. But losing Hanna... it was just too much. He blacked out and he barely remembers what happened. He feels awful. But it wasn't him in control."

"Part of him wanted to do that though, didn't it?" I say, hurting. "Even if it's the beast that he pushed far down."

Phoebe, not knowing what to say, simply plays the video again. Eclipse starts to speak on the screens of Sanctuary.

"You may have heard, as the news has spread like wildfire," Eclipse starts, *"but I am your new Emperor. My name is Eclipse."* I can sense his embarrassment at addressing so many, but he also looks determined. Princely.

"All hail, Emperor Eclipse!" the citizens shout in the streets down below.

"I'm sharing my role with Empress Hanna, who you knew once as Empress Demetria. She is fighting a savage illness, and I ask you all to have her in your prayers. Many of you may not want Hanna or myself as your rulers, but Empress Galvanize is dead. Her cruelty, her madness, and her failure to deal with this war have led to so many Shadows dying for no reason. Part of me wishes I hadn't been chosen as Emperor," Eclipse says honestly. *"That I hadn't been given the burden of Emperor, especially in times as dark as these. What happened today is a tragedy unlike any other. The sights from our cities are beyond*

imagining, and we are supplying all of the aid and support we possibly can to the survivors. I know how many of you have lost loved ones, and my heart goes out to you.

'I know you will want to avenge your loved ones, but you know how this war will end if we do: in blood. Our blood and theirs. The cycle has to stop. Because no matter what the Empire has preached up until now, there is a link between ourselves and humans that cannot be denied. Tens of millions of humans dropped dead the moment they bombed us. Each of our lives is tied to a human life in the other world however much some of us want to deny it. This is a war that cannot be won.

'So, in my first act as Emperor, I have approached the GSA myself. I have asked them to help broker a deal between our world and the human world. My first action as Emperor will be ending this war.

'These losses... they've changed everything. The GSA has helped to negotiate an agreement between myself and the United Nations. We are calling it 'The Treaty of Total Separation.'"

My heart stops.

"Calvin," I whisper. "Eclipse took Calvin's proposal to the Shadows. The worlds both actually went for it."

"*All of the portals will be closed,*" Eclipse says. "*All of our troops are coming home, and the humans are leaving these shores, forever. Now, with your blessing, I will head to Brisbane to sign the peace treaty. The worlds will remain separate forever...*" as he says it, I swear I see a sharp shard of pain in my Shadow's eyes, "*...just as they were before.*"

The video ends.

"Every single Shadow and human without exception will return to their own world," Phoebe says in a rush, as if desperate to share the burden of the news.

"Everyone?" I say faintly. "Even the GSA?"

"Especially us. We have to make an example, if both the worlds are going to cooperate." She clears her throat and I can see the emotions playing out dangerously behind her eyes, threatening to eat her alive. "We all have to say good-bye. We all have to let our counterparts go."

"You can't!" I burst out. "They can't do this."

"It's done, Grif. They humans and Shadows are going to sign the Treaty of Total Separation. All the newspaper headlines are calling it 'The *Nevermore* Treaty.' No one ever wants to see a conflict like this ever again. The troops are already retreating from both worlds back through the portals. Yay, us."

"How long have I been out?" I whisper.

"A day and a half."

"A *day* and...?"

"This thing with Eclipse really messed with you. All of the portals have already closed but one. Tomorrow the GSA is going to oversee the ceremonial signing of the treaty, then all our Shadows are going back home. The final portal will close forever."

I try and imagine it. A future where there's no chance of being with Eclipse. After what I did, after what happened between us... I know there's no tomorrow for us. My heart breaks. But there should be for everyone else. That's what Mum and Silvaluna wanted. That's my destiny, it's been my destiny my whole life.

Without it, without Eclipse, who am I?

The two bright threads of our lives, always tied in a knot, are being severed in a single swing. I try and imagine that future where the Shadow world is closed off to us forever but all I see is blackness. It's impossible to imagine. Even after all the horrors we've seen in the war, this somehow is the most unspeakable. I feel the deep fear of oblivion growing and growing, the hopeless despair of it spreading through me.

I recall the anger and hatred in Eclipse's eyes as he chased me, and suddenly I want to start crying. I can feel Phoebe watching, and force myself to blink back the stinging tears. I don't want to look weak or selfish in front of her, I don't want her to see me like that.

Phoebe wordlessly reaches out and she holds my hand, gripping it tightly.

I can't believe that it's so soon. All *over,* just like that.

"Calvin's betrayed everything Mum stood for," I say violently.

"He thought that we should be prepared for a scenario like this, yes," Phoebe tells me. "He knew it might be the only outcome both worlds would accept. No humans and Shadows coexisting, but at least no more death and bloodshed on our conscience. He also knew you would never accept it and that you'd probably try and do something stupid to prevent it. He wasn't wrong. He knew how blindly loyal you are to Melissa's cause."

"Who do you think taught me that? What does our family have to show now, for all our work?"

"Saving billions of lives, I guess," Phoebe says dully.

"I can't believe that *you're* lying down and accepting it," I say heatedly.

"Don't," she says dangerously, and that single word makes me jam my mouth shut at once. "I'm tired of living with the guilt of causing all this, aren't you? Ever since we opened those portals, we've given every inch of ourselves to trying to end this. You and me both. I'm prepared to say goodbye to the one I love more than anything if it stops more people dying needlessly. So don't tell me that I'm weak."

"Phoebe," I say, my voice breaking. "How can you... how do you even go about saying goodbye to Ember? How do you live without her when you've just got her back after all this time?"

"I don't know," Phoebe whispers.

"Were you there at the negotiations?"

"Yeah. Zephyr and Calvin too. Calvin's taken over as the face of the GSA, while you... while you get better."

My head swims.

"He's taken over as head honcho?" I say wryly. "A little opportunistic."

"You know we're a team, really. '*Leader*' is just a title."

"So Calvin's having me locked in here and declared an insane traitor so he can push his agenda through when I'm out of commission?" I say, blood boiling.

"Thickhead," Phoebe sighs. "You still don't get it, do you? Calvin loves you. He's trying to protect you from doing something you'll regret."

"Protect what, my *innocence?* Doesn't he know the things I've already done?" I laugh bitterly. "He has no idea what I'm capable of, what I'm prepared to do for the cause."

"He knows. He just wants to save you from following through with actions you can't take back. The actions that will haunt you, the ones that you'll struggle to live with. Calvin's trying to protect your *soul*. The guilt you feel over what happened to Sophie... he never wanted you to feel anything like that, Grif."

I can't look at Phoebe. She's being far too kind. Part of her must despise me for what I've done. Part of her must barely be able to look at me.

"Calvin was hardened by trying to fulfil your Mum's mission," she reminds me. "He lost the joy of living, and he never wanted that for you. It's why he lied about Shadows being real when you were growing up, however misguided that was."

I shake my head. It's all too hard and inconceivable. Phoebe's already forgiving Calvin for pulling this on us? Surely part of her must blame him as the one who's taking Ember away from her.

"What about Raven?" I ask suddenly.

"The human world negotiated to keep Raven in the world where he was born and prosecute him here. The GSA is going to hold onto him here until the trial, once the portals are closed."

"So all of the GSA have to give up their Shadows because of the treaty?" I say disbelievingly. "Calvin's just going to wave goodbye to Zephyr? Everyone here has to split up with their counterparts forever? They're never going to see each other again?"

I remember when Phoebe was reunited with Ember, the love I saw between them. Phoebe has been so happy since she got Ember back at long last. I try and imagine what their goodbye will look like, but it breaks my heart to even try.

"I know," Phoebe says heavily. "It's going to feel like hell, but at least we can do it knowing…" She sobs suddenly, violently. "I don't want to lose Ember."

"Hey, hey," I say soothingly, taken by surprise. She might present her calm, in-control exterior to everyone else, but right now it's too much, and I see her let her disguise slip in front of me.

"I don't want to lose her, I just got her back Griffin, they can't take her! I can't just give her away… she's me," Phoebe whispers. Her head rests on the bed as I stroke her hair comfortingly. "She's me."

"Don't worry," I say, wishing I had more words to make her happy. More words to stop the wild fear in her that I feel in myself. "We're not going to let this happen. We're going to stop it."

"We're not," she sighs, closing her lids. "Can't you just…"

"Pheebs…"

"We started this war, whether or not Raven planned for us to," Phoebe says, her voice level again. "When we started this place we said we'd do whatever it took to stop the killing."

"The worlds were already falling apart before," I insist, "and you know it. Humans and Shadows need each other more than ever now."

"At least now we know," she says, brushing those tears away sardonically. "Things can always be worse."

I see it in her. That courage I've never seen in anyone else. If Phoebe believes this is the only right thing to do, if she really believes it's the best for the helpless and down-trodden out there who've borne the cost of this war more than most, then she'll go to any lengths to see it through, even if it means tearing herself in half.

"I'm so sorry, Phoebe," I whisper. "I'm so sorry that you have to… that I couldn't…"

"Griffin!"

I'm barely aware that I've fallen out of the bed before I hit the floor.

Flashes are ricocheting through my skull. I can hear Cirrus' laughter all around me, then I'm in the chapel again, seeing Cirrus spasming as he starts to transform into Eclipse. Now I'm seeing the cool endless sands under the stars, as Eclipse offered himself up knowingly to the Empire to save his people...

When the fit breaks I'm shivering, and Phoebe has fallen to the floor too. She's on her knees and she's pulled me into her, cradling me in her arms.

"I'm okay," I mutter feverishly, before she calls Zephyr or some medic. "I'm okay."

"No, you're not," Phoebe says, crying. She smoothes back my hair. It's matted with cold sweat, and I can't stop shivering. "This is all coming from being at odds with your-self. Shadow and human counterparts aren't meant to turn on each other. I've seen this so many times in the field. Humans and Shadows going insane until they become more like monsters. This feud with Eclipse is ripping you apart from the inside and I hate just sitting here having to watch it happen. You two need to make your peace before it's too late, okay? You need to before he leaves for good. Please. I don't want to lose you, I..."

She strokes my cheek with a thumb.

"I love you," she confesses tenderly. And before I can digest the shock of hearing those words, Phoebe's leaning down toward me, and her lips touch delicately against mine. It's one single moment of beauty. My heart leaps even in the middle of so much sadness.

When we finally part, I stare up at her in awe. I'm holding onto those three words, spoken in her voice.

"That's all I ever wanted," I say.

The corner of her mouth quirks up into a smile.

"I know."

But then, like the inevitable waking from a very, *very*

good dream, I remember my brother, and my one great moment of happiness is shadowed by an equal amount of pain.

"What?" Phoebe asks uncertainly.

The door crashes open.

"Griffin," a hoarse voice says. "I need to talk to…"

I turn to see Calvin standing there. He's staring at Phoebe and me, white as ash.

23
RAGNAROK

Calvin looks at us, frozen, and I can't possibly imagine what thoughts are crashing through his head. The guilt surges in, quick and fast, polluting the brief spark of happiness that I just found here. Suddenly I want to be a million miles away.

"What is this?" my brother finally says. He sounds surprisingly young and uncertain.

I jerk away from Phoebe, disentangling myself. I open my mouth, but my jaw gyrates, nothing useful seeming to come out of it no matter how many times I mentally search for possibly acceptable answers.

But Phoebe, likely due to everything that's happened and in the face of losing her own Shadow, doesn't even flinch.

"Stop trying to talk before you injure yourself," she tells me. I can hear her shame and her regret, but just for a moment. Then, looking to Calvin with resolve, she bluntly confesses: "I'm sorry, Gecko, but I have feelings for Griffin."

Time seems to stand still.

Calvin and I meet each other's eyes, and I don't know how to describe what passes between us. Then Calvin tears his gaze away, shaking his head in shock, in denial.

"But... he's just a kid," Calvin protests.

"So am I," Phoebe says simply.

"What," Calvin says, his face screwing up in pain. He sounds lost. "You're saying I'm too old for you? That you need someone your own age?"

"No. Just that I'm pretty sure you've known how Griffin and I have felt about each other for a while. Can't we all stop kidding ourselves for a moment, maybe?" Phoebe looks at both of us. "Don't pretend you didn't suspect something when you first told me how you felt on the beach, Calvin. You must have sensed that something had grown between me and Griffin on our journey there."

"Ridiculous," Calvin mutters, shaking with anger. He's pacing like a caged animal.

"I should have told you sooner," Phoebe says in a smaller voice. "That was wrong of me, and I should have talked to you. I'm sorry. I didn't mean to hurt you. I guess I've just been denying it for a while. I didn't want things to get complicated, but now... this doesn't seem as world-endingly scary anymore. I'm done with lies."

Calvin's gaze is piercing me as if he's about to explode, but Phoebe cuts him off.

"Listen, each of you," Phoebe says emphatically, and we turn our full attention on her. "I care about you both. I know that's not convenient, but I refuse to be part of a drama-filled love triangle. That's not my style. We have enough crap to be focusing on, you know? So... you two sort it out. Try and overcome your differences, and maybe nobody has to break up." She stands, making her way past Calvin toward the door of the cell.

The wheels in my head are still grinding and I think Calvin's are too, trying to understand exactly what it is Phoebe just said.

"I'm sorry," I say, highly confused, "are you saying that you and I could... date? And that you and Calvin could still keep dating? But... like, all at the same time?"

Even just framing that thought in my head is flummoxing enough that my brain has to shut down and reboot itself all over again.

"You two have a lot to talk over," Phoebe says casually. "Me? I'm going to go spend the rest of the time I have with my Shadow. I suggest you both do the same."

She leaves.

I don't think I've ever seen Calvin more stunned. He stands there rigidly. He opens his mouth to speak, than closes it again, like a perplexed goldfish.

"Can she *do* that?" I say, sweating. "Feel free to correct me, but was she suggesting... polygamy?"

"Polyamory," Calvin says. He clears his throat awkwardly. "Polygamy is when, er, multiple people are married. Polyamory is just when they're dating. I think."

"Ah. Thanks."

I'm pretty sure we both want the floor to swallow us. I turn to Calvin bleakly.

"I'm sorry," I whisper. "I tried to bury how I felt about her and give you two space. I didn't mean to ruin things and I didn't want to hurt you. I know what she means to you."

Calvin finally meets my eyes, and it's like the anger he's

been trying to suppress suddenly bursts forth, the dam breaking.

"Do you realise how utterly you've betrayed this organisation?" Calvin demands. "How you've betrayed me? You let Raven out of his cell. You worked side by side with him as if you were equals when you knew the unspeakable things he's done to us, to our parents, to our *family*."

"Yeah, what does that say?" I comment. "I had to turn to our worst enemy just to find someone who'd listen to me. You were too busy cooking up your own little betrayal behind my back."

"Because I knew you wouldn't understand about the treaty."

"So how's that any different from what I did with the Siren again? Just remind me."

"Well, my plan didn't break a girl's mind."

The words escape him before he can stop them. It hits me like a punch to the gut. I think Calvin instantly knows he's crossed a line, but his anger about Raven and Phoebe are taking control.

"No," I retaliate evenly. "You're just going to doom two worlds forever. Let their people shrivel into nothing, cut off from everything that they're meant to be, cut off from their potential, cut off from the one person in the universe who can bring each of them joy and peace. You can't possibly be planning to follow through with this. Help me, let's find a way to fix the Siren and activate it. There's still time. But it has to be now."

"Your Siren is a lost cause."

"It's not," I say, with heat. I realise I'm standing now. "I've seen the Siren work. We all have."

"You can't force everyone to accept their other half,

Grif," Calvin says. "Look at you. You and Eclipse spent your early childhood together, and this conflict between you has ended you up in here."

"You always had to feel superior to me," I say in wonder. "You were always so reluctant to admit I was right."

"We can analyse my child-rearing another time," Calvin says, rolling his eyes.

"You held me to an impossible standard, and now that I'm on the verge of finally meeting it, when I've achieved the unthinkable and found a way that could make Mum and Silvaluna's vision real... you refuse to acknowledge it."

"This '*Siren*' you invented to force the minds of counterparts to hear each other..." Calvin shakes his head. "You know it doesn't work that way. You should have known and anticipated the shock that would cause some individuals. We warned you. Each of us had to come to know our counterpart. Confronting someone with the true face of who they are, so suddenly and so violently... is unspeakably immoral."

"Immoral? Since when has that bothered you? Ever since you became a Majestic you've lost the steel in you that made you Calvin Cameron. You know it. You don't have the conviction anymore to do what has to be done."

"Grif, you're my little brother," Calvin says with exasperation, his fingers twitching, "and I'm trying very hard to help you, and to be on your side. But I'm also trying really hard to not punch you in the face right now."

"All that time you spent down in the lab analysing Raven's tech, trying to get inside his head... you always wanted to be him, didn't you?" I say. "You always felt like you fell short. Well, you know what, Calvin? I think you're just jealous that you didn't figure out how to make the Siren a reality before I did, and now instead of being proud of me you can't stand it."

In a flare of rage Calvin shoves me backward. I stumble, and now he's advancing on me, and I've got nowhere to go…

He pins me against the wall of the cell, hard. The spongy surface seems to deflate behind me.

"Why are you always so determined to screw everything up?" he pants. "You know, I thought we were actually making some kind of progress to fix things between us? Maybe you didn't notice because you're so used to always painting me as your villain, rather than taking responsibility for your own issues. Or maybe it was just that you were just too busy trying to steal my girlfriend."

"Oh, come on," I gasp, trying to writhe free. "*Stealing* implies Phoebe doesn't have more free will in this than either of us combined."

Speaking Phoebe's name seems to inflame my brother even more. He presses his arm into my windpipe. I flail like a pinned butterfly.

"As a kid, I thought the sun shone out of you," I manage, incensed. "You were the hero who could always pull off the impossible, who would do what was right. That Calvin could never have possibly thought this treaty was a win."

"It's not a loss," Calvin fires back. "Everyone gets to live."

"If you do this, you know that no one will open portals between the worlds ever again. The war is all they'll remember about each other."

"The improbable utopian future our family dreamed of isn't the only thing at stake here, little brother," Calvin says with cold fury and... is that *fear?* "Ever since we lost Cameron Technologies, we've been running for our lives. Starting up the GSA only put a bigger target on your head. At least when this war is over, even if the paradise our family dreamed of doesn't exist, you'll be safe. We all will be. We can lead normal lives, which is what I wanted for you back before you ever went to the Shadow world. So I'll do whatever it takes to make sure this treaty goes off without a hitch. I'm your big brother, and what you were going to do with the Siren... I couldn't let you become that. I'm supposed to protect you, no matter what." Calvin's whispering now, haunted. "I tried to do what Mum would have wanted. I always tried to do my best for you."

"Yeah," I wheeze, his arm still crushing my windpipe. I sound like I've had too much helium. "You're doing a super stellar job of that."

As if noticing what he's doing for the first time, Calvin staggers backward, appalled. He looks at me, like waking from a daze.

"If you still want me to believe you've become a better person since being a Majestic, sorry," I tell him, hurting at more than one level. "Not convinced."

Calvin backs away, feeling for the doorway. I reflect that soon because of him, Shadows will for all intents and purposes no longer exist to us. They'll only be a memory, a fantasy, just like Calvin spent so much time and effort trying to convince me while I was growing up.

"Go spend the time you have left with Zephyr," I say, rubbing my throat. "You know, the Shadow I nearly died trying to bring back to you."

Calvin holds up a hand, and for some reason I stop. He has his eyes closed.

"Fine then," he says softly. "Push away the only people who care about you, just like you did spectacularly with Eclipse. You're right, Griffin, you're an adult now. My job of taking care of you is over. You've made your own choices, and its time you faced the consequences."

I try to tear away the padding on the walls of my cell, hoping to find a fault or flaw that I can use to break out of this place, but it stubbornly resists my nails.

Phoebe left her tablet with me so I'd have some entertainment, but after combing through news reports on the tragedies and the treaty for hours, and discovering that Phoebe deactivated any hacking capabilities it may have had to get me out of here, I leave it lying abandoned on the floor.

Letting out a cry of frustration I look back at the straps that had bound me to the bed. Even freed from them, I'm still trapped in here.

I'm strangely reminded of the Norse myth of Loki, the trickster and shape-shifter. I loved myths and legends growing up, especially anything to do with Loki. Half-giant and half-God, Loki had never really belonged to either group. He ended up tied to a rock deep underground by the Gods who were once his friends, as punishment for his treachery and the death of another God: a bright, beautiful and innocent soul called Baldur. Raging, Loki had struggled against his bonds, helpless to do anything but wait as Ragnarok, the end of all things, approached.

Loki: trickster, shapeshifter, liar.

I guess that's me.

. . .

I'm staring at the roof with my own tortured thoughts when Phoebe comes to see me. I know it must be morning, because the artificial light coming through my window has brightened slightly.

"I just came to say goodbye," Phoebe whispers. "We're heading out to the treaty signing at the Brisbane portal, and to… to say goodbye to everyone."

She means their Shadows. Zephyr and Ember and all the others.

"Do I not get an invite?" I say humourlessly.

"You should, Grif, you should really come along and… you deserve to be there," Phoebe says adamantly on my behalf. "I want you to come; I want you to be there with us." Stepping closer, she takes my hand in hers. The feel of her skin against mine fills me with emotion; but I don't want to break down right now, I want to stay strong. I just can't see any way out of this. It's a nightmare I'm powerless to stop. "It's not right; you helped this happen as much as anyone. Calvin just thinks…"

"He doesn't trust me not to create trouble."

Her lack of an answer is a definite yes.

"Zephyr says your brain scans all look fine, so that's good news."

"Huzzah."

"But you should still be kept under observation for a bit."

The lack of any medical evidence just proves that whatever is happening to me is definitely something between Eclipse and me, something deeper and not yet within the purview of modern neuroscience.

"Yeah," Phoebe says briskly, seeing my expression. "I know. All of this is crap."

Understatement of the century.

"Are the others all leaving now too?" I ask.

"Yeah. A lot of them… they're still coming to terms with what you were planning with the Siren. I'm sure they will, in time. Some of them do want to say goodbye," she says, "before they go home through the portal."

"I don't want them to see me. Not like this."

"Grif, you have to talk to Zephyr and Ember…"

"I can't. I'm so sorry Phoebe, I just can't."

If I say goodbye to them, it means they're really leaving. It means that half of our family here will really be gone.

She shakes her head, softly tracing my hand with her fingers.

"Did you…" Phoebe exhales nervously. "Did you and Calvin talk anymore about… you know."

"We had what passes for a brotherly conversation with us."

She sighs.

"That bad, huh? Have you thought about it anymore, though? I mean… what are you feeling?"

I wonder how to even start to articulate my feelings, even just about us, let alone everything else.

"I know you care about Calvin," I say finally, "and I… and that you care about me too." It feels strange, even presumptuous saying that last bit aloud. Phoebe nods though, and doesn't correct me, so that's promising. I exhale. My brain and heart are struggling to work through this. "I also know you're not planning to break up with Calvin anytime soon," I say.

Phoebe presses her lips firmly together, giving me a reproachful look.

"No, I'm not," she says awkwardly.

"Right," I mutter, feeling suddenly like I was wrong to push her. "I know that. Sorry."

"It just... it feels like you're trying to make me feel guilty for feeling how I feel, and I refuse," Phoebe says honestly. "I refuse to be ashamed for being in love with two extraordinary people. I just won't. My feelings for you and Calvin can't be compared and contrasted. They're two separate things. I seriously don't mean to seem greedy or selfish. It's just that if one of those loves has to break apart for another one to exist, if one has to be sacrificed for the other, then I don't know if that's a kind of love I'm interested in. You both mean so much to me, and I don't want to disrespect either of you."

Startled, I stare at her. I slowly shake my head.

"I'm not trying to shame you. I think you're the most magnificent person, I really do. What you're suggesting... that you keep dating Calvin *and* me... I think it's pretty mind-twistingly weird," I confess. "But, I mean, these are pretty mind-twistingly weird times. And after all the suffering we've seen, I'm all for us each finding our own little bit of happiness, however we can, no matter how weird it seems from the outside, no matter what other people think. Life's so short." I take in a breath. "With us though... I just... I can't, Pheebs. I'm sorry. I don't want to lie awake at night, wondering if Calvin does things better than I do, if he's a...." I'm about to say *'if he's a better kisser,'* and I shudder at the thought. I'm too embarrassed to voice the insecurity out loud.

"It's not a comparative thing," Phoebe says in a flat voice. "What happens between you and me, and what happens between Calvin and me... those are two separate things. Love isn't pie. There's not a finite number of slices to deal out."

"I get that, and I'd do anything to be with you. Calvin's family, though. It's too hard and it's too strange and I think it's going to break me apart. I'm sorry, Pheebs."

A tear makes its way down her cheek.

"I understand. Sorry. I don't mean to be stupid," she mutters. "I just really wanted at least one good thing to come out of all of this."

"I guess we won't have to live here anymore, at least?" I offer. "That's not bad."

"Yeah. The GSA are being granted immunity for making this treaty happen. We can go back to Auckland, or what's left of it. We can start normal lives."

It's strange. After so long spent loathing this place and fighting claustrophobia on a daily basis, the thought of leaving it suddenly makes me ache. This ship is home. Without the Shadows though, it will feel so empty.

"What's the mood like?" I ask. "Out there, in the base."

"Awful," Phoebe says simply. "Everyone's saying goodbye. It feels like twenty break-ups at once."

"When you come back from seeing Ember off," I say, "you and me can eat ice cream from ridiculous sized tubs and watch cheesy movies and cry for like a week. We don't even have to shower."

Phoebe finally laughs. A snotty laugh, as she's crying.

"I'd like that."

"What are friends for?"

She nods, smiling sadly.

"I've got to go," she says. "Spend some time with Ember, before...." All of a sudden it looks like Phoebe is going to break down. She gathers herself though, blinks back the tears with a will of steel.

"You should go," I say softly. "Thanks for visiting me, but go. Be with her."

"There seem to be a lot of goodbyes today," Phoebe whispers, and bending down, she gently pulls me close to kiss me. But this kiss is as sad as it is sweet, and I know this is her way of saying goodbye to what could have been *us*. I'd never imagined that anything could simultaneously be this pleasurable and torturous. Her lips linger tenderly on mine, my face wet with her tears before she pulls away.

"Well?" Phoebe says, almost mischievously. "That didn't change your mind?"

"Close, but there was a lot of snot."

She snorts, and punches me in the arm.

"Yeah, well, you deserve it." Phoebe straightens. "I'll see you soon."

"Right," I say, my stomach sinking as reality settles in.

"Um, Griffin..."

"That's me."

"Eclipse wants to see you. He wants to say goodbye."

My insides tighten. I don't answer for a moment. Opening my mind slightly, I can feel Eclipse's getting closer. So he's still here in the base. I can feel his colours brushing against mine. I don't know whether to run from them or toward them.

But then I push Eclipse's mind away, hurting.

"I don't want to see him," I whisper.

"Griffin... this is your last chance. You'll never see Eclipse again."

"He tried to kill me."

"He lost control. He'd just lost his friend because of

something you... just *talk* to him. If you don't, you'll regret it for the rest of your life. I don't want you to have to live with that."

I keep my mouth determinedly shut. I can't think of anything but the fact that this treaty betrays all of Mum and Silvaluna's dreams for a more joyful universe.

Phoebe opens her mouth again. For a moment she looks like she might want to hit me over the head for being so stubborn, remind me of how much I'll regret this... but then I think she remembers how Eclipse hunted me through the base, and what I've been through.

She nods, troubled, and leaves for the door.

"Phoebe?"

She looks back at me on the threshold.

I want to tell her that I'll still be there with her when she says goodbye to Ember and signs the treaty. I want to tell her that she's strong enough for this, that she's the strongest person I know.

"Please don't do this," I say instead. "It's wrong."

"Grif," she says tiredly, "for God's sake..."

"I've never told you this," I whisper, and she pauses. "I've never talked about it to anybody. But there used to be a kid called Rick in my school. He and his friends used to bully me, mercilessly. I don't know why. He was smart and athletic. He had it all going for him. Maybe it was a power trip for him. Or maybe he was just bored. When I first went to the Shadow world, I killed someone in battle for the first time. She was a Shadow called Nugwai. And when I got back to this world... Rick was dead.

'I *knew* that Nugwai was his Shadow. I could just feel it. When I looked into her eyes when I killed her... it was like Rick was staring back at me."

Phoebe is looking at me, shocked.

"If we don't use the Siren," I say past the lump in my throat, "if we don't help every single human to hear their Shadow, then all of this was for nothing. None of their sacrifices mean anything. Rick and Nugwai. Mum and Silvaluna... Dad. Sophie and Hanna. Mr Falco."

Phoebe slowly bows her head against the door frame.

"This isn't easy for any of us, Grif," she says. "I can't do what you're asking me to do with the Siren. Frankly? It terrifies me that you thought you were capable of using it in the first place."

"I just..."

"It's over, Grif," Phoebe says, unable to look at me. "It's time for goodbyes, not misguided last-minute heroics. I'm sorry."

Only after Phoebe has left and I'm lying on the bed does a familiar, giant golden head looms into sight on the other side of the window. A single wide, dark eye stares in at me, anxious and inquisitive.

"I'm so sorry," Eclipse says softly through the glass. "I don't know what happened, Grif. I still can't believe I lost control like that. I didn't think that darkness was still in me. It scares me. I can't believe I could do that to you." He doesn't speak for a moment, like he's still waiting for a reply. "I'm ashamed, but I'm also so hurt and so... confused. I know you didn't mean for what happened to Hanna, of course you didn't. But I still can't make sense of it. It just feels like everything I shared with Hanna, everything we built together was for nothing..." I feel the pain swelling in his chest, taunted by his memories of her. "So many of the best moments of my life have been with you," Eclipse says to me. "But I have to go and do this. It's what Hanna and I fought for. The end of the war. I know you believe it's a mistake, but can't we just have this one moment to say goodbye? Just for one minute let's act like we never got separated, as if we spent our entire lives together. I need this. I'll need this moment to hang onto in all the days and years to come when you're not there."

I roll over, turning my back to Eclipse.

You think I like this? I hear him say. *You think I want this anymore than you do? We're not kids anymore, Grif. We're not dreamers. We just have to find some way to move forward.*

I can sense him bowing his head. I've blocked his mind, but I can still hear a parting whisper make its way through my barriers, so very faint.

I'm so proud of who you've become, even if sometimes you can't see it in yourself, Eclipse thinks to me with all of his heart, *and I'll always be with you, even if you can't see me.*

And then he's gone. I turn to see his eye has vanished from the other side of the glass, and his consciousness is already too far away, fainter, fainter, fading...

When I can't bare it anymore, I cry out into the mental space between us. I cry as the pain finally sets in, the realisation that this really is happening. I'm really losing him forever. But there's no reply, and all I can feel is nothingness. And that's when I know Eclipse is too far away, that he's flying away from the base and I left it too long. I run to the glass and hammer it with my fists. My hands hurt, but it's an easy pain. The harder pain would have been to confess to Eclipse that I was too reckless with the Siren, to tell him that I know I'm responsible and how badly I wish I could give Hanna back to him, whole.

Eclipse? I cry out.

But he's gone.

Then I feel terrible as the guilt sets in, unrelenting and pitiless. I already miss Eclipse more than anything. I miss him like a deep, physical pain, like a piece of me has been forcefully ripped out. I damn my pride at losing my last chance. I lie there curled up in the Asylum and I cry at how powerless we really are in the grand motions of the universe, and how indifferent it seems to all of us.

24

AIN'T NO PLACE FOR A HERO

I have to get out of here. I have to find some way to stop this treaty from going ahead, even though I have no clue how.

Time has run out. The hands of the clock are on midnight. There's no way I can fix this in time. I run everything over and over in my head but there are too many variables and possibilities. Even if I was free from this cell… Raven and I think we've fixed the Siren, but how can I be one hundred percent sure? I wanted to do more rigorous testing with much larger sample sizes to know for sure that no one else would be adversely affected like Sophie and Hanna were. Are Sophie and Hanna completely unique in how they reacted? What exactly was it between the nature of the signal and their brains which caused the reaction? To figure out if I've really fixed the Siren, and rule out any chance of this happening to anyone again, requires far more time than I have.

I scream for help. I scream and scream but no one can hear me. For all intents and purposes, the universe is ending out there. It's Ragnarok, the end of all things. The end of hope, the end of unity. And the leader of the GSA is locked in his cell.

Maybe it's my fault for putting up a wall, for keeping my distance from the others here in the base. Eclipse was right. I'd been so angry at Eclipse after he betrayed me at the station, that I'd taken it out on the others here. I'd separated myself from everyone. Eclipse had helped me to start reconnecting with them, but it was too little too late. I should have trusted more of my team with the truth of what I was working on. If I'd had their help, the extra hands could have made all the difference.

Sitting on the bed with Phoebe's tablet, I watch the live stream of the treaty signing ceremony in Brisbane. The fanfare and troops collected around the enormous, reflective orb. Shadows marching through it, returning to their home dimension for good.

It feels like an out of body experience seeing the black limos lining the streets outside Parliament House, metal barricades holding back an enormous crowd of onlookers who watch wide-eyed as history unfolds before them. The nine months of the war seemed to go on for multiple lifetimes. Now it's officially ending. I can see shots of the Brisbane portal too, a giant, mirror-like sphere that rears up above the city. Its surface seems to reflect the buildings below but if you look closely you can see that it's actually showing the buildings from the Shadow world version of Brisbane on the other side.

The live stream cuts to the interior of the room where the treaty is being signed. Everyone is arrayed around a long, dark wooden table, and at either end are countless rows of flags; representing the nations of Earth and the

Shadow world. Flowing down the walls like grand tapestries are two giant flags. Behind the Shadow representatives hangs the crowned heart of the Empire in dazzling gold, crossed with talons, wreathed in flames. Opposite it, behind the human representatives is the flag of the United Nations, the white world map emblem surrounded by two olive branches on a blue background.

It hits me hard when I recognise so many of the faces arrayed around the table. It's a strange thing to see them all there, the focus of billions of other eyes across the two worlds besides mine.

I recognise the faces from the United Nations Security Council, of course, but it's a shock seeing Eclipse opposite them. Chairs have been cleared to let him stand freely, because there's no chair that could hold him, and it would be logistically tricky to add in a giant perch to the meeting room. Behind Eclipse, Imperial guards stand at attention, now armoured in resplendent gold to match him. I feel a fresh pang as I see the empty throne beside Eclipse. A seat reserved in honour of the other leader of the Shadows, Empress Hanna, in absentia.

Then there's the GSA members seated on both sides, overseeing the signing of the treaties. There's Calvin and Zephyr, and Phoebe, beside a small empty perch. I frown. Where's Ember? Has she already returned through the portal, not wanting to stay and watch the proceedings? Phoebe's face is definitely hard as she watches the negotiations, referring to some notes before her as Calvin reads out the text of the treaty.

The treaty in question is impressively and, it seems to me, unnecessarily large. It's laid out on the table for the two parties to sign before the final portal closes. Before our two peoples say goodbye for good.

I reach out to touch the image of Eclipse on the screen, as if I can pass through the glass and have a chance to say the goodbye I squandered.

But then I hear a noise.

I pause for just a fraction of a second. Then I look up at the door of my cell. Did I imagine that? The sound of movement from the other side?

"Get down," a voice says through the speakers.

I throw myself down onto the bouncy-castle style floor just as the lock on my door begins to glow the colour of magma. The door blasts open, a trail of fire escaping into the cell. The flames whip narrowly over my head.

"Was he down?" the voice asks. "I couldn't actually see if he was down." I recognise that voice. But I still don't understand.

"What the hell?" I exclaim. "*Ember?*"

"Oh, howdy Griffin. I didn't know that was you in there."

Tentatively, I step toward the opened door.

"You realise you just had to open my door from the outside?" I say.

"Ah, I may have forgotten," Ember replies. "Good thing you enjoy theatrics as much as I do."

As I get closer I make out Ember waiting for me, as well as other faces clustered excitedly on either side of the flaming bird of prey.

It looks like half of the GSA are here.

Tears well up in my eyes.

"I thought everyone had left for the portal," I say

emotionally, still dazed. This definitely *feels* like a breakout, but I don't want to count my eggs before they hatch.

"We're meant to take the second jet and meet them there. Calvin, Zephyr and Phoebe don't know what's going on yet."

"Ember, why aren't you with Phoebe at the treaty signing?"

"I told her I wanted some time to process things on my own and that I'd be on the second jet." Ember casts her gaze down just for a moment, hinting at the agony playing out inside of her. "Phoebe wasn't happy; it gives us much less time to say goodbye, but I couldn't tell her the real reason I stayed behind. She wouldn't understand."

"What reason?" I look at all of them, still not cottoning on. "Are you planning to run away and hide, so you don't have to give each other up? What's your plan here, exactly?"

"Well, that's a complicated question," Ember posits. "One that we're really hoping you'll have a good answer to."

I raise an eyebrow, not quite understanding.

"Not everyone thinks that Calvin and the others were right to block your research on the Siren," Arian speaks up. "I understand why they were worried about playing with other people's minds, but you're just amplifying what's already there. How could that possibly be worse than this war? How could it be worse than the agony of forcing all of us to farewell our other halves and splitting us in two?"

"As you can see, we're not all in support of Calvin and Emperor Eclipse's treaty," Ember says evenly. I catch only the tiniest spasm of emotion as she mentions Eclipse's name, and his new title. "Consider this something of a mutiny. We are on a ship, after all. We believe in you. We believe that your Siren is the way to fix this, we've seen what it can do when it works. And we're with you all the way, no matter what the others say."

I look around at them, overwhelmed. Nearly half of the GSA has stayed. Nam and Ashwind. Sien and Pixie. Jade and Arian, Georgia and Tovii, even Celeste and her counterpart April. April was once so afraid of Shadows she actually tried to shoot Eclipse. How people change. Some of our new recruits have stayed too: Blanca's here, the only one apart from Sophie who hasn't met her own Shadow, as well as Molly and her fearsome Shadow Grindelbark.

I want to say something, but I can't get the words out. Just minutes ago, I'd felt like nobody in the two worlds was still on my side, that I had no one.

"We won't go to the portal. We'll fight and die if we have to. I'm not going to let them take me and Grindelbark away from each other," Molly says fiercely, hugging herself into her giant, honey-furred bear.

"But... there's hardly any time until the portals close," I say slowly.

"So we have to act fast. Calvin told us that the Siren and all of your equipment had been destroyed," Ember says, "but if I know anything about you Griffin, it's that you're too smart to put all of your eggs in one basket. I'm sure with something this important, you had a back-up hidden away somewhere."

I hesitate. She's right. I was smart enough at least to think there was a chance that Eclipse or someone would uncover and destroy the Siren.

"Okay, you got me there," I confess slowly.

"Oh, you did make another one? Thank God, I wasn't sure."

I made another copy of the Siren which was up to date with the fixes Raven and I made to it since Sophie's adverse reaction. But if Calvin destroyed the other equipment then I'm going to have to improvise with what we have on the ship... I'll need more time.

It feels far too real now that we're here. What if my brain isn't enough for this? What if I hurt more people, the way I hurt Sophie and Hanna?

Still, this is our one chance. It's all or nothing now. For the first time, there's a flare of hope.

"There's no time to waste then," I say quietly. "I'll start taking a look at the Siren, fine-tuning it, run some last minute tests..."

"Grif, have you been watching the news?" Ember says uneasily.

"Yeah, I saw some of the signing. Why, how long do we have until they close the last portal?"

The others all look at each other uneasily.

"A few hours," Ember says, "tops."

My victorious high at getting released is just as swiftly crushed.

"A few hours?" I repeat, shocked and broken. "How...?"

I look between their hopeful, happy faces. Then, realising what they're asking, I recoil violently.

"No," I say, horrified. "No way."

"Griffin, you invented a way to end the war, and bring all humans and Shadows together at once. You're not going to use it?"

"You don't understand. It had... terrible, terrible side effects for some people. We need more tests..."

"We know what happened with Sophie was because of the Siren," Ember says softly.

"It happened to her Shadow too," I confess, haunted.

Which is the greater evil right now, doing nothing, or risking everything? Which of the two evils am I going to let define me?

I feel like I'm standing at the very edge of a jutting cliff, about to step off into empty air.

"But we know that it worked! It worked for everyone else you tried it on! Sophie and her Shadow could just be a freak accident, an outlier, an isolated incident..."

"Do you really want to risk being wrong? I've altered it since then, I've tried to fix what caused that reaction in Sophie, but I can't be sure. We haven't even trialled the new version."

"Look, I don't like this either, Griffin," Ember says, blazing. "But we all know in our gut that closing the portals is a temporary solution. Without our counterparts, both of the worlds will drown in loneliness, violence and self-destruction, just like before."

"We have *hours*," I say, incredulous. "A few hours before the last portal closes for good. And you want to take this chance with the mind of every single intelligent life form in this world and the other? There's no telling what will happen. It's chaos. It's playing with lives."

"It's our only chance," April says softly. "We believe in you, Griffin. You were there for us when no one else was, you started this whole place. I know what happened with Sophie shook you, but I think you know you've fixed what went wrong. You just need to believe in yourself again."

"We wouldn't have met our humans without you," Celeste bursts out. "That would have been, like, a total travesty. You gave us this place where we could be together. Everyone else deserves that too."

I try not to show them how overwhelmed I am. I'd thought I didn't have any real friends here.

"What I think everyone here is agreed in saying, Grif," Ember says, with that dangerous, ruthless twinkle in her eye, "Is that you are our leader. Everyone here pledged their fealty to you, and they'd do it again in a second. We trust you to lead us where no one has ever gone before."

But I can still feel the anxieties inside of me, as if the ground under my feet is tilting. It feels like the first signs that something was off before I broke down into hysterical laughter in front of everyone. I don't like the feeling of not being able to trust my own brain. Usually it's the one thing I have to rely on.

I need to decide. I need to take action. When I try to visualise a path to victory for us though, a way that this could work without hurting anyone... all I can see is Sophie's face, her smile the moment before it all went wrong.

"I need to see Sophie," I say. I don't know why, I just do. Am I looking for her permission? Can she even give it, even if she'd want to?

"Griffin, we don't have time..."

"Let me see her. Please."

Ember looks at me, getting the measure of where I'm at. Then she nods.

Jade walks over to Sophie's cell with me and opens the door. I enter.

Its occupant seems unaware of my presence, as if I'm a ghost. I kneel down in front of her. She looks so pale, hunched on her hind-legs, her hands clasped together.

"Hey Soph. It's me, Griffin," I say quietly, smiling sadly. "I'm here. I'm sorry I haven't been here more. I was working to try and fix what happened to you. I was trying to make this right, but I think I was a scaredy cat too. I was afraid of seeing you like this, and I should have spent more time with you." There's still no reaction. "I just want you to know how much you mean to me. You would have made a great apprentice, you know. You're so brave and fearless. You have so much kindness in you ..." I shake my head. "But I already knew what you were capable of. I knew from the first time I laid eyes on you at school. You talked to me when no one else wanted to talk to the weirdo, the outcast. I remember how you believed in magic back then, like me. You believed that there were still wonderful impossible things in the world that nobody understood. You still dreamed of heroics and adventures in the books that you read on the bus on the way home. I adored you from the moment we met. I thought you were a real-life princess, and this light seemed to come from you no matter what." I sit down beside her. Sophie's looking at the wall of her cell with interest, seeing something play out in the distance that no one else can see. "When I first met Hanna, I felt the same way," I tell her. "What Hanna wanted more than anything in the entire world was her human. She was trying to find you, Sophie. She loved you; she would have fought for you and died for you if she could have, even though she'd never even met you.

'Hanna's suffered through so much darkness, Sophie. Part of her became that darkness as she reflected the evil that had surrounded her for her whole life. But part of her was always still with you. There was always that bright spark that was you hidden down deep inside her. Nothing could erase that. It was thanks to you that Hanna chose to save her friend Eclipse and abandon Raven, even though Raven had been her entire world. Hanna tried to make life better for all Shadows, to save her people from this war. It meant that she would never get to meet you, and I'm sure that hurt more than anything, but she thought that's what it would take to save everybody else. It's crazy to think that my Shadow and yours were working together all this time over there, trying to build something good."

I want to hug Sophie, but she's started muttering feverishly again, and I'm afraid she might freak out if I invade her personal space. So I just watch her with a roaring in my ears. I can feel the burden of the decision I'm about to make, crushing me.

If I refuse to activate the Siren and send its video out to all the humans and their Shadows, then I know the grim, lonely future that awaits both of the worlds.

But if we attempt to connect all of the counterparts together and fail, or even if the Siren only works on some people for whatever reason... we could put the peace that Phoebe, Calvin, Zephyr and Eclipse have all painstakingly achieved into jeopardy. Whatever choice I make right now, the universe will never be the same.

Helplessly, I search for answers as I huddle there beside Sophie in the silent room.

Then Sophie suddenly reaches out in front of her, and it's as if she's pressing her hand against the hand of someone that only she can see.

"You're beautiful," Sophie whispers dreamily. "You're the most gorgeous thing I've ever seen." Sophie cocks her head, quizzically, listening to a voice that I cannot hear. "You're alone?" she says to the invisible person, saddened. Then she brightens. "That's okay. I'm alone too."

I feel pained seeing Sophie like this. Imagining things, as if she's talking to an imaginary friend...

Then it hits me. She's not imagining anything.

Sophie is glimpsing her Shadow on the other side. She's seeing Hanna a world away.

You're jumping to conclusions, I tell myself, but then I remember how the last time that I'd visited Sophie in here she had seemed to know about Hanna's past feelings for me. Things I've never told Sophie, things she could never have known.

Sophie's been talking to Hanna. Somehow, the two of them are communicating, even in this mentally foggy state, between worlds. And the quiet joy of that in Sophie's smile, the love for Hanna in her eyes, is what seals it.

When Sophie first reacted to the Siren, she hadn't been able to speak. She hadn't been able to sense her Shadow. She's getting better. I know it. This isn't permanent.

Maybe I'm believing what I want to believe. Maybe I'm reading into things which aren't there. But that hope is all I need. Hope is what life needs to have a chance to grow. Hope for something better.

Shadows and humans are symbiotes. We depend on each other. Mum knew that. We both need each other not just to survive, but to thrive. A universe without each other would be missing the point of living.

I stand. Staring down at Sophie, I know that I've made my choice. The path before me is clear.

"I'm going to bring Hanna to you," I promise her. "Maybe together, you can find a way to fix each other. I really hope that you can. Because the new universe that's coming... it's going to need you, Sophie. It's going to need people like you with giant hearts to lead. To show people how to live in peace. Everything you've done to make it this far... you're a hero. You're my hero."

I'm not a hero. That much I'm pretty sure on. A hero wouldn't take this kind of a risk with the Siren. A hero wouldn't betray his friends, his family and his Shadow. I reach out to tenderly tuck a soft wisp of blonde hair behind Sophie's ear. "The universe doesn't need a hero right now," I tell us both. "It needs something else. That's what I've got to be."

When I step out of the cell, the others are all standing there, still silent, waiting for me. Some of them look fairly anxious, desperate to know what's going to happen so they can take some kind of action. Others have their game faces on, standing resolute like they're ready for anything. I feel my insides glowing with pride as I look at them all.

A wide smile graces Ember's face as she sees mine. She can tell from my face what path I've chosen.

"Ember..." I say, having no idea how to broach the subject, "...what did you say to Phoebe? How did you convince her that you wanted to spend your last hours apart?" The pain that Phoebe must have felt, the confusion that Ember didn't want to spend every last minute of theirs together must have been devastating. I wish Phoebe hadn't had to be hurt like that for this to happen.

"It was the most awful thing I've ever done," Ember says matter-of-factly. "I had to sell it that I was still angry at her about the treaty, so that she wouldn't cotton on to what we were all up to. I told her I wanted to be alone, that I'd see her at the portal to say goodbye. So we sure as hell better succeed. Phoebe wouldn't understand or agree, but you and I are the same Griffin. We know what must be done, and we know that it looks ugly to some. But I didn't spend my youth working with

Melissa for this to happen. I didn't start Winghold as a safe place for humans and Shadows who wanted to be together just to let them be taken away from each other. I didn't start a Resistance that rose to liberate entire nations just to let everything return to the status quo. It all has to be for something. This creation of yours, it will not fail. We won't let it."

I'm strongly reminded of that time after Winghold had been burned to the ground by the Empire, after the Empress had been captured and I'd freed Ember and her rebels. Together, Ember and I had joined forces to commandeer the airborne ship New Redemption, flying toward Sanctuary City. A gutsy, last minute, reckless move for us both. She did it to take out Raven, and I did it to try and get Cirrus back. It feels good, it feels right, to be standing with her now.

If I couldn't be here with Phoebe trying to change the worlds again, at least I can do it with her other half.

"Phoebe will understand eventually, and Eclipse," I comfort Ember. "Once we show them that the universe they gave up on creating is still possible, once we make it real for them, everything will be okay."

Ember takes something from Blanca and carries it over to me. The others watch as she struts forward with what looks like a blue cloak dangling from her beak.

"We thought it was stylish," Ember says once I take it from her. "It's long overdue." She smiles. "Our glorious leader should have a uniform, after all."

I feel the fabric between my fingers. It's blue and gold, the colours of the GSA. I reflect on how long I've longed for this, without knowing it. To feel really accepted by the team here, as if I'm one of them, instead of being marked as the

freak whose Shadow abandoned him. Finally, at long last...
I feel like I belong.

Gently, I turn the cloak over in my hands. Embroidered along the collar of the cloak it reads:

'Griffin's Shadow Academy.'

I laugh, feeling a wave of emotion toward everyone here.

"Thanks, folks," I say. "I feel super dramatic now." Sien and Pixie step forward, helping shrug me into the cloak. The fabric flows elegantly down my back.

"When you arrived at Winghold and I saw you for the first time since you were a child, I felt so much excitement," Ember says proudly. "You'd arrived fully formed to help me so that we could finish what your Mum and Silvaluna had started. This is what I wanted all along."

I smile.

"Do you want your own leadership cloak?"

She snorts.

"I'm done being in charge. But I do promise you this. I will follow you until the very end, no matter if that's hours or years away."

"Thank you." My throat feels like it's constricting, and I clear it. "Be my number two, at least."

"You don't even have to ask," Ember grins.

As she does, I see so much of Phoebe in her; and from the look she gives me... I think she sees Eclipse in me too.

I look around us at the humans and Shadows crowded into the passage between the cells. Looking at them gives me hope. The space falls silent, all eyes on me.

I walk in the darkness to protect those in the light, I think, comforting myself as I prepare to face what's ahead. I try to remember where I first heard those words. *Hanna.* It was Hanna who'd said it once to Eclipse. I smile.

I can do this. This is what my entire life has been building toward. I breathe in, reflecting how far I've come since being bullied in the Burger Max toilets, since making my own birthday cake in the hope that my oblivious brother would cotton onto what day it was. That was just a year and a half ago. It feels like eons.

They others stare at me, hopeful, and in that moment I feel the responsibility of holding all their lives like stars in the palm of my hand.

"We can do this," I say resolutely. "You've all felt what I have since you were born: something in the back of your mind, telling you that this world isn't how it was *meant* to be. You're all risking your lives for this, but it's to build the beautiful universe that we know is possible. We're not doing this just for ourselves; we're doing it for everyone else out there who hasn't had the joy of experiencing what we have: meeting their own counterpart. It's time to fix that."

Everyone cheers, some of them whooping. There are even a few battle-cries.

But Jade approaches me, handing me her tablet anxiously.

"Grif, you should see this."

I take it from her. I'm looking at a live stream of the treaty signing room in Brisbane once again. What drew my attention was a sudden buzz of activity; a ripple of unease has disturbed the carefully choreographed moment, throwing it into chaos. Eclipse and Phoebe are on their feet arguing heatedly with Calvin as well as the UN representatives.

Something's changed. The humans look angry, like

they're accusing the other two factions of something...
but then I see the UN reps starting to confer with each
other.

Suddenly Eclipse turns to face one of the cameras,
staring directly out at me. As if he can sense me.

I suppress a shiver.

"He knows," I say, without any doubt.

"Who?" Ember asks.

"Eclipse. Phoebe too."

"That's impossible," Ember says, shocked. "We can't
read each other's thoughts over this distance."

"They're our counterparts, Ember. They felt it. Don't
ask me how, but they did. They know what we're
planning."

I look up at the watching, apprehensive faces.

"They're coming," I say, suddenly feeling very calm. I
watch as the faces before me pale. "The Shadow and
human forces, maybe even the GSA. They're in Brisbane, so
those jets could reach us in minutes. We have to activate
the Siren first."

"What would you have your second-in-command do?"
Ember asks.

"We need to get high," I tell her briskly. "Very, very
high."

I see their confusion, then the shock as they all
understand.

"I'd say it's time this vessel had its debut flight at long
last," I say, feeling buzzed.

"It's never flown," Ashwind says, flabbergasted. "We've
never even test-driven it."

"It can do it," Celeste says with a determined grin. "I've
run some checks over the last month, making some repairs

and tune-ups. I'm quietly confident we can fly this bad boy."

"When Empress Galvanize hijacked our world's communications to transmit her message, it inspired me that we could get the Siren's video out there the same way," I explain. "The humans have put new security in place to prevent that, but I've written a code that will bypass it. This ship's formidable communications array is going to help us hijack the satellites to transmit across emergency civil defence and military channels, but to do that we need a good line of sight to the satellites in question. Hence, the higher we are the better. Got it?"

They nod.

"Then Celeste, take some peeps with you and get this baby flying, go go go!"

She salutes me, then tags a few of the others and they all scamper.

"Secondly..." I say, turning to Ember. "I need Raven freed. We're going to need him."

Ember shuts her eyes.

"Give me strength," she mutters. "Do we really have to strike a deal with the devil?"

"Two heads will be better than one. He's the only one who knows how the Siren operates as well as me. If we have any problems with it, I want him there with me to figure out a solution. He *is* still here, right?"

"Affirmative. But he's going to be guarded at all times, okay? No way are we going to let him screw things over for us, no matter what he says about us being a happy, reunited family."

Blanca hands me a headset and a gun. I prefer my handy crossbow but I know reloading bolts is going to be less convenient if our pursuers manage to board. I just hope I don't have to use it.

I nod at Ember.

"For Mum and Silvaluna."

"For Melissa and Silvaluna," she says softly.

Ember heads toward the bridge. She's going to launch the ship from the underground home that's kept it hidden ever since it was constructed. Meanwhile, I make my way to the end of the Asylum and Raven and Winter's cell. I unlock the door and wrench it open.

"Griffin, thank God," Raven breathes, sounding relieved. He looks up at me, smiling wryly. "Are we making a run for it? Is this a breakout?"

"It's time to activate the Siren," I tell him. "It's now or never." Ula hands me the keys, and I fumble as I unlock the bonds anchoring Raven's limbs to the floor. The heavy metal hits the ground with clang. As I unlock the final chains around Raven's wrists, I feel a moment of doubt and fear. What if I've made a mistake? What if the two of them have been biding their time until this moment to make their move?

This moment requires trust. We won't have time to pull off what we have to if I doubt my judgement the entire time. I have to take Raven and Winter at their word. The three of us are on the same side now.

I free Winter. After hesitating, I unlock the clamps restraining his wings, and he stretches them gratefully.

"Come on," I say, as Raven rubs his wrists. "This way."

I swallow. I turn, exposing my back to them. If they're

going to seize the moment and take me hostage before the others can even move, this is their chance.

But then they're alongside me, Raven striding on one side and Winter waddling along on the other.

"What do you need us to do?" Raven smiles.

A long, slow grinding sound reverberates through the base, like a long-buried beast from a forgotten time. Our ship, belonging to a future that was thought lost, is slowly awakening.

The GSA members flank Raven, Winter and me as we leave the Asylum. I take the tablet from Jade again, to take one last look at the live stream of the treaty signing. I'm staring at an external shot of Parliament house. The humans, Shadows and the GSA are rushing out of the building surrounded by soldiers and security, rapidly conversing, trying to make calls. Aircraft lie in wait in front of the building: human jets and Shadow vessels like hovering pirate ships, their sails billowing in the wind.

I guess it's humorously ironic that in the end the threat great enough to force the UN and the Empire to unite in a common cause is me. I'll try not to let it go to my head.

I can see Eclipse and Phoebe standing outside, preparing to board. They're two still figures at the centre of the commotion. The camera slowly zooms in on the two of them, as Phoebe stares up into Emperor Eclipse's face, looking as solemn and haunted as he does. Eclipse bends his neck to gently rest his head against Phoebe's. The two of them close their eyes in a single moment of shared grief at what lies before them. I ache at the sight.

They both know that they'll do whatever it takes to stop Ember and me, and how high the cost may be.

The screen cuts to black.

25

Nevermore

We race for the lab. Everyone is hushed as we pass quickly through the dimly lit corridor of the base. Our home is airborne. The *Ambassador* is banking through the clouds, the massive vessel guided carefully by Ember. She's in the cockpit, piloting the vessel higher and higher into the atmosphere. Away from Brisbane, out toward the ocean. I get the uncanny sense of the ship being alive around us, overjoyed to finally be doing what it was built for. Not just flying, but being a symbol of hope for bringing Shadows and humans together forever. I can feel the hum of life from the engines coming up through the floor as we ascend into the sky. Now and then the vessel groans, as if it's still waking from its long slumber.

The others have their weapons out in case the ship is boarded, though it's far more likely we'll just be blown out of the open sky. I get that the idea of having a clear enemy to shoot at might be comforting, but I think they know as well as I do that our real enemy is time.

Raven and Winter are out ahead of us now. Their arms and wings are raised compliantly, a dozen weapons aimed at their backs. Even if his reputation didn't precede him,

Raven was also responsible for kidnapping and caging most of the GSA members. It doesn't foster a deep kind of affection.

An incredible impact shudders through the ship, and the floor tilts upward at a shocking incline. There are a few screams.

"*Our pursuers have engaged,*" Ember says cheerfully and unnecessarily over the speakers. "*Fasten your seatbelts, kids. It's show-time.*"

As we fight to get our footing, the ship groans again, straining to meet Ember's demands for evasive manoeuvres. This ship wasn't built for combat, it was built for a new era of peace. This isn't a fight; it's going to be a chase. The United Nations, the Empire and the rest of the GSA are hot on our tail, their aircraft all faster and more agile than ours. Ember has to do whatever she can to keep us one step ahead until Raven and I can activate the Siren.

I imagine the combined Shadow and human armies hunting us down right now. I think of Calvin and Phoebe with them, the other members of our GSA, now racing to arrest their own friends and comrades.

This ship doesn't have any weapons itself, except for the ones on board to non-lethally incapacitate any violent or uncooperative passengers. We did prepare for some hiccups with bringing humans and Shadows to meet each other for the first time. Still. The force we saw being mustered against us was more than enough to wipe us out. Hell, Eclipse on his own can take down pretty much anything he wants to. It's like the humans and the others just wanted an invite to watch the fireworks.

Eclipse won't do it. He won't kill me in order to stop us,

will he? It's not fair that I've forced him to weigh what he feels is safest for his people against his own life and mine.

My hands are shaking as I replay what I'm about to do over and over again in my head. How many others may end up like Sophie and Hanna as a result? What will others make of my actions and choices when history is written?

It doesn't matter, I tell myself. I have to kill the boy I used to be. I left the child Griffin behind a long time ago, left him crouching in the rain in the gutter, holding a bedraggled, half-drowned bird in his hands. Now, a giant dragon-parrot is soaring through the sky after us. An alpha predator, searching for a weak point so he can tear his way inside here.

I can already feel myself fracturing again. The conflict between Eclipse and me is tearing my atoms apart, but somehow I need to hold myself together just a little bit longer. I search inside myself for some warmth to shield me against the horror and madness.

I recall messages I've received from people across my world, people who emailed me after they saw my video online where I told the truth about Shadows. I used to read them so often, whenever things felt too dark in here, that they're imprinted in my memory. I cling to those now.

Dear Griffin, one of them had read. *In your video, when you asked: 'Have you ever felt that part of you is missing?', it really resonated with me. It does with my friends too. So many of us have felt broken, alone, like we're incomplete. This war has been so hard, so hopeless, but your story has helped me find my hope again. Thank you.*

. . .

Another one:

Dear Mr Griffin Cameron, I hope you read this. I have always wanted a best friend who believed in me. I have always felt very alone and I sometimes imagine I have a Shadow who is always with me so that I'm never lonely, someone who I can talk about all my problems with. That's what I long for more than anything. Actually, the idea that I might never meet mine breaks my heart.

It feels like those voices are clustering in on me. All the lost and dispossessed of our world, wishing for their Shadows. They're the reasons I keep going.

I'm here, Griffin, says another voice entirely, seeming to come from all around and inside of me at once.

I gasp, staggering. My hand flies out against the wall for support.

Then the voice flickers out again, like faulty TV reception.

"Grif! Are you okay?"

"We have to hurry," I gasp. "He's close."

"Double time!" Sien orders everyone.

One foot following the other, I force myself to sprint down the corridor with them, toward the stairs which lead to the lab. My vision swims, and suddenly I see a flash of the world through Eclipse's eyes. He's launching himself from the bow of a Shadow world ship, his gaze fixed on our massive metal vessel out in front...

For the first time, I *see* how grand our base really looks. Even though we were inspired to make a version of New

Redemption that was a force for good, there are distinct differences between it and the *Ambassador*. The *Ambassador*'s metal hull is the colour of copper but it glints crimson in the light. It has flapping wings like the leathery wings of a bat, covered in a metallic foil that gains additional power from the sun. I can't see the front of the craft from Eclipse's position, but I know that if I could I'd see three roving orange spotlights piercing the clouds, looking like quirky, goofy-shaped eyes fixed to the head of some airborne creature.

Hey, buddy, I say to Eclipse, falsely bright. *Who are all your new friends?*

Griffin, please... stop this. I can feel his desperation. But he's distant, only just in range of our telepathic connection as he tries to keep up with the ship. But he's getting close.

I think you know that's not an option for me anymore, I say in a mental whisper. *It's not too late for you to join me. I mean, I know you ran for Emperor on the whole platform of separating the worlds, and that reneging on that might be a little embarrassing what with the promises you made to your citizens. On the upside though, you would be saving both the worlds.*

I told the humans that the peace treaty is off if they choose to fire your ship out of the sky, Eclipse tells me, with the mental equivalent of gritting his teeth. *I think they saw that killing the Emperor of the Shadow world by taking you out wasn't a great step in the peace proceedings.*

Thanks, I appreciate it.

Griffin, the humans will risk war again in order to stop you. There's something going on, some double meaning or hidden intention to his words, but I can't quite glean what it is that I'm missing. *They've allowed me a short window to talk you down and bring you in...* Eclipse cuts out again, like a radio disrupted by static. *I have Calvin with me,* he says when I can hear him again. *Phoebe, Zephyr... they all want what's best for you. Just like I do.*

Calvin wants to freaking murder me, I expect, I mutter. *So this is your idea of what's best for your kind, leaving them feeling like shells of who they really are? Not even giving them the choice to ever meet their humans?*

I know what we're both thinking, even as we dance around with words. If one of us dies, we both die. Either we both leave here alive, or it ends for us right here.

Look, I know how messed up things are with us! I hear Eclipse cry, trying to reach me. *Can't we at least for now say this is a strange way of us being even? Can't we stop fighting?*

I know it's a desperate last attempt. His final hope.

I can't, I whisper.

I don't want to fight you. I don't want to watch my best friend be blown out of the sky for a lost cause.

My vision seems strangely wobbly.

It can't be all for nothing, I mutter feverishly, pelting with the others toward the lab. *Eclipse, you've seen so much suffering that you've given up on living the life we dreamed about as kids. But I'm going to remind you that it can be real. I'm going to show you.*

Griffin....

But I push him out, focusing my mind again on the memories of all the people who need me to succeed. I can feel their loneliness, their uncertainty and their longing for someone to hold on to. I'm carrying all of their pain inside of me like it's my own. Bitter tears sting at my eyes with the intensity of it.

They're all counting on me, all the other young Griffins of my world. I can't let them down. I refuse to.

We must go on.

"Ember, faster!" I yell into my headset.

"I don't know if the ship can take it."

"Try anyway! Everything depends on it!"

Our team sprints toward the lab, even as the floor tilts again. We can feel the ship shuddering all around us. The mammoth vessel surges onward, powering through the clouds, carrying us all toward our destiny.

We rush down the corridor, our breathing impossibly loud in the close, dark quarters...

"GRIFFIN!" Ember's voice crackles suddenly over the overhead speakers. Everyone bristles, raising their weapons at the warning in her voice. Ashwind's feathers burn in alarm with blue flame. *"The humans, they've latched on somehow in a stealth craft, avoiding our sensors! They've boarded through another access point, they're..."*

Ember's hardly finished her sentence before masked black figures are exploding out of the side passages, and everything's chaos. There's gunfire.

Someone pushes my head down, avoiding the crack of bullets flying overhead, but then everything is close combat and the entire corridor of the ship is a warzone. I see Grindelbark throwing two humans so high in the air that they hit the roof. I see Jade and a soldier grappling on the ground, the soldier fighting to reach for her knife before Jade's buck Shadow Arian butts the soldier with his antlers, knocking him out cold.

I see Raven and Winter just up ahead.

"RUN! Get to the lab!" I yell.

Raven hesitates. Winter sends a flurry of ice to freeze one of the soldiers against the wall, but his gun goes off and bullets clip the air above Raven's head. Alarmed, Winter forces Raven along with him, the two of them bolting off down the passage.

I take out my phone to activate the security system then hesitate, torn. They're all too close together. I could try and knock out all the humans but that would come at the price of incapacitating all of us too.

Suddenly Blanca is there, grabbing me by the arm.

"*GO!*" she cries. "Get to the Siren!"

It only takes one beat for me to realise that she's right. I press my phone, with access to all the defence systems, into Blanca's hand. Something tells me this is only the first wave of the forces being sent to stop us changing their universe irrevocably. Then I hurtle through the bodies, staying low. The fighting rings out around me, and I fervently hope that some of us will live through this to tell our story.

25

THE BROTHERS CAMERON

Our ship is plunged into darkness. The attacks against it must have knocked out the power. My way is lit only by the odd sparking light. I hold my gun in one hand, scanning the darkened corridor, imagining things crawling in the corners of my vision as I proceed toward the lowest level.

Every corner I reach seems to whisper of a malevolent threat lurking around the bend. The terrors of my own mind multiply in the oppressive blackness around me. Just the thought of the invaders breaking into our home outrages me.

None of that is what's really setting me on edge though. I feel like I'm breaking apart. The further I get, the louder the screaming in my head. It's a screaming that I can't pinpoint the source of, but it's not stopping, and the louder it gets, the more my head hurts.

The corridors around me swim in my vision. For a moment it's like I'm back on New Redemption, trying to rescue Cirrus, hearing my Shadow's helpless screams. The pain of losing him, of seeing him mutate into someone unrecognisable... it's like I'm living through that, again and again. He's haunting me.

"*GRIFFIN!*"

I shake my head madly. It's Cirrus' voice, and I can't escape him. The ghost of Cirrus has been taunting me ever since Eclipse abandoned me in the station. He won't leave me alone.

A violent eruption courses through the ship. It feels like a missile has struck the *Ambassador*, and for a moment I'm scared the entire craft is about to be ripped apart in roiling flame. But it holds together. I stagger sideways before the floor rectifies itself.

Damn it.

Shakily, I get my balance back, pressing further down the corridor...

"He's playing you."

I've never had such a shock in my life. I spin around, aiming my gun, nearly firing. With shock, I make out Calvin standing there in the darkness. There's no sign of Zephyr. Calvin must have boarded the ship with the soldiers... either that, or I'm really starting to lose it.

"Are you real?" I whisper. A light flickers above, illuminating him briefly.

"Raven's been playing you all along, Grif."

"No," I say, aiming my gun directly at my own brother. He seems too real for comfort. I try to detect if this is a trap. I check again to see if anyone is coming up behind me. "You and me have been the ones playing each other. I was working on the Siren right beneath your nose, just as you were working on this treaty under mine. And when you found out what I was up to, well, you didn't hesitate using that to your advantage, did you? You always need to get your way."

Calvin raises his hands into the air in a gesture of peace. My mind is racing. My forehead's slicked with sweat.

"You can't collaborate with a psychopath. That's what Raven's always been: a killer."

"Raven's changed, Calvin. Just like I was hoping you had."

There's a pain in my head, one that's been building all this time. I press my free hand hard against my temple, trying to contain it. I can hear whispers, mocking voices... things that aren't there.

The gun is shaking in my hand.

"You won't do it, Grif."

"Don't let us find out," I say. "Walk away."

"You're in pain," Calvin says, seeing how I'm clutching my head. "Are you injured?"

"I just want it to be quiet," I whisper, my words anguished. "I just want the noise to stop, a moment of silence where I can actually hear myself think! It's so loud!"

"Griffin, what are you talking about?"

"I can hear it all the time, can't you? Cirrus. His screaming."

"You've got to stop pushing Eclipse away, Grif," Calvin says, his voice broken. "It's tearing you apart. Listen to yourself. You need to make peace with your Shadow to stay whole."

"I can't. I'm the only one who can't have his Shadow, who can't hold him tight. Because if I do then no one else will ever meet theirs. If I show weakness, he'll stop us. And we have to finish this, no matter who stands in our way."

"You don't have to do this."

"Of course I do. I'm the one who walks in the darkness to protect those in the light. I'm the one who always does what has to be done. I brought you back Zephyr. I cracked the Oracle. I brought you back from being stuck as a Majestic. When you thought everything had ended, I started this organisation which gave you purpose and hope, at least for a while. All so that you would love me!"

The words ring out around us, bouncing from the walls. The truth, out there at last.

"I do love you. I always have."

Calvin takes another step.

"Stop there!" I warn him, my voice high.

"All your life I've been trying to protect you. At first I thought we'd die in the same fire that Mum did, that it would be kinder than going on in a world capable of so much cruelty." Another step. "We were lucky enough to live, but I hid Shadows from you, so you wouldn't know the pain of missing Cirrus like I missed Zephyr. But instead I made it worse, because a nameless loneliness was eating away at you and you didn't even know who it was you were missing." Calvin's too close. "Don't fall for the walking in the darkness crap, Grif. It makes for a miserable life. All I ever wanted for you was for you to know more happiness, more joy than I ever did."

"I can't stop now," I whisper, the gun shaking in my hand. "This war started because of me, and if I don't reach the Siren all of this has been for nothing."

"I can't stop either," he says. "I can't let you follow through with this, little brother. I can't watch you tear your soul apart with an act so evil, or there will be no difference between us at all, can't you see that? The guilt will either swallow you or you'll become it, and realise one day that you're nothing but pain."

"Stop!" I scream, clutching the grip of my gun with both hands to steady it.

"No," Calvin says softly, with finality. "I let Taylor take everything from me. But I won't let him take you."

Calvin lunges for my gun.

"No!" I cry.

The gunshot is deafening.

26

BEST FRIENDS

"No, no…" I mumble feverishly. I'm bowed over Calvin like a terrified child. My cloak is bundled against his stomach as I try to staunch the blood flow. "I'm so sorry, I'm so sorry… what have I done?"

I've stumbled into a nightmare.

Calvin mumbles something. Then he gasps with pain and the sound is a knife to my heart.

"Calvin, talk to me. Where's Zephyr?" I shout at him. Zephyr's our only hope now, the only one who's known for healing mortal wounds with the touch of a scaly hand. But if he's far away, if they left him behind…

My stomach turns, unable to contemplate losing Calvin.

"He's on board," Calvin wheezes, and relief and frantic hope flood through me. "We split up to find you. He's on his way."

And feeling pretty murderous towards me, I expect. But my own survival is a secondary concern to Calvin getting out of here alive right now.

He's Calvin. How did we get to this point? I'm crouched

beside my intelligent, magnificent brother who's bleeding out from a wound that was dealt by my own hand, I don't feel like the universe's best and last hope for liberation. I feel like a six year old. I feel like little Griffin who would get chocolate from sundaes smeared around his mouth and need Calvin with a napkin to gently help remove it, little Griffin who wasn't terribly bright and was a bit of a danger to himself, yet the brilliant prodigy and leader of a global corporation still made the time of day to play games with him, to listen to him, to make him feel the world revolved around him, even just for a moment. Those moments got more fleeting as time went on; as Calvin withdrew because of the psychic baggage of everything he'd suffered, and it felt like he slowly escaped through my fingers.

"You really were trying to protect me," I whisper as the life drains out of him, "all this time."

"Sometimes I was just being difficult... by being myself." He screws up his face at the pain, which must be agonising, but he plays it down well. He's playing it down for my sake so I won't feel any worse about what's just happened. He's still looking out for me.

For some reason it hits me then, and I feel like the world's biggest idiot. The numbers which Eclipse gave me as the password to Calvin's computer, the ones which let me discover the information about the treaty. How lost in my work have I been, how far have my thoughts been from ordinary everyday life to not recognise them as I typed them in?

"Your computer password," I say, wiping tears away. "It's my birthday."

"You only just realised that?" Calvin wheezes.

"That's not terribly secure you know," I sniff.

"I know I'm not easy at times, Griffin. But I tried. I really tried."

"You did. It was my fault, I couldn't let go of all the anger, but that anger wasn't meant just for you. I never should have blamed you. You coped with it as best you could. It was just hard getting used to you being flawed, after I'd thought you were perfect for so long."

Whispers are crowding in around us, whispers that I know are just in my head. Not really audible, or tangible, more like a slow pressure that keeps building.

"Calvin, I'm so lost," I whimper.

"No," he says, and I've never heard so much kindness in his voice. "You've just forgotten what you learnt in the Shadow world the first time round."

"Which was what?" I whisper.

Calvin cringes, forcing himself to speak through the pain.

"The importance of loving who you are, no matter what. Because wherever you go, you'll always take *you* with you. We can't run from our demons, Grif. We have to face them or be destroyed by them. Also..." Calvin hesitates, his face white from blood loss. "I didn't mean to disregard the love between you and Phoebe," he says. "What's between us shouldn't cancel out what's between the two of you, especially if each is just as real."

"Calvin, you don't have to say this. Just rest, Zephyr will be here soon."

"After this... if you and Phoebe want to explore your feelings, the fact that her and I are together shouldn't stop you from doing that as well."

I stare, incredibly moved, while also grossed out.

"Shut up, you're delirious," I tell him. "It's the blood loss talking."

"All that matters… is love," he manages, with feeling.

"Oh my gosh, please stop."

There's a flash down the corridor and I don't have time to react before there's a white velociraptor there, bristling, all fangs and talons.

"I didn't mean to…" I say to him, shaking. Zephyr lunges to Calvin's side, then reaches out with his stubby arms to place his claws gently against Calvin's stomach. My brother yells. It's a wrenching sound like nothing I've heard from him before. The gun I used is on the floor beside me, incriminating me. "It was an accident," I whisper.

"I know," Zephyr says, shocking me. He doesn't look livid with rage, just… grief-stricken. "I know. It's okay, I'll see to him." I see fear in his eyes, and it's not just for his counterpart. "Grif, you've got to go. Now." Zephyr takes Calvin's headset and activates it. "GSA," he orders, and I realise that he's transmitting to Calvin's members who boarded the ship to stop us. "This is Zephyr. Fall back. End the pursuit of the ship, all of you. That's an order. Anyone on board should return to their own vessels."

"Zeph, no!" Calvin moans. "Don't let him do this!"

"You're a good man, Gecko,' Zephyr says softly. "You really are. You always have been. But I've served the Empire, Cameron Technologies and the GSA. I've seen too much suffering on all sides for our worlds to part from each other permanently. Griffin and I understand the Siren is our only option, no matter how grisly it seems. War is a time for those who are prepared to consider all of the options." Zephyr looks to me. "Do you believe your Siren will work this time?"

I think of the changes I made with Raven. I think of Sophie's new signs of lucidity, her conversation with a Shadow invisible to anyone but herself. I nod. Any other answer isn't an option.

"Good. Then go. End this."

I look at Zephyr, thrown off-guard. We met for the first time so long ago, as enemies. But as I watch him crouched beside my brother, healing him, I see the similarities between the two of them more than ever. Having Zephyr believe in me means there's one small part of Calvin which trusts too that I can do this... and that it's right.

"Look after him," I whisper.

"Don't even think about it," Calvin manages. "You won't make it out alive before the soldiers catch up to you. They'll be here any moment."

I can't hug him without hurting his wound, so in a moment of instinct I bend over and I do something I've never done before. I kiss my brother on his head, in a moment of tender protectiveness. Like I'm his guardian, and he's the child.

"Thank you," I whisper, "for looking after me. For fighting for me. For caring. But the Siren is going to work. You taught me to invent things to solve the problems of the world. You taught me that fortune favours the bold."

"I also taught you to eat your greens, but that never caught on."

"Just hold on," I whisper to my brother, retrieving the gun.

"No, no, Griffin!" I hear him growl, a guttural cry, but he's already behind me and I'm running. I hear him curse in pain and then his voice subsides.

• • •

I'm fleeing through the darkness. Zephyr may have called off those in the GSA loyal to Calvin, but they were the least of our problems. I can't stop imagining a bullet from the UN soldiers flying silently through the air to end me, or Eclipse and his guards smashing down through the hull to end any hope we have of succeeding. Calvin's GSA members have left, but mine are still fighting in the passages of our ship right now to hold the enemy off for me. All of this so I can complete the task which Cirrus and I had always dreamed of completing together. I can't let them down.

"Griffin," I hear Ember's voice crackle through the speakers above, panicked, *"she's coming for you, I can feel her, get out..."*

Pain explodes in my side and I'm knocked sideways, slamming into the floor. I land with an *'oof'*, my elbows flaring with carpet burn. Scrambling in the dark to face this new enemy, I bring my gun up to shoot...

The weapon is kicked from my hand, flying into the darkness. Someone tries to pin me down and we scuffle, rolling across the floor. I try to get on top of her to pin her down with my weight, but she kicks me off like her legs are spring-loaded. Then she's on her feet, standing over me, her gun aimed directly at my chest. The lights flicker, and I finally get a proper look at my opponent.

It's Phoebe. Her hair is tied up in a ponytail, and she looks deadly.

"Wow, all that combat training really paid off, didn't it?" I pant. "You really going to fire that thing?"

"Some of us have to grow up. If you do this you'll become someone else. You'll cross a line that I know, I can *feel*, you won't come back from."

"Still, that kick was a tad unnecessary." I grin weakly. "No warning first?"

"I'm taking no chances." Her voice is strangely devoid of emotion. "How did you get Zephyr to call off the others?"

"I didn't. He knows that this is our only option, just like Ember does," I say, "and he knows that the Siren isn't a weapon, it's our salvation. It's what this organisation was really formed to do."

"Drive people insane? I don't think so. Hands in the air."

I slowly rise to my feet, raising my hands. I look at her, and feel my heart contorting. She's so beautiful. Even now, even in this nightmare scenario we've stumbled into. It feels like it was only a moment ago that we had our second ever kiss. I'm sure she can feel the heat of my love for her coming off of me in waves. That doesn't stop her from treating me like a terrorist.

I take a step forward, and then another, making it clear that my hands are still visible and that I'm unarmed. When I reach her, she's so close I can feel her unsteady breaths.

"Phoebe," I say softly. "I didn't go to all the trouble of getting you back your Shadow just to watch you be forced to let her go. I know you don't want it to go this way. We can still finish what we always set out to do, together, but this time it's going to stick. Don't make me do this alone."

"It's too late," she says, but for the first time her voice reveals a hint of the emotions storming inside of her. "You have no idea what will happen when you activate that thing."

"No. But I know what will happen if that portal is closed and our Shadows leave us forever. It's up to us, Phoebe. It's just on us now."

"I would have followed you anywhere you know,"

Phoebe whispers. "I would have followed you to the furthest reaches of the universe, but I can't follow you down this path you've set yourself on."

"Part of you already did," I say softly. "She's in the bridge, flying this ship."

Slowly I step up to her so that there's only inches between us. I know what we said, I know I talked about things being over between us, but in this moment I'm feeling so many things. I'm asking her not to let me take this step alone.

My lips search for hers. Then I feel her stiffen, and something presses into my sternum. It's the muzzle of her gun.

"I can't," Phoebe says hoarsely. "You know what my first thought was in that treaty room when Eclipse and I felt what you and Ember were planning? My first thought was that I had to *save* you. That's why Eclipse, Calvin, Zephyr and I tried everything we could to board this ship first to try and stop you from a death sentence or a life in prison. I wanted to stop you from doing something stupid you couldn't take back.

'But then I thought about how I didn't stop Taylor, because he was my best friend. I didn't have it in me to kill him. Look how much suffering has happened because of my act of mercy, because of my own feelings for him. If it comes to it, I'm not going to let a new wave of suffering ripple through the worlds because I'm too emotional to do what has to be done."

I blink slowly at her, troubled.

"Phoebe, it's me," I say. "You're not going to hurt me. I'm not Raven."

"That's up to you," she says through tears, but her gaze

is formidable. "You still think this is all some game, Grif. I wish I knew how to save you. But I didn't come here just for you. I came here to protect those who don't have a choice. Tell me: where's the back-up Siren you made? Clearly you hid another one on the ship."

"You know I can't tell you that."

Without warning, Phoebe swipes my feet out from under me with her leg. Before I know it I'm lying on my back, gasping in surprise and pain.

Phoebe appears over me, and places a foot squarely against my shoulder, holding me down. Her face looks like she's in hell, but to her credit she doesn't waver.

"Griffin Cameron, order your people to stand down."

"Your friends in the UN and the Empire started attacking us first!" I growl. "Ask *them* to stand down! They're hurting the GSA members on this ship, your own family!"

"I will if you tell me where the Siren is," Phoebe says, tears wetting her cheeks. I know she's hoping to have the courage to do what must be done, even if it destroys her. In that aspect, we're mirror copies of each other.

I gaze up at the girl of my dreams, the only one I've ever loved this fiercely and proudly. I wonder what our lives would have been like, without the war, without the GSA or Shadows. We could have lived a life like normal teenagers our age. I imagine us in school uniform, sitting around with our bags on the beach on a hot summer's day, the free stretch of the holidays in front of us now that our exams are over. I imagine the sense of peace I'd feel as Phoebe lay her head in my lap, hypnotised by the sound of crashing waves.

But then I'm brought back to reality, with Phoebe's foot pressing down on me.

There's no normal life waiting for us in an alternate universe. There never was. My whole relationship with Phoebe has relied on the strange, topsy-turvy time we live in. If Cirrus hadn't saved her by freezing her into stone only for me to revive her later, maybe we never would have fallen for each other. She would have just been my brother's age; they might even have been married by now. If Calvin and I had succeeded in joining the worlds the first time around, maybe I never would have brought Phoebe back and the two of us would never have bonded through our journey to the station. The connection between us has relied on so many chances of fate only to lead us here. It's no use trying to imagine another life for us. This is the price for all the special moments we shared. We were always headed to this moment. Eclipse and Phoebe on one side; Ember and I on the other.

"Where is it?" Phoebe repeats. I still don't respond, my mind racing through my options. She increases the pressure, and I cry out. "Please, don't make me do this," Phoebe says, a treacherous sob escaping her. "Hand it over before you get us all blown out of the sky."

"This isn't you," I say through gritted teeth, "and this isn't us. You're hurting, and that's why you want to hurt me."

"You're the one breaking my heart," Phoebe says simply. So honestly that I stare up at her, speechless. I feel like part of me is dying as she looks at me like that. Like I've betrayed her. Betrayed *us*.

"I can't believe you and Raven are teaming up," she says, shaking her head like this situation is beyond any nightmare she could have imagined.

"I think you know a bit of pain isn't going to make me

break," I breathe. "You don't expect it to. You're not really trying, Pheebs."

"Shut up."

"You grew up on the streets. You saw the worst of humanity, the apathy, what can happen when we're at the mercy of each other. How many other young Phoebe's out there are you letting down? How many are you keeping from their Shadows who could keep them warm and tell them everything is okay?"

I'm the only one who knows where the back-up Siren is, and soon Raven and Winter will be apprehended as well. It might as well be goodbye Shadows. I try to think how the hell I can get out of this. Phoebe's gaze is determined, even with the tears glinting there. She looks like a warrior. A hero of legend.

Except she's standing on the wrong side of history.

Suddenly the passage glows with hot orange light, and we twist our necks to see Ember flying toward us. She gently lights down just short of our little stand-off.

"Hey, babe," she says to Phoebe cutely.

"Please tell me someone else is flying the ship," I groan.

"I'm at least seventy percent sure of that. Now go, Griffin. I've got this."

Phoebe pales.

"Em... you can't do this."

"Phoebe, if I'm doing it, then you know part of you knows that this is right."

"I know that this isn't my call," Phoebe says. "It's not our choice."

Ember's tangerine feathers start to lick with flame. They spill over with molten fire, curling up the walls, across the floor...

"Seriously?" Phoebe says, arching an eyebrow. "What, we're going to fight each other?"

"No, that would be silly."

Flames suddenly shoot up all around us and I cry out. A wildfire has erupted in the hallway, consuming me and Phoebe as well as separating the two of us. But then I realise despite the overwhelming heat, I'm safe. The fire's burning around me without touching me, as if I'm protected by an invisible force field.

"You've got this, Griffin," Ember's voice speaks, seeming deeper and more layered than her usual voice, and for a second it's like I can hear Phoebe's voice in her own.

Then I'm rushing down the passage. I look over my shoulder, and see a swirling inferno, knowing that Ember is keeping Phoebe trapped safely and securely inside it.

I make it to the bottom of the ship. The sounds of the fighting are growing closer behind me. I think of my GSA family. They chose me as their leader. If any of their lives are lost I'm going to have to carry that with me, always.

Weaving between the water tanks I enter into the room I shared with Eclipse. The memories of the few magical days we spent here are thick around me. I come to stand in front of the piece of paper hanging there with paint prints of Eclipse's massive claw beside my small hand. Gently, I pull up the paper to reveal the deep cut in the wall behind it. Stowed safely in the accidental alcove is a golden handset. When my hand closes around its cool surface, I feel a dizzying relief, followed by a deep pang.

I wish Eclipse was here, and I wish that he wanted to be part of this. That he could share in the beauty of this moment with me. I hope, I wish right now with every single inch of me, that somehow this future that I'm about to create will enable the two of us to be together again.

The glass doors of the laboratory slide smoothly open, then close behind me, leaving only silence and the distant roar of the ship's thrusters. It's disorientating for a moment as the lab is lit by natural daylight, something that feels alien and unfamiliar in here.

The last time I was in the lab was to have Sophie checked out by Zephyr. I take in the vast space, and the giant shelving racks looming above me, stacked with equipment that we thought we'd need for the transition. Surgical devices and magnifying appendages run down from the roof and hang above our heads like shiny tendrils along with the familiar array of screens and monitors. At the far end of the lab is the wall made entirely of glass, and through it is a breath-taking, soaring view. I can see the ocean rolling out far below, as our ship hurtles down through wisps of low-lying cloud.

But what matters is that I see Raven and Winter, alive, their faces etched with anxiety. Raven whirls toward me as the glass doors slide open, but when he sees me, his relief is palpable.

"Thank God, you're okay," he says to me with so much feeling that I'm taken aback.

"How's our progress?"

"I've uploaded your hacking program; the satellites are under our control. We're just rotating them into position. The Siren?"

"Check." I run to the colourful interface up against the

wall. This is our only chance now to take over the ships' communications system and broadcast our signal to all corners of this world. Don't even ask me why, but the interface very much resembles a DDR stage. You know, Dance Dance Revolution, the interactive game with all the directional arrows you're meant to dance on? I can't remember who added this into the ship's design. It could have been anyone.

Hopping up on the raised platform, I move to the interface's screen and place the Siren down on the pad in front of me. A twinkling sound confirms that it's recognised the device. Quickly I check that Raven has calibrated all of the settings correctly, and confirm the satellites that the transmission will target. Everything looks perfectly on track. I take back the Siren, clasping it as if it's a fragile egg. The glass face of the Siren is now displaying a loading icon as it uploads the video file that will change everything.

POSITIONING RELAYS/ARRAYS, it reads, 7%.

The ship sways dangerously, the lab instruments hanging above my head swinging this way and that as our ship evades the human and Shadow vessels still in hot pursuit. I pray that any missiles headed our way have the decency to at least hit us the second *after* this has worked.

"We're just about there!" I shout to Raven, as I watch the glow spread up the bars. The ship's system is preparing to transmit the signal to the satellites and then out across the entire globe, igniting a revolution.

I look down at the golden Siren cradled in my palms. Its screen is illuminated, blinking slowly.

57% OF ARRAYS IN POSITION.

Raven turns to me, smiling warmly, and claps a hand on my shoulder. There's a quirky kind of humour in his eyes.

It's not like I'm looking at Raven in that moment. It's like I'm seeing Taylor. The kind of man that he was meant to be.

Other than Winter, it's just the two of us here together, Taylor and Griffin, at the death of the old universe and the beginning of the new. Meanwhile two worlds are trying to bring down our ship before a bold new era can be born.

62% OF ARRAYS IN POSITION.

Come on, come on!

Then I hear a crashing sound echoing from beyond the lab doors.

NO! Not now, not when we're so close...

Then, silence. Nothing.

"What was that?" Raven yells, but I already know who it is. I already know we're too late.

Eclipse slowly descends into sight, landing on the other side of the lab's glass doors. His feathers shine in the daylight, making him appear as an avenging angel. As he sets his sights on me and Raven, he doesn't look at all exhausted from the flight to reach our ship. The opposite, in fact. All that Eclipse has suffered, all that he's been through and overcome up to this point only seem to have made him more formidable, like forged steel.

27

MY SHADOW

The wide glass doors to the lab don't slide open for Eclipse. So instead he smashes through one with a claw, grabs both doors by the frame and then tears them out of their fixtures, flinging them behind him. They crash in the distance, which is possibly the sound of the water tanks shattering. It's a small reminder of his total and unstoppable might.

I remember him hunting me through the ship when I thought he was going to kill me. I remember a little toddler and his scruffy dragon-parrot snuggling under the blankets in Cameron Technologies to watch a movie.

Eclipse steps into the lab with heavy, earth-shuddering steps. Raven calls for me to fall back, buying time for the Siren to be ready.

Instead I stride forward to meet Eclipse. I can't explain why.

We stop only a metre from each other, blazing. Eclipse bows his head until his forehead is inches from mine. I glare at him and he glares back.

Emperor vs. Leader of the GSA.

"I dare you to!" I challenge him. "I dare you to stop us, but you won't!"

"I know," Eclipse says heavily, and I drop my arms to my sides, staring dumbly. "I'm here to help you."

There's a ringing in my ears. I'm truly flabbergasted.

"Don't say that," I say, hushed. "Don't joke about that, or mess with me. No more tricks, Eclipse. I just can't take it."

"No more tricks," he says softly. "I've told all of my soldiers to drop back from the ship."

"But I... I don't understand. You don't believe in this. You think Shadows and humans are better off apart, you created an Empire based on that belief. How can you turn your back on all that? You agreed to the treaty..."

"I thought I could do it, I thought I could follow through. But I don't believe I know the answer anymore. I don't know what future is best for them." Eclipse bows his head, like part of him is breaking. "I *attacked* you," he says in a small voice, unable to look at me.

"This isn't on you. I was reckless," I say, a tear streaking my cheek. "I took away someone you love."

"They think I'm the Messiah," Eclipse exhales shakily. "They think I'm the one who's going to lead them into the light. But I never asked for this. I never wanted it. I'm still just a kid. I'm trying to lead them, I'm trying to make a universe which is safe for them... but I'm just making it up as I go along! And now I don't have Hanna, my partner in all of this. She was my guide; I needed her experience in running an Empire across an entire world. I'm a teenager, Grif. I don't know anything."

"You know that's not true. You're better than any of them."

I can see him as he truly is. I drop my mental barriers too. It feels so good to let them go. There are no more secrets. No more lies.

I can see everything in Eclipse that led to him standing here speaking these words. I see the times when Eclipse's faith was challenged in the desert, when he wondered if he and Hanna were doing the right thing. The laughter and intense happiness he'd felt while he was back here with me. Losing Hanna and then losing himself to the primal beast within when he hunted me. Hearing of the nuclear attacks that stole millions of his people's lives in an instant.

Standing in that treaty room, feeling sick.

"Seeing our two kinds living together in here... it reminded me of Winghold. It showed me the good that I needed to see again. I need to believe that all this suffering... that it *meant* something. Don't go where I can't follow," he tells me, broken. "We belong in this together, Griffin. I won't let you do this alone."

"What if I haven't fixed the Siren?" I whisper. "What if there are more Hanna and Sophies?

"I believe in you, Grif. You won't make the same mistake twice. My world has lost too much. We can't heal without the help of your world, and vice-versa."

I clutch the Siren tightly in my hands.

90% OF ARRAYS IN POSITION, it reads.

"Here's to our Mums," Eclipse smiles emotionally.

"Here's to our Mums," I agree softly, feeling goosebumps, preparing to press the button.

There's an explosion from behind Eclipse, further

within the ship. I can hear the sounds of fighting echoing down to us, far too close.

"I'll do this with you," Eclipse says, "but not him." I turn slowly, following his glowering gaze to look at Raven. "You can't trust this monster."

"Eclipse," Raven smiles shyly, stepping forward. "I've made mistakes. We both have. But I've been trying to make the universe better for everyone, like you. We were just both going about it in the wrong way. This is our chance to finally work together, as we were always meant to!"

Eclipse takes a step toward Raven, his expression dark and thunderous. Winter rushes to Raven's defence, spreading his dark wings intimidatingly to send a flurry of frost up at the towering Eclipse...

"No!" Raven cries in anger, and lashes out at Winter, his fist connecting with Winter's beak. The skeletal crow retreats on those strange, humanoid legs, wailing.

Eclipse grabs Raven in his claw. Lifting him, he smashes Raven against one of the beams of the giant shelving unit above us.

"Stop!" I cry, horrified.

"You treat your Shadow the same way you treat all of us!" Eclipse screams at Raven who's writhing, asphyxiating as he's crushed between Eclipse's claw and the beam. "Winter loves you and gives and gives, and yet you only despise him. He deserves better!"

I can see Eclipse's fury for all that Raven has done; how he corrupted Hanna, how he hurt the Shadow world, how he spread the insidious beliefs that caused Cirrus so much suffering growing up just because Cirrus wanted to meet his own human.

"Eclipse, you don't understand..." I begin.

"I know you want him to be better," Eclipse says. He doesn't lessen the ferocious pressure crushing Raven. "I know that you believe if you can redeem him you can redeem yourself, because that's what I thought with Hanna. But Hanna found good inside her despite her upbringing. Raven had people in his life who loved him, but he chose to inflict pain."

As Raven writhes there, I see him manage to slip something from his pocket. It looks like a remote.

He jams one of its buttons.

The tendril-like appendages hanging from the ceiling suddenly come to life. I watch as the silvery tentacles undulate, fixing their attention on Eclipse. Then they lash out, striking at him...

I cry out in shock. Eclipse flings Raven away and roars. Spinning around he snaps through some of the tendrils with his beak, severing them...

...but the others keep jabbing at him like the stingers of a scorpion. That's when I notice what's at the end of each of the tendrils. A needle. Of course. These were to tranquilise and subdue Shadows for surgery if necessary. Raven activated them to save his own life.

The needles jab Eclipse again and again as he fights them off; mad, he strides toward Raven to finish the job. Raven slides himself back across the floor, looking up in shock and awe as Eclipse fights the sedative that would have downed any other organism.

"Idiots, stop this!" I shout, irate. "We're on the same damn side!"

Eclipse strikes but the drugs have affected his coordination. Raven rolls to the side and the massive claw misses him by inches...

Then Eclipse finally sways and crashes to the floor with a titanic impact. He tries to struggle back to his feet, but the dosage has become too much. I cover my mouth as I feel Eclipse's mind go dark with sleep. He lies still.

"No!" I scream. I sway, feeling that same sleep taking over my own mind. Just how I'd blacked out from our connection when the missile had struck Eclipse at Troy. But this time I expect it, so I can fight it, telling my mind to stay conscious rather than follow his into slumber.

I run to Eclipse, and Raven does too. Eclipse is still breathing, but it's shallow.

No. We're meant to do this together.

"What did you do?" I whisper.

"He's just knocked out," Raven says anxiously. At least he looks upset at having to hurt Eclipse, even if it was for his own survival.

"You were just protecting yourself," I mutter. "But we have to wake him up. Eclipse wanted to do this with me... as a family."

The Siren feels hot in my hand. I stroke the feathers on Eclipse's head with my other. There's no time, I know that. He's going to come to in an entirely new universe.

"I love you," I whisper to Eclipse, my finger moving to activate the Siren.

But then I look across from me, and I see Raven's hand stroking Eclipse's feathers too.

Something feels very wrong.

The hairs stand up on the back of my neck as I watch Raven comforting the Shadow he just knocked unconscious. I see the tender way he runs his fingers over Eclipse's golden feathers. I shiver. It feels like a violation, having my Shadow touched by another without permission. Especially knowing quite clearly what Eclipse's real feelings are for Raven.

"What is this?" I say, sounding far away. "What are you doing?"

Raven draws his hand away, embarrassed.

"What? I just... I just wanted to make sure I didn't hurt him. How close are we to transmitting?"

I look at the Siren in my hand and take in the glowing read out on its screen.

95% OF ARRAYS IN POSITION.

I hesitate. I look suspiciously at Raven, thrown by how tenderly he rushed to Eclipse's side. I know that I'm missing some of the picture.

"No," I whisper slowly, shaking my head. Something's wrong. I look at Raven with new eyes, backing away from him. Eclipse could sense something about him, something that I've missed that I should have seen. I can feel a rising hysteria. My whole body is shaking.

I don't know what to do! I cry, but no one can hear me. Eclipse's colours are all dormant in slumber. I'm the only one of us here now who can change things. I'm the one who has to take action.

"Griffin, keep it together," Raven says. "You're freaking out."

97% OF ARRAYS IN POSITION.

We are so close. So, so close.

My finger hovers over the button that will finally end it all. Or start everything.

"This is a trap, isn't it?" I whisper to Raven, dreading the answer. "I don't know how, but this whole time... you've been using me, you've been manipulating everything to get to this point... something about this isn't right."

"Grif, all of your people are fighting to buy us time to complete this," Raven says, exasperated. "They're risking their lives." But I catch something in the corner of his eye. Something that looks like guilt. "You can't quit now. Everything is happening exactly as it's supposed to."

I tackle Raven, hard. We fall together, hitting the floor of the ship...

"Griffin, what the hell!" he yells.

But then I'm blasted off of him, caught in a blizzard. The force of the frosted winds flings me into the air slamming me against the far wall of the lab. I stay there, stuck like a fly in a spider web. I struggle, but my legs and arms are encased in ice. It's burning cold.

"Hey, hey!" Raven says, concerned, getting to his feet. He displays his palms to me disarmingly as I try to struggle free. "Woah! It's okay. You're okay, Grif."

I spot the Siren on the floor where it fell, out of reach. I wrench at the ice binding me, struggling against it until I'm scared my limbs will be wrenched from their sockets.

"What did you do?" I shout. "What did you do to the Siren? Did Sophie and Hanna happen because of you?"

"The Siren works exactly as you designed it," Raven says, sighing. He kneels to pick it up from the floor reverently. When he looks at me, he looks proud of me. "I don't know for certain what caused Sophie and Hanna to react that way anymore than you do, but we have to trust that we have it right this time. I haven't lied to you about the Siren, Griffin." He smiles crookedly, almost self-conscious. "I mean, you're my only friend."

Winter bows his head sadly.

I study Raven, trying to figure him out. Searching for any signs of deception.

"If you haven't lied, then I'm sorry for freaking out," I say, feigning calm. "Let's do what we came here to do then. Let me down, let's activate the Siren."

Raven looks torn.

"We will. I would love to. But first, there's something you need to know." He wrings his hands, and it takes me a moment to realise that he's anxious. It's a strange emotion to see on Raven. "I haven't lied, but I *have* concealed something important from you."

"You know, we call that lying too," I say, gritting my teeth. I try to swallow my temper and hear him out. "We're running out of time. What is it?"

"I think you've known," Raven says quietly, unable to meet my eyes. There's something wrong with his voice. It's thick with guilt and... longing. "I think you've known deep down, for a while now."

"I.... really don't think I have."

"I remember when I finally found Winter again," Raven muses. "I'd been so excited to finally meet my counterpart who'd been stolen when we were children, to discover who I really was. But I was appalled. I felt *nothing*. No matter what Phoebe or Winter thought, I knew he wasn't mine.

'Years later I engineered Ammut from the most superior Shadows I could find, to try and create the Shadow I could love. The Shadow who truly reflected who I was in all of my potential. He was unstoppable and yet there was still something missing. That love I saw between Melissa and Silvaluna or Phoebe and Ember... it still wasn't there.

Everything changed when I faced you beneath Sanctuary City. I was so lost back then. Nothing but darkness and rage. But then I saw a Shadow unlike anything I'd ever seen."

I blink in confusion, feeling a deep sense of unease.

"A giant who shone with heavenly light, with feathers and scales of pure gold. One who could mimic and improve on any power he wished. I'd never seen or heard of anything like him in my entire life of studying Shadows."

I'm going to faint. For a moment, I think I already have.

"You think Eclipse is *your* Shadow," I say. The words don't make sense.

"His courage, his beauty... it spoke to me, Griffin. It was more than that though. I just knew he was the one I was destined for. I told Galvanize to bring Eclipse to me in Aeyu Palace, but in the end Eclipse came of his own accord. I tried to convince him to join me, to be my partner in all of my work. But he wasn't ready. He still thought I was his enemy. You can't imagine how much that hurt," Raven whispers. He's standing very close. I can feel his breath on my skin. "Eclipse is who I've been searching for ever since I first learnt of Shadows. *He* is my redemption. I look at him, and I see all the things that I could be. Everything I've ever known I was on the inside. He's me, Griffin. I know it."

There's a roaring in my ears. So many pieces are falling into place.

'*He was meant to love* ME!' Galvanize had moaned when Eclipse found her. What she'd meant was that she had wanted to be Raven's favourite. But in the end, she could never replace Eclipse. No wonder she'd always hated him so much.

Galvanize had tortured Eclipse, so Raven had found a way into Opal Towers and murdered Galvanize. He hadn't done it out of revenge for himself, but for Eclipse.

This nightmare can't be real.

"You want to steal my Shadow," I hear myself say. "You want Eclipse for yourself."

"I know you think he's still your Shadow," Raven says, troubled, brushing aside a lock of my hair in a paternal gesture. I try to head butt him but he steps out of reach. I strain against my ice bindings but they refuse to break. "But you have to let him go. He's not your Cirrus. We'll find you someone special, someone who can make you happier than you ever dreamed. But Eclipse is mine, Grif. I've known it since I first saw him. It's fate. He is me, I am him. Soon, we will be one."

I'm flashing back to when Hanna had taken Cirrus captive, trying to break his link with me so that she could have me all as her own human. I remember how it felt as he was slowly torn from me, his mind artificially paired with Hanna's instead.

I shudder.

I don't know if it was the trauma or the black, murderous rage toward Hanna that had erupted deep within me which transformed Cirrus into Eclipse. I just know that was the worst night of my life. Now I'm reliving that horror again on another flying ship. But this time I'm contending with Hanna's dark master, someone ruthlessly intelligent who's always planning twelve steps ahead. Someone impossible to out-manoeuvre.

Someone completely, irretrievably deluded.

"You're going to artificially bind Eclipse's mind to yours," I say hoarsely. "The same way that Hanna tried to do with me."

Raven moves away, setting the Siren softly down on a metal trolley far out of my reach. Reaching the controls for the storage shelves, he fiddles with them for a moment. An enormous silver cube the size of a small house slides from its place and is slowly carried down to the floor of the lab.

I start screaming, and I don't stop. I know what that is. Calvin told me.

Raven presses his palm against the cube and steps away. He looks up as it unfolds, morphing as if with a mind of its own, unfurling into a contraption of pure terror.

The fusion machine reminds me of the one I saw in the Underworld. But once it has expanded and unfurled fully, there's no questioning that this model has had some upgrades. At its base is a wide rectangular tank, connected by organic pipes like intestines to two pods suspended above it.

I thrash against my icy bonds, sounding more animal than human.

"Eclipse and I will become a Majestic," Raven declares, euphoric. "We will be blissfully whole. Imagine his power combined with my intelligence. We wouldn't be an angel, but a god to rule over this new universe of joined counterparts. We'll find you a new Shadow, and soon the two of you along with Calvin and Zephyr, Phoebe and Ember... you'll all join me in our paradise. Our family will rule together, like the gods on Mt Olympus." Raven's gaze slides to the Siren sitting on the silver trolley. "This is the day of creation. This is the day it begins."

Giant, artificial claws on cables unleash from the machine. The multiple talons encircle Eclipse delicately as if he's the greatest prize of all, heaving him up toward one of the pods. The pods both started off human-sized, but the one the claw is moving toward is already inflating, expanding like a human lung, growing larger and larger...

closer and closer to Eclipse's size. A hole at the top of it opens like a hungry, gaping maw. It's as if the machine itself is alive. Then Eclipse hangs limply, dangling above the pod.

"I've perfected the process," Raven explains, as if the more I understand, the less terrifying this will be for me. "All of those experiments at Aeyu Palace have paid off. Don't worry. It will be over very quickly. You'll see that this was all for the best. I just don't want to start our new universe with the Siren until I'm with the one I've always meant to be with."

The claw descends toward the mouth of the pod. I watch the talons loosen. When they withdraw, Eclipse is no longer in them, and the mouth of the pod seals with an awful sucking sound.

The front of the pods are made of a transparent material, like there's a window in each. I can see Eclipse's face, his lids shut, as the interior slowly fills with what looks like red, amniotic fluid, rising to consume him. I make out something dark whipping up toward Eclipse's face, expanding to fasten around his beak. An oxygen mask.

The machine, something from my worst nightmare, raises two metal arches so one hovers above each pod. They crackle with sinister crimson light.

Raven starts disrobing, dropping his clothes to the floor. Completely naked, he approaches a row of metal steps leading up toward the unoccupied pod. The transparent window peels away for a moment, the round passage expanding as if inviting Raven in.

"It will be over quickly, Griffin," Raven says softly. "Then we can activate the Siren together, and begin this new era for the universe, as we always meant to."

"Winter!" I beg, speaking to the creepy humanoid crow. He's standing there to the side, obedient and miserable as I plead with him. "Winter, please, you know that this isn't right! He's your human, you love him. Don't let him do this! Don't let him tear you from him just so that he can replace you with Eclipse!"

But Winter, trembling, looks down shamefully.

"I just want him to be happy," Winter croaks.

Raven steps onto the stairs leading up into his pod.

"All of this has finally been worth it," he says, almost too quietly for me to make out.

And with that Raven ascends the stairs, striding naked up toward the glowing, crimson cradle.

I force myself to think through my panic. At some level Raven must know that Eclipse isn't really his. He's convinced himself that he has to artificially bind Eclipse to him to correct a cosmic mistake. Raven believes that my Eclipse is the part of him that's been missing, the reason he's always felt a loneliness that he tried to numb with his destructive acts, the reason he's never felt *right*.

Raven is going to turn into a Majestic with my Shadow.

But is that even possible? I wonder, breaking inside. If Eclipse isn't really Raven's Shadow, can they still become a Majestic? My family always liked to believe the human-Shadow connection was something intrinsic and sacred, something unbreakable. But nobody has studied how far science can mutate the human-Shadow connection like Raven has. If anyone can pull this off, he can, and he's been planning this for the last year and a half, ever since he first saw Eclipse.

Majestics are power without limit. When Calvin and Zephyr were a Majestic, their strength was greatly suppressed, because Raven was drugging them to keep them on his leash. But if the Majestic has Eclipse's strength, and is fully in control of his own power...

Then Raven will be invincible. A dark god to rule over two worlds.

This is why Raven was experimenting with Majestics in Aeyu Palace. We thought he was trying to build some kind of army. But really he wanted to become a Majestic with Eclipse all along. That was his end goal.

I fight against the ice restraints, feeling a rising wave of vengeance. Yes, Eclipse and I have been on opposite sides of this war. We were prepared to fight each other for what we believed was right. But he's everything to me, and I love him more than anything or anyone.

I gave Raven a second chance he didn't deserve. He's repaying me with the ultimate betrayal.

They can't turn into a Majestic. The good in Eclipse is going to negate the evil in Raven, somehow, surely. But even as I try to convince myself of that, I can't ignore the fact that Raven wouldn't become a Majestic if he didn't have reason to believe that he'd still be in control. For all of Raven's hunger for a Shadow, Raven could never open himself up and trust someone fully enough to really be equals. That's what being Shadow and human is really all about. Perhaps this new machine will make Eclipse more a slave than a partner.

Raven stands at the entry to the pod.

"Taylor, please!" I beg. "I know my Dad did this same thing to you, but you don't have to become him. He was wrong to steal your Shadow from you just because he believed it was his own. He had all of this love for his other half but he misplaced it. He was confused and that love drove him to do something terrible to you. I know how badly you want to be loved. I know that feeling. But sometimes trying to fix our own loneliness in the wrong ways can lead to the greatest evils. You can still learn to love Winter. *Please.* Please don't take the most precious thing from me."

"I love him every bit as much as you do," Raven says softly, looking across at Eclipse's pod. "How is it fair you should get two Shadows? Your counterpart was Cirrus, and I'm so sorry he was lost. But Eclipse is mine. I know it."

"You're wrong; they're the one and the same. Why are you doing this? We just have to push that button on the Siren and we can be heroes together! This was meant to be your redemption!" I yell. "Why do you have to sabotage yourself every damn time? Why are you determined to destroy everything good?"

"I'm not. Just once, I want one good thing for myself. I want one shred of the light," Raven says quietly. "Eclipse will be enough. Once we're together the Siren can be activated, and the new universe will begin."

Raven raises a foot to step into the pod...

"Griffin? What's going on?"

Twisting my head, I see them, and my spirits soar.

Ember flies into the lab, and Zephyr comes running in after her over the shattered glass. They have Phoebe with them. Calvin, I'm overwhelmingly relieved to see, looks very much alive. He's draped over Zephyr's back.

Seeing my family come for me, at this darkest moment, floods me with hope.

"Stop Raven!" I shout. "He's trying to fuse with Eclipse so he can become a Majestic! He thinks Eclipse is his own Shadow!"

There's not much time for them to take this in as they rush toward Raven and his infernal machine, fanning out around him. Ember lands beside Zephyr. The people I care about most in the world stand against Raven as the badass team they are.

Eclipse is visible through the window of his pod, slumbering. As glad as I am that the cavalry has arrived, I worry that if Raven or Winter do the wrong thing that maybe Eclipse could be hurt while he's in that pod.

"It's over, Taylor," Calvin declares. He slides down off Zephyr's back, taking his own weight with a grunt. The bullet wounds must be healed but his shirt is still bloodied. He clutches his side as he limps toward the steps where his old friend stands. "Give up. You've played on Griffin's kindness for long enough."

"You can all join me too, you know," Raven breathes. "We'll rule the worlds as a family... as a pantheon. Phoebe, imagine what an incredible Majestic you'd make with Ember. You and I would be King and Queen of the universe, just how we always dreamed. I told you one day it would come true. You can join us too," he says to Calvin and Zephyr. "Don't pretend you don't miss it, how intoxicating the infinite strength was that I granted you. That was just a taste."

Ember launches herself toward Raven, blasting fire. But her flames freeze in mid-air, falling to shatter on the stairs. Ember is tackled by Winter, and the two go flying, fighting and blasting each other with their respective powers.

Zephyr roars and races up the steps, rushing Raven. The metal tendrils dangling from the roof of the lab hurtle downward to attack him, and I cry out to warn them all about the danger from above. Raven's put them on autopilot somehow. The needles stab at Zephyr, the tendrils writhing around him, as if trying to bind him in place as well as sedate him. Zephyr struggles against them, pushing back with his immense strength. He's injected again and again, but he tears his way through them, his crazy metabolism fighting the drug. His eyes are fixed on Raven, vulnerable up there on the steps, determined to take him out...

Phoebe has raced to the machine's controls and she's yelling for Calvin's help to decipher them. Calvin barely has a chance to limp toward her before he's struck down by one of the tendril's needles.

As Calvin slumps, I realise sickeningly that Zephyr and Ember have also collapsed from the injections. Ember's feathers are crusted with ice from her battle with Winter too. Winter's so shy and demented I forget how potent his power can be.

"Taylor!" Phoebe cries to her old friend as she fights the drug. She's also been injected and I cry out as she slides slowly to the floor, trying to hold onto the machine's controls for support. She clambers across the floor toward Raven. She grits her teeth, fighting to keep the defeat of unconsciousness at bay. "Don't do this," Phoebe says ferociously, but a sob breaks out of her. "This is exactly what Alex Grove did to you, don't you see that? I know you don't like to think of that event as what defined you, as what made you who you are, but you know that it broke something in you, don't try to lie to me. Now you're doing just the same thing Griffin's Dad did. You've done a lot of awful things in your life, Taylor. Draw the line here. Don't do this."

For a moment Raven seems to hesitate. But it's only for a fraction of a second.

"Alex Grove was deluded," Raven's voice says with a flash of cold malice. "I am not. I know who I am."

With that, Raven climbs through the opening into his pod. The fine, transparent skin that acts as a window expands behind him to seal him inside.

That's when I realise what Phoebe is trying to do. She's been crawling across the floor to where Zephyr dropped her and Calvin's confiscated headsets. Phoebe grasps one of them, and holds down the button to speak.

"Transmitting all channels," she says, struggling to form the words. "Raven is the threat, he's in the..."

A missile of ice flies from Winter and strikes the headset from Phoebe's hand, sending it flying. Phoebe struggles toward it then slumps, passed out. Another blast from Winter strikes the machine's controls, freezing them in place. There's no stopping the machine now.

NO! I cry inwardly. For a moment I thought Eclipse was saved, only to have my hope cut down so quickly in front of me. I look at the still bodies of our family, praying that their hearts are all still beating. Frozen to the wall by Winter all I can do is watch, a futile, helpless spectator.

I'm wracked by childish longing as I think of little Cirrus and Griffin, safe and snug as their Mums wrap them up under the blankets for sleep. The last night of our innocence, of our bright, glowing time together. I remember wrapping my tiny arms around Cirrus for the night and I feel an ache so great I fear I'll crack in two... and worse, that if I do crack, I'll never be able to put the two halves of me back together again.

28

BECAUSE IT IS MY NAME

The amniotic fluid in Raven and Eclipse's pods rises. I see Raven floating, suspended like a baby. His eyes are closed peacefully. There's a terrifying smile on his face.

The others are all unconscious on the floor. Phoebe. Ember. Zephyr.

That's when I notice that Calvin is moving. He struggles toward me weakly, fighting the effects of the drug. He's been shot and drugged in the space of half an hour, but somehow he's still crawling toward me. There's no way he's going to make it, but that doesn't stop him trying.

"I'm so sorry, Grif," he manages. He's crying. "If I'd just destroyed this damn thing, none of this would be happening. Raven knew that I wouldn't get rid of this machine. He knew that I'd want to figure out how he invented it so that I could best him. He played me too well." His lids flicker, as if they're about to close.

"Calvin!" I yell, desperately trying to keep him alert.

"You've been studying this thing, trying to learn from it. There's got to be a way to shut it off!"

I don't know what I'm thinking. Calvin is almost gone, and I'm powerless to break free of the rock-hard ice crystallising me to the wall. I keep trying to reach Eclipse telepathically, but I can't wake him up.

Surely some of my GSA members are going to make it down here to help? The fact that they haven't tells me that they're still giving everything they have to hold back the invading UN soldiers, both sides completely unaware that the true threat to all free things is being birthed down here. Raven is poised to become an unstoppable dark god with all of us as his puppets, and no one is here to stop it happening.

It's not just my life and Eclipse's that depend on stopping him, but everyone's. If the process rides itself out, Eclipse will be gone. Raven's Shadow forever, a part of him. The man I hate and the friend I love will be inseparable.

"You have to have found something," I plead with my brother, "or there has to be something you missed."

Calvin's given up moving, realising it's a waste of energy. He twitches there on the floor. I can see him fighting to come up with a solution, rebelling against the drug tranquillising his mind.

Then I see a light bulb switch on behind those steely grey eyes.

"Cal!" I shout, worried he'll pass out before sharing the epiphany. "Tell me!"

"The machine locks onto the DNA of whatever subject is in there," Calvin manages. "But if Eclipse was to be taken out of the pod, if another Shadow was in Eclipse's place instead... the machine would detect the change and halt operations. The interference would... force the machine to reverse its processes, and shut down automatically."

"But how?" I cry. "Calvin, no one is coming!"

And even if I wasn't stuck here, I can't haul Eclipse out of there on my own.

Calvin looks up at me, his lids barely open, but then I think I see something in them. A moment of realisation. His lips move, but I can't make out what they say.

Then he's hit in the face by a gust of frost, icing his mouth shut. He struggles, then his eyes roll back and he slumps to the hard metal floor.

I scream, but there's nothing I can do. Winter strides over to Calvin to inspect him, prodding him with a foot. Satisfied, Winter looks sadly back toward the machine. His attention now entirely fixed on where his human is using the full weight of his scientific research to finally strip Winter away from him, replacing him with a Shadow that he believes is actually worthy.

What did Calvin mean? I strain my brain. What does it matter that if we replace Eclipse with a different Shadow, that the machine's process will be reversed and he'll be saved? What does he expect me to do frozen to the wall over here?

I work my brain over the clue, and when the answer hits me I gasp as if I've been winded.

It can't be. No, it *must* be. That's what Calvin mouthed to me before he was silenced by Winter. One single word.

Cirrus.

My insides lurch.

When Cirrus became Eclipse, his DNA changed too. If there was some way that Eclipse could revert to being Cirrus...

I can barely breathe for a moment.

The Majestic Machine would shut down. The universe would be safe from Raven. But then... wouldn't Eclipse be gone?

How much of my Shadow would still be the same? Would he lose everything that's happened to him since he changed on New Redemption? Would he still be the same inside? Would his personality be the old one, or stay the same?

Too many questions. I shake my head fiercely to clear it. I have no time. I have to do something.

We don't even have any idea how Cirrus became Eclipse in the first place, Calvin. How the hell am I meant to get him to change back now, on command? Don't you think that might have already happened if it was possible?

But Calvin's out cold and not in the mood for an imaginary argument.

Time's running out. I'm going to lose Eclipse if I do nothing too. Taking a breath, I reach out for Eclipse's mind, and I delve into it. His mind still feels foggy and dark, but I call on the full strength of our connection and pull my consciousness into his...

I'm floating in pure inky blackness. Thin tendrils of mist float through the void around me, reflecting a ghostly light... even though it doesn't seem to have any clear source.

"Eclipse?" I call, searching the darkness. Awkwardly, I try to flip myself around. Eclipse's mind feels weird with him being unconscious. Being in here is a cross between being underwater and being in outer space. I can propel myself slightly through his mind, but it's hard.

Then I see him. Eclipse floats there, drifting through space. Unmoving, like a puppet gone slack. His eyes are jammed shut.

The golden light in him feels like it's died, and he looks destroyed, ravaged. His feathered tail hangs down below him like the broken mast of a ship.

Kicking, I swim over to him, slowly driving myself through the dark toward him. We're just two lone objects in space.

I grip onto the ridge of his great outstretched wing.

"Eclipse?" I say, heart-pounding. I can feel him slipping away from me. "Oh Eclipse, please tell me you're still alive. Tell me you're still with me. Don't let him take you. He doesn't own who you are. Only you do."

I feel his panic, the claustrophobia of the tank and the thick liquid pressing in at him on all sides, swallowing his enormous form whole. But overall Eclipse seems defeated. Accepting of his fate.

"Eclipse, you've got to fight this!"

"I can't, Griffin," he says softly. "It's my time. I fought hard. I tried to do what was right. But this is how I go."

"You can tear your way out of the pod! You're Eclipse. Blow this place apart. Tear Raven out of his pod and squeeze him into silly-putty. Nobody trifles with you."

"I'm fighting the tranquiliser, but I think Raven put a paralytic in there too for good measure." I feel Eclipse struggling. A low, desperate roar gathers in him, but then he slumps, rendered powerless. "I want to go bravely," he whispers. "This is the end for me. Let me face it with you, Grif, in courage, not in fear. I'm so grateful for the life I've had and for the friends I've made. I've been... so lucky."

"You have more courage than anyone I know, but there's nothing noble about this!"

"There's nothing we can do," Eclipse swallows.

"But what if there is?" I shout at him. His eyelid flickers open and he looks at me strangely. I feel him searching my mind.

I hesitate. I can't stand to speak the words, so instead I show him. I open myself up to him, and show him what Calvin said. I reveal what we might have to try in order to stop the greatest of evils taking over the worlds. I see his reaction before he even speaks.

"No," Eclipse says, recoiling. He shakes his head. "No."

"This could keep you alive," I say in a small voice.

"But I wouldn't be me anymore."

"Eclipse," I say urgently, "this is the only solution. Can't you feel it? You're barely even here anymore. This space keeps feeling colder, emptier. He's taking away who you are already. You're becoming just a ghost."

"We don't even know how to turn me back into Cirrus, or if it can even be done. Let alone with no equipment, and before Raven's machine finishes doing this to me? It's impossible. We know nothing about how it happened in the first place!"

"We know some things," I say desperately. "Whether it was the psychological trauma of that night or something else, it hit some kind of switch, enabling Cirrus' genetic makeup to be altered. Doesn't this feel like New Redemption to you all over again? The ship, the machine... it's like we're reliving that night. Maybe that's not an accident. Maybe these are the conditions we needed to mirror that moment and undo what happened. When you changed, that wasn't to do with what Hanna did to you. I've always known it deep down, and I know you have to. Somehow that change came from inside us. We can find a way to do this. What about those dreams you've been having of turning back into Cirrus? What if those are a prophecy? I think part of you has known this moment was coming this entire time."

"Those weren't dreams, they were nightmares."

I stare at him pleadingly.

"I'm not going to do it!" Eclipse says with a burst of thun-

derous anger. "Even if I knew how, I'm not going to just switch back to being Cirrus, as if being Eclipse, being me, was all some kind of magic trick, just some cheap illusion."

I shake my head, frustrated.

"You think I want this?" I say hotly, tears sliding down my cheeks. "I know how much being Eclipse means to you. I don't want to lose you, no matter how much I loved when you were Cirrus too. But if you don't change, I'm going to lose both of you. There's no time left. I love you, you're my best friend no matter what version of you you are."

"I can't."

"I saw how you gave yourself up to the Empire in order to save your own people," I swallow. "You were prepared to die then, to give your life to save them. Why are you afraid now of just turning back into Cirrus?"

"I don't want to be Cirrus again. Everyone thought he was stupid and nobody believed he could do anything. All that Cirrus ever did was love people and get kicked down. Once I became Eclipse, people started to notice me. I started to matter. They even started to love me. I could change things as Eclipse, I became somebody that I wanted to be. Not a loser, but the Emperor of my entire world!"

Eclipse yells in agony. I cry out with him. The process is well under way. It's like pieces of me are being forcibly removed. It's unbearable.

"It's one thing dying for what you believe in, for the people you care about," Eclipse gasps. "But you want to take away my name, my identity. You want to take away everything I've become, everything that makes me me."

"You're being stupid," I choke.

"Then you don't understand, Grif. I'd rather die as Eclipse than live as Cirrus."

"But you're not going to die," I sob. "You're going to be part of Raven. What if you're a prisoner in your own body, forced to watch all the evil he carries out, for all eternity? Surely nothing can be more horrible than that."

I feel Eclipse shudder at the thought of being part of a human who isn't his. But still he fights my idea.

"If I turn back to Cirrus, it's like this was a mistake, a blip. To take this away would mean that none of this meant anything, that it was just a phase. There has to be another way to stop Raven."

"There is no other way! Why would you rather die than get to...?"

"Because!" Eclipse explodes. "Because when I came here as Eclipse, it was like Zephyr and I finally started to get close. Ember never saw me as an equal until I became Eclipse either. Cirrus was nothing more to her than a crazy little hatchling. If I turn back into Cirrus, then I might find out for sure that all of that was only because I was Eclipse. And I don't think I'm strong enough to take that, Grif. I really don't think I am. Maybe I chose to become Eclipse subconsciously because this was what I wished for more than anything. This is who I wanted to be. And I'm not ready to give that up."

"Eclipse... this will save your people. The people you pledged to protect. It will save my people too. I'm begging you."

"I'd do anything for them," Eclipse says, crying. "But it's cruel for the fates to ask for this. I gave everything. But I shouldn't have to give up who I am."

I cling to Eclipse's wing as we float through the hungry emptiness, feeling the colour and beauty of our connection being stripped and eaten away from within.

"The reason your people care about you, the reason they've followed you and chosen you as their leader isn't because you're

Eclipse. It's because of who you are on the inside, who you've always been. It's just that being Eclipse made you brave enough to show the world who you'd really been inside all along," I say. "A kooky dragon-parrot who's different but cares about others more than anything. A kooky dragon-parrot who can't stand to see injustice run unopposed." I snivel into his neck. "If you choose to change back, if you choose to stay with me, I'll never leave you again. I'll spend every living moment beside you until we die, sometime very far from now. Even if you try and leave me again, this time I won't let you. I'll come after you. I'll always come after you." I start crying freely into his feathers. I can feel the turmoil inside of my Shadow.

There's an agony like nothing I've ever experienced. It splits through me, tearing at me with ruthless, cold claws inside my body, my brain, my heart...

"Arrghhh!"

I'm unravelling like a ball of yarn. Half of everything I am, half of everything I know is being stripped away by force. Griffin and Cirrus, Griffin and Eclipse... our stories are being erased.

"I don't want to lose Eclipse," I tell him with feeling. "But even if you turn back to Cirrus, you'll still be him. Even if Cirrus' brain goes funny and wonky sometimes and he gets confused or acts strange in ways people don't understand. Maybe you won't feel as... impressive. But know this. You are loved. You will be safe, and you will be loved. You've come so far. Who you grew into as Eclipse will always be a part of you, no matter what you look like."

"I won't change back, Griffin. I can't. I just... that's the one thing I can't do." I can feel Eclipses agony. He doesn't want his legacy to be leaving the worlds to darkness and destruction either. But this is the last straw. This is too much for him to give.

"Eclipse," I say, brokenly, "We share a soul."

He looks at me.

"I don't know what will happen to me if Raven takes you from me, if I can continue to exist without a Shadow..."

"Griffin," he whispers. "I didn't even think... I didn't realise..."

"Maybe that wouldn't be so awful if I knew I was going to see you on the other side. I don't know if humans and Shadows really do become Majestics after we die, like when we saw Mum... but I want to believe that there's a chance. If Raven becomes a Majestic with you though, he'll take that from us too."

Eclipse is wracked with emotion. He bows his head. Then he says it, what's really haunting him, the one thing that he can't stand to face.

"What if Hanna doesn't recognise me anymore?" Eclipse chokes. "The way she is now, she barely recognises me when I'm there with her. If I change my face, my whole appearance... I'll be a stranger to her forever. She matters to me, Griffin. She matters to me so much and I've only realised now that she's gone. Eclipse is the version of me that she became best friends with, the one that she really cares about. You know what things were like between Hanna and Cirrus. If I go back to being him, all she'll ever see is the mad little Shadow that she hurt. She'll never be able to look at me without the guilt of what she did to me on New Redemption. Even if we find a way to cure her, Hanna and I might never get back what we had. What if we only work together as Hanna and Eclipse?"

There's a long silence before I can formulate a reply.

"You can't let Hanna live in a world where Raven is a god," I say honestly. "You know she betrayed him, you know what her upbringing was like with him, how he used her... do you really want to let Raven take over the worlds and not be there to protect her? And maybe even worse, to be part of Raven, Hanna's

tormentor? You don't deserve this after all you've been through. I wish I could make this sacrifice for you, but I can't. You have to choose."

Very slowly, Eclipse finally nods.

"I'll do it," he whispers. "I'll try. For you. For her. For everyone."

29
TRANSMUTATION

So we do. We try.

We think back to that horrible night on New Redemption which we've tried to forget and everything that led us there. Eclipse recalls all of his suffering as Cirrus leading up to that point.

Being disowned by his brother when Zephyr found out that Cirrus had reunited with me.

Attacking his very own brother on the beach to save me from being drowned.

The hurt of seeing me falling for Hanna.

The agony as the contraption on New Redemption tried to tear our connection in two.

I relive everything I'd been through too: being bullied by Rick and his cronies, discovering the portal beneath Cameron Technologies and my first experiences of the Shadow world. I remember how much it had hurt when Cirrus' mind was being separated from mine on New Redemption, just like the hurt I feel now. I remember holding Cirrus in my arms thinking he was dead, feeling that the world would break apart from the force of my grief.

But nothing happens.

The pain at our core is nearly unbearable, an emotional and psychological wound so deep it feels physical. Our separation must be nearly complete. I can feel Eclipse being taken away from me.

"Keep trying!" he cries.

I try to focus on Cirrus, to remember everything about him. How it felt to hug him. He'd smelt of straw and sugar, of the warm breeze just before a summer storm...

The happy memories are torn apart as memories that aren't mine suddenly force their way into Eclipse's head and mine.

I scream.

I see a young boy crying out in the night for his Shadow, missing the feel of his best friend's feathers. I'm forced to watch as that same boy runs away from home and starts living on the streets of Auckland, knowing that part of him is missing. Every day he looks up at the tower of Cameron Technologies standing proudly above the other buildings in the skyline, and he knows that it holds the answers to the questions he doesn't know how to ask. I see the wet, wind-swept night on Queen Street when the homeless boy meets a girl, saving her before she steps into traffic. The girl has vivid red hair.

Now I see the boy lying in the centre of a burned out house, staring up into Phoebe's eyes. She's smoothing the hair away from his face.

"I'm not going to lose you," she tells him.

Raven strokes Phoebe's cheek sadly. His fingers gently touch the ghostly burn scars along her cheek.

"What if I lose you?" he whispers.

I shudder, feeling violated as the images are forced into my mind, inescapable, replacing parts of me and Eclipse that were meant to be just our own.

We're seeing into Raven's past. We're seeing the moments that made him into who he is today.

It all plays out for us:

Raven entering Cameron Technologies with Phoebe.

The moment when Raven was finally reunited with Winter, only to feel nothing.

"He's not mine!" I hear Raven say, deeply distressed. His eyes burn with intense vulnerability as he looks at Winter. "If it was my Shadow, I'd know. I'd know straight away, wouldn't I? If Shadows really are what you all seem to think they are. I would know when I looked at mine, instantly."

"Maybe not. You just need time," Phoebe says soothingly.

"That's not my Shadow, Phoebe. It feels like... like a patch of nothing."

"Taylor!" Phoebe says, shocked. Winter stares at Raven with deep hurt in his eyes.

"It's someone else's," Raven gasps, shaking. "Don't force it on me."

"Tay-lor," Winter whispers. He reaches out for Raven timidly, longingly...

Other memories now, flashing far too quickly as the merging process between Raven and Eclipse nears its end:

I watch Raven screaming as Phoebe blasts him into the portal, banishing him to the Shadow world even as she lies dying.

I see Raven descending into the dirty cellar to find little Hanna. She was so small, so innocent. She was also abused and malnourished, vulnerable enough for him to mould her into the puppet-dictator he needed.

I watch Eclipse and myself fight Raven beneath Sanctuary

City, and the moment where Raven saw my blood on his hands. He suddenly recalled the family he'd once had, and realised how far he'd fallen. Then Raven looked up to see Eclipse poised above him. Raven's eyes drank in the sight of those feathers that shone with the light of a thousand suns. For the first time ever, Raven felt a sense of peace. He finally felt love for a Shadow.

I see the moment in our old lab when Raven shoved my Mum and I watched in shock as she falls, her head colliding with...

"NO MORE!" I scream in grief, clinging to Eclipse as we float in the darkness, trying to protect him from Raven with my entire body. "Please, stop this!"

But then something more horrifying happens.

There's a tear in the very fabric of the inky blackness where Eclipse's consciousness and mine meet. The personal space, shared just by the two of us, is split open by an invader, and someone starts to crawl through the tear.

Eclipse is too drained to react. His mind is growing quieter and quieter by the moment. I'm left on my own to face the invader, as Raven comes crawling through the tear into our joined minds.

Raven's hair floats about his face. He's panting, his eyes alight with hunger as he crawls into the private space shared only by me and Eclipse. He drifts out of the tear, reaching toward Eclipse longingly...

"NO!" I scream, but I feel my voice is sucked away from me. My connection with Eclipse is so eroded that he can't even hear me in his mind anymore.

There's only one thing for it. Using Eclipse's slumped form, I launch myself from his side, propelling myself toward the invader.

I've got to protect Eclipse. I can't let Raven merge with him, or absorb him... whatever his plan is.

Raven shakes his head, mouthing my name disapprovingly. I see his reluctance to hurt me. As if he isn't already taking everything from me.

I sail through the darkness of me and my Shadow's disappearing universe, and I tackle my worst enemy.

The two of us spin around as if in zero gravity. Locked in a mental duel, I go berserk, punching and kicking, attacking like a wild animal, anything to stop him, anything to slow him down and buy us time...

Every second I delay Raven is another second that I still have Eclipse.

But then Raven kicks me free and I fly away, spinning, losing my bearings. I can just make out Eclipse's broken form, drowning in the blackness moving in on him...

... then my eyes open. I'm back in my own body.

No.

I lost the mental battle with Raven and he's forced me out. I'm stuck to the metal wall of the ship by Winter's frozen bonds. It feels like I have frost burn around my arms and ankles.

Mentally I reach out to the slumbering giant in that machine but it's like a wall is up between us now, keeping me out. It's a profound loneliness worse than anything I'd felt growing up without my Shadow. The sensation of reaching for Eclipse, right there, and feeling nothing. Inside that pod the unspeakable process is fusing him and Raven into a single form: mind, body, soul.

"Winter!" I shout, pleading. He's staring at the machine too and I swear I can see thick, sloppy tears running down his feathered cheeks. But he doesn't interfere, following his counterpart's orders to the very end. "Stop this madness!

This isn't love, what he's making you do! Love isn't just doing whatever he asks of you!"

But Winter just trembles. I growl helplessly, looking around the space for anything I can use to break my frozen shackles...

Then I spot something that shocks me. For a moment I'm sure I must be hallucinating,

Someone new is entering into the lab. She's arrived without making the slightest sound. Innocently she stares up at the Majestic machine, as if she has no idea of the horrors that are happening.

She can't be real. She *looks* real though. Long dark hair, violet wings and all. Her skin is very pale.

It's Hanna, and she's standing only metres away from me.

Winter hasn't seen her yet; all of his focus is on the machine where his human is replacing him with another. I hear the low moans of pain from him, and I know he must be feeling what I am. It's the most awful sensation in existence.

"Hanna?" I whisper across at her. "Hanna!"

She flinches in shock. Turning to me she brings up her arms to shield herself. *Hanna, please!* I mouth. *Help me! Let me go!*

But her eyes are foggy, and her expression is vague. It looks like my hope of her freeing me was poorly placed. She's just like Sophie: not fully tuned into this plane of reality.

I made her that way. I made them both that way.

How is Hanna here? She looks barely lucid enough to find her way out of this lab, let alone stow away on an Imperial ship and sneak past the fighting to make it down here. But somehow she was drawn here. She came to this ship looking for something.

Sophie, I realise, aching. Hanna is still being called toward her human here on the ship, and Hanna came, no matter what it took. Maybe she didn't even know why she was coming. It gives me hope. Hope that I haven't broken the two of them apart forever.

It's stupid, but I've dreaded seeing Hanna again. In the Underworld there was so much going on that I'd had plenty of distractions from her, though that hadn't changed the red-hot animosity I'd felt toward her. But now I'm surprised that all I feel at seeing her is gladness. In this dark moment, I have someone else with me who loved Eclipse, even if she doesn't fully understand that we're losing him.

Now, staring at Hanna, it's impossible not to see how much of Sophie is in her. It feels ridiculous that I didn't see the similarities, their shared quirks of expression, all along.

Then Hanna steps up to me.

"I'm sorry," she chokes at me suddenly. I stare at her. Her voice is the barest whisper.

"Sorry for what?" I whisper back. Everything around us is chaos and pain. For the moment, all there is is this moment just between the two of us.

"For..." her face screws up with emotion. Hanna moves closer to me, and she looks like she's fighting hard to place memories together. "For putting that knife in your back. For hurting you. I was terrified that you were leaving me; it felt like the world was ending. But that's not me anymore. I was so lost. You and Eclipse made me stronger. There was so much goodness in you, so much happiness, Grif. I hate the thought that I'm the one who broke it."

It's more coherent than anything Sophie has said since

being exposed to the Siren, though I get the feeling that Hanna is only experiencing a brief moment of being lucid. She could be gone again any moment.

"Hanna, it's fine, please, just free me!" I say desperately. She blinks, seeming to finally notice my predicament. Hanna looks around us. Winter is bowed over before the machine, sobbing. He doesn't seem in a position to even notice an escape attempt. Hanna grabs a scalpel from a nearby trolley and brings it back over to me. She chips away at the ice, freeing my left ankle, then working on my right...

"*I'm* sorry," I whisper to Hanna. "I messed with your head. It's my fault that happened to you." I choke on a sob. "You mean so much to Eclipse. Thank you for looking out for him. Thank you for being his friend."

"You forgive me?" Hanna whispers, her lip trembling.

"Of course I do," I say, crying, and a weight lifts from me that I'd never realised was there, a weight that had been with me ever since that night on New Redemption.

Hanna shatters the last of my icy cuffs and I drop to the ground. Then I take the scalpel from Hanna and sprint toward the machine's controls. I can't hear Eclipse at all anymore.

I start hacking at the thick ice Winter covered the controls with. As I do, Winter slowly turns toward me.

The machine containing Raven and Eclipse whines, reaching a crescendo, its operations nearly completed. I hack away the ice, harder and harder, determined to shut this thing off before an unspeakable horror can be birthed within it...

WHOOSH.

Without any warning, the machine catches fire. The

windows of the pods burst, and flames flare upward in plumes from the metal shell. I feel the last faint shred of Eclipse's consciousness flicker and die.

"No!" I scream with Winter, as we watch our counterparts burn.

30

HEAVEN ON YOUR MIND

"No!" I shout. "Eclipse!"

Sparks fly from the machine and a dangerous whine begins to sound from it. Smoke streams from the flaming pods. The central pod is unharmed so far, but if there's a chance that Raven and Eclipse hadn't yet combined into a single form, then they're about to be burnt alive.

Winter launches himself toward Raven's pod with his surprisingly enormous wings. Landing on top of the steps he tries to prise open the strange organic window there, but it seems to be jammed or something. He coos, a small and desperate sound. He's helpless to stop the person most precious to him in the two worlds from meeting a slow agonising death.

Leaving the controls, I race up to the machine, bounding up the steps toward Eclipse's enormous pod. Smoke makes me cough and wheeze. The air feels like heated metal. The warning sound from the machine gets louder the further the fire spreads, enveloping its other components.

I can't see Eclipse's face anymore through the window, but it could just be that the smoke is too thick. The fire hasn't consumed the front of the pod, so I can still access the window... but how do you open this thing?

Desperately I press my hand against the transparent surface. It's still cool enough to touch. With a sucking sound, the translucent layer peels away, surprising me. Red, thick fluid drains out of the opening, and I steady myself, gripping onto the pod to avoid being washed back down the stairs in a flood of crimson.

Holding onto the rim of the opening, I lean in to search for Eclipse.

The giant pod is empty. Eclipse is gone.

I feel an icy fear. Oh God, no. The machine did what it was intending to. The process is completed.

Eclipse and Raven are joined as one.

But then I spot something dark at the bottom of the pod, visible through the amniotic fluid. Something that looks like a body.

Without hesitating I dive into the pod. The crimson fluid is thick and disgusting against my skin and it would make me shudder if I wasn't so intent on finding any sign of my Shadow. The liquid is growing hot from the flames licking the pod's exterior, and soon I'll be in danger of boiling alive. I don't even know what I'm doing, it's obvious Eclipse isn't in here...

But someone is.

My hand closes on the ridge of a wing. I feel blindly to get a better picture of what I'm touching. Then I realise, and feel a bolt of shock.

My hands are shaking as I wrap my arms around the Shadow, so much smaller than Eclipse, and pull him close. Heaving, I kick off from the bottom of the pod to bring us to the surface.

Clambering out of the pod, I drag the Shadow up out of it with me. Helped by the force of the crimson liquid I guide him down the stairway away from the orange glow of the hungry flames, away from the volatile-sounding machine. Then I collapse with him on the floor of the lab. In my peripheral vision I can see that Winter has managed to get Raven out of the other pod too. But I don't think about him right now. I can't.

My attention is all for the Shadow I just rescued.

His giant powerful body has shrunk. He looks so small, even though he's about the same height as me. His wings spread out on either side of him, with bat-like membranes and green, matted feathers.

"Cirrus?" I whisper, trembling.

Eclipse changed back. He did it. That must have been what stopped the machine, what caused the violent reaction.

Cirrus' eyes are closed. His feathers are red and sticky from the substance in the pods. He's not even responding. It looks like he's...

"No," I cry in shock, terribly afraid. "No, Cirrus, come on, please! Cirrus!"

I shake him, but he doesn't respond. The colours of his mind are awfully dark.

Opening his beak, I check for obstructions to his airway. Then I start trying to pump his chest. If he swallowed fluid in there then there might be a chance to bring him back.

I feel sick. I wish that I'd paid more attention during our

class demonstration of CPR back in school. I didn't know at the time that watching the strange demonstration on a rubber mannequin might mean saving my best friend's life. Also, Cirrus has a beak, and I don't know if breathing into it would even work, or if that's a bad thing to do if he's already got fluid in his lungs... and do you even pump a dragon-parrot's chest the same way you do with a human? Does it work the same?

"*ZEPHYR!*" I scream. He's still over with the others, lying further away from the machine, unconscious. "Zephyr, Cirrus needs you!" I beg.

Getting up, I stumble over to Zephyr.

"Hanna," I shout. She's standing there idly, looking lost and confused. Damn it. From the look of things, she's not lucid anymore. "Please, Hanna," I beg her. "Help me."

She seems to get the gist. With Hanna's help, I drag Zephyr over to beside Cirrus. Then I take Zephyr's claw, and place it against Cirrus' chest.

There's no response. Nothing. I take Zephyr's claw away and place it back again, hoping for his healing power to take effect. When nothing happens, I pump Cirrus' chest again and again, screaming at him, until I realise Cirrus is truly gone and I bury my face in his feathers, sobbing uncontrollably. I cling to Cirrus' cold body for the second time.

I'm too late. He's gone. Soon I will be too, crossing over after him into the void.

Who knows? Maybe we'll be together there. Maybe we'll be a Majestic, like Mum and Silvaluna were when I saw them. Magnificent. At peace, together forever.

But all I really want is to hug my bonkers dragon-parrot again and play games with him and to never ever die.

I cry softly. Distantly I'm aware of the Majestic machine's whine growing higher and higher. It sounds like the entire thing is about to explode from the pent up Majestic energy within it, like a nuclear warhead. But still I can't bring myself to care. There's no point in moving away. I'm already lost. I just crave an end to this pain.

Hanna kneels beside Cirrus. She looks at him and I think that maybe she's confused as to who exactly he is. The moment of lucidity is gone, and she looks as if she's trying to search through her jumbled memories to place him exactly.

I look across at Hanna and suddenly I understand how Eclipse turned back into Cirrus, foiling the machine.

I remember that night on New Redemption, when I'd finally freed Cirrus from Hanna and stood over her, rage flowing through me, my sword poised at her heart. The girl that I thought I had loved had tried to steal away my Shadow. I remember how I'd felt that killing Hanna then would have been justice. I remember the roar in my ears, a roar foreshadowing the one that I'd soon hear from Cirrus' own beak as he transformed into Eclipse.

That was it, I realise. That was the moment when I turned down a darker path, when I betrayed who I really was. I recall the dark rage that had nearly pushed me down a path into becoming someone else entirely. With me and Cirrus both in such altered and volatile states, somehow the sheer strength of our connection caused him to transform.

Forgiving Hanna was the key. Making peace with her was what changed Eclipse back. If only it hadn't all been too late.

"This is Cirrus," I tell Hanna hoarsely. "I know you two

never got on… but he's Eclipse too. Eclipse just looks different now, that's…"

But then I see a glistening tear has already streaked down Hanna's cheek.

"You remember him," I whisper. "You know who he is." I smile sadly. Together, we look back down at Cirrus, at my fallen Shadow. I stroke his cheek-feathers gently.

"Hanna remembers you, Eclipse," I whisper to him. "She's here, and she misses you. We both do."

Hanna looks down at Cirrus, dazed. Heartbroken.

"Why?" she croaks.

"I don't know," I confess, choking. "I don't know why this happened." All I know is that in this moment I'm gladder than anything to have someone who feels this pain, the loss of this light, as acutely as me. I'm glad to have someone else who understands that the world has ended.

I holler with animal rage at the universe. I wish that a million things could have worked out differently. After Cirrus had died in my arms on New Redemption, I'd thought nothing would feel that bad ever again. Maybe this is my punishment for all of my mistakes: having to relive the worst moment of my life all over again.

I look to the enormous glass window at the rear of the laboratory. The ocean is gone and now we're hurtling over a coastline. I watch a city unveil itself in the distance across the ranges covered in bush. I recognise it.

Auckland. I wonder if Ember piloted our ship back home on purpose, or if it was subconscious. Seeing the place laid out before me where I spent my childhood with Cirrus and our family is as happy as it is sad.

I hear Raven cough.

A wave of hate consumes me. Raven still has a pulse. I

look over to see Winter lovingly reassuring him, but Raven's first action is to push Winter away. Raven looks around, scared. He's searching for Eclipse, I realise.

How can that man still be allowed to have the gift of life running through him, that same gift that he took from Eclipse?

Murderous fury blooms through my veins. It feels powerful. It feels like it could annihilate an entire universe, and that's all I have right now.

So I brush Cirrus' feathers lovingly one last time, and I close his eyes.

Then I stand. I forgave the man who'd taken everything from me. This is what he did with his second chance.

"Winter," I hear myself say. "Get out of the way."

Winter steps in front of Raven to protect him.

"Move aside," I say.

The darkness of nonexistence is coming for me. Cirrus… Eclipse… is dead. I'm going to follow him soon, into the afterlife. But I'm still here, for this minute. My heart still beats. I'm still here for one purpose.

To avenge him.

"You can't kill him," Winter wails. Spirals of ice appear in the air beneath each of his wings, swirling. "He's all I have."

"Aren't you tired?" I rasp. "Of all that you've been through, all that he's put you through?"

Winter hesitates. The spirals of ice vanish, and he turns to regard his counterpart. Raven stares up at me, disorientated. I think maybe for the first time he's realising that he's lost. He's reflecting what brought him to this point, and beginning to understand the consequences of his actions.

I look at him and I see Raven and I see Taylor too. I see

the boy who cared for Phoebe on the streets, wishing that the world recognised his gifts. I see the boy who would go on to cause more pain than anyone in history.

"Let him," Raven whispers to Winter, resigned. "Stand aside. That's an order."

Grief contorts Winter's face. Loyally obedient to the last, he stands aside.

The Majestic machine is howling now. I can hear screams and shouts, and I realise that Calvin, Phoebe and the others must have come around. But if they're screaming for me to get out of here before the machine blows, or telling me not to kill Raven, I don't know.

I just don't care anymore.

I take a step closer to him. Another step. Close enough to see the fear in Raven's eyes.

My foot hits something, sending it skittering a few inches along the floor.

Dully, I look down. I see a glint of gold, lying there innocently on the floor of the ship. A glass screen encased in an ovular golden frame.

The Siren. It's just lying there, ready to change everything.

Kneeling, I pick it up. It feels cold in my hands.

100% OF ARRAYS IN POSITION, its screen reads. *READY TO ACTIVATE.*

As I straighten, I distantly hear Calvin and Phoebe screaming in horror, yelling at me not to do it.

But Eclipse can't have sacrificed himself for nothing.

Winter is tugging at Raven with his beak, trying to pull him away from the Majestic machine. Smoke is billowing from it, and something like lightning is crackling around it in multiple colours, including colours I haven't seen before.

I barely pay it any attention. I don't fear death. Not anymore.

All I need to do is touch the button on the Siren and the video will be transmitted out across the human world. For every human who sees it, their Shadow on the other side will be forever changed as well. A spark will be lit that can't be snuffed out.

Anything might happen, obviously. I might wreck the universe. But I'm willing to risk infamy if there's an equal chance that this makes everything everywhere better. I want others to be spared the misery that my Shadow and I have suffered, I want them to have the chance to live their lives together. The chance that Eclipse and I didn't get.

"I'm coming, Mum," I say softly. "I'm coming, Cir."

I return to kneel back down beside Cirrus' body, where Hanna is crouched in silent vigil. It's fitting. It was just the three of us in the beginning, racing through the trees of Kashlak. Just the three of us against the world.

I rest one hand on Cirrus as I prepare to press the button. Beneath the scream of the machine I think I can make out the sound of human troops shouting, crashing their way through the ship toward the laboratory. They'll be coming through those shattered doors in seconds. The Majestic machine is deafening, its sound volatile.

I see Phoebe trying to drag herself toward me, disorientated. I see her fear as she stares at the Siren clasped in my hand.

"Griffin..." she moans. "No..."

"We all win," I mouth to her, serene. My finger moves to the Siren's button.

Which is when Cirrus suddenly lurches upright.

"Holy heck!" Cirrus screeches, eyes bulging. "Get me outta there! This machine is all kinds of messed up!"

Hanna gasps.

I nearly have a cardiac arrest.

He's alive.

He's *alive!*

"CIRRUS!" I throw myself into him, hugging him so fiercely he's in danger of asphyxiating.

"Okay, okay…" he says, laughing.

I can't stop trembling. I'm a snotty, tear-flooded mess. *He's alive!*

As I hug Cirrus, I feel a familiar tendril of consciousness. Tentatively it reaches out to wind around my mind in a mental hug.

"Oh my God, you're alive!" I've never felt so much joy. I've never been so thankful to the universe.

"Eclipse," Hanna whispers softly.

Then it feels like everything happens in the space of seconds.

The UN soldiers erupt into the laboratory. Fanning out, they scream at me to put down the Siren. Their guns are aimed toward Hanna, Cirrus and me.

I feel Cirrus' claw on my hand. The hand that's hovering over the Siren.

"We'll do it together, dude," Cirrus croaks.

"Together," Hanna mumbles.

A dangerous howl rises from the Majestic machine, splintering with light, and too late I realise the danger we're in. Oh, crap. Bolts of rainbow energy lance out of it, sending sparks flying from the roof and walls.

I lock eyes with Cirrus. Together, we hit the Siren's button, wiping away everything that we've ever known.

All of the screens around the lab start playing the Siren's video, the same flashing images that billions of humans are simultaneously watching worldwide. The video's entrancing music fills the lab. I look at Raven to see him staring up at the video with an unreadable expression.

I wonder why the UN soldiers haven't fired yet, and then I realise they're transfixed by the video too.

For a sickening moment, Cirrus and I have no idea what's happened. No idea of the impact of what we've done. We've rolled the dice, but we don't know how they're going to land. We hold onto each other, not breathing.

The not knowing is unbearable.

Then...

"Winter?" I hear Raven whimper, as if seeing his Shadow for the first time.

The Majestic machine explodes, tearing the lab apart with all of us in it. A shockwave ripples through time and space, scattering our atoms like stardust.

THANKYOU
FOR COMING ALONG ON THE ADVENTURE

Hey There! I'm Sam.

I hope you enjoyed *Eclipse* as much as I enjoyed writing it. For exclusive free stories and behind-the-scenes news on upcoming books, you can join my mailing list at:

www.samblood.com

It would be great to have you there!

Wishing you and your Shadow all of the very best adventures,

Sam Blood

ABOUT THE AUTHOR

Sam lives in Auckland, New Zealand, where he enjoys writing and playing King of Tokyo with his quirky and highly charismatic friends.

The Shadows Series originated when Sam started telling bedtime stories to his Godsister when he was nine; the stories were about magical creatures called Shadows. He completed the first version of Shadows at fourteen, and redrafted it countless times before he published it in its current form.

Sam loves hearing from readers, and you can contact him at sam@samblood.com.

www.samblood.com

www.facebook.com/sambloodauthor

www.instagram.com/sambloodauthor

9 780473 499419